THE
$\mathfrak{K}$INGSBRIDGE
$\mathfrak{P}$LOT

THE

Kingsbridge

Plot

An Historical Mystery

16030

Maan

Meyers

A Perfect Crime Book
DOUBLEDAY
NEW YORK LONDON TORONTO SYDNEY AUCKLAND

A PERFECT CRIME BOOK
PUBLISHED BY DOUBLEDAY
A division of Bantam Doubleday Dell Publishing Group, Inc.
1540 Broadway, New York, New York 10036

DOUBLEDAY is a trademark of Doubleday,
a division of Bantam Doubleday Dell
Publishing Group, Inc.

Book Design by Gretchen Achilles

Library of Congress Cataloging-in-Publication Data
Meyers, Maan.
    The kingsbridge plot : an historical mystery / Maan Meyers.—
1st ed.
        p.   cm.
    "A Perfect Crime book."
    1. New York (N.Y.)—History—Colonial period, ca. 1600–1775—
Fiction.   I. Title.
PS3563.E889K56   1993
813'.54—dc20   92-47058
                                                            CIP

ISBN 0-385-46951-9

1   3   5   7   9   10   8   6   4   2

DEDICATION

We dedicate this book to Joseph Meyers and Sara Goldberg Meyers, Paul Brafman and Esther Weiss Brafman, who came before: Ellis Island immigrants, with rights of memory in this nation, and heroes all.

In loving remembrance.

ACKNOWLEDGMENTS

Thanks to Lola Fiur, Rabbi Joseph Telushkin, Salva Siegel, Boston Hebrew College, Yael Penkower, Reference Librarian, Jewish Theological Seminary, Z. Paul Lorenc, M.D., Ann Bushnell, Chris Tomasino, the wonderful staff of the library of the New-York Historical Society, and William S. Ayers, past Director of the Fraunces Tavern Museum.

And particular thanks to our editor, Kate Miciak, a kindred soul who nurtured our vision.

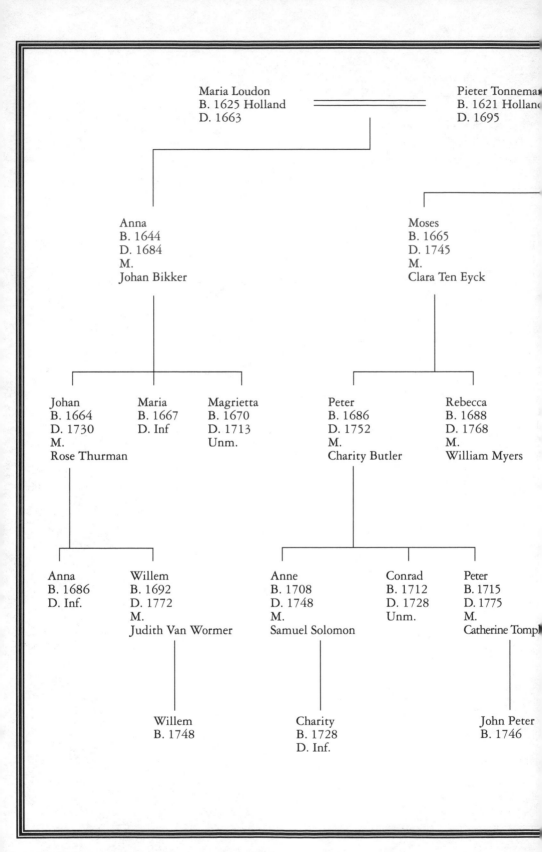

Maria Loudon
B. 1625 Holland
D. 1663

Pieter Tonnema...
B. 1621 Holland
D. 1695

Anna
B. 1644
D. 1684
M.
Johan Bikker

Moses
B. 1665
D. 1745
M.
Clara Ten Eyck

Johan
B. 1664
D. 1730
M.
Rose Thurman

Maria
B. 1667
D. Inf

Magrietta
B. 1670
D. 1713
Unm.

Peter
B. 1686
D. 1752
M.
Charity Butler

Rebecca
B. 1688
D. 1768
M.
William Myers

Anna
B. 1686
D. Inf.

Willem
B. 1692
D. 1772
M.
Judith Van Wormer

Anne
B. 1708
D. 1748
M.
Samuel Solomon

Conrad
B. 1712
D. 1728
Unm.

Peter
B. 1715
D. 1775
M.
Catherine Tompl...

Willem
B. 1748

Charity
B. 1728
D. Inf.

John Peter
B. 1746

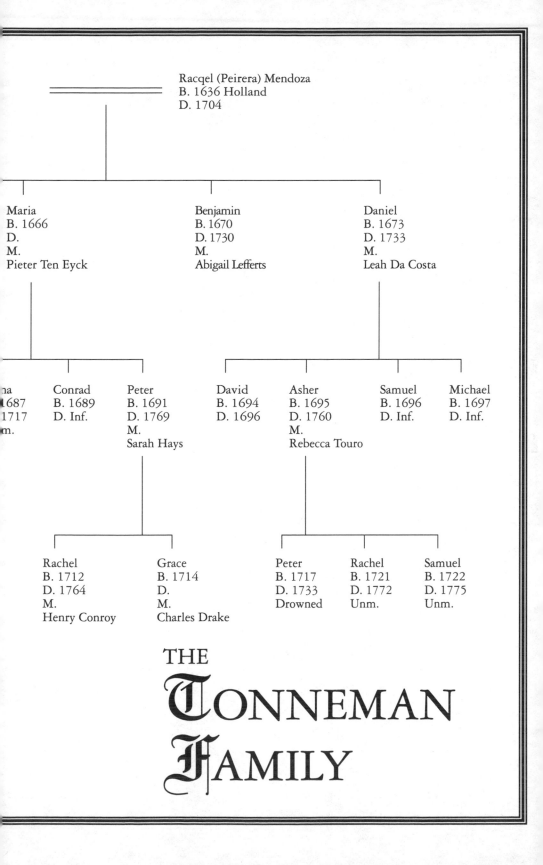

Racqel (Peirera) Mendoza
B. 1636 Holland
D. 1704

Maria
B. 1666
D.
M.
Pieter Ten Eyck

Benjamin
B. 1670
D. 1730
M.
Abigail Lefferts

Daniel
B. 1673
D. 1733
M.
Leah Da Costa

na
687
1717
m.

Conrad
B. 1689
D. Inf.

Peter
B. 1691
D. 1769
M.
Sarah Hays

David
B. 1694
D. 1696

Asher
B. 1695
D. 1760
M.
Rebecca Touro

Samuel
B. 1696
D. Inf.

Michael
B. 1697
D. Inf.

Rachel
B. 1712
D. 1764
M.
Henry Conroy

Grace
B. 1714
D.
M.
Charles Drake

Peter
B. 1717
D. 1733
Drowned

Rachel
B. 1721
D. 1772
Unm.

Samuel
B. 1722
D. 1775
Unm.

THE
𝕿ONNEMAN
𝕱AMILY

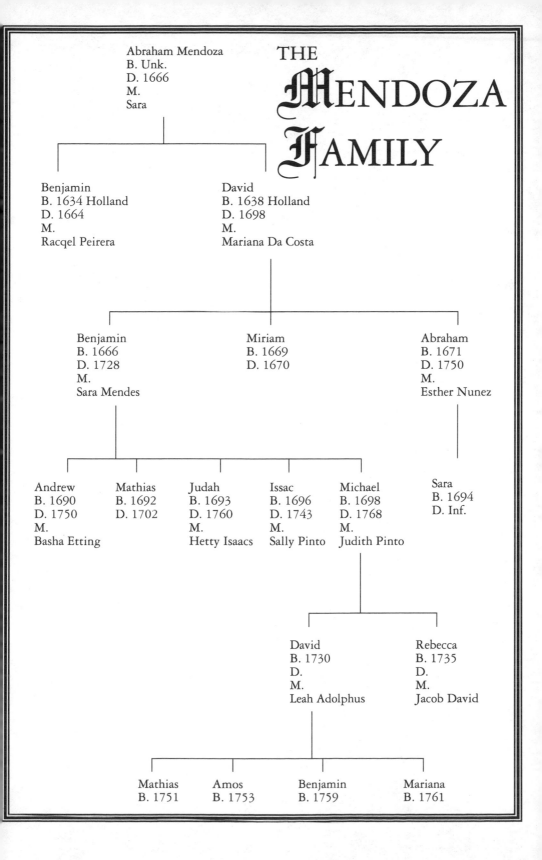

THE MENDOZA FAMILY

Abraham Mendoza
B. Unk.
D. 1666
M.
Sara

Benjamin
B. 1634 Holland
D. 1664
M.
Racqel Peirera

David
B. 1638 Holland
D. 1698
M.
Mariana Da Costa

Benjamin
B. 1666
D. 1728
M.
Sara Mendes

Miriam
B. 1669
D. 1670

Abraham
B. 1671
D. 1750
M.
Esther Nunez

Andrew
B. 1690
D. 1750
M.
Basha Etting

Mathias
B. 1692
D. 1702

Judah
B. 1693
D. 1760
M.
Hetty Isaacs

Issac
B. 1696
D. 1743
M.
Sally Pinto

Michael
B. 1698
D. 1768
M.
Judith Pinto

Sara
B. 1694
D. Inf.

David
B. 1730
D.
M.
Leah Adolphus

Rebecca
B. 1735
D.
M.
Jacob David

Mathias
B. 1751

Amos
B. 1753

Benjamin
B. 1759

Mariana
B. 1761

AUTUMN

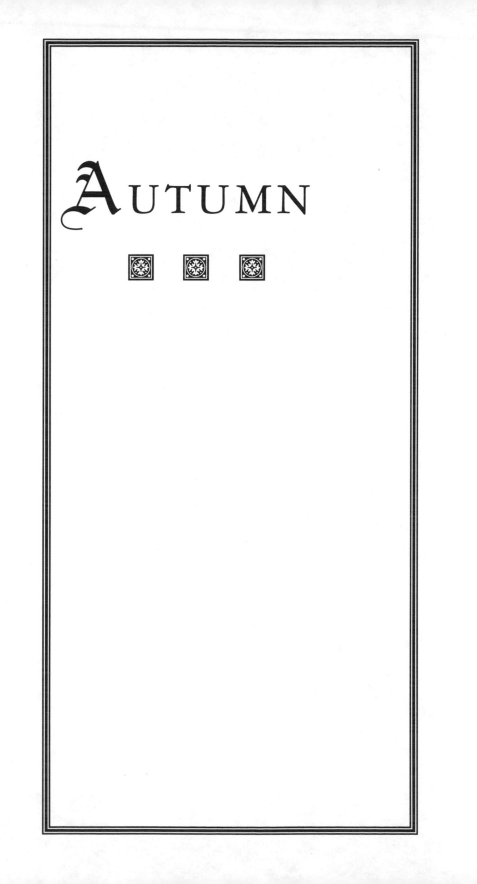

ℙROLOGUE

𝕀t had started snowing early, before daylight. The first of the season. Kate Schrader could smell it before she saw it. It had a fragrance she couldn't explain, that she'd never encountered anywhere else.

Now, the snow had stopped. A thick fog hung over the Collect Pond. Perhaps the proximity of the pond to the marsh had something to do with the smell of the snow.

She shivered, laboring to light the tinder. Everything was damp. She rubbed some lard from the black cast-iron pot into her ashy elbows and neck and pulled her shawl close.

When at last she got the fire going, she filled her kettle from what remained in the bucket. She'd have to get more water. Firewood, too. That was for certain. She shook her head. Served her right for depending on that scamp Jonas Wheeling. Here it was past first light and he hadn't come by to do what he was supposed to. And his poor mother with all those youngsters and no man, God rest his soul, depended on the trade of eggs and milk for Jonas's chores.

Kate shoved the shawl into the collar of her leather jerkin to warm her scranny throat and put her bony backside to the fire for a moment, then opened her back door.

Thick as cotton batting, the fog hung over the water like a pall. This time when she shuddered it wasn't from the cold. Bad fortune to think of death. She should know better.

Nanna bleated at her from the shed.

"I'm coming, I'm coming." Kate took the milk pail from its nail just inside the door and trudged out back in her cracked shoes. "Chick, chick, chick," she called, then clucked her tongue. The chickens were all outside, but they didn't come running. Instead they were pecking away at something they seemed to think was better than corn.

They could wait. Kate went into the shed. Nanna butted her gently. Kate set the bucket under the goat's swollen teats and sat on the stool. Nanna stood patiently while Kate pulled. Soon the bucket was more than half full of rich warm milk.

Kate carried the steaming pail back to her hut, took a nice long draught, and set the pail on the half-log table. Before she could have her samp and birch tea, she had to feed the chickens. She filled her apron with corn, holding the ends to form a basin.

The snow had started again, a fine white powder. "Here chick, here chick, here chick, chick." She cast corn all around. Still the hens took no notice. Usually they were all around her, under her feet. She drew closer to them. "Here chick." She wanted her breakfast. She kicked snow at them, calling, "Shoosh."

What was wrong with those birds? Her hands clutched the apron ends tightly, then dropped, spilling the yellow corn over the white snow.

The birds paid no attention. They were too engrossed in savaging the remains of a human head.

CHAPTER I

The lone rider reined the black mare to a halt. The snow had almost stopped. To his left, across the road, were the lights of the Cross Keys Tavern. Off to the right, the barn. About ten feet shy of the barn, a fire blazed in an open pit where people paused for a last-minute warm before going inside.

The horse and rider were strange to Kingsbridge. Their trappings, while not rich, were not what countryfolk were used to seeing. The horse's leather and brass were somewhat shinier than folks about this part of the country troubled with. The man was swarthy, and though no aristocrat, certainly not a farmer. His greatcoat had a military look to it.

After scrutinizing the faces of the people around the fire, the rider rode his horse into the barn. His mare, glad to be out of the snow, neighed and showed her teeth. The horse stalls to the left were filled. The mare went forward, following a trail of hay on the muddy dirt floor, bumped a man in her way, and nearly trod on his box of tools.

The carpenter snatched up the box, dropping his saw onto the foul floor. He retrieved it, then whipped around, his eyes narrow. "Leave that stinking, wet nag outside," he complained as he brushed barn muck from the canvas covering the saw.

The swarthy man paid no heed. Frig him, the animal was wet, winded, and heated. In this cold weather she'd die on him if he left her out there without drying her off and cooling her down. He wiped the snow from his face, then patted the mare's heaving, icy flank. "Steady, Vixen." She continued chewing stoically at the bits of hay.

A tall ox of a boy stood before him, his palm up. "Tuppence."

"Go away." Immediately one knew from the stranger's voice and the way he spoke that he was an Irish.

"Tuppence to come in, sir."

The Irish glared at the boy. He didn't mind cheating others, but if there was one thing he hated it was being cheated himself. Pulling a ratty green leather purse from his jacket pocket, he dropped a coin into the boy's hand.

This place stank worse than even a barn had the right to smell. Both men and women waved perfumed handkerchiefs in a vain attempt to dispel the oppressive stench coming from the steaming compost heap in full rot in the rear of the barn.

Candles in iron holders hanging on the walls and support posts contrived flickering shadows. In the middle of the dirt floor was a wide circle, enclosed by a three-foot-high fence of loosely woven twigs. Arranged around the fence were rough-hewn log benches. Here, oil lamps provided more light so the players could see the action.

There were about twenty-five people in the barn, including a couple of local lewd women, a short one with pendulous tits and a skinny one, with no dugs, whose hacking cough could be heard above the other noises. The men and trollops alike drank beer or rum.

Acrid perfume mixed with the baser odors of the human condition, alcohol, tobacco, candle and lamp smoke, the compost heap, manure, bird droppings, and blood. An olfactory feast.

Just inside the two large doors a man, dressed in the rough clothes of a countryman, stood alone. A large handkerchief, knotted about his head, hid most of his red face. From the soft groans he emitted every so often and the way he stroked his cheek it was plain he had a toothache.

He was bloated, with small snake eyes, and he wore a hat but no wig. Obscured by the tooth rag or not, he was ugly. What little could be seen of his skin was smooth like a snake's, as well.

The Irish spied the man with the toothache and stared without subtlety. Urging Vixen forward, he would have spoken, but the fat man shook his head violently. Surely such a motion had to bring pain.

The first contest was about to begin. The Irish had turned away to watch when a boy in ragged clothing, toting a large tray loaded with pewter pots of beer, tugged at his sleeve.

"What?"

"Beer, sir?"

He grunted yes.

The potboy handed him his drink.

"Tuppence."

"Wait." The man drank deeply and presented the cup. "More."

The boy took the empty and gave him another cup. "Four pence."

Pulling the green leather purse out again, the Irish paid.

All about, men were calling out their bets and others answered.

The cocks were flapping and slashing, their bloody metal spurs shimmering in the lamplight. Red-stained white and brown feathers flew wildly.

Men cheered, the two women screamed. Those in front shielded their faces from splattering blood.

The white bird seemed to be winning. The boisterous, frenzied congregation shouted encouragements, backers of the white telling him to finish the brown off, backers of the brown urging the cowardly miscreant cock to fight. Even at this stage the crazed revelers were making more wagers as to the outcome.

Out of the corner of his eye the Irish noticed a grizzled old gaffer holding a burlap bag to his puny chest. Whatever was in the bag was moving. Recognizing the hen dodge, the swarthy stranger called out, "Cocker, odds on the brown?"

A squat chap with a face full of boils laughed. "Ten to one."

The brown rooster skirled and tried to run but was thwarted by the twig fence.

"Blind me," the cocker cried. "Make that twenty to one!"

"Five shillings," the Irish called out. He was certain he was going to win.

At that moment the white flapped the brown down with its wings. The end seemed obvious: The white was preparing for the killing blow.

The gaffer let open his bag. An orange chicken popped its head out. The old man released the leather thong about the bird's beak. The hen flapped its wings and cackled.

The white fighter paused, and instead of finishing off the vanquished bird as all nature demanded, it swaggered about, head raised, crowing.

A mistake. Its enemy distracted, the brown rooster attacked, flying at the white and raking its upturned throat. Blood gushed from white feathers. The brown cock vaulted and plunged its spur deep into the base of the white's head.

Watching the blood spurt, the swarthy man licked his lips. He'd been a butcher once; he missed his trade. This night brought it all back to him.

His heart was racing. Vixen felt his mood and snorted and danced a few steps. The skinny whore jostled her way next to Vixen and caressed the Irish's thigh. "Excitin', ain't it?"

"Not now," the Irish said, reining the horse so it shoved her away.

She tossed her stringy blond hair and moved on. A strangled screak came from the white bird. Though finished, it ran a few paces till it hit the opposite side of the fence, spun wildly, then fell, finally admitting death.

"Fraud," someone called.

The gaffer was gone.

The brown inspected his dead foe, then preened, strutted, and crowed, announcing victory to one and all, especially the local chickens.

Nearby, a flock of hens gave off an answering clamor.

Stunned, the gamblers set up an equal commotion, victors cheering, losers grumbling. Especially loud in his jubilation was the Irish. "Five pounds, cocker!"

The squat chap glared suspiciously. "Something's wrong here."

"Not my concern." He hoped this weasel would try something. He'd have his throat cut before he could blink.

Softening his face, the squat chap paid off. All in shillings. The Irish didn't care. He stuffed the coins into his green purse. What didn't fit he crammed into his saddlebag, as he salivated over the thought of a night of drinking. Rum, not beer. And in the company of a whore whom he would then frig till she screamed. Whores was better. If you paid for them they knew you owned them. No trouble from whores.

Two Negroes, a man and a wall-eyed boy, pushed through. The man scooped up the still excited brown cock, kissing and petting it until it was calm. The boy threw the dead white bird in a basket and quickly cleaned up the rest of the bloody dirt and feathers with some water and a twig broom.

The Irish tilted his head to glean the last drops from the cup; it was empty. Sneering, he threw it to the dirt floor and cast his eyes about for the whores. The short one with big, low-hanging melons smiled and came to him. "I'm Joy."

"Yes, you are," he growled, leaning to her and pinching one of her soft breasts.

"Ow. Hands to yourself. Those are all mine until I see some silver." While one hand was squeezing his arse the other was picking at his saddle-bag.

He grabbed her wrists. "And those are all mine until I say different."

"You're hurting me."

"I will not be trifled with. Bite your arse, I will. There are those that know I mean what I say." His laugh was nasty. "But they're not around to speak, are they?"

"Prick."

He raised his hand as if to strike her. "Ah, get away."

Joy ran a feathery hand up his saddle, twixt pommel and groin. "I can make you very happy."

But he had forgotten her. Wheeling Vixen about, the Irish looked for the Fat Man, but he was no longer to be seen.

CHAPTER 2

The Irish, Thomas Hickey, for that was his name, pressed hands on saddlebag, pockets, and purse to make sure his winnings were secure and prodded Vixen out of the barn away from the babble of drunken bettors who were reliving the cockfight.

The night was raw, but at least it had stopped snowing. Hickey rode to the pit fire for one last feel of warmth, thinking again how sweet a bit of rum and a slap, a tickle, and a frig would be. But he wasn't getting that. Not just yet. He ambled his horse to the roadway past the Fat Man with the toothache. His royal lard-arse was fussing with the dapple gray's stirrups, all the time moving those snake eyes. They settled on Hickey, hesitated meaningfully, and shifted away.

Mounting, grunting heavily as he did, the Fat Man slowly walked his horse south down the road. Hickey looked regretfully at the lights of the Cross Keys across the way, listened for a moment to the laughter from the tavern, then followed the Fat Man, taking his own sweet time.

The town of Kingsbridge didn't offer any sort of light along the wayside to help the poor weary traveler. Hickey shivered and pulled his collar up against the cold wind blowing from New England.

When he peered into the gloom of the dark road, the road was empty and eerily quiet. Then he saw the glimmer of light coming from the right. Hickey turned.

By the sign out front, this tavern was The Fighting Cock. It seemed cocks was all the people hereabouts had on their minds. The dapple gray mare was tied to the rail in front of the tavern along with three other horses. The miserable beasts kept pawing the snow-frozen ground and whinnying.

Inside the public house, the redolence of coffee and sweet cakes blended with that of ale, rum, tobacco, a smoky fire, and the pungent smell of burnt roast mutton, raising hunger and thirst.

A short man with a large wen in the middle of his bald head was tending the bar. Four others sat about the tables. The Fat Man was not in evidence. A tiny potboy struggled by with a pitcher of ale half as big as himself. "Did a fat man just come in?"

"In the back, sir." The youngster pointed with his chin to a closed door at the rear.

Hickey stepped up to the bar. "Rum." He drank it in one draught and dropped some coins. "Again." This he carried with him to the back room. He didn't knock.

He entered a small cold chamber and took a seat at the rough-hewn oak table opposite the Fat Man, who still had the cloth tied about his head. Snake eyes never blinking, the oily-tongued Fat Man spoke. "I understand you're loyal to His Majesty."

"For a price I'm loyal to anyone." Hickey stretched his thin lips across yellowed teeth. "I've worked for Mad George before, I can work for him again."

The Fat Man leaned across the table, started to speak, but was stopped by the timid tapping on the door. "Damnation! What is it?"

The boy appeared with another immense pitcher of ale. This he set down on the table. Back to the doorway he ran, returning with a tray bearing platters of mutton and potatoes and bread and two pewter tankards he'd left on the floor outside the door. When the boy started to arrange the victuals on the table, the Fat Man snarled, "Get out."

"Yes, sir." The boy backed off, but lingered.

"Give the kid something for his trouble," Hickey prompted. Annoyed at the lack of a fire, he pulled his greatcoat closer against the piercing cold.

The Fat Man frowned, then flipped the boy a penny. The boy caught it deftly, grinned, and scampered out the door, closing it.

"What can you tell me?"

"A certain gentleman who's been busy in Boston will be coming to New-York. I've given my simpleton lieutenant three bottles of brandy and in return he's promised me good duty. Pretty soon he's going to need guards for this certain gentleman when he comes to New-York."

"This is nothing new." Grunting pleasure, the Fat Man took a mutton chop in his hands, hurrying it to his mouth.

"He'll be in Kingsbridge before midnight," Hickey said, lifting his tankard. "He's been sneaking down from Cambridge now and again. Uses

Kingsbridge as a way station to New-York. I haven't found out yet why he comes south. Could be a woman. When he's in Kingsbridge he stays at the Cross Keys Tavern, across the way from the barn."

"We know all that."

"He's to meet a man in New-York."

"We know that."

"If you know so much, what do you need me for?"

The Fat Man cleared his throat and drank some ale.

"Fellow from Connecticut, name of Bushnell." Hickey chewed on a roasted potato soaked in mutton grease.

"We've heard of him."

"There you go again. Stupid bastards. Fellow's coming from Connecticut, our man has come from Cambridge to Kingsbridge, and still they're going to meet in New-York. You know why?" Hickey laughed. "He doesn't trust the barkeeper at the Cross Keys. Alfred Abbott."

"People are like that," said the Fat Man. He squeezed his mouth in distaste at the sight of some gore on Hickey's coat sleeve. "What's that on your sleeve?"

Hickey sucked his teeth noisily as he rubbed his coat sleeve on the ale-soaked table. "One of them birds gave me a sprinkle. Amazing that it could squirt so high."

"Appears to be a whole rooster's worth."

"All right," said Hickey, tucking away food and ale as fast as he could. "What can I do for you?"

The Fat Man removed the large handkerchief from his head, and poured himself a mug of ale. He drank slowly, then wiped his lips with his fingertips and his fingers on the handkerchief.

Hickey stopped eating and waited.

"We want you to kill the man, Mr. Hickey."

Hickey sucked food from his teeth. "Tell me when. I could do it tonight. A knife between the ribs as he sleeps."

"Not yet. Don't be impatient. The timing must be exactly right. And we may not want it to be a blade or a gun."

"What, then? Do you want me to hang him?"

The Fat Man took a deep, noisy breath. " 'A consummation devoutly to be wished.' "

Hickey resumed eating. "Why don't you take him yourself?"

"We prefer this way."

"Afraid of the Sons, eh, what?"

"Never mind that."

"No skin off my nose. How much?"

"More than enough. Is that all you care about? How much you'll get paid?"

The Irish tilted his head back and drank deeply of the ale. "I care about women." He belched. "Juicy women who spread their legs and scream and scream and scream."

"You're a disgrace."

"Ain't I, though? How about some rum?"

CHAPTER 3

"Ahoy! What ship?" The sea was rough and the harsh wind was punishing, but the sailor's voice cut through. "What ship?"

Captain Boulderson lowered his spyglass. It was useless in the snow-shrouded gloom. Where he had moments before seen only stygian darkness, he could now make out pale flickers of light, then vague images of flags and pennants amidst masses of sail. The Union Jack, even through the dimness, was hard to miss. Another few minutes and they would be right in the middle of the Royal Fleet. "Hard to port, helmsman!" Boulderson shouted.

"Aye, sir."

"What ship?" came again through the creak of rope and sail.

"Tell the man, boatswain."

"Packet, *Earl Of Halifax,* out of Falmouth," the boatswain bellowed on the horn. "Captain Boulderson commanding. Who the hell are you?"

"*Duchess Of* frigging *Gordon,* if it's any of your bleeding business. And that's the *Asia* sniffing up your arse. What are you doing going to New-York?"

"That's our business."

" 'Twill be our business one of these days soon. Don't you know New-York is a tinderbox?"

"Good, that'll warm things up."

"What news from London? Is it going to happen?"

"Can't tell by me."

"Me, neither, to tell the truth. Proceed with God's speed, *Earl Of Halifax.* Stand you a drink in New-York by-and-by."

"I'll drink it and ten more."

Thus, in November, in the year of our Lord 1775, the *Earl Of Halifax,* taking a young man home after seven years abroad, continued without incident through the Narrows and on to New-York, a city under siege, in a way, and with, at the moment, two governments: the King's and the Patriots'. It was the eve of a war that no one really believed would happen and everyone knew had to happen. It was the eve of war and the eve of a new world.

Holding tight to the rail on the sea-swept deck of the *Earl Of Halifax,* the young man was grateful for his heavy garb. Winter in New-York was as cold as he remembered.

They had been at sea since early October, seven weeks and two days before. When they passed through the Narrows, he knew he was almost home.

The sight of the Royal Fleet was a shock at first, but it gave the newcomer only a moment's pause. The City was considered a nest of Tories, loyal followers of King George. And the brawny English fleet's job was to safeguard that nest. The trouble would pass soon. Just something that had to be worked out between the obstreperous Colonies and the King.

Day broke as they entered the Bay. Ahead, to his left, through the drifting snow, the cliffs of New Jersey rose above the fog. To the right, the City of New-York. He peered into the fog-shrouded island, anxious for the first sight of the city of his birth.

Shifting his weight impatiently, he bumped his boot on the black leather bag at his feet, then moved it beside the two large brown leather portmanteaus.

His companion grinned. "A little eager, what?"

"Rather," he answered. A tall, broad-shouldered man of twenty-nine years, he wore close-fitting blue velvet breeches that buckled just under the knee, an equally close-fitting blue velvet coat, knitted white stockings, not-quite-calf-length black boots, and a heavy black wool cloak. Unlike his friend, he disdained the wig fashion of the day, choosing to wear his thick, blond hair tied back with a black velvet ribbon. Just now it was covered with a flat-crowned beaver hat.

The color of his hair and his ruddy complexion gave away, to those who cared, his Dutch lineage. His name was John Peter Tonneman.

Like a ghost ship, the *Earl Of Halifax* traveled the last leg of its journey through the wet fog. Around them, the sounds of a working ship were real enough: voices raised from the deck and below, the strain of sail against wood. A fair wind suddenly billowed the sheets and seamen called out to one another. The wind began to blow away the fog created by the early snow meeting the unready earth, and the City of New-York emerged dense and beautiful, crowned by the pale glow of street lamps.

Though heavy of heart, Tonneman felt a surge of joy at his homecoming. He had been in London these seven years, having gone to learn surgery after completing his studies at the King's College in New-York.

He hadn't been in London a fortnight when his betrothed, Abigail Comfort, informed him by letter that she considered being an officer's wife preferable to that of a surgeon's, and had chosen to wed one Captain Richard Willard. She had written the letter the day he'd left.

Tonneman had always dreamed of working side by side with his father, practicing the art of medicine together, but now he would not be joining his father's practice; he'd be taking it over. His father's death of the Pneumonia five months before was what had finally brought him home from London Hospital.

Tacking sails snapped overhead as they made their way past Fort George and the Battery into the East River and weighed anchor finally opposite Peck's Slip.

"Welcome to my city, Jamie."

Tonneman turned to his companion. Professor of surgery, Maurice Arthur Jamison, a man of perhaps thirty-six years, was slightly shorter and slimmer in stature than Tonneman, with the intense nature and the rounded shoulders of a dedicated scholar. Jamison wore a black bicorne and a small, powdered wig over his fine copper hair. Below were the straight nose and a face that would be very much at home in the highlands of Scotland. Instead of the expected high Scots color, however, he had exceeding white skin that made him appear ill although the man was decidedly robust. His velvet breeches and coat were tan, his boots and wool cloak brown. He had made the journey to New-York to be the teaching Chancellor of the college of medicine at the King's College.

Looking at the small English city of mostly brick homes, Jamison breathed the clean air and thought how unlike the fetid stink of centuries-battered London it was. He liked what he saw. He'd had enough of the stodgy Old World. This was decidedly the place to spread his wings.

Tonneman and his friend bade farewell to the captain and with the other ten passengers took a short ride on the barge to Peck's Slip. An officious Negro boy helped them with their baggage and promised them a carriage. As the barge neared the shore Tonneman could feel his heart pounding. At last he was home.

John Tonneman was an Englishman of his century, outwardly calm, composed, imperturbable. He had learned to contain what Jamie referred to as his "wild Colonial passions" in order to fit in in London. His laughter was loud, quick, and deep; his anger red-hot and furious.

Abigail's betrayal had hurt him deeply and had brought to the surface feelings of which even he had not known himself capable. For a time he could not imagine a life without her, and he had plunged himself into both the society and the underbelly of London life with identical fervor, subsisting on bachelor's fare of bread and kisses and often more spirits than his head and digestion could handle, becoming more the drinker and brawler than the physician.

Now, he had little clear memory of those first three months of his London existence. All he had was a memento: the jagged scar that dented his left eyebrow—testament to an angry blow and God's grace that had kept the blow from cleaving his skull. Who'd dealt the blow and why was a mystery.

It had been Arthur Jamison, head of surgery at London Hospital, who had found Tonneman lying in a filthy tavern bed and who had cleaned him up and brought him back to the living. Jamie became John Tonneman's mentor, and order came out of chaos.

Not that Jamie was a saint. Jamie drank and fought with the best of them, but his true passion was women. All classes, all shapes, all sizes, all ages. Tarts, widows, even married women, as long as they could spread their legs and bring him pleasure. He preferred the beauties, but any port in a storm.

When old Doctor Tonneman began urging him home, Tonneman had invented reasons to delay. He was an Englishman now. And for almost five years he had evaded, made excuses, for New-York meant seeing Abigail, married and with children who might have been his.

What had changed all this was his father's unsteady script with each of the last few letters, filling him with guilt and doubt and with them, thoughts of returning.

Then, his father's spindly hand had firmed; his writing took on a new character and seemed steady, sure of its way again.

In the end, the shocking truth belied all the hopes Tonneman had based on the paltry excuse of a steadier hand. The news of his father's death staggered him, igniting all his buried, turbulent emotions.

The month before, Jamie had been offered the position at King's College. When Tonneman announced he was going home, Jamie promptly accepted the appointment. And now here they were.

Shifting his black physician's bag to his left hand, Tonneman wiped the feathery snowflakes from his face, and stepped carefully onto the slippery cobblestones of Water Street. The old town seemed the same despite all the contretemps.

The first sight and sound to greet them were swine snorting as they foraged for titbits among the snow-covered litter of the streets.

"Just like London," his friend Jamison said amiably.

But this wasn't London.

Countinghouses and taverns, solicitors and merchants lined Water Street. The two men were immediately swept up in the daily bustle of the port of New-York, the air sharp with spice and tar, wet rope and fish. In the river, sewage mixing with salt water sent up brackish odors. Peddlers shouted out their wares. Of immediate interest was the gnarled-fingered hot potato monger. The two physicians exchanged coppers for 'taters and had their breakfast in the falling snow.

Tonneman wiped his mouth and doffed his beaver hat, shaking snow from crown and brim. If the snow continued and stayed on the ground, sleds and sleighs would soon be out. He grinned broadly. "It isn't cold enough for the Collect to freeze over, Jamie, but you'll see it soon enough."

Tonneman's New-York was a thriving metropolis, a mixture of old and new. The southern tip of the island was crowded; many new homes had been erected in the years he'd been gone. His father had written that there were now three thousand houses to shelter some twenty thousand people. The new structures, he could see, were very English indeed, three-storied red brick buildings, embellished with marble. Here and there the City's Dutch origins were proclaimed by houses that gave their shoulders rather than their faces to the street, and now and again, by the names of their residents.

Trees, now bare-limbed and dusted with snow, lined the streets, giving everything a clean, peaceful aspect. But that was just the surface. Beneath, Tonneman knew his City was a powder keg of warring philosophies and viewpoints.

He was not political in any sense of the word and in his years in

London, he had, if anything, become more English in his allegiances. At least, on the outside. But he was well aware of the independent Dutch blood in his veins and the hardheaded Dutch streak he'd not always managed to control. That was his legacy from his ancestor, Pieter Tonneman, who had been the first Sheriff of New-York.

On Water Street the Negro boy waited for them with a carriage.

Tonneman took a deep taste of the bracing winter air. "What say, Jamie, we go to Bowling Green?" He frowned, remembering. "To the Blue Bell Tavern. We'll have mulled wine to wash down those 'taters."

"A capital idea."

"After that I'll take you to my home." It was so strange to say that when he meant his father's home.

The house on Rutgers Hill and John Street had been his grandfather's. When his father married, his grandfather deeded the house to his son as a wedding present and Tonneman's grandparents moved up to the country, near Bowery Lane, past the Jews Burying Ground.

Jamison nudged Tonneman with an elbow. "What have we here?"

A slender young boy, his face cruelly scarred from the Pox, stood before them. His gray breeches and blue frock coat were both much too large for him. With the same movement he hiked his dragging breeches and lifted his tricorn. "Mr. Tonneman, sir?"

"Yes, boy."

"The Mayor requests your appearance, sir, at your convenience." The boy waited expectantly.

Tonneman let out a sigh and watched it gather into a puff in the cold air. "I have been summoned, Jamie. That means now."

"Quite all right. My thirst isn't that bad."

"I would rather have seen to our thirst first." Tonneman handed the boy a penny. "Thank you, boy. At the Hall?"

"Yes, sir."

"Run along then and tell the Mayor we're right behind you."

The boy raised breeches and hat again and scampered down town toward Wall Street, keeping his balance amazingly well on the slippery stones.

Tonneman gave the Negro lad several coppers, and the coachman a shilling. He instructed the coachman to take all their baggage, excepting their medical bags, to the home of Dr. Peter Tonneman at Rutgers Hill.

Then he and Jamison set off for City Hall. As the two men turned from Queen Street to Wall Street, they saw a crowd gathering near City

Hall. The snow, a thorough blanket, made everything white—men, carts, peddlers, trees.

Laughter came tittering from onlookers. Some were yelling raucously.

Hanging from a street lamp was a body wearing the red coat of an English soldier.

CHAPTER 4

The two men pushed forward. "What have we here?" Jamison asked. "Murder most foul?"

"Not at all, sir, just the rabble showing their dirty arses to the King." This muffled declaration came from a burly, well-turned-out man in claret velvet. He had a scented handkerchief to his nose. "That's not a corpse, though they might wish it to be. It's an effigy."

It was easy enough to note, even to those newly arrived in the City, that there were two contentious factions in the crowd, those who were loyal to the King, and the Patriots. Or as the Loyalists would label them, the Rebels.

"Tory sons of bitches!" somebody yelled.

"Rebel bastards."

"Frigging inimicals!"

A Loyalist was hit in the face with a snowball.

"Who did that?" the inimical King's man screamed. "I'll have your bloody eyes!"

His comrades held their ground, unsure in the middle of the jostling club-wielding rabble. By this time a larger throng had assembled. They began hurling snowballs and chunks of ice from the streets, Rebels advancing on Tories.

One of the pieces of ice struck a young woman, carrying a full and heavy market basket. She slipped and fell to the ground and was in danger of being trampled. Tonneman darted into the middle of it all and scooped her up in his arms.

"My eggs," she cried.

"To hell with your eggs," he said, running her back to the sidewalk where he set her on her feet.

"Withdraw," called one of the Tories, in a military manner.

The Tories fell back. The one who'd been hit with the snowball yelled, "Face us man to man, you foul bastards. We can best any Sodomites of Liberty."

He was heartily jeered. "Inimical sons of bitches! Cowards!"

One of the Tory clan, a thin lame man, stumbled. As he righted himself, he pulled out a large tailor's scissors from beneath his coat.

"He's got a blade!"

A hush came over the street.

"That won't be necessary, Andrews." The man in claret velvet stepped forward. "Sheathe your weapon, please." The firmness of his words contradicted his agreeable countenance.

The scissors wielder quickly complied.

"Why don't you all go home," the man in claret velvet called out. "Royalists and Patriots alike. Go home. You'll be spilling one another's blood soon enough."

Each group of partisans milled about and muttered imprecations but did not leave.

The man in velvet squared his shoulders. To Tonneman he said, "The Sons of Liberty they call themselves. Nothing but a rowdy rabble who have no respect for King and country." He dabbed his nose daintily with his scented cloth. "Move on, you people. Disperse. Andrews, cut that damned thing down. Move on. Move on. The game is over for the day."

Amidst low grumbles, while members of the Tory group cut the effigy down, the two groups began to wander away as others arrived to ogle. The Tories took charge of the effigy and carried it off as one of their own. Tonneman and Jamison exchanged looks, but neither made comment. The new onlookers chattered and swarmed about them, eager either to see what was happening or to join in on one side or the other.

Tonneman now turned his attention to the young woman he had rescued. She had a bump and a raw spot on her forehead. "You'll be fine," he said. "It's only a small scrape."

"I know that." She made a face. "My eggs."

Jamison had gone and fetched the young woman's basket. He presented it gingerly. The basket had lost its handle and its side was crushed. The only thing left in it were the eggs, also crushed. "More like iced omelet," he said, handing her the destroyed basket, with a small bow.

"Ah, me." The young woman wrapped her orange scarf tightly around her neck. "I must hurry back to the market before everything is gone. It wouldn't do for my husband to have no food for his guests. Good day, gentlemen." She curtsied to Tonneman. "Thank you, gallant sir." With great dignity and a modest smile for Tonneman, she took her leave.

Jamie chuckled. "What a champion you are, John. Not only did you not get her name—you could have gotten a scissor up your arse for your bravery, running out into the throng like that."

"Not likely. And didn't you hear? She's married."

"Bloody likely. That nice bit, married or not, might have been worth a tup at that. Still, you're a fool."

"That's bloody likely, too."

Flurries of snow speckled them, flying in their faces. Tonneman shook his head. "The entire affair might have been worse. That cripple with the scissors was certainly edgy."

Jamison gestured with his medical bag. "Judging from the *mobile vulgus* I daresay everyone in your City is edgy."

"So it seems, Jamie," Tonneman agreed. "But we have always been an excitable lot, fond of giving opinions, dearly loving debate." As he spoke he was amazed at how quickly he had once more adapted to his birthplace. The City had already worked its magic on him.

"That was no debate we just witnessed," Jamie said. When Tonneman didn't respond he commented, "Lovely little cottages," referring to several houses they could see from their vantage point on Wall Street. The area around City Hall was majestic with many fine and spacious Georgian homes.

Tonneman stamped his feet. They were starting to numb. "Let's to the Hall. I need a fire. And the Mayor will not relish being kept waiting."

Jamie nodded. They moved at as brisk a pace as possible over the snowy ground, past the public wells.

Ahead, on the corner of Wall Street, where Broad Street to the left became Nassau to the right, was the "new" City Hall. Completed in 1747 on the same site as its predecessor, it was a formal brick structure of three stories and a basement, with a three-arched, columned entrance up a short flight of steps. Its shape resembled a capital I, lying on its side. A tall chimney heated the chambers in each leg of the I. Smack in the center on the roof was an ornate cupola, on top of which a rooster weather vane spun erratically in the blowing snow.

People pushed past them, to and fro, fixed on their business and complaints. A bustling woman fell flat on her backside at the foot of the stairs; passersby paid her no heed, intent on their own problems. She was barrel-shaped with tiny feet. Tonneman and Jamie each seized an elbow and helped her up.

"Thank you, good sirs," she said in a thick Irish accent, "I'm going to take them to law, I am. You're my witnesses. That icy walk near to killed me."

"Are you all right?" Jamie asked, trying not to smile.

"Right as rain, I am. Plenty of padding, that's the trick. Good Irish suet on my arse." Her winter-red cheeks were puffed with indignation, but her eyes and smile were full of cheer. "Well, can't stand idling all day long. Good day to you, gentlemen. Thank you for your kindness." And off she went into the Hall in a flurry of skirts and pettiskirts.

Two New-York militiamen standing guard eyed them suspiciously as Tonneman and Jamison mounted the steps to the Hall. At the top of the steps under one of the arches was the pockmarked youth who had brought the summons from the Mayor. His deeply scarred face lit into a smile when he saw them, and he began to leap about with a kind of frantic energy, tugging at his oversized breeches with every other leap. In this manner he conducted them through the wide brick-floored entrance hall and up a flight of stairs to the second floor and the office of the Mayor of New-York.

The boy knocked.

"Come. Come."

The boy opened the door and waved them in. A fire blazing at one end of the spacious chamber gave the large room some comfort from the early chill.

A sleek-skinned fat man standing near the desk stopped speaking in midsentence. His small eyes were almost buried by expanses of broad forehead and meaty florid jowel. His powdered peruke was askew and seemed more a lopsided white hat than a wig.

His brown breeches were swollen with flesh, and his red waistcoat appeared set to burst its buttons. The silver buttons on the buff coat and the ostentatious silver buckles on his shoes reminded Tonneman of the dandies he'd met in London—those who liked to pretend they knew the King. The fat man picked up his ranting about there being too many of "them" in the Provincial Congress. "They're a pack of hypocritical, swindling, canting miscreants."

Sitting in the middle of the room, behind a desk, listening patiently, was Whitehead Hicks, the Mayor of the City of New-York.

"Calm down."

"Why, in heaven's name, would I want to calm down?" The fat man's face was turning purple. "All those sons of bitches of liberty in the Provincial Congress . . . Who is running this City, anyway? This is the King's city. You should—"

"Do what? Our honorable Governor Tryon hides on a ship in the Narrows and you expect me to do what he can't?"

"The one in their ridiculous congress that galls me most is that hermaphrodite, John Morin Scott. Years ago Jim De Lancey told me that the filthy beast dances with and kisses men."

"Enough." Favoring his right foot, the Mayor came out from behind his graceful inlaid cherrywood desk, decorated with false brass drawer pulls on all sides. The niches for papers on either end were overflowing, covering the ink standish. Several quill pens could be seen among the papers.

The Mayor shook Tonneman's hand. "I'm genuinely sorry about your father, boy." The man winced in distress. And it was from more than respect for Tonneman's mourning. Was it the fat man, Tonneman wondered.

"Thank you, sir. Are you not well?"

"It's this damnable gout. Rain or snow, it plagues me until I want to cut the leg off."

The two physicians lifted their black bags at the same time. Both laughed and Jamison gave way to Tonneman, who said, "It's not the weather. Does it appear without warning?"

"Sometimes." Hicks limped back to his desk and sat.

Tonneman knelt and lifted the Mayor's right foot to his lap. "For one thing, your boots are too tight." With a struggle he removed the right boot.

The Mayor groaned loudly. "Damn it, man, are you trying to kill me?"

Tonneman touched Hicks' big toe, lightly.

"Ow."

"Is that tender?"

"Good God, man, what do you think?"

"I think you've got some corrupted humor. Does the pain occur after a big meal or too much spirits?"

Mayor Hicks nodded glumly.

Tonneman placed the foot carefully on the floor.

"Gently, damn it. That's my foot, not a leg of lamb."

Tonneman got to his feet, nodded to Jamie. "It's the gout."

Jamie nodded back.

The fat man paced fretfully from his spot to the fire and then back to the desk.

Tonneman opened his bag. "I can offer some relief and perhaps if you do as I say, even cure you."

"I would be in your debt."

"A little concoction of dried meadow saffron seeds, handed down through the generations in my family—"

Jamison shook his head. "*I* was going to offer laudanum, not some old wife's brew your father got from the Indians." After a pause Jamie added, "With all respect to your late father, sir."

Tonneman did not respond to his friend's gibe. They had had this debate before.

Mayor Hicks raised his hand. "Not laudanum, sir. It puts me into a stupor."

The fat man fidgeted impatiently, then, licking his fingers, bent to polish his silver buckles.

Among the chaos on the Mayor's desk were a salt-glazed stoneware pitcher and several cups. Tonneman measured the pulverized seeds from a jar into a cup. "I'm putting in willow bark for the pain." He added the powdered bark from a small twist of paper into the cup with the meadow saffron seeds, and after sniffing to see if it was indeed water in the pitcher, poured some. Then he stirred the concoction with a metal rod from his bag. "Drink this. It will lessen the pain."

"We'll see about that." Hicks sat down behind his desk and tasted the potion. "Bitter."

"But the cure will be sweet," said Tonneman in his best physician's manner. "Drink up."

The Mayor did so with a scowl.

"I'll prepare more seeds and send them over. Four times a day for two weeks, then we'll see how you feel. But you must avoid organ meats. Liver, so forth. Rich foods. Spirits."

"Why not bury me and have done?"

"And you may have a bit of diarrhea from the meadow saffron."

The Mayor groaned. "Now he tells me."

"Aside from the gout, how are you, sir?"

"When I'm not aching, splendid." The fat man cleared his throat

loudly, and Mayor Hicks turned to him. "You know Alderman Matthews?"

"Your servant, sir. This is my friend, Maurice Jamison, doctor of
physick and—"

But Alderman Matthews jerked his head violently at the Mayor and
was out the door without so much as a beg your pardon.

CHAPTER 5

"Politics," the Mayor offered by way of explanation. "We had an election five days ago. The Provincial Congress. They have *grievances*. Things are topsy-turvy here. Governor Tryon holds his office on the *Duchess Of Gordon*. I have to try to run this City with the likes of Matthews constantly sniping at me. Town soldiers, Sons of Liberty, you name it, I've got it to contend with. Now this new thing. We'll get to that by and by. Come, warm yourselves." Waving the physicians to the fire, the vexed Mayor hobbled to join them, and for a moment, toasted his bootless aching foot. He then went back to the desk and sat heavily in a maple-and-hickory slat-back armchair. He smiled. "Your father was my friend."

"I know that."

"And you're my friend." The Mayor clapped his hands together. "But we carry on. Since your father was Coroner, I think it only proper that you be appointed interim Coroner until one is named." Winking, he added, "I'm sure the position is yours for the asking." He pointed to the stout beechwood sidechairs in front of his desk. "Gentlemen."

Tonneman advanced to the desk, eyeing Hicks warily. "What's up your sleeve, you crafty old bugger?"

"Sir?" The Mayor contrived to look shocked.

"I've known you since I was a lad, and you never gave away ice unless it was winter and it's winter now."

Jamison, still taking warmth from the fire, smiled.

"Just like your father," said the Mayor. "Do you swear to be loyal to the King?"

"I do."

"Good. You're the Coroner." The Mayor ran soft fingers over his cleanly shaven throat. "One thing, Coroner. A discovery has been made over at the Collect. Would you please look into it?"

Tonneman rolled his eyes and glanced at Jamie. "I thought as much. Of course."

"Reuben."

The pockmarked boy came running in, hiking his breeches. "Yes, Your Honor."

"Fetch the bundle you put out back for me."

Reuben raced from the office. He returned quickly, carrying a bushel wicker basket which appeared to be filled with crisp snow. The boy dug into the basket and produced a bundle wrapped in jute cloth. Brushing away the snow, he wiped the bundle down.

"Put it on the desk, that's a good fellow. And run along."

The Mayor waited until the door closed behind the boy. "Constable Daniel Goldsmith is at the Collect." The Mayor undid the cloth wrapping from the bundle.

Revealed was a human head, so ravaged by birds or animals its gender was impossible to guess at first glance. The eyes were gone, and scraps of flesh had been gouged from the cheeks and forehead. Little was left of the nose and ears. But the hair was of reddish hue, long and matted with mud and dirt, caked with bits of dried blood.

Tonneman banished the emotions that still plagued him. The obscene object he studied with narrowed eyes had once been human.

Jamison left the comfort of the fire and joined them at the desk. "Interesting." He looked to Tonneman. "Woman?"

"I would think so," said Tonneman.

"The amputation is trim enough to have been done by a draughts-man."

Tonneman nodded. "With the eye and hand of a surgeon and the strength of a woodman."

Jamie's mouth curled in an ironic smile. "An angry hand?"

Tonneman's smile matched his friend's. "I would think one would have to be very angry to cut off someone's head."

"A Negro woman up at the Collect found it yesterday morning in her yard," said the Mayor. "Her hens had gotten at it. Goldsmith has been out at the Collect these two days looking for the body, thus far with no result. When it's found I want to know how she died, just to be certain she didn't have the Plague, or Cholera or the Pox, or some such. Then have the Constable bury the lot in Potter's Field."

There was a knock at the door.

"Come."

Reuben pushed open the door. Behind him a large black man with a ragged piece of canvas about his shoulders appeared, gasping for air. "I ran . . . all the way. . . . Constable Goldsmith says to say . . . he found the rest."

CHAPTER 6

If one were to follow Broadway north past the Common, and then veer east, one would come to Fresh Water Pond or the Collect, known in Dutch times as Shellpoint. Here in rundown huts lived a motley collection of humanity: descendents of the freed Dutch West India Company African slaves, other free Negroes, poor whites, and mixed bloods.

Between Fresh Water Pond and the marsh, a large area of spongy lowlands, was a patch of dry land. The area was bountiful with wild fowl, and the streams which fed the Collect teemed with fish.

In this patch Kate Schrader and others like her had their homes. It wasn't much, especially not in comparison to the grand estates, the wedge-shingled and elegant brick homes on the southern tip of New-York, but here they had their freedom and for the most part, control of their own lives. And though harsh winter winds did blow through their flimsy huts, firewood from the surrounding forest was plentiful, and in the summer one could sit out in front of one's own house, shelling peas and catching the fragile breeze from the pond.

Hills perhaps a hundred feet high encircled the Collect like tiers of an amphitheater. In the winter when the pond froze over people would stand on the hills and watch the skaters.

The Collect, nourished by springs that had slaked the thirst of the red man for centuries before the coming of the white man, had been considered a treasure by the Dutch of New Amsterdam and until recently the same by the English-Dutch community of New-York.

The last leg of this short journey was up a steep grade and down another. When the carriage carrying the Mayor and his party pulled to a halt, the bay and chestnut team snorted and shook their heads, filling the air with the frosty cloud of their labored breath.

Quintin Brock, the black man who had brought the news, jumped down from the roof of the carriage and stood waiting patiently as Tonneman and Jamison descended just behind the Mayor. The Negro led the three men away from the pond to the edge of the marsh. In spite of the wet snow and frigid wind, those who lived around the Collect had gathered in a ragged and uneasy group near a steam engine, stacks of logs piled high as the Mayor's carriage, and an excavation. The steam engine was still. A stubby, thickset man was bending over an object in the snow.

The crowd stepped quickly aside to let the people from City Hall have a look at what had brought each of the Collect dwellers out on this hard day, which had begun so violently the morning before with Kate Schrader's tortured howl.

"What have you got, Constable?" the Mayor called as he approached.

Startled, the Constable straightened up, losing his precariously perched beaver hat in the process. He pointed to the excavation. "One of my Watch who guards the well hole during the night found it there." The Constable picked up his hat and used it to point to the excavation again. "Why we missed it yesterday I'll never know. If it hadn't got caught on a root, it would have fallen to the bottom and he never would have seen it."

Puzzled, Tonneman turned to the Mayor. Jamie went ahead.

Hicks sighed. "There've been complaints that the City water is foul and the reserve perilously meager in the event of fire. The Common Council engaged the services of a civil engineer to construct a reservoir at the bottom end of Broadway at Pearl Street, near Fort George."

Tonneman nodded, fretting at the windy explanation. He was eager to be with Jamie at the body. He edged away. But Mayor Hicks, once started, was not to be stopped. He hobbled after Tonneman, still explaining. "Water is to be pumped to the reservoir from a well or wells to be dug here at the Collect by that steam engine, and it will be circulated by pipes that will be laid in the City come spring. Digging is stopped until then."

Jamie was standing over the headless corpse, thoroughly absorbed. Tonneman circled the body. No matter how many he had seen, and Jamie had arranged for him to see and dissect many, it always felt like the first time. Even though he knew it was a lifeless shell, to Tonneman the body represented the person who had been, and he had a reverence for that person and for the life that had been lost.

The two physicians had been together for seven years. They were more than friends, they were brothers. Each knew the other's thoughts and intentions almost immediately. Without a word they knelt on either side of the body.

"Woman, then," said Jamison.

"Really, Jamie?" Tonneman teased, but he did not smile.

"How did she die?" the Mayor asked impatiently.

"That's easy," said Quintin. "She lost her head."

The group of Negro men laughed uneasily.

Jamie's lip curled in distaste.

"No more of that," a thin woman in faded calico scolded. "Have some respect." She clutched her shawl around her shoulders and curtsied to the Mayor and the two physicians. "Kate Schrader, Your Honors. I found the head."

"I'm Robert," declared a small black man. "I found the body."

There were titters from the Africans.

"Quiet," the Constable ordered.

The victim's build was slight, though long of limb. She wore a short cambric gown of green, red, and yellow stripes over a long gown of the same colors, which was torn to reveal a green calamanco quilted petticoat, and new black boots. All of these were splattered with blood and thoroughly marked by mud from the excavation.

Jamison put his face close to the corpse and sniffed. "What's that odor? Tar?"

"That's me, sir," Quintin said. "I work making tar."

Once more Jamie's lip curled. He waved the black man away. Quintin lowered his head compliantly and moved off.

Jamison now attempted to raise the several hems of the corpse's clothing, but they were frozen stiff. "Young?"

"I would guess. Was there no greatcoat?" Tonneman lifted the rigid white hand and brushed the snow from it. The fingernails were ragged and blue.

The Constable stepped forward. "No. No coat."

Tonneman shook his head. "She's so stiff from the cold it's impossible to estimate how long she's been out here. Ah. See here," he said to Jamie. A red scar stood out against the white of her skin, running from hand to thumb.

"Recently healed," Jamison said.

"Oho," a shout came.

Tonneman placed the hand down gently across the woman's breast. He attempted to fold the other over it, but it was too rigid. Conscious of the chill in his lower limbs, he stood. His boots and breeches were covered with rust-specked marsh mud and snow.

A Negro, the one who had just shouted, shouted once more. "Oho." He was coming from deep in the marsh as best he could on the partially frozen quagmire. Tonneman could see as the man drew closer that he was waving something black. He ran up to them, out of breath. "Pardon me, sirs. I've been in the marsh . . ." The man was forced to stop to take in air. The something black was a worsted cape with a blue lining. In his other hand was a black satin bonnet with blue and yellow ribbons on the crown. The sheen under the marsh filth made Tonneman think the bonnet was new. And though they were soiled, there was no evidence of blood on either cape or bonnet.

Jamison, his attention diverted only momentarily from the corpse, remained on one knee, this time examining the stump of the woman's neck where her head had once rested. "Clear evidence that you have animals in the colonies, too."

"Was this done by a wolf, then?" the Constable asked.

Tonneman shook his head. "He means human animals."

"Those who live in cities and towns," said Jamison. He unbuttoned the top of the woman's gown and prised the frozen garment open. "Look here, Tonneman," he said in a low voice.

"Not the Pox, I hope."

Jamie shook his head and opened the outer garment further. The dead girl was wearing a silk-and-lace undershift, the quality of which far surpassed her outer clothing.

Tonneman turned to the Mayor. "At first blush, there is no illness here, no danger of contagion, but I want to perform an autopsy to be certain."

Jamie nodded his agreement.

"Constable."

"Sir?"

"What's your name?"

"Daniel Goldsmith, Constable of the Out Ward."

"Very well, Constable Goldsmith of the Out Ward, I'd like to have these remains delivered to my surgery on Rutgers Hill."

"Yes, sir," the Constable answered smartly.

Mayor Hicks slapped Tonneman on the back. "I leave this in your obviously very capable hands, young Tonneman. You're a chip off the old block. Yes, indeed, the apple doesn't fall far from the tree. I have business to attend in town. Governor Tryon has a royal bug up his arse." So saying, the Mayor went off in his carriage, leaving Tonneman, Jamison, and the Constable to ride back with the body.

CHAPTER 7

They traveled back to town by way of the snow-covered, unpaved route that led to Queen Street, past open stretches very thinly populated, past an area on the eastern outskirts of the City where several tanneries belched hideous essences into the air. Down Queen Street, the population was denser, the streets lined with trees, the roadway paved with cobblestones.

A right turn brought them to Golden Hill. Just as they made the turn, wind gusted and the snow-and-ice-laden trees bordering the road spilled their icy burden in front of them. The tired black mare whinnied and shied, and the wagon wheels slipped and slid, almost causing them to collide with a sleigh coming rapidly from the other direction.

"Sorry, sirs."

Tonneman and Jamie grunted and pulled their cloaks tighter. Only minutes later they were delivered to Tonneman's home along with the corpse and its supposed head, in its burlap wrapping.

The house on Rutgers Hill stood three stories. It was shingled with white pine and surrounded by tall oaks and elms that foretold a leafy shade in the summer. Smoke drifted into the pewter-gray sky from two of three chimneys and the place had a cozy, inhabited appearance.

Tonneman noted with satisfaction that the smokeless chimney was the one at the rear the house. The surgery would be sufficiently cold to preserve the corpse and its head. It would not do to have the evidence rot away on him. "Goldsmith, take these things to my surgery around back. Then you're free to leave with my thanks."

"Sir, do you plan to do the autopsy right away?" The Constable had an earnest expression on his plain face.

"As soon as I get out of these wet boots and have some mulled wine, yes."

"If it may be permitted, I'd like to stay and watch you work. I have an interest in the procedure."

Jamie raised his eyebrows. "Planning a career in physick and surgery, Goldsmith?"

"I'm only a Constable, sir."

Tonneman looked from his friend to the ruddy-faced official. "That doesn't mean you have to die a Constable, Daniel."

"No, sir. Thank you, sir."

"Very well. I'll have someone bring you hot wine."

"If it's all the same to you, sir, hot soup would be better."

Tonneman grinned. He liked this man. There was something stubborn and perverse about him which he found charming. Jamie, he knew, would not agree. "Soup it will be, Constable."

When Tonneman opened the front door, he was immediately greeted by the smell of stewing meat and sweet cakes and a shout of throaty joy. Gretel Huntzinger barreled from the direction of the kitchen, drying her toil-coarsened hands on her apron. Somewhere behind her a dog whined, then barked excitedly.

"Ach, ach." Gretel clasped Tonneman in her muscular arms. She had come from Saxony with her husband Kurt in '53, when Tonneman was five. After only a week in the new country, her husband had been killed when the house where they boarded burned to the ground. Gretel was left severely burned about her body and homeless, without friends or resources. Tonneman's father, Peter, who had lost his wife in childbirth only the year before, had taken Gretel in and nursed her back to health. She became his housekeeper and had looked after the two of them, Tonneman and his father, from that moment on.

"Ach, my Johnny," she cried between hugs. Her German accent was still as thick as her barley soup. "My Johnny *herr* doctor has come home at last." She kissed him full and wet on one cheek, then the other.

Flushed, Tonneman hung his cloak and hat from one of the maple knobs on the wall. Jamie did the same.

"This is my friend, Mr. Jamison. He is also a surgeon."

"You are welcome. Johnny's friend is always welcome."

Jamie smiled. The woman was an Amazon from classic Greek myth. Taller than he, and broader.

"Gretel, we are starving for your cooking. We have had but one potato since we arrived." Tonneman saw with a catch in his throat that her once red-ginger hair was tinged with gray.

"Don't track your muddy boots through my clean house. I have unpacked your bags. You change your clothes and I will feed you and make everything clean again."

"Too hungry," Tonneman said, marching into the kitchen.

The gray mastiff, eyes veiled milky by cataracts, threw himself at Tonneman, received a loving pat, then found a place by the back door to sleep.

"My floor, my floor." The large woman trailed after Tonneman, bending and wiping the wood floor with a rag as she went.

"Nice dog."

"He's a good-for-nothing, but your father loved him. Didn't he, Homer?"

The huge dog opened one eye at its name, then closed it.

Tonneman smiled at his father's choice of name for a dog. "Constable Daniel Goldsmith is in the surgery. He is in dire need of some of your hot soup. What kind today?"

"What else? Your favorite. Barley with hamhocks. Dinner will not be ready for one hour but you will have your *suppe* immediately. Herr Goldschmidt will have his next, when I go to feed Chaucer."

Jamie looked questioningly.

"The horse," said Gretel.

Tonneman smiled. Just like the old man. Chaucer.

The broad-beamed kitchen was enormous, holding a large oak table and six ladder-back rush-seat chairs among sundry wood storage boxes and more chairs. A huge brick fireplace and bake oven lined one wall. Cast-iron kettles and pots and tongs of assorted sizes clustered the floor space around the hearth. A fat-bellied kettle hung from a crane over the fire, which was kept alive day and night, winter and summer.

A spinning wheel stood to the side, and a large basket of wool. Next to the spinning wheel was a four-legged table holding dried herbs, small pots of ointment, bitters, and salves.

The corner cupboard, its door open, revealed burnished pewter utensils. It was from here that Gretel took two large yellow majolica bowls.

While Tonneman and Jamie ate, wordlessly but not silently, Gretel went to take the Constable his soup. Tonneman looked around at the familiar chamber where he had spent so much of his time as a child, studying his lessons and eating little titbits from Gretel's generous larder.

Appetites appeased for the nonce, they went upstairs.

Gretel had put Jamie in Tonneman's boyhood room, and Tonneman in his father's. A chipped orange majolica pitcher of fresh water stood waiting to be poured into its corresponding basin. Tonneman ran his hand fondly over the pitcher. This was his, from his room. It was the first thing he saw when he woke each morning as he was growing up, and had been in his family for generations.

He removed his waistcoat and shirt, then poured the water and plunged his hands into the basin, splashing his face and upper body. A fire burned in the small stone fireplace, but the room would have been snug without it. He dried himself with the cotton cloth waiting for him on the bed and put on clean linen, a clean shirt, stockings, and breeches.

The spartan chamber still held his father's presence. On the blue-painted floor was the worn Persian carpet with the colors even more faded than he'd remembered. Next to the bed on a round maple table was a brass candle stand and his father's wire-framed spectacles resting on an open book. Tonneman picked up the spectacles. The book was Chaucer, of course. *The Canterbury Tales.* The Wife Of Bath's Tale. The story in which the Wife of Bath contended that the married state was happiest when the wife had sovereignty. Tonneman's father loved that tale because it was a theory he never got to prove or disprove in real life, and for some strange reason it helped him to remember his wife and their brief tender marriage.

Tonneman now considered the spectacles, probably where his father had set them for the last time. He lifted the wire frames to his face. The metal's touch conjured up his father's gentle expression, the deep-set eyes, blue like his own, under bushy eyebrows, his voice deep with a slightly hoarse quality, but still soft and caring.

As a young boy Tonneman had nestled in his father's lap and listened as Peter Tonneman talked about his cases, hardly understanding. As he grew older and came off his father's lap, young Tonneman understood more and more.

He closed his eyes and felt his father's hand on his head, and heard his voice, gentle as a summer wind. *"What do you think of that, boy?"* Then, in a sadder tone, *"You should have come home sooner. When I was still here."*

"I know that now. Why didn't I?" Tonneman passed his hand across his face as if to wipe away the guilt.

"I needed you with me, boy."

Anguish, swirling like a maelstrom, filled him. He'd always believed the old man would live forever. Why hadn't he answered his father's call?

After Jamie had rescued him in London from total dissipation and given him new life as the young physician and blade-about-town, Tonneman had lived only in the present, day to day, without a thought to ever going home again. It was as if the picture of home was frozen in time, and when and if he ever chose to return he would find everything as he had left it.

But that was never to be.

Tonneman balanced the spectacles in the palm of his right hand, then set them on his nose, striving to find his father in them, attempting to view the world through the old man's eyes. But he saw only a magnification of his surroundings—and his grief. His father was gone. Gently, he removed the spectacles and set them down on the open volume.

The rich aroma rising from the kitchen saved Tonneman from becoming maudlin. The soup had barely slaked his hunger. He tapped on Jamie's door, and opened it, but the room was empty. Tonneman headed for the stairs, following his nose, with great anticipation.

But standing at the foot of the stairs was his friend, a grim look at his face.

"Jamie, what's wrong?"

"I'm afraid this headless woman incident is more complicated than we thought."

"Why is that?"

"I've just had a closer look at her. . . ."

Tonneman waved his hand. "Go on."

"There are pieces of flesh missing from her chest."

"Done before or after she died?"

"I pray after. Impossible to tell, what with freezing and thawing. What is significant is how the wounds were made."

"And . . . ?"

"Teeth. Human teeth."

CHAPTER 8

The surgery consisted of two connecting rooms, the second of which could only be reached through the first, the study. The study had been a special place to his father. Peter Tonneman had called it his thinking room. Right now it was dim and cold as a tomb.

A half-expended candle stood unlit in the turned walnut candlestick on the maple desk, beside two neat mounds of medical books and pamphlets, some newer than others. Many of the texts Tonneman himself had sent to his father from London. The only light was feeble sunshine filtering through the sole window.

The rest of the study was as precise and neat as the desk. The senior Tonneman had been a meticulous man, exact in his methods and totally immersed in the care of his patients. As he thought of his father's patients, Tonneman made note to place an advertisement in the *New-York Gazetteer* and perhaps one of the newer journals to announce his arrival and his intention to take over his father's practice. Handbills and broadsheets might serve as well.

"Tonneman." Hearing the impatience in Jamie's voice, he continued through the study to the surgery, the same room that had fascinated him so much as a child.

The headless body was laid out under a cloth on the examining table; the head, still in the burlap bag, was on the floor beneath the table. Also piled on the floor was the woman's clothing, including the expensive silk undergarments and the boots which had barely a mark of wear on their soles.

Goldsmith stood uneasily, shifting from one foot to the other, studying his hands, looking everywhere but the table. Tonneman smothered a smile under his hand.

Candles burned from iron holders. Next to one stood a microscope, pots of unguent, an ink pot, a quill, and sheaves of paper filled with notations and sketches.

The surgery was equipped with counters, tables, cabinets, and several large pitchers, bowls, sundry mortars and pestles, pliers for pulling teeth, pincers for making spectacles, and two large enclosed cabinets, one an apothecary cabinet, containing pots and jars, all of them labeled. The other was where his father kept surgical knives and clamps and other operating apparatus. This cabinet, as Tonneman remembered, held blankets. When he pulled open the drawers in the one table that had any, he discovered rolls of linen bandaging cloth, neatly lined up. There was a fireplace. He didn't even consider asking Goldsmith to light it. If it weren't for the blessed cold, the cadaver would be stinking them clear into Pennsylvania.

One worn brown leather medical bag lay open on a counter, most likely where his father had left it the last time he had returned from his rounds. On the counter were two oil lamps. Tonneman lifted each in turn. Empty.

"Shall we begin?" Jamie, who was already suitably garbed, handed Tonneman an apron and his medical bag. Jamie's own surgical gear was already waiting on the wooden counter nearest the operating table.

"Goldsmith, fetch me some water and tell Gretel to keep our food hot. We'll not be long." The Constable took one of the pitchers and ran to do as he was bid. Tonneman tied on the apron and started to lay out his tools, then stopped. He went to his father's bag and then the equipment cabinet. When he had the assortment of tools he needed for the autopsy, Tonneman took them to the table. By this time the Constable was back, hugging the pitcher of water to his chest. He was perhaps more nervous than before.

"We begin," said Tonneman.

Jamie removed the cover cloth. Goldsmith averted his eyes. "None of that, Constable," Jamie said. "We are not here to ogle but to learn." Reluctantly, Goldsmith brought his eyes to bear on the body.

As cold as the room was, the body had thawed somewhat. Bloodless, it was a ghastly gray-white and pitted here and there with pockmarks. The small breasts sagged. Even though the belly was swollen with death's poisons, the pelvic bones protruded. She had been a young, slim woman and, not too long ago, very much alive.

After examining the bite marks, Tonneman felt under the armpits and ran his hands over the limbs. He then probed between the legs.

"That's disgusting." Goldsmith turned crimson. "Begging your pardon, sirs."

"It's my job, Constable," Tonneman said without looking up. "We need to know if she was violated." He continued for a moment. "Well, she wasn't a virgin, that much is certain."

"And no rings on her fingers," said Daniel Goldsmith brazenly. "So she was just a whore. Well, that's a relief. If you'll forgive my saying so, sir."

"See here," said Jamie. A small, thick, brown mark that looked like an *f* or perhaps a *p* was on the right arm near the shoulder. The brand suggested that at one time she had been a felon.

What was the letter for? Prostitution? Or, Tonneman thought ironically, for being poor? Probably an indentured servant paying her debt to the Crown, working for whoever had bought her indenture. "Turn her, please."

Goldsmith complied, but not eagerly. When he was done he shuddered, but it wasn't from the cold.

There were further bite marks on the dead woman's buttocks. After sketching the savage lacerations and those on her breasts and belly and making an overall sketch of the woman, with measurements, Tonneman said, "We have a cadaver that with her head would measure sixty-six inches, somewhat tall, and weighed about nine stone. I'm of the opinion that she was a healthy woman of under thirty years at the time of her death. Her hands and skin are weathered, rough and raw, and there's a burn scar on her left hand and thumb. In spite of the fancy underclothes, I would say it's most likely she was a house servant."

When he began cutting with his father's scalpel, he experienced a glow of comfort, continuity.

"Only one kidney," Jamison said. "The other's not in evidence."

"Dear God," said Goldsmith. "Did someone steal the poor girl's kidney? How can that be?"

Tonneman shook his head. "No. She was born that way, Goldsmith. This one was quite healthy, though, able to do the job of two. None of her organs are diseased." Another twenty minutes passed before Tonneman said, "I'm finished." He held his hands out to Goldsmith. The Constable poured the water over hands and tools. "I think," said Tonneman, as he cleaned gore from his nails, rinsing his hands in the flowing water, "that we've earned the right to our supper now. You, too, Goldsmith."

"That's good." The Constable set the pitcher down, rubbed his hands, and blew on them. "I'm near to cold as she is."

Jamie cleared his throat. "Careless talk drives away wise thoughts."

Chastised, the Constable dropped his eyes to avoid Jamie's stare. He took a twig broom from against the wall and swept the filthy water out the side door.

"There's one thing you've overlooked," said Jamie.

Tonneman wrinkled his brow. "What is that?"

"Come on, boy. I've trained you better than that, I hope."

Tonneman put his hand to his head. "Oh, my God. I forgot to fit the head to the body."

"And . . . ," Jamie prompted. "There's no way of knowing if the cape and bonnet found in the swamp belonged to this unfortunate creature. Which leads us to one important question."

Tonneman nodded. "What if we're talking about two different murders?"

CHAPTER 9

The head, what remained of it, matched; the teeth confirmed Tonneman's estimate of the victim's age.

They'd helped Daniel Goldsmith wrap the woman in the burlap in which she'd been transported. After the Constable had his second bowl of Gretel's soup he was on his way to Potter's Field with his two parcels.

At last Tonneman and Jamie had eaten their midday meal. Now they were drinking Port in the dining room. Above them, more heavy beams showed the sturdy construction of the house. Here the fireplace was smaller. Eight high-backed walnut chairs surrounded the cherrywood dining table. Tonneman, his boots off, was comforting his feet on the old red rug from Turkey which lay over the wide-board floors.

A large wedge of Stilton, and two bowls—one of juicy winter apples, one of walnuts—lay on the small table that stood between worn wing chairs in front of the crackling fire.

Jamie trailed the silver cheese knife along the vein of mold in the waxy white cheese as if plotting a course, and with a sudden movement of his fine surgeon's hand, carved himself a thick wedge. "What do you think?" he asked, chewing.

"About what?"

"That unfortunate woman."

Tonneman savored his Port. He could hear Gretel's guttural voice singing in the kitchen as she worked. It was satisfying to be home, sharing good food and drink and talk with his closest friend. His sorrow was that he had not spent any such nights over the past seven years with his father. "She was a servant by the look of her."

"Indentured?"

"I would think." Tonneman cracked a walnut. "Probably not from the

City. Upcountry or New England. New Jersey. Who knows? But not local. I'll wager she ran off and met with the wrong company. No purse was found. Very likely one of her new friends robbed and killed her."

Jamie's expression was scornful. He drank more Port and refilled both glasses. "What could a woman like that have that was worth stealing?"

"Aha," Tonneman answered, while he concentrated on digging the meat out of his nutshell. "There's a question worth answering. Solve that and you solve the mystery."

"If her killer was a stranger, why chop off her head?"

Tonneman nodded. His theory no longer made as much sense as it had. But that's the way it was with him and Jamie, the way it had been for most of the last seven years. Jamie asked the right questions in the Socratic method to develop a latent idea in Tonneman's mind. By never answering the question himself the older man helped Tonneman come up with the answer on his own. "To hide her identity?"

"My thought exactly. If so, your story of her meeting strangers is not as good as mine."

"Which is?"

"You tell me."

Tonneman dusted his lap of shells, picked up his father's briar pipe from the side table, and filled it with the burly Virginia leaf from the blue Delft tobacco jar. Dry. He put a taper to the fire and then to the pipe. It was a sweet pipe, and in spite of the dry leaf there was no bite. An answer came to mind. "She ran off with another servant. He, and it would have to be a man—no woman could have managed cutting the head off like that—"

"Not even Gretel?"

Tonneman laughed, put a finger to his lips, and said softly, "Gretel excepted." He cut a small slice of the apple and put it in with the tobacco. "The other servant. This man . . . took her head because if the body were found and she could be identified, he would be the first one suspect."

"Very good, my boy. Well done. As far as you've taken it."

Tonneman wasn't listening. He had another question of his own. "But what of the undergarments?" He puffed the briar pipe. The heady scent of the Virginia leaf laid claim to the room.

"Yes, what of them?" Jamie brought a snuffbox from his waistcoat, sniffed the powdered tobacco into each nostril, and sneezed lightly into a large handkerchief. He shoved the handkerchief back into the lace-cuffed sleeve of his dark blue coat. "That's why I say as far as you've taken it. The undergarments put your theory of the other servant, the man, to question."

Tonneman stood and looked out the window. "The snow has stopped." Trees and fields, now decked with snow, separated his house from the Comfort estate. And it seemed, as he stared, that he could see his Abigail again with her parasol raised against the sun, her hand in the crook of his arm, her fair hair and milk white skin. He heard her laugh that tinkling laugh, saw her cornflower blue eyes glistening.

"Damn it, boy, where'd you fly off to?"

Tonneman turned, startled out of his reverie.

"It couldn't have been another servant." Jamie fairly shouted. "Those undergarments speak of wealth."

Tonneman nodded thoughtfully. "She had a protector."

"Yes."

"It may be he was the one who cut off her head."

Jamie reached for the Port bottle. "At last."

$\mathfrak{C}$HAPTER 10

$\mathfrak{T}$he afternoon brought sun and warming temperatures; the snow began to melt. With Jamie dozing in the big wing chair, his feet resting on a stool in front of the fire, Tonneman collected his father's latest casebooks and went back up the stairs to his bedroom.

He put another log on the fire, sat himself in front of the window, and gazed fondly for a moment at the old oak tree he'd climbed as a boy. The tree's bare branches fairly caressed this side of the house. In the summer it furnished lovely shade. Many a day as a youth he'd spent sitting beneath that shade, alone, and later with Abigail.

The September casebook was the last one. He opened it. Odd, it appeared as if his father had two distinct handwritings. One shaky, one steady. Tonneman was familiar with this in older people. The years simply caught up to them. Of course, it could have meant that toward the end his father was suffering from palsy.

Reading, Tonneman admired his father's painstaking day-by-day account of the patients he saw and the treatments prescribed. But soon the Port and the fire had their way and the words began to blur on the page.

Perhaps only moments later he woke with a start and was astonished to find a face staring at him. A loud snap and a cry set him on his feet before he was fully awake.

He opened the window and thrust his head out. The small figure of a boy lay on the melting snow beneath the oak tree. Tonneman couldn't help thinking as he ran downstairs that the boy had climbed the tree to spy on him.

Coming out the surgery door he saw the boy, tangled in a brown greatcoat much too large for him, struggling to his feet. Next to the boy was the broken limb of the oak tree. The slight youth's russet-colored breeches were torn. Tonneman shivered at the cold wind; he knew the boy was feeling a draught through that tear. Snugly pulled about the stripling's head was a knitted hat of red wool. The boy, who had perhaps ten or eleven years, seemed foreign. An exotic, with a tiny chin and red lips, and olive skin. Spanish or Italian perhaps.

"I'm Dr. Tonneman. Who might you be?"

No answer.

"Do you understand English?"

Still no answer.

"Are you all right?"

"Fit as a fiddle." The boy answered in a small voice. He slapped wet snow from arms and legs, then attempted a little caper. But he stopped short, a cry of pain belying his words. It was obvious that his left foot had been hurt in the fall.

In spite of this the lad was as graceful as a deer in the wood. And just as skittish, Tonneman thought, watching him back away, his dark eyes darting this way and that. There was wariness in those eyes. And defiance. The boy picked up the oak limb. To help him walk or to beat off an attack?

"Come," said Tonneman, reaching out his hand, beckoning him into the surgery. After a moment, the boy followed, limping. Inside, Tonneman took the tree limb, dropped it to the floor, and lifted the youth to the examining table. No weight to him at all. Under the russet coat he wore a clean white linen shirt and a brown waistcoat, each as oversized as the coat.

Tonneman probed the left foot carefully with his fingers. The black boots were a mite too dainty for a boy who climbed trees. Tonneman tugged at the boot. The boy winced but said nothing. "That's a brave lad." The boy sneered, then smiled. Finally the boot was off. Tonneman rolled down the wet cotton hose. The area around the ankle was swollen and beginning to purple with contusion. He probed more thoroughly to be sure there was no fracture. The ankle didn't appear to be broken, but it would be sore for some time. All the while the youth stared at him, silent and stoic. "Only a sprain."

"I knew that," the boy responded saucily.

"I'm going to bind this up and you'll be climbing trees again in no time." He grinned at the tiny solemn face and wrapped the small ankle in a linen bandage.

When he was done and stood back, the boy lifted the injured foot to his thigh, inspected Tonneman's handiwork, nodded, and with much difficulty pulled his wet stocking on. He looked down at the floor for his boot.

Tonneman picked it up. The boy took the boot and attempted to put it back on his foot. "It won't fit, I'm afraid," Tonneman told him.

The boy expelled a huge sigh, shoved the boot into his greatcoat pocket, and slid off the table.

"Aren't you going to tell me who you are?"

Biting his lips, the boy picked up the oak branch and used it to limp towards the door of the surgery.

"Where do you live, boy? I'll take you home."

"No!" The word was an explosion. The boy shook his head vehemently. He stared at Tonneman. His dark eyes were fringed with dark lashes. "Dr. Tonneman died."

"I'm Dr. John Tonneman, his son, home from London."

"Dr. Tonneman was my friend. He was teaching me physick and surgery."

"I see."

The boy looked indignant. "You don't believe me?"

"Of course I do." What a pugnacious little fellow he was. "Why don't you let me take you home?"

The youth shook his head again.

"Very well, then. What say you to a cup of chocolate before you go?"

The lad's eyes lit up, then hooded. "Gretel will be angry with me."

"Nonsense. Gretel doesn't anger easily. And her bark is worse than her bite. She certainly doesn't devour little boys."

The boy still appeared doubtful.

"I can promise you that from my own experience."

Chewing on his lower lip the youth moved slowly to the outside door.

Tonneman blocked him easily. "Very well. I won't tell her it's for you." He lifted the boy back up to the examination table, oak branch crutch and all. "You be a good lad and wait here. I'll see if I can round up a pair of boots." This was doubtful. Even boots large enough to accommodate the swelling on that small foot would have to be very small, indeed. Still, there might be a pair from his boyhood in the attic.

Tonneman passed Jamie having a good snore before the dining room fire. From the kitchen came a whirring and intermittent banging sound. There he found Gretel at her wheel, spinning a basket of flax into linen thread. On the hearth pots large and small were in process. She looked up from her work and gave him a generous smile, showing her strong, oversized teeth. Not brown at all, thought Tonneman, the dentist.

"Spinning? I would think the variety of cloth from England—"

"*Ja.* This is why I am back to the wheel."

He was confused, and said as much.

"I am a Daughter of Liberty," she stated proudly with a set of her jaw and a firm nod of her head. "The Daughters do their part. We are all agreed. Just as we will have no tea in this house we have resolved to buy no English finery and instead will spin our own cloth, coarse as it may be."

Surprised by her ardor, he tried not to smile. "And when did we get political in this house? Surely my father . . ."

"Your father was a fine man." Gretel's movements were fluid, the smooth motion from basket to wheel and the vigorous dipping of her foot that kept the wheel moving. "He knew what was right." She halted the wheel and rose to stir the fragrant mixture in the smallest of her kettles. Every bit Tonneman's height, she was as broad as the old oak outside. "I have some good sweet chocolate, enough for you and your friend and then some."

"And where, may I ask, did the chocolate come from?"

"*Ach,* you." She struck him on the rump with her meaty hand. "Not from England, I'll tell you that." She tasted from her smallest pot. "*Gut.* Very *gut.*" This was succeeded by a deep, contented sigh.

Tonneman took a pewter mug from the corner cabinet and held it out to her. Gretel ladled the thick, steamy, dark brown liquid into it. She waited, hands on hips, for him to sip.

The flavor was rich and coated his tongue with the sense of well-being he'd had in his childhood. Was his father, in fact, teaching the boy physick as he'd taught Tonneman when Tonneman was hardly older?

"*Gut?*" Gretel prompted, piercing his trance of memories.

"Yes, more than good."

Pleased, she wiped her hands on her apron and sat back in her chair, once more setting the wheel in motion.

Tonneman turned, then stopped. "Tell me, was my father training anyone to be a physician? A youngster?"

Gretel frowned. "There is that one who was always here. A wild animal, if you ask me." She stopped the wheel. "Why?"

"No reason," he said quickly and made his way back to the surgery, careful not to spill the quickly cooling chocolate. "I beg pardon for taking so long," he said, pushing open the door, "but this is a treat worth waiting . . ."

Tonneman was talking to an empty room; the boy was gone.

CHAPTER II

Private Thomas Hickey of the New-York Volunteers, dressed in mufti but carrying his weapon, unslung the musket before he entered the warehouse on Pearl Street at the southern tip of Manhattan Island. He was smiling. Not fifteen minutes earlier he had watched old Gunderson, his landlord, carve up a carcass. He still had the sensual scent of blood in his nose.

Lieutenant Plunkett was standing amidst dozens of barrels. Of what, Hickey wondered. Not gunpowder. He sniffed the air. Flour. Well, there was money in that, too. He would have to consider ways of pilfering this cache.

Hickey peered about. It seemed as if he and the lieutenant were the only ones in the warehouse. What did the ninny want him for this time? Was it to elicit another present from the affluent private? Or was it the special assignment that the lieutenant had been hinting at?

Out of the shadows came a tall man with a pockmarked face. He stood well over six feet, with long arms and legs. Thick of torso, his aristocratic head seemed small for his body. His blue eyes were set far apart under prominent brows; his thin lips always remained pursed to hide his ill-fitting false teeth and ease the discomfort.

His dress was simple and well tailored; the only embellishments on his blue coat were gold epaulets. He wore buff breeches, white hose, and soft black leather boots. His hands were large and rough like those of a farmer, which he had been, although a gentleman. A blue cocked hat sat like a crown atop his powdered brown hair.

No matter what he felt, Hickey's years of training brought him to immediate attention. "General . . ."

"Hickey!" Plunkett shouted.

The gentleman half smiled. "Has someone been nailing my likeness on trees? At ease, Private. Lieutenant?" He had a deep, low-pitched voice.

"No word of this gentleman's presence. To anyone. No mention of any name that might occur to you. Understood?"

"Understood, sir."

"This gentleman has come to meet another gentleman at The Queen's Head. Since I know you to be a formidable soldier and familiar with the ways and back ways of this City, I have trust that you will perform this task diligently and well. You will escort this gentleman to and from the tavern. He will give you further instructions in the carriage that is waiting outside. You will guard this gentleman's person with your life. Understood?"

"Understood, sir."

"There will be you, another private soldier, Ned Smith, and a Negro driver. This gentleman has been traveling with them from Cambr—"

The gentleman cleared his throat sternly.

". . . from a different place," Plunkett finished lamely. He turned respectfully to the gentleman. "Will there be anything else, sir?"

"No." The gentleman nodded to Hickey. "Guardsman, the carriage."

Hickey took the statement as an order. He stepped quick-time to the front door of the warehouse. His face showed no emotion, but his black heart was singing. The prize he sought was in his grasp. He finally had the man he was going to kill.

The unadorned black carriage stopped at Pearl and Broad Streets in front of the three-story brick mansion. Above the door a sign swung from a ratchet, creaking in the wind; it was a picture of Queen Charlotte Sophia, wife to His Exalted Majesty George III. This establishment, then, was The Sign of Queen Charlotte, better known as The Queen's Head Tavern.

The mansion, which had been built in 1719 by Stephen De Lancey, had become the property, in 1762, of one Samuel Fraunces, who immediately converted it into an inn.

Because of Fraunces's swarthy complexion he was given the nekename of Black Sam. Whether his skin color was due to mixed West Indian blood or Spanish or Portuguese origins, no one knew for sure, and Black Sam never told.

The driver of the carriage that stopped in front of The Queen's Head on this day was Nathan, an ancient white-haired Negro. Surprisingly agile for his years, Nathan climbed down and opened the right-hand door to the carriage.

Out bounded a barking black foxhound with tan and white markings. He danced, then circled in the mud left by the melting snow, splattering anything near. He lifted his leg on the wheels of the carriage and again on the steps to The Queen's Head.

Hickey stepped down from the carriage. "Quiet," he ordered. The dog continued barking.

Whistling "Yankee Doodle" softly under his breath, Hickey walked around the outside of the building carefully, making a great show of looking behind barrels, probing the stack of firewood in the backyard with his bayonet. After peering up and down the street, he returned to the carriage. People were out and about, but not the way it had been before the exodus began.

Finally satisfied, Hickey walked quickly to the front door of the inn, on which a sign had been tacked: CLOSED UNTIL FIVE. He ignored the sign and knocked on the heavy door. Almost immediately it was unlocked and flung open by Black Sam himself, revealing a vast room filled with cherrywood tables, bright with the afternoon sunlight coming through the many windows. In the center, a special table was set for two.

Sitting at this table was a thin, light-haired man of about thirty years: David Bushnell. His right hand was thrust deep into the commodious pocket of his threadbare black broadcloth jacket. Though he was doing work for the American Navy, which had been created only the month before by an act of the Second Continental Congress, Bushnell had no rank. He was neither a sailor nor a soldier, merely another Patriot.

The foxhound raced into the tavern, ears alert, and went at once to Bushnell.

"And good day to you, dog." Bushnell scratched the hound's hanging ears with his left hand. His right was still in his pocket. "Are you Rebel?"

The animal wagged his tail and roamed, sniffing under the tables, benches, and chairs, lapping up errant crumbs. Then, weary of this game, he lay prone near the fire, muzzle flat on the floor, eyes shiny and sad, even as his tail swept the wooden floor. The fat black-and-white kitchen cat pushed its nose out of the kitchen. Rebel growled, and the cat spit and withdrew.

Hickey came to the doorway, measuring Bushnell. The dog stopped licking his muddy forefeet; he bristled at Hickey, then stood uneasily, the skin on his neck trembling.

The Irish raised his weapon and the animal growled. "Shut up, you dumb cur, or I'll have you for breakfast." Hickey now brought his musket almost to bear on the light-haired man. "Name?"

"Bushnell."

"The word, please."

"Shell," said Bushnell, bringing his right hand out of the roomy jacket pocket, showing his cocked small Queen Anne flintlock pistol. "The answer?"

"Back," said Hickey. An annoyed grimace pulled at his lips.

Bushnell carefully eased the hammer forward and set his pocket pistol on the table next to a blue willow-patterned china plate.

Black Sam, who'd been standing nearby watching the terse exchange, picked up a large silver spoon from the table, polished it against his brown breeches, and replaced it in its place setting. As a final thought he straightened the Queen Anne pistol so it lined up with the silverware, then grinned at Bushnell who had the humor to grin back. Hickey did not grin. Black Sam shrugged and retreated to his kitchen.

The whitewashed walls of the tavern had recently displayed English regimental flags and banners. Now in their place were objects Black Sam had brought with him from his younger days, when he'd traveled to Africa: exotic shields, one zebra-striped, the other made of antelope hide, wrought-iron spearheads on light wooden shafts, and two curved, single-edged, serrated swords. The scimitars had no hand guards protecting the brass double-ball hafts. The surface of the blades had a wavy pattern particular to the Damascus steel from which they were made.

On his way to the kitchen Sam stopped at the martial arrangement and righted one of the swords, which was hanging crooked.

Warily, the dog trailed Hickey as he inspected the room and looked into the kitchen. Black Sam was tending a mutton roast. His wife, Elizabeth, a comely, plump woman of twenty-five, as swarthy as her husband, dressed in blue calico, her jet hair captured under a white ruffled cap, was bent over the fire stirring the contents of a great cast-iron kettle. Two little girls, the image of their mother, sat on low stools near the hearth, paring winter apples into a large wooden bowl. The smell of roasting meat and juicy ham bones made Hickey's nostrils twitch.

Backtracking, he tested the rear door to see that it was secure. He placed his hand inside his coat and scratched, strolled back to the front door, opened it, and looked up and down the street again. At last, he whistled.

"I'm not a dog, Mr. Hickey," Nathan said wearily, from his post at the carriage door.

"You're a frigging slave, for Christ's sake."

"I'm still a man."

Hickey spat on the ground.

Nathan ducked his head inside the carriage. "We can go in now, sir."

With eminent ease, the big man uncoiled himself and stepped out, slouching then in an attempt to appear smaller than he was. It was a wasted effort; there was no disguising that giant frame, that commanding walk, bend or shape it as he would.

Next out of the carriage came a tow-haired boy by the name of Ned Smith, another guardsman. Smith, like Hickey, wore mufti and was armed with a musket complete with bayonet. He, too, scanned the terrain for possible trouble. When the gentleman entered the tavern, Smith, eyes still peeled, backed in, musket at the ready.

Bushnell leaped to his feet at the gentleman's entrance.

"Be at ease." The gentleman settled in the chair next to the young man's. "Sit. You must be hungry. I am."

As Hickey closed the front door and took up his position, Smith ran to the kitchen to guard the rear door.

"Innkeeper!" the big man called, smiling through his severe expression. "Present arms."

Black Sam, his darkish skin glowing from the heat of the kitchen fire, came out beaming, bearing a large Wedgewood tureen. He was followed by Elizabeth, who on a tray carried a loaf of fragrant bread, a bottle of Madeira wine, two goblets, and two china bowls.

"What have we here, Sam?"

Black Sam set the tureen in front of the gentleman. "Your favorite, General Washington. Pease soup."

CHAPTER 12

Hickey was angry.

There they sat, stuffing their faces full of real food while he had to do with leftover dregs of pease soup and a meatless ham bone. The damn soup was swill, fit only for swine. His old red-haired whore of a mother, bless her soul in hell, had made a good thick bean soup, when she had a mind to, and with chunks of ham a man could sink his teeth into.

The afternoon sun glinted through the street-facing windows into Hickey's eyes. He moved his weight and leaned his back against the front door to avoid the glare. Infuriated, he watched Washington, sprawled there, waited on like he was Mad George himself. Hickey smirked.

The General picked up Bushnell's Queen Anne pistol. "Weapons on the table? It hasn't come to that yet. But your instincts are correct, Mr. Bushnell. Soon enough that will be the way everywhere in the Colonies." He drew out his own all-metal Scottish pistol, made certain the hammer was safe, laid the weapon alongside his silverware, and uncorked the wine.

Hickey's eyes shimmered with cupidity. He wouldn't mind making that Scots gun his very own. And the pair of silver-mounted Hawkins pistols the General kept in his saddle holsters when he rode his white warhorse.

Outside a heavily laden wagon rumbled by. Rebel, who had been happily engaged with the crumbs under the table, ran barking to the front door. After the wagon had passed the foxhound started back for the table, taking a snap at Hickey's boot en route. Hickey lifted the boot in a kick; the dog snarled, sidestepped expertly, and moved briskly back to his scavenging.

When the General glanced at the guardsman and the dog, Hickey put on a phiz as if butter wouldn't melt in his mouth. The General frowned and addressed himself to his soup.

Washington's attention prompted the Irish to stroll about the room as if inspecting the area outside the windows. He stopped when he got to Black Sam's display on the wall. Nigger stuff, he'd heard. From Africa. The heathens were like to chop each other pretty good over there. He wondered if that uneven edge would make the blade a more efficient head chopper. It would be interesting to find out.

Hickey could see himself in a red uniform with heavy gold braid, commanding a large army, riding Washington's white charger, the General's silver pistols blazing, then the nigger sword flashing and slashing when the guns were empty. He coveted those African swords. And Washington's horse. Not the dog, though. He would kill the dog.

"I know I should properly wait for our meal to be over, sir, but the *Turtle* is very important—"

"Patience, Mr. Bushnell. All things in due time."

"Yes, sir. I'm surprised you wanted us to meet here, sir. It would have been simple for me to come to Cambridge."

"What you're saying, with ever so many manners, is that it would have been eminently more logical. That's why I chose not to do so. The secret of good warfare is to use logic but not always do the logical and obvious thing. Keep the enemy guessing, son."

"Yes, sir."

"First things first. I want to hear about the two floating batteries we used last month and the month before on the Charles River against the British in Boston."

"I had nothing to do with them, sir."

Washington rubbed his lips. He seemed in pain. "These choppers were not made for tough meat. Sam!"

The tavern keeper hurried out. "More Madeira, General?"

"Yes. And this mutton's a bit stringy."

Sam Fraunces looked dismayed. "Suet pudding?"

"Fetch it, then." To Bushnell, Washington said, "I take my intelligence where I can get it. Tell me what you know about the floating batteries." He drained his glass, refilled it, and topped off Bushnell's.

"Sir, the two barges have superstructures of heavy timber. There are two eighteen-pounders, one forward, one aft. Wooden doors mask the embrasures through which they are fired. A three-pounder is set on each side of the stern, and four small one-and-a-half pound swivel guns are mounted atop the superstructure."

The voices of several pedestrians arguing in front of the tavern were heard. No one, not even the hound, paid them any heed.

"I thought," said Washington, "that the guns forward and aft were twelve-pounders."

"I heard eighteen, sir."

"Small arms?"

"Loopholes on the sides for muskets. The barges were driven by oars on each side."

"How many rowers?"

"I don't know."

"How effective were they against the English?"

"I heard piddling."

"As did I. Would they work on the North River?"

"Based on my limited knowledge, no."

"My thoughts, too. Ah, my suet pudding."

Sam placed a new bottle of Madeira and two dishes in front of the General. His voice was taut with embarrassment. "My apologies about the mutton, sir. I wasn't thinking." Removing the cork, he filled their glasses.

"No need to fret. It's not your thinking or your cooking that's at fault; it's my chewing. Ah, turnips, and you've mashed them. Good man."

Sam went back to his kitchen, somewhat mollified.

Washington was now able to eat with ease and gusto. "I delight in food," the General exclaimed. "It irks me that there are times when these damn teeth act up on me and I have to settle for baby pap." Rebel nosed at his leg. "I delight in you, too, dog." He gave the hound a bit of pudding. "You have quite an adventure planned," he said, around a mouth full of suet pudding and mashed turnips. "If we come to some sort of agreement."

"Yes, sir."

"In the meantime, when you're not working on your adventure, I want you to be my agent in New-York."

"But, sir, this mission will require—"

"I understand all that. Of course your mission is first. But I need people I can trust. Watching, listening. Be calm, young David. You are not my only eyes and ears in this City."

No, Hickey agreed silently, nor anybody else's eyes and ears, for that matter.

The meal was over. Sam bustled out with brandy, tobacco, and several new clay pipes. He poured, and was gone.

Washington sipped the brandy, then set about packing his pipe. "Now then, tell me about the *Turtle.*" As much as his mouth hurt, the General couldn't help the small smile when he spoke the name.

"I'm a graduate of Yale College, sir. I know what I'm talking about."

"No need to be prickly, son." The General lit his pipe and blew billows of smoke.

Bushnell did not smoke; he was too involved with what he had to say. "Yes, sir. My Water Machine works, it truly works. I've tested it on the Connecticut River and on Long Island Sound. It works."

Bushnell's enthusiasm was contagious. "I believe you."

"What I've invented is a one-man sub-marine . . ."

"Go on."

"A sub-marine is a boat that sails—paddles actually—under water. I've also made gunpowder that will work under water."

Hickey, once more at the door, started. He knew something about gunpowder. Bushnell had to be mad. And a boat that sailed under water? No doubt Bushnell was crazy. All the same, the guardsman listened intently.

The General seemed to be taking the younger man very seriously. "Could this vessel row unobserved to a man-of-war and secure a mine?"

"Yes, General, it most definitely could."

Hickey's lips tightened. What was that word again? *Sub-marine.* The Fat Man might pay good money for this little bit of lunacy.

"You realize," said Washington, "that if I approve of your scheme, your mission would be the key to my New-York campaign. One of my greatest concerns is a possible invasion from the sea. If the British forces were to take New-York, they would control the North River. It would be their road to Rome. They would then be in position to attack north or south, from Canada down to Virginia and the Carolinas. This City is vital. Winning or losing it could change the face of the war."

In his excitement Bushnell rose, then, embarrassed, sat down.

"Yes," Washington declared, his deep voice booming. "It's mad, but it's just what I've been waiting for. As soon as the weather is clement, I want a demonstration of your *Turtle.* Subject to my final approval after that, I'll want you in the water as soon as possible. If your invention succeeds, we will blast the English fleet to the bottom of the sea. Victory will be ours, and long live the Colonies."

Hickey, noting every word, pretended to be scraping the last remembrance of soup from his plate.

The General leaned back in his chair and stretched his long legs. "Once we know that your plan works in an actual circumstance, we can repeat the stratagem and destroy the British ships in New-York waters. The destruction of those ships will give us control of New-York. With their navy decimated and our forces in control of New-York, it can be a short war. If we don't control this City, the war will be long, hard, and, I'm afraid, bloody."

It was all Hickey could do not to dance a jig then and there. The Fat Man would pay a fine sum for this piece of information. Whistling "Yankee Doodle" softly, Hickey placed his wooden bowl on the floor. Damn pease soup was loose shit. Looked like green paint. Hickey knew a man once who'd died from swallowing green paint. The Irish scratched his belly thoughtfully. He was ready to dance another jig. He'd just figured out how to kill the General.

CHAPTER 13

She felt no pain. Chilled to the bone, she had sneaked back into the house by the rear door. The wrapping on her foot had become soaked in the snow and had frozen.

Crawling up the back stairs she smiled to herself. He had thought she was a boy and treated her like one. She paused at the top step, the one that squeaked—but she wasn't quick enough.

"Mariana? Is that you?"

"Yes, Mother." A trail of melted snow was puddling on the polished maple of the staircase. "I'll be there directly." Quickly, she limped to her room, tore off the boy's clothing, and pushed everything under the high four-poster bed. Without bothering to put on a petticoat, she struggled into a pale blue cotton day dress and buttoned it carelessly over her bosom.

The dress was getting too tight, but no one had noticed. She put out her tongue, made a noise, and fastened a missed button over her ripening breasts. She was becoming a woman. And in this house, it meant she would be expected to be a lady. Why was everybody always hectoring her about that? It was no fun being a woman, less a lady. The men got to do all the good things. The Daughters of Liberty stayed home and spun and sewed while the men went out and did exciting things in the dark of night.

Being a lady made you a prisoner. A dress and all its accouterments were the ties that bound. It was impossible to climb a tree in a dress.

"Mariana!"

She started for her mother's room. Her lopsided walk reminded her that she was wearing only one boot. Off it came and under the bed it went with the rest of her boy things.

The swelling in her foot had not worsened, and she was able to put on her slippers. The red wool hat was still on her head when she went into her mother's bedroom.

Leah Mendoza lay propped up against colorful pink and yellow satin pillows, her face as white as the counterpane she had draped over her, except for the faint blue tinge around her eyes and mouth. A book of Shakespeare's sonnets lay under her frail hand. The warmth of the fire did not warm Leah Mendoza. A glass of weak laudanum rested on the bedside chest.

Mariana dutifully kissed her mother's cold cheek and went to the fire. With the tongs, she pulled out some bricks and wrapped them in the small blanket.

She took her warm offering and tucked it under the covers below her mother's feet, far enough away not to harm her.

"How does that feel?" Mariana sat down on the bed beside her mother. Her mother answered her with a weak smile. Mariana held the glass at her mother's lips. Leah Mendoza sipped the elixir of opium, rum, and water, and moaned. The woman had a wasting disease that made her short of breath and subject to fainting spells. She looked much more than her forty years. Her eyes, though deep-sunken, burned with intermittent fever.

"Oh, Mariana, why do you hide your lovely face under that dreadful hat?"

Mariana set the laudanum tonic back in its place on the chest and pulled off the red hat, scolding herself for not remembering to do it earlier. Her hair, a mass of deep brown curls, tumbled past her slender shoulders. Her mother reached up and stroked her daughter's face. "Oh, my dear, my sweet baby, what is to become of you?"

"I'm not a baby. I'm almost fifteen years old."

"Oh, darling . . ."

Mariana held her mother's fragile hand in her strong one until the laudanum eased her into sleep. When her mother fell ill, Mariana had determined to make her well. To do that, she had to become a physician. And to this end she had taken to spying on Dr. Peter Tonneman to learn the physician's magic. But when she had impulsively announced her ambition, her father was derisive. "Why not become King of England—that's a job you could do, too. Don't be a silly child. You will marry and have children and be a good wife and mother. You'll see."

Her brothers Amos and Matthias had laughed heartily and mocked her. Only the youngest, Benjamin, had taken her seriously. And it was only Benjamin, but three years older than she, who understood her need to be free. In this world it seemed solely the men were their own masters.

Benjamin had provided her with his cast-off greatcoat and breeches, shoes, and other clothes so she could pass herself off as a boy.

Only to old Dr. Peter had she divulged her secret. What Mariana didn't know was that it was difficult to keep such a secret in a small place like New-York, and the even smaller community of the Sephardim of the City. No matter. The other Jewish families thought her odd to begin with, and even if she were to become the wonderful lady her mother dreamed of, they would not want their precious sons to court the mad Mendoza girl despite her father's wealth.

David Mendoza was a prosperous merchant with a thriving business in imported silks and woolens, and carpets from Persia, China, and Turkey, on Broad Street near the General Post Office. His beautiful home was on Maiden Lane.

Both Matthias, the eldest son, and Amos, next in line, were in business with their father.

When Matthias married Caty Da Silva eighteen months earlier, and Amos married Hannah Frank a year later, their father built each a brand-new home. Matthias now lived to the left of the family house and Amos to the right.

Mariana's mother's first seizure had occurred the previous December. Lilly, the hired girl, had run to her friend Gretel on Rutgers Hill because Dr. Jacoby was in Haarlem tending patients. A tall man with white hair and piercing dark eyes had come quickly: Dr. Peter Tonneman. Mariana knew who he was, because for the past year she had been watching him through the window in his surgery. The way he scrutinized her when he came to the house for her mother, Mariana wasn't sure that the old physician hadn't recognized her.

After he had brought her mother back from her faint and Leah had fallen into a deep sleep, Dr. Peter had taken Mariana's elbow and said, "Well, young missy, you bear a startling resemblance to an inquisitive lad who's been my silent companion these many months."

She busied herself with the bottle of tonic he'd taken from his black bag. "I don't understand, sir." Her mother's color was still poor. "Is my mother going to be well?"

"For now, but she's to stay in bed. And no excitement, mind you." He gave her a sober smile. "It's too bad you don't know what I'm talking about. Because the next time I saw that young fellow I was going to invite him in for cakes and chocolate."

"I think he likes ale."

The old physician laughed, banishing the lines and creases on his face. "Ale it is."

The next time the boy peered through Dr. Tonneman's surgery window, the physician did invite him in. Mariana quickly confessed both her masquerade and her fascination for the science of medicine while she sipped her ale, trying not to grimace at its bitter taste. Dr. Tonneman agreed to teach her and keep her secret. Thereafter, she drank chocolate and they became friends. When the tremble in his hand couldn't be controlled, she became his writing instrument.

On April 23, after Paul Revere rode in from Boston to tell of the battle on Bunker Hill, Ben's friend Joel Higgins, the mason's son, was stuck in the left leg with a bayonet, during a night raid of the English arsenal by the Sons of Liberty. Mariana led Ben and Joel to Dr. Tonneman while the redcoats were still pursuing the Sons through the streets. The old man had cleansed and sewn up Joel's wound.

Mariana had fitted the bandage. Much to her joy and Ben's bafflement, Dr. Tonneman said he was proud of his prized pupil and pronounced the bandaging an excellent piece of work.

The four of them had then talked into the dawn about the Cause, drinking chocolate dosed with rum, all fervently aware that the war for liberty had begun.

CHAPTER 14

THURSDAY, 16 NOVEMBER. MORNING.

Constable Goldsmith spent the morning as he always spent it, walking the entire Out Ward from the Jews Burying Ground, starting at the foot of Catherine Street near the East River and Cherry Street. He then followed his route along Division Street and Orchard, named for its stands of fruit trees, through De Lancey Square, around Bullock, crossing Bowery Lane, which that far out was Mr. De Lancey's road to Albany and Boston, past Mount Pleasant, along Mary Street, and back around Bayard. From there the Constable continued to the bottom of the Collect, wishing for a cup of hot soup. Draped across his back, the leather wallet he had made from an old saddle bag held food, but if he ate it now what would he have for later? Goldsmith could not remember such an early onset of winter; it didn't bode well for the next few months.

The open area around the pond offered meager shield from the blustery wind, even with the surrounding hills. Its ferocity whipped through his greatcoat, making him tie his gray wool scarf tighter about his neck and clutch his beaver hat down over his ears. Cold it was, but the snow had all but disappeared and though his feet ached they were dry and that was a blessing.

The City of New-York was divided into seven wards: The South and Dock Wards covered the tip of Manhattan; the West Ward ran along the North River; the North, East, and Montgomery Wards covered the central part of town, with the East and Montgomery extending to the East River. The Out Ward, for which Goldsmith was responsible, lay on the far side of the Collect Pond.

At night he had three full-time and two part-time Watch Men to walk about making sure nothing adverse was happening and to call the hour and *all's well.* The Collect was really a no-man's-land where the Negroes lived, but since the City had started digging for water, and what with the hospital going up on the north end of Catherine Street, Goldsmith had been told to include the area in his rounds. That was before the headless maiden had turned up. A good jest. No maiden, she. Since that day Goldsmith had kept a special eye on the Collect.

Now, as he reached the intersection of Cross and Magazine Streets, the stench of the tan yard on Magazine Street greeted him. Holding his breath he proceeded first to the well excavation, which had been partially covered with planks on the Mayor's charge. Satisfied that the planks had not been disturbed and no one new had fallen in, he made his way to the east side of the pond and started north, using the rope walks to guide his footing and keep him from straying into the marsh.

"Cold enough for you, Constable?" Elias Goodsell, who worked in Van Pelt's Rope Walk, called.

Goldsmith waved at the rope worker but didn't answer.

All looked peaceful among the shabby houses about the Collect, but then all had looked peaceful the days before the head and the body were found. Just beyond the pond was frozen marsh. Still as death, but Goldsmith knew there was an active life underneath of fish and water critters.

His tour brought him to the two tar houses at the northernmost end of the rope walks. About two hundred and fifty yards to the right of the tar house the frozen ground was topped with walk boards. This was where the soldiers' encampment started. A collection of huts and tents, the camp stretched to Bayard Street right onto the grounds of the Bayard mansion. The camp was quiet. The men were probably drilling on the Common or taking one of their marches, which the sergeants loved so much, or drinking in the taverns to stave off the cold.

Beyond the tar houses was the smelly tar fire set in a large hole in the marshy ground that had been lined with matted earth and grass, plant roots and moss, filled with coniferous wood, then nearly covered with more sod. Deprived of almost all air the fire burned slowly, making a great putrid stink and smoke. Tar collected on the bottom of the pit in an iron pan that was drained via an exit tube. The tar was in demand for coating timber in exposed places and for ointments, lotions, soaps, cough mixtures, and medicinal vapors for pulmonary troubles.

Even twenty feet back what little remained of the snow on the ground was specked with tar. The earth just short of the fire was wet and pulpy, sticky with tar. The mixture of scorch and tar squished beneath the Constable's feet. He could feel the heat through his boots.

Goldsmith held his hands over the smoldering flames. The fire warmed him, but at a price. Smoke streamed up his nose on its way to darkening the sky. Coughing violently, he pulled his heavy gray wool scarf over his mouth. The thick viscous liquid sprayed his clothing. Worse than the tannery. He watched and listened as the tar bubbled and boiled in the immense pit. The acrid smoke at last drove him inside the nearest tar house.

No one was about. It was just a bare room, a place for storing tar till it was transported elsewhere. Barrels of tar were stacked, waiting to be moved. In the center of the dirt floor was a fire too small to be of any consequence. In the flames was a large rock on which rested a pot of cooking liquid. Goldsmith placed his wallet on a large coil of rope and sat next to it.

He was thinking of eating some of the dried apple in his wallet when Quintin appeared like a specter. The Negro who had fetched the physicians to the Collect the day before stood in the doorway of the work hut, a worn squirrel hat in his hand.

"Good day, Mr. Daniel."

"Good day to you, Quintin. Put on your hat. It's too cold to stand bareheaded."

"Yes, sir." Quintin replaced his hat firmly and adjusted the frayed piece of canvas he used as a scarf around his neck. He seemed ill at ease.

Goldsmith waited for him to speak.

Instead the African stomped his feet. Heavy blobs of black adorned his shabby boots. "You here for me, sir?"

"Only walking around, seeing what I can see. It's bitter cold today."

"You didn't find another head, did you?" Quintin laughed, sounding like a fool.

This troubled Goldsmith. Quintin was no fool. The Constable rubbed his nose.

"You find who killed that woman, sir?"

"No."

"You don't think any of us had anything to do with it, do you?"

"That's a notion. What do you think?"

"I don't think nothing. I do my work, mind my own business. You're welcome to birch tea, Constable. It's mostly water but it's hot."

"Yes, hot tea would be good."

While he poured the tea into a rough bark cup, Quintin's forehead wrinkled. The Negro seemed to be deliberating, as if seeking the right words.

Goldsmith took the cup and drank, all the while watching the African struggling with what was on his mind. The Constable was cold. The tea and the modest fire didn't help. Impatiently he stood up. "If you're trying to say something, say it."

"The night before Kate Schrader found that head . . ."

"Yes?" Goldsmith warmed his hands on the cup.

"I saw a man walking from the pit where we found the rest of her. He wasn't one of us. And he wasn't a poor white man like what we got living hereabouts."

"Did you see his face?"

"No, sir."

"Was it one of my five Watch Men or the military Night Watch?"

"No, sir. . . . But I think he was a soldier."

"What do you mean, you think? Did you see a uniform?"

"Not exactly."

"I don't understand. Was he from the Bayard Camp or the New-York Militia?"

"It was dark and I couldn't say for sure. That's why it took me till now to tell you. This man was going away from the Collect that night. Not towards the camp, towards town. He was maybe five and a half feet, not heavy. I didn't see the color of his coat. Just something about him made me think he was a soldier. The way it fit him, the way he walked. Like a soldier." Quintin shrugged.

"How old a man?"

"I couldn't say."

"Did you hear his voice?"

The black man shook his head.

"Were you drinking that night, Quintin?"

Deeply insulted, Quintin pulled himself up to his full six feet. "I'm a Christian, Mr. Daniel. For ten years now, since my fourteenth birthday, I have taken Jesus to my heart, and I haven't drunk spirits."

"I truly beg your pardon." The Constable flushed red. "Thank you for telling me this."

"Yes, sir. Only doing what I'm supposed to do. Now if you'll excuse me I've got work to do." Quintin, still indignant, took his leave without lifting his hat.

Chagrined, Goldsmith followed the man outside. Quintin was very busy tending the fire, poking at it and grunting with the effort. The Constable stood and watched him. Quintin took no notice. It was as if Goldsmith wasn't there.

Goldsmith, sighing, doubled back on his route till he was once more on Cross Street. He thought about Quintin. The black man was twenty-four, the same as Goldsmith. But they lived in two different worlds.

The Constable's intention had been to do what he did every day. After he walked the east side of the Collect, he walked the west. But there was something he meant to do and this would break the routine of his rounds.

In the West Ward, on Church and Barkley Streets across from King's College, just north and west of the Common, was the area known as the Holy Ground, for the bawdy houses and the bawds who worked in them. Goldsmith went to a red door at the side of one of the houses and knocked.

"What?"

"It's me, Molly."

There came a sound of feet moving quickly. The door was flung open, and a woman with black silk hair pulled Goldsmith in. "Oh, my sweet Danny, where have you been? I've missed you."

He grinned shyly. "Saw you yesterday."

Molly pursed her heavy red lips in a childish pout. She was wearing a rabbit coat which had seen better days. She opened it. Underneath she had on a thin pink chemise. Her legs were covered with heavy woolen stockings. She wore no shoes. "Well, I've missed you since yesterday."

It was a small dark room with no fire and only one candle for illumination and heat. A narrow bed, a chair, and a wooden box on the floor for the girl's meager clothing were the only furnishings. On the wall was a peeling, ornate, gold leaf mirror.

Molly sat on the bed and pulled him toward her, trying to get his hand to touch her plump breasts. The whore smirked, smiling wantonly and watching herself in the mirror. "Are you ready? I'm always ready for you." She had a particular musky odor about her that was not unpleasant.

Gently, he brushed her away. "None of that now, Mistress Weiss."

"What if I don't listen?" She pushed his beaver hat up on his head and toyed with his hair. "Will you spank me?"

"Do you know a girl? Pretty. Twenty-five. Tall. Five and a half feet. Slim. Nine stone. Small here." His hands made motions on his chest.

"Why are you asking for a skinny bitch like that when you've got me?"

"This is serious, Molly."

The girl put on a false serious face. "I'm sorry. Go on. I'll be good."

"Hair red. A scar along her hand to the thumb. Brand mark on her right shoulder. F or p."

"Doesn't sound like anyone I know."

"Any complaints from the other *ladies* about a customer who likes to bite? On the arse? Anywhere?"

"You jest?"

"What do you mean?"

"That's hardly uncommon in my trade."

"You mean they bite you? And you let them?"

"I don't have a choice, Daniel. This is how I make my living."

Someone knocked loudly on the door. "Jew Molly?"

"Be right there, love," she called.

Goldsmith sighed. "Let me know if you hear anything about my red-head. Or my biter."

"Yes, Constable." She brushed her cheek against his. "Don't be a stranger."

Outside, Goldsmith sighed again and stepped around a tall man muf-fled against the cold. He watched as the man entered Molly's room and the red door closed. The Constable readjusted his hat, returned to the foot of Collect Pond, and continued his rounds. He went past the hair powder and starch factory on Magazine Street and turned north again, this time walk-ing the west side of the pond. As little as there was on the east side, there was less on the west: the Gun Powder Magazine and another tannery and more marsh. Goldsmith walked along vigorously but noticed little. His thoughts were no longer on Molly.

So absorbed was he by Quintin's information about a strange white man that he found himself on Catherine Street, where they had broken ground for the hospital, without knowing how he'd gotten there. His breath came out in white puffs. A soldier. What did it mean?

The City was full of soldiers. But they all didn't look like soldiers. Nor did they look alike. They could be in rags or hunting shirts or Continental Army blue. If Quintin was right, it had to be a seasoned regular. Most Continental soldiers looked like anything but soldiers.

But this didn't have anything to do with the war. This was just murder, plain and simple. Horrible murder.

He had to tell someone, and he had no idea where Alderman Brewerton was. Rutgers Hill was closer than City Hall and the Mayor. Dr. Tonneman it was then. He would tell Dr. Tonneman that he had a witness who'd seen the murderer.

CHAPTER 15

Fronting Hanover Square was the print shop Tonneman sought. The establishment, which was also a bookshop and stationer's shop, took up the first floor of the white-painted brick house.

Above the print shop sign was another, carved and painted to look like a pocket watch, which told Tonneman that this was also where he could find Joseph Pearsall, watchmaker.

The front door burst open, ringing a small bell attached to the door, and a white-haired boy with a bundle of newspapers dashed out.

A wagon rattled behind Tonneman. "Move it, move it," cried a young voice, and another boy jumped out of the wagon and brushed by Tonneman to the door. The boy from the tree.

"Frig you, Ben," said the first youth, plunking his papers into the wagon bed. He ran back inside the shop, slamming the door. The frisky bay mare hitched to the wagon nuzzled a small mound of snow.

"You, stop."

The dark-haired youth turned. "Sir?"

Tonneman was mistaken. This boy was older and sturdier. Still, he had the same exotic face and dark eyes. "I'm looking for Rivington's Print Shop."

"You've found it, sir," the lad proclaimed proudly, opening the door. The small bell rang again, announcing them. Tonneman could hear the rhythmic thump of the press. The boy held the door wide and recited: "Here be the establishment of James Rivington, bookseller, printer, stationer, and gazetteer. I'm his chief apprentice, Benjamin Mendoza. Every Thursday Mr. Rivington puts out the best newspaper in New-York City,

Rivington's New-York Gazetteer. Subscriptions are one dollar and a half per annum, two coppers for a single copy."

"Well spoken," said Tonneman, stepping through the door. At once the distinctive odor of printer's ink filled his nostrils. The thumping sound of the press was louder now, coming from the rear of the room where the monster stood. Separating the front room from the press room was a wooden counter on which were stacked a dozen or more books with fine leather bindings. Shelves to the left, flanking the fireplace, held other books and many quires of tidily stacked paper.

In spite of the cold day the fire was not blazing, a sensible precaution considering the danger of a conflagration to the house. Perhaps that was why the sleek ginger tomcat slept so close to the flames, its tail coming alive every so often as feet came too near. To the right of the fireplace was a staircase. A finger sign pointed the way up the stairs to Joseph Pearsall, watchmaker. The white-haired boy was speeding toward the front door, another bundle of papers on his shoulder.

Tonneman could see a rather portly man operating the press. He had a prominent high-bridged nose, thick dark brows, and a high forehead. A box hat fashioned from the page of a newspaper protected his powdered white wig. He wore a grimy leather apron over his silk breeches and shirt. The elegant shirtsleeves were rolled back, revealing massive forearms. He seemed out of place and at the same time completely at home in the print shop.

"Ben," he called to the boy Tonneman had met at the door. The lad rushed to him and took over the operation of the press.

The man in the paper hat wiped his thick hands on torn sheets of newspaper, dropped them in a barrel, and picked up the single large sheet of paper that the press had just produced. He then displayed the sheet to a well-dressed, older gentleman in yellow satin, blue tricorn, and periwig. The ribbon on the wig was the same yellow satin.

There were two tables nearby. At the first, a stocky apprentice with mouse brown hair laboriously picked type from large trays, composing a page.

Rivington called out. "This is not the time to practice, Arnold. Stack papers."

The stocky boy rushed to do as Rivington had ordered.

At the second table a thin, balding man was bent over an account book. Windows on both sides and on the rear wall offered light enough so that candles were unnecessary.

Everywhere—under tables, on the brick floor—were pottery jugs and other containers, logs for the fire, tied-up parcels. Sheets of paper dried on strings, strung from wall to wall. From the bare brick walls hung pages of newspaper, notices, handbills, and broadsheets—samples of the printer's work. Sheets of clean paper lay stacked on several tables.

The gentleman in the blue tricorn leaned on his walking stick, shifted his weight from one hip to the other, and nodded. "This will do very well indeed, Mr. Rivington."

Abruptly, the noise of the press stopped; the boy Benjamin wiped his brow, grateful for his respite.

"I'll be with you in a moment, sir," Rivington said to Tonneman, as he came front to the counter to write a bill for the old gentleman. "Pardon the bedlam. Today's the day we get the paper out. What can I do for you?"

"I'd like to place an advertisement—"

"Ben, if God had meant you to rest all day he would have put a chair where your arse is. Show this gentleman samples of our advertisements." Rivington pointed to a block of set type. "Mr. Morton, the latest broadside is waiting to be scrutinized before printing."

"I'll tend to it." The tall bald man at the accounts picked up a small black wig from his table, placed it none too carefully on his head, and crossed to the type sitting on a rack next to the press.

"Thank you, Mr. Morton."

Ben quickly gathered sample papers and brought them to Tonneman. Tonneman couldn't help wondering at the resemblance this boy had to the other, the one from the tree. Surely it was the same olive skin, the same fine features.

"Do you have any brothers, boy?"

"Two, sir. I'm the youngest."

"Benjamin Mendoza, correct?"

"Yes, sir."

"Spanish?"

"No, sir. My family came here from Holland over a hundred years ago . . ." He was about to say something else but held the thought.

"Well, Benjamin, let us see what you have there," Tonneman said. There were a number of advertisements for services: shopkeepers; houses to let; notices of runaway slaves and indentured servants.

Benjamin cleared a small space for Tonneman at a table crowded with pamphlets, set a stubby quill pen and a pot of ink in front of him, and returned to his press. While the press noise continued, Tonneman scratched out the notice he had in mind.

Dr. John Peter Tonneman, of London, is practicing Physick and Surgery, the art of the Dentist and the Oculist, on Rutgers Hill. Treatments for Palsy, Rheumatic pains, Sciatica. Treats and pulls Teeth. Manufactures Spectacles. Prepares and sells Medicines.

James Rivington, having seen his well-dressed customer to the door, returned and ran his eyes over the advertisement. He smiled at Tonneman's name. "I knew your father, sir. My sympathies for your loss."

"Thank you."

"I understand you have taken over his duties as Coroner."

Tonnemann nodded.

"As Coroner, do you have anything to tell me about that grisly event at the Collect?"

"Only that the body of a young woman was found."

"And her head?" Rivington prompted. The man obviously knew some of the story.

"The head was severed from the body. Anything more should come from the Mayor."

"Obviously the woman was murdered."

Tonneman looked for a smile on the man's lips. There was none. "Obviously. I can say no more."

"Very well, sir. I respect your decorum. Six coppers will run your advertisement for one week."

Tonneman nodded. "I may want it to go on longer."

"Fifteen coppers for three weeks."

"I'll let you know."

Rivington took a moment to inspect the papers coming off the press now being stacked by Arnold. Then he handed a paper from a bundle on the floor to Tonneman. "This is our current edition. It's a bit smudged. The ink doesn't get enough time to dry, I'm afraid."

Tonneman put six coppers on the counter and crammed his bill in his wallet. "Benjamin is a good worker."

"The best. If you've an eye for an apprentice, this one is mine, heart and soul. His father wanted him for a merchant like the rest of his family but the boy's got printer's ink in his blood." Now Rivington did smile.

"There's the lass, of course. Fourteen, perhaps." Rivington laughed. "I thank God I'm not her father."

"Good day to you then, Mr. Rivington."

"Anything else I can do for you before you go? Paper? A book perhaps. Medical books? Books for children?"

"Not at this present time. Medical books I have. As for the children . . . I am not married and so have not been blessed."

"Ah. Just the thing. I recently acquired a handsome edition of *Gulliver's Travels.*"

"Thank you, but over the past seven years Gulliver and I have been boon companions during many a lonely London evening."

"Then I wish a good day to you, Dr. Tonneman. Thank you for the custom."

"Oh, I owe you for the *Gazetteer.*"

Rivington shook his head. "For a paying advertiser the paper is free."

"Thank you again," said Tonneman, going out the door to the tinkle of the little bell. He stood for a minute on the stone sidewalk in front of the print shop, then looked down at the newspaper in his hand.

Except for the note stating that on the previous Friday, November 10, the Continental Congress had established a corps of marines, there was nothing of interest. He ran his gaze over the first page at the advertisements.

One in particular caught his eye; he looked closely.

FIVE DOLLARS REWARD

for the return of a Scotch servant girl named Jane McCreddie. She is twenty-five years of age, about five foot six inches, red hair, pretty, but pitted with the Smallpox. Well set, speaks very much the Scotch dialect, came from Greenock in September last. She had on and took with her when she went away a short cambret gown with green, red, and yellow stripes. A green callemance quilted petticoat, a long gown about the same color as the short one, a new black satin bonnet, lined with blue and yellow ribbons on the crown. What is most remarkable, she has a scar on one hand and thumb.

REPLY TO J. RIVINGTON, PRINTER.

CHAPTER 16

Tonneman burst back into the print shop, and without preliminaries said loudly, "The murdered girl near the Collect." He pointed to the advertisement. "She was wearing garments as described here as those worn by a Scotch servant girl, Jane McCreddie."

Rivington pivoted from his position at the press. The two boys looked up, eyes frogged with curiosity. Mr. Morton, unperturbed, was back at his account book.

The ginger tomcat yawned, stretched, and leaped down from a stack of packages, rubbing his length against Tonneman's boots.

"Ah, that would be David Wares, a Yorkshire man. He owns the Cross Keys Tavern in Kingsbridge up above the Heights. He won't be happy to hear this, he bought her indenture and from what he said, paid dearly because she was comely and a good barmaid." Rivington shook his head. "I'll dispatch a message to—"

"Don't trouble. I'll have a ride Upcountry and tell him myself. . . ." Tonneman puzzled himself with this last. He was only the Coroner, but admittedly with a curious mind. Perhaps he should search out Goldsmith. The Constable was properly the one to deal with this.

Tonneman came back onto Hanover Square, bemused. It was cold in New-York, colder than he remembered. Perhaps he was getting old, but the cold dug into his marrow and left him chilled to the bone. And New-York seemed sadder, for all its vitality.

People's faces were grimmer. Many shops were closed, their doors boarded over. Gretel had told him, and he had seen some evidence himself, that riotous mobs periodically toured the town, looking for trouble, or looking for Tories they could make trouble for. A third of the population, fearing the lawlessness, fearing the worst, had packed up and left town.

A Rebel government consisting of a Provincial Congress, with committees for everything, ran the colony without much direction because no one wanted to put himself in the line of fire.

The Royal Governor, William Tryon, who had been in England for his health, had returned to New-York in June and found that in his absence the City had become totally politicized. The Provincial Congress continually ignored the Governor's orders. Worse, the Sons of Liberty and other Rebel groups openly taunted him, threatening his life.

Shortly before Tonneman's arrival, Tryon had escaped to the frigate *Duchess Of Gordon,* sitting in the harbor under the protection of *H.M.S. Asia*'s nine guns, eighteen and twenty-four pounders. Gretel claimed the *Duchess Of Gordon* ferried Tryon back and forth, up the Narrows and down the Narrows, and whenever he got within land's view, the cowardly Governor surveyed his little kingdom of New-York through a spyglass.

This, then, was John Tonneman's New-York, the home of the legal Royal government, and at the same time the home of the Rebel government. Rumor was that the City would be either an English garrison town or destroyed.

On the previous Friday, November 10th, the same day they established a corps of marines, there had been a new election because the term of the Provincial Congress was over. People didn't know which way to jump. Danger was manifest on both sides. If they voted for a Rebel delegate, the Crown would have its revenge; if they voted for a Tory, the Sons and others would exact their revenge.

It was clear to Tonneman that the best course would be to take no side. On this day in November the autumn sun was nearing its midpoint, giving little warmth but abundant light. The shops still open about the square were bustling, though their custom was sparse.

Located near Old Slip Market and only one block from the waterfront, Hanover Square was desirable property. At least, this had been so before the trouble began. Owners had been able to charge rentals as high as two dollars a month. Now it would seem to be a different story.

Tonneman pulled on the bit of black ribbon hanging from his fob and brought out his watch. For the first time in a long time this gave him pause. In the back compartment of the watch was a lock of Abigail's hair which he had never been able to remove. He flushed at her memory as he looked at the watch. Only past eleven. He was to meet Jamie at noon at Burn's Coffee House on Broadway opposite Bowling Green. He had a short interval to reacquaint himself with the City.

A kiosk in the square posted arrival and departure notices of ships, packets, and stagecoaches. On the thick column a handbill advertised the information that for two shillings, one H. Gaine would sell a report of the proceedings of the Continental Congress.

Tonneman looked away. He was a healer. The rude and rough-cast politics of the Colonies were not his concern.

"Mr. Tonneman, sir." A tiny Negro boy of perhaps nine years, dressed in scarlet satin breeches, a black cloak, and a white powdered wig, presented himself to Tonneman with a bow. The silver buckles on his shoes gleamed in the bright day.

"Yes, boy?"

"My mistress—" He pointed, with an elaborate twist of his hands in imitation of a courtier, to the small but elegant dark green coach stopped on the far side of the square. "She would have some words with you." The boy bowed again, deeper than before, like some poppet on a string, not a real person. But he wasn't a real person. He was a slave, or at best a servant whose food for the year most likely didn't cost as much as his scarlet costume.

Tonneman squinted in the sunlight. On the coach's door was a family crest, painted in silver, of crossed swords, a crown in their crux, and a hawk above. The boy in satin had already started back to the coach. Provincial troops from Connecticut, in their bright blue coats, small beaver hats set off by black bands and silver buckles, mingled with the civilians. The soldiers had been encamped on the Herring farm near the Village of Greenwich since July to protect the City from the rumored arrival of four regiments of Redcoats. The City was tense, an undercurrent Tonneman was slowly beginning to comprehend. Perhaps he had been in London too long.

The coachman sat in a red coat like a fat ham on a shelf, his skin sallow and pimply, his pudgy fingers loose on the reins of the sleek brown gelding.

The black boy opened the coach door. With the sun's glare in his eyes, Tonneman could barely make out the form of the young woman inside: dainty feet encased in dark, soft red leather boots, a dress of deep blue, small hands covered with dark red leather gloves, and a cloak of cornflower blue with silver fox trim.

He drew nearer, brushing the sun from his eyes. The cloak's hood could not hide the familiar golden hair, a lock of which he had in his watchcase. The cornflower blue hood framed her pale cream face. Her eyes were of the same hue as the cloak.

"Abigail," Tonneman said, feeling his blood rush uncontrolled. She was even more beautiful than she had been seven years earlier, if that was possible.

"Welcome home, John."

He took the perfect little hand she held out to him. A modest pressure invited him into the coach.

He would not, could not enter. He had no desire, or was it too much desire, to sit surrounded by her perfume. He swallowed. Abigail had stirred feelings in him which he had thought long dead.

"I'm sorry about your father. He was a good man."

"Yes. Thank you." He tore his eyes away, seizing on a small altercation between a pompous white-wigged gentleman and a cart driver. Apparently the cart had almost run the man down. Or at least that was what he was claiming.

"It's cold, John. Please step inside and close the door."

He said nothing but did not move.

She smiled, and the two dimples appeared where he knew they would. She tucked the fine dark blue lap robe around her. "Are you home for good?"

"Yes."

"Do dine with us a sennight hence. Our house is on Crown Street just west of Broadway. Six o'clock."

"I have a guest with me. Mr. Jamison, also a surgeon."

She sat straighter and folded her hands in her lap. "I will send you both a proper invitation later in the day."

About to close the coach door, Tonneman was halted by the reappearance of the small Negro boy, this time laden with wrapped packages of sundry sizes, piled higher than his head. Tonneman moved to help the boy, but the fat coachman had swung down and gathered up the goods, placing them on the seat beside him.

The child clambered past Tonneman into the coach. The door swung shut.

"Thank you, Rudy," Tonneman heard Abigail say. Then, louder, "Go on, Phelps."

Phelps slapped the gelding's rump with his whip. The coach made a slow turn around the square and started off on Queen Street.

Suddenly, from out of nowhere, the coach was bombarded with eggs. The coach did not stop. As it careened around the corner, Tonneman could see the dripping yolks forming a yellow scar on the crown and hawk of the family crest.

Chapter 17

Every day now at nightfall one could see carts loaded with trunks and household goods, carriages full of families, Tory and Whig, quietly slipping out of the City.

Houses were shuttered, closed and empty, their owners gone north to the counties or the hinterland. Others, who leaned toward the rebellious illegal government, but feared that the Rebels could not hold New-York, moved further still into Connecticut, Whig country for sure.

His Majesty's ship *Asia* had been off the coast of New-York for months. Its ominous presence reminded one and all of the incident of last August 22 about an hour before midnight. Patriot artillery was positioned along the Battery to stop any troop landing the *Asia* might attempt, while some patriots hauled away English cannon emplaced near the Fort.

When an English barge stationed offshore saw what the Rebels were doing, it came inshore and fired. The Rebel artillery in turn fired on the barge.

A broadside from the *Asia*'s nine guns followed. Next, the Asia let loose a scattering of grape and its marines fired their muskets. These bombardments may have been meant only for the thieving Rebels, but the City was hit. Citizens ran out of their houses screaming, thinking war had begun.

The result was three men wounded and some waterfront houses damaged.

The town soldiers—the New-York Militia—were boiling to fight.

The wavering, cautious Provincial Congress said no.

About one third of the citizens of New-York had had enough, and so began the exodus.

Now, since so many businesses were shut down, men with time on their hands gathered in coffeehouses and public houses and told stories based on truth or air and exacerbated the fears of the population with their rumors.

Those yet uncommitted to one side or the other who chose to remain in the City were distraught. Many delegates to the "Committee," the arm of the local illegal Rebel government, were not willing to risk their necks by pledging to outright rebellion. They found a variety of reasons not to attend meetings of the Committee. Quorums were infrequent, leading to adjournment and frustration.

Meanwhile the radicals fanned the flames of discontent.

The City of New-York sank down into the unusually early frigid winter with almost a sense of relief that there was something other than war and patriotism to think and talk about. Even the strange murder near the Collect was a momentary distraction, although murder did occur often enough in the "Holy Ground" beyond St. Paul's, where the prostitutes dwelled and roamed freely.

In Philadelphia, the Continental Congress grew concerned about the indecision of New-York. Some delegates of the Congress began to refer to the City as the "nest of Tories."

Gusts of wind flailed the City, unhinged shutters, and chilled bodies and souls. Only the women, who still had households to run, seemed to have purpose as they spun, cooked, cleaned, mended, and worried.

Finally, it was decided that the streets leading to the East River should be barricaded, and cannon were placed at points strategic for return of fire should the bombardment reoccur.

Tonneman walked down to the waterfront through the somewhat deserted streets, past brick and stone buildings. The previous day's thaw and today's frosty cold had not given the melting snow a chance to disappear, thus making the flat stone sidewalks slick under his boots.

A sure-footed boy, his tricorn tied down with a large brown scarf that covered his face from the cold, ran by and thrust a pamphlet at Tonneman, who tucked it into his greatcoat pocket.

From Jasper Drake's Public House a crowd of drunken rowdies spilled out onto Water Street shouting and singing, celebrating something or other.

As Tonneman edged past they shouted oaths about bloody Tories, barely comprehensible and yet menacing, boldly inviting him to join the festivities. Tonneman saluted them and hurried on. These men and their idleness troubled him. It was this sort of indolent inactivity that led to discontent and to drinking. The men hereabouts had too much time on their hands, what with trade and business at a near standstill.

As a boy, Tonneman had watched, fascinated, the wharf construction along the waterfront of his City. Pine trunks had been tied with heavy rope and sunk. Next had come a layer of stone, and finally earth. There was so much construction that Manhattan Island, which had once ended on Pearl Street, had been extended into the East River by this man-made land.

The harbor was cluttered with ships, large and small.

Gulls swooped from the rugged sky, shrieking. The pungent smells of salt, rotting seaweed, and tar filled him with nostalgia for his idyllic boyhood.

Shading his eyes, Tonneman could see clearly the offending *Asia* out in the Bay. He turned away from the waterfront, the sun high overhead. The smell of fried oysters coming from a rickety hut open to the street tingled his appetite. He headed for his rendezvous with Jamie.

Just beyond Trinity Church was Burn's Coffee House, a brick building with large mullioned windows on the first two floors. The third floor showed four dormers to the street. Left of the door, in the brickwork, the numbers 1737 declared the year of construction.

A wooden sign above said simply: "Burn's Coffee House." Two large brass carriage lamps hung in front; they would be lit at sundown. Inside, the ready pots of chocolate and boiling coffee mingled with tobacco in the dim, low-ceilinged chamber of heavy wood beams and whitewashed walls, covered with notices of ships coming and going, goods for sale, services to be rendered, and political statements. Many political statements.

The floors sloped from the years of men's feet tramping in for their daily hot brew, which was incidental to the more important purpose of conversation and male conviviality.

Booths were positioned all along the walls of the long room. Most of them were occupied. Some had their heavy curtains pulled for privacy.

Tonneman knew that women were often secreted behind some of those curtains. How did they get in and how did they get out? He grinned; he'd always found the question amusing.

The center of the chamber was crowded with stained pine tables and wide-seated chairs. Tonneman sat at one of the tables, ordered a penny cup of coffee, and pulled from his pocket the pamphlet the running boy had thrust upon him: *"Attention Patriots,"* it said. *"The moment is now, the time has come to Choose. We herewith quote and support the eloquent Words of a southern Patriot, Patrick Henry, from a Speech in the Virginia Convention, at St. John's Episcopal Church in Richmond, Virginia on 23 March of this Year. 'Is Life so dear, or Peace so sweet, as to be purchased at the price of chains and slavery? Forbid it, Almighty God! I know not what course others may take, but as for me, give me Liberty or give me Death!' "*

CHAPTER 18

"All right if I sit?"

Putting his hand over the broadsheet, Tonneman looked up guiltily, as if Gretel had caught him with his fingers in the honey.

The question was asked again over the hubbub of masculine voices.

Before him stood a bull of a man, blond as the sun, his face apple red from the cold, a yellow knit stocking cap sitting atop his head. Tonneman looked about. All the tables were filled.

"Please." He gestured at the chair opposite.

The man sat; the rough-hewn chair creaked in protest. "What are you reading?"

Tonneman looked at the man again, this time more carefully. By his dress he was obviously a countryman. He wore no greatcoat or scarf, and was splitting out of his shirt and hide jacket. A single-strap canvas haversack was slung from his beefy right shoulder. "Words of a man named Patrick Henry."

The man scratched his short blond thatch vigorously through and around his cap and considered the name. "Don't know him."

"Neither do I. He's from Virginia."

"That's one of them places down south where they grow tobacco. I'm going to have some chocolate. You want some?"

Tonneman shook his head.

"I know that's not frugal of me but since it's my first day in town and I've sold my goods, what the dickens."

Loud laughter came from one of the booths with drawn curtains. The blond man's eyes twinkled. He covered his mouth with his hand and whispered. "There are women in there. Some stuff." Then he blushed. "What's that you're drinking?"

"Coffee."

"Is it good? I never had none. At home we drink beer or milk."

"Have the chocolate. And please, as my guest." Tonneman raised his hand, beckoning the serving girl.

"That's mighty kind of you." The blond man thrust out a very large hand across the table and pumped Tonneman's. "William Bikker. My friends call me Bear. I'm a farmer from up Haarlem."

The farmer's grip was firm but not punishing. "Mr. Bikker. My name is John Tonneman. I'm a physician. What brings you to New-York?"

"My horse. Ha. A joke. Applesauce and cider, winter potatoes. Sold out everything at the Fly Market. I'm going to be a soldier. But I figured, I'm not going to be a soldier without I have my last visit to New-York first. So, here I am. Tonneman? You're a Dutchman, then?"

Tonneman nodded. "A little bit."

"Nobody's a Dutchman a little bit. A Dutchman, eh?" Bikker pounded the table several times enthusiastically.

"Why are you joining the army?" Tonneman asked. "Do you think there's going to be fighting?"

"I hope not. I wouldn't want to hurt nobody. But I'm afraid so. Else, why would they want people to join up? And these English give us no choice."

"Why do you say that?"

"Look what's been happening. Everywhere we turn, they push. They should learn—you push a man too much, he's got to push back."

The skinny serving girl was at the table. "Another coffee, please, and a cup of chocolate for my friend here."

The woman nodded and bobbed, lank black hair showing from under a ruffled white cap.

"Well, if I'm to be your friend, you've got to call me Bear." Bikker fixed Tonneman with a curious stare.

"Very well, Bear, have you seen anything of the City, yet?" Tonneman was fidgeting with the pamphlet, rolling it in his hands.

The countryman was watching him as if he had two heads. "No. Just got into town. Sold my goods. Now I'm having my chocolate."

"And after that?"

"After that . . ." His eyes grew bright. "Whatever the Lord presents to me . . . I'll be a skunk in a hole if that don't beat all. Tonneman, eh?"

"Yes, John Tonneman."

Bear delved into his haversack and pulled out a folded square of paper.

"Letter from my granny." He read a section to himself. When he looked up, his face was as full of sunshine as his hair. "That would be John Pieter Tonneman?"

"Peter, not Pieter."

"I'll be plowed." Again he offered his huge hand. "Put it there, coz. Go back a hundred years we had the same granddaddy."

CHAPTER 19

The surgery was empty.

Goldsmith put his head into the study. "Anybody home?" There was no answer. He would leave a note. He was about to enter the chamber when he remembered that his boots were fouled with tar. He removed them, left them in the surgery, and walked gingerly into the study. The small fireplace was lit. He was sweating under his heavy wrapping.

"Mistress Gretel?"

No response. On the desk were a pot of ink and several quill pens. What he lacked was paper on which to write his message. Afraid to touch any of the doctor's papers, Goldsmith remembered the broadside he'd been handed on his way to the Out Ward from his home on Water Street. He had shoved the sheet in his coat pocket to read later.

The Constable unfolded the paper. At the top was the legend: "AU-DACIOUS REBELS." He shuddered. Loyalist language, not to his liking. He turned the broadside over, dipped one of the pens into the ink, and wrote:

> *Mr. Tonneman. I have encountered a Witness who has information which we may find useful in Apprehending the Murderer of the Headless Woman. I will return shortly after Sundown.*
> *Respectfully.*

He signed *D. Goldsmith* with a flourish. Not since his childhood when he had been his father's scholar had he had much reason to put anything in writing and sign his name to it.

He placed the note on the kitchen work table, then retrieved his boots from the surgery. The rest of the day was spent on his rounds, eating his cold chicken and dried fruit as he walked, asking people in the Collect area if they'd seen the man Quintin had described, and pothering all the time whether he should inform the Mayor, try to find Alderman Brewerton, or return to Dr. Tonneman's house on Rutgers Hill.

Thus his tour of duty ended not a moment too soon. Darkness had come on quickly, as it did during the cold months. The lamplighters were already lighting the lamps over on Broadway when he gathered with his Watch Men on Cross Street and saw them off on their rounds, after telling them to keep an extra eye out for Quintin's soldierly man.

The Constable was already feeling the gnawing pains of hunger and thinking about his supper. The way things were, it was probably only chicken soup and noodles, but that was more than many were eating in these hard times. Except for the rich. Goldsmith's shoulders were stiff and his feet ached in his heavy boots. But food and respite would have to be delayed until he told someone in authority about what Quintin had said. Then and only then could he eat in peace and spend a restful night, knowing he had done his job.

Horses and vehicles bulging with furniture and household items rumbled past him. Slowly but surely, people were fleeing the City. Not just the carts of the common man. Even the carriages of the wealthy. War was something the rich with all their wealth couldn't buy away. His father would have called it the wrath of Jehovah. Thanks be to God, he was through with that religious nonsense.

His eyes widened in recognition. One of the carriages passing by bore the crest of the family Lopez. "Jacob!" he called to the driver. Jacob Lemco was his wife Deborah's cousin.

Lemco, a wispy-bearded, religious man, slowed the double team of matched chestnuts to a walk.

"Where are you off?"

"Rhode Island, Newport, God willing. Just the young ones and the nurse."

The brown velvet curtains covering the windows opened a fraction, and Goldsmith saw bright eyes peering out at him. Goldsmith waved to the eyes and smacked the chestnut closest to him on the flank. "Get a move on, then, Jacob. Have a safe journey."

"God willing."

As the carriage rumbled away, Goldsmith wondered if he ought to send his wife and young ones off to Flat-Bush where his cousin Solomon had a farm.

A cloud of leaflets came at him in the high wind and he reached up and grabbed one. Standing under a street lamp he read: *"Who can seize Life without Liberty?"* He folded the piece of paper and placed it in his sleeve. He would read this at home; these words held substance for him.

By the time he got to Rutgers Hill, the Constable was too tired and hungry to think. He knocked at the front door, wondering if perhaps he should go to the surgery.

Gretel greeted him with a big smile. "Ach, Herr Goldschmidt. Herr Tonneman has gone out. Herr Jamison has also gone out."

"Could I come in and sit by the fire for a bit?"

"Ach, the fire has also gone out."

He looked at her strangely, without comprehension.

"That is a little German joke. Funny, *ja?*"

Goldsmith nodded politely.

"Herr Jamison left this *Zettel* for you." And she handed Goldsmith the same scrap of paper he'd left. "Come in my kitchen, you can warm there."

Jamison had written beneath Goldsmith's message: *Dr. Tonneman and I will be at Burn's Coffee House on Broadway opposite Bowling Green.*

"Sit," Gretel commanded. "I'll give you some ham and bread."

With a mild reservation at keeping the two physicians waiting, and another one about his wife and mother-in-law, who were keeping his supper for him, and only the barest thought to his father and his father's religion, Goldsmith followed the large German woman into the house to eat pork.

CHAPTER 20

By late afternoon, with darkness falling quickly, the serving maids went from table to table lighting candles while the barkeeper dealt with the sconces and the wagon wheel chandeliers overhead.

Tonneman had progressed from coffee to ale. Bear Bikker had not yet had his fill of chocolate. "I am," the big farmer was saying, slurping his syrupy drink, which left a brown ring around his lips, "the last Bikker. The last of my line." He thrust the letter at Tonneman. "Here, see."

"I'm sure you're mistaking me for someone else. I know of only a distant cousin who used to live up in Peeks-Kill. She was older than I by some twenty years. She did marry, but I have no idea of her name or where she lives. Or if she lives." Tonneman, being a man of manners and because Bikker was so insistent, took the letter and unfolded it.

The paper was worn silky and brown around the edges and the words were foreign. Tonneman shook his head. "I read sparing Dutch." He returned the letter.

The farmer took another gulp of chocolate. When he put his cup down he was all smiles. "I will tell you what it says."

Tonneman looked about the large chamber. Where the devil was Jamie? He was exceedingly late. His business at King's College must have delayed him.

Burn's Coffee House had filled to its limits as more and more men poured in through both doors, crowding into the main room. The booths were jammed and spilling over, resounding with the raucous noise of argument.

Bikker had to shout to be heard. "See here. It says that I should always be proud of my family, that we are descended from Pieter Tonneman, the last Schout of New Amsterdam and the first Sheriff of New-York."

Tonneman was dumbfounded. "I, too, am descended from Pieter Tonneman. Do you know what the English called him?"

"Do I know? What else? The Dutchman."

With that Tonneman's reserve was finally broken. "Yes, the Dutchman." He offered his hand. "We are indeed cousins."

Their hands clasped across the table. The farmer's eyes were jubilant. His acceptance of their connection notwithstanding, Tonneman was still cautious.

It was at that moment that Jamie appeared out of the dark smoky haze of tobacco, shoving his way through the crushing pack of men. Tonneman stood and waved, making sure to keep one hand on his chair lest it be spirited away.

Bikker, suddenly shy, stood, too, his haversack to his shoulder. "I am happy to know I have a cousin. As your friend has come I will go now."

"Sit down, Bear. We'll find another chair."

"I'll get it," Bikker said eagerly, and he disappeared into the crowd just as Jamie arrived at the table.

"It seems we've landed in a bed of nettlesome Rebels," he announced. "Never mind, it might prove interesting." He sat and draped his cloak over the back of his chair. Tonneman couldn't help but notice that his friend smelled unfamiliarly of rose scent and that there was rouge on the ruffle of his shirt. "I've completed my survey of King's College, which was followed by a long and dreary inspection of the site of the new hospital. After all, what can one say about a pile of bricks and stones after one has said *very interesting* for the fourth time? When they invited me for coffee at The Queen's Head, I could not refuse. That man Fraunces has several extraordinary African swords. Have you ever seen them?"

"I don't believe I have."

"The blades have serrated edges, supposedly for a more efficient cut. I don't see how that would be the case, do you?"

Tonneman sniffed the air audibly and ran a finger over his friend's rouged shirt front. "I believe you, Jamie. Of course I do. You've been all this time inspecting bricks and stones and sitting in The Queen's Head Tavern looking at swords."

Jamie grinned. "Well, perhaps a detour *à la femme*. I have discovered a pleasant *mélange* of ladies not far from the College."

"I thought you abjured the woman-for-hire, and prided yourself on your seductive powers and those of persuasion."

Jamie sighed an immense mock sigh. "When we are at Rome, we do there as we see done. I assure you, my—"

He was interrupted by a whoop. The giant Bikker was holding a high stool aloft in his right hand, a bucket in the left, all the while fighting his way to them.

Jamie's eyes followed Tonneman's. "What apparition is this?"

Tonneman grinned. "This," he said solemnly, as Bikker lowered the stool from his great height, oblivious to all around him but Tonneman. ". . . is my kinsman, William Bikker from Haarlem upcountry. Cousin, this is my friend, Dr. Arthur Jamison." He poked Jamie. "He's called Bear."

"I wonder why?" Jamie extended his hand, as he examined Tonneman's face for any sign of a ruse. "Jamie."

"Pleased to meet you, Jamie." Bikker levered Jamie's arm as if he were pumping for water. Then he whacked the bucket on the table. "Fried oysters. My treat."

The serving maid stopped at their table with a tray containing a pitcher of beer, three mugs, and bowls of pickled pigs' feet, pickled beets, and walnuts. Jamie and Tonneman reached for their purses.

"Away," said Bear. "Away. Your money's no good at this table. Not this day. Not the day I find my coz, the illustrious great-great-great-grandson of The Dutchman, Sheriff Pieter Tonneman."

Tonneman, hungry as the Bear's namesake, fell to at once, delighted to see that Jamie's reaction to Tonneman's so-called cousin was dubious to say the least. Although he hadn't had that much to drink, Tonneman felt drunk. And he felt an enormous sense of liberation. He was home. He was assuming his birthright. He had met a relative he never knew he had. For the first time since Abigail's rejection, he was feeling his own man. With another whoop, Bear dug into the oysters, equaling Tonneman's gusto.

A voice louder than all the others broke through the din of the crowd. "Brothers for Liberty!"

"Heaven forfend," Jamie said, his right eyebrow lifting sharply.

Tonneman and Bear turned to see the speaker. It proved to be a man about Tonneman's age, in the bloody smock of a butcher. The chamber went silent. "We have already shown our mettle as fighters at Lexington!"

"Here, here!" was the answering shout.

"Were you there, butcher?" Jamie muttered.

"And we'll show it again and again, till Doomsday if need be!"

"Amen to that!" Bear banged the table with his massive fist. Empty oyster shells spilled to the floor.

"Doomsday might be sooner than you think," said Jamie. "Tonneman, old fellow, dear friend, this is no place for a true Englishman." He made a move to rise.

Tonneman put an arresting hand on his friend's arm. He needed to assuage his curiosity. "Let's hear what he has to say."

"When Patriots bleed and die in Massachusetts, can it be long before Patriots bleed and die in New-York?"

"Amen," someone shouted, and other voices said "Amen" and "Amen." A rumble of agreement rolled through the coffeehouse.

The speaker swept on. "The Patriots at Lexington and Concord and Breed's Hill were our brothers. When they bled we bled!"

"Praise God, we stand together."

"Yes, let that be our battle cry. Stand together we must. Then what can King and Parliament do?" The butcher sat to cheers and many claps on the back.

Another stood. "They will raise their army of hirelings, carry provisions across the vast ocean, and fight . . ."

"Smart man."

Jamie's hoarse whisper carried. Bear turned and eyed him strangely, as did several men behind Bear. Jamie raised a supercilious eyebrow.

"These hirelings will be strangers in a strange land," said a voice from behind Tonneman. The voice was familiar. Tonneman turned. Constable Goldsmith, bundled up against the cold, his eyes shining with excitement. "We have been chosen by the Almighty for this fight. God is with us and our Cause is just."

"Very eloquent, Constable," Tonneman said to an accompaniment of mugs pounded on tables. Another rose to speak.

Goldsmith leaned toward Tonneman. "Good evening, Dr. Tonneman. Might I have a word with you?"

"Yes. As matter of fact, we were just leaving."

They stood and pushed through the crowd to the door.

Outside, the air was crisp and Broadway was bright and filled with people. They hadn't gone three steps when a shout echoed behind them.

Constable Goldsmith cried out, then stumbled. Blood flowed from his head.

CHAPTER 21

Goldsmith sank to his knees on the ice-slick sidewalk, groaning. Blood streamed down his ashen face. The horses tied to the rail in front of the coffeehouse whinnied and tugged on their reins, frightened by the scent of blood. In the glow of the street light, Tonneman knelt beside the Constable while Jamie and Bear silently faced the five men who approached them, taunting, "Stand and fight, you Tory bastards."

Bear seized the first two by their necks and knocked their heads together. One fell to the ground and crawled off, whimpering. The other was made of doughtier stuff and traded blows with Bear.

Jamie feinted to his right, drawing one man to him, then stopped short and struck the man squarely in the throat.

The other two attackers closed in on the kneeling Tonneman and the injured Constable.

The first, a burly dockman, swung a stick at Tonneman's head but Tonneman, seeing it coming, dropped to the sidewalk and into the street, amidst the horses' hooves. The man with the stick pursued and struck again, cursing when he missed Tonneman. The terrified horses pulled despairingly at their reins. One jerked free and galloped up Broadway. Tonneman had all he could do to keep from being stomped. He rolled out from under, only to see the dockman still coming after him. Crawling backwards, crablike, he found a brick under his hand, perhaps the same one that had been hurled at the Constable. He threw it, hitting the man in the solar plexus. The man gasped and went down.

In the meantime the dockman's partner aimed a vicious kick at Goldsmith's head. A groggy Goldsmith grabbed the man's boot and pulled. His attacker fell heavily on his rump. "Desist, friend," Goldsmith said, getting to his knees, wiping the blood from his eyes with the sleeve of his coat. "I'm an Officer of the Law."

"Frig you and the Law." The man bounced up and kicked again. Goldsmith clasped both hands together and dealt him a solid blow in the groin. The man doubled over and fell to the ground whimpering, a problem no more.

Bear and Jamie dispatched their opponents at the same time and grinned at one another as only victorious men of combat can. They joined Tonneman, who was helping Goldsmith up. The Constable's head wound was still running blood. Tonneman tied a handkerchief around the wound. "You'd best come along to my surgery."

"Well done," Jamie stated ecstatically. "Well done, all."

Bear nodded, his blue eyes gleaming like triumphant beacons in the pale light. "Aye, we all did well." Then the triumph ebbed from his face. "But for the wrong cause. Those men are more my comrades than you." He turned to Tonneman. "Cousin, I'm glad to know you, glad we met, but we are different men. You are the King's man. I am my own man. We have chosen different paths." He took a deep mournful breath, turned, and went to the aid of their assailants.

Jamie's face was grim as he watched the big man leave. "Indeed. These scum are nothing but canaille. The King's army will make short work of them."

"Sir . . ." Goldsmith began. He was stopped by the slight pressure on his arm from Tonneman.

"Constable," Tonneman said firmly. "It is late. You mentioned a word with me. I, too, want a word with you. We can have our words together while I attend your wound. Can you walk?"

The Constable wiped blood from his forehead and forced his eyes wide and his stocky body alert. "I'm ready."

Tonneman offered a bracing arm, but when he approached, Goldsmith made a face. "Phew. Excuse me, sir, but you're a bit ripe."

Tonneman sniffed, then looked down at his clothes. "It seems I've been among the horses."

"Couldn't you tell?" Jamie guffawed loudly. One of their attackers groaned and lifted his head. "Shouldn't you arrest these ruffians, Constable?" When there was no response, the surgeon persevered. "Very well, we'd better leave posthaste, before that fellow finds out he's lost his horse." Jamie laughed again, altogether enjoying himself.

In spite of the stink of manure, Goldsmith accepted Tonneman's support. As they made their slow way to Rutgers Hill, Jamie delivered an extended peroration on the perfidy and cowardice of all thirteen of the American Colonies. It was nearing seven o'clock; darkness had long fallen, but the street lamps cast a vivid, serviceable light along their path. The half-moon hung in a sky dense with scudding clouds. It was intensely cold.

Candles glimmered behind shutters in the Tonneman house; smoke lifted lazily from the chimneys.

"I have need of a drink and a smoke," Jamie said, leaving them for the house proper as Tonneman led Goldsmith into the surgery.

Only after the wound was washed, shaved, stitched, and bandaged did Goldsmith speak. Diffidently he asked, "Are you a Loyalist, sir? Or worse, are you a Tory like your friend?"

"I'm not political." Tonneman poured water from a pitcher, rinsing his hands of blood. "I take no sides."

The Constable hesitated, then plunged in. "That won't do, sir. Not in this place, not in this time. There's going to be a great battle. For men's lives, their liberty, perhaps for their very souls. Every man of us will have to declare himself. It—"

"I feel much better." Jamie came through the door from the study, puffing away on his pipe. "We've had a communication." He was holding a torn broadsheet with only a few words printed large and bold. "To wit: *He who is not loyal to the King will lose his head.*" Jamie smirked. "And now it is my turn to say Amen."

CHAPTER 22

Jamie leaned against the surgery door, studying the few words of the broadsheet as if they were holy writ, chuckling as he did so.

Tonneman helped Goldsmith from the examining table. On his crown was a white patch. "There you are, Constable, five stitches, nice and neat. See me in ten days and I'll pluck them out for you. Other than that, you're good as new."

Goldsmith moaned. "From the way my head aches, I find that difficult to believe, sir."

"A bit of willow bark in rum should help."

"It will no doubt put me to sleep right here."

"Do you want to take it home with you?"

"No, sir. Ah. My head feels like the brick that hit me is still in it."

Tonneman went about preparing the mixture. "By the by, Constable, I have some information for you."

"Sir?"

"The dead girl. I believe her to be a Scotswoman, Jane McCreddie."

Jamie lifted his eyes from the broadsheet with amazement. "Now how would you know that, my dear fellow?"

Goldsmith was immediately attentive.

"There was a notice in Rivington's *Gazetteer* about a runaway. An indentured servant girl. The description of her clothing is exact. The notice said the girl was twenty-five years, about five foot six inches, and pretty. Well, we can't tell about the pretty but the rest is the same. The notice also mentioned pox scars and the fact that she has a scar on hand and thumb. That also fits our dead girl."

"Who placed the notice?" the Constable asked.

"Rivington told me the notice was placed by one David Wares, proprietor of the Cross Keys Tavern in Kingsbridge."

Goldsmith's weariness dropped away. "That's wonderful news, sir. Thanks to you, we know who she was."

Jamie sneered. "Now all you have to do is find out who relieved her of her head."

Goldsmith shot as hard a look as he dared at Jamison. Was the physician mocking him?

But Tonneman did not seem to notice the edge in his friend's words. "Now that that is out of the way, Constable, what was the word you needed to have with me? And how'd you know where to find me?"

"He left a note here and I left him one with Gretel in return," said Jamie.

"Same subject, sir. The dead girl. Quintin, the black who fetched you to the Collect, told me that the night before the head was found he observed a man walking from the pit where the body was later discovered. Quintin said the man wasn't one of his people and he wasn't a poor white man."

"What did he look like?"

"No help there, sir. All Quintin could tell me was that he was of moderate height and not a heavy man."

Jamie yawned loudly. "So sorry."

Tonneman gave Goldsmith the willow mixture in a phial.

"Thank you, sir." Goldsmith quaffed the medicine in one gulp. "Well, if I don't feel better at least I'll *think* I feel better. And I'll get a good night's sleep . . . if my wife lets me."

Jamie raised an eyebrow. "Ah, lucky man, an amorous woman."

Goldsmith hesitated. He didn't know if Dr. Jamison was being insulting, but considering their stations and that the man was Dr. Tonneman's friend he let it pass. "No, sir, a complaining woman." Goldsmith brought himself back to the matter at hand. "There was one more thing about the man Quintin saw. He said he thought he might be a soldier. He didn't see a uniform or anything like that. Said the man walked like a soldier."

"Niggers." This from Jamie. "The things they say. He was probably drunk."

"He swore he wasn't a drinking man."

Jamie laughed derisively. "And I'm the Emperor of the Holy Roman Empire."

Goldsmith inclined his head. "If you say so, sir."

It was Jamie's turn to give the Constable a sharp look.

Tonneman took the phial from Goldsmith. "Have you children, Constable?"

"Yes, sir. Two girls. A boy next time, the good Lord willing. If that's all, sir, I think I should be getting home."

"Of course."

Goldsmith frowned, searching his mind. He brightened. "One more thing. The man Quintin saw was walking in the direction of the City." He fixed his beaver hat gingerly on his bandaged head. "I'll say goodnight, sirs."

"Constable?"

"Sir?" Goldsmith paused, hand on the door latch.

"I thought I might ride up to Kingsbridge tomorrow and have a word with David Wares."

"What of your practice?" Jamie asked.

"It's waited for me this long, it can wait for me a day longer. Constable? Would you care to join me?"

"Alderman Brewerton would have to approve. One of the Night Watch would have to walk my rounds, and I would have to pay him out of pocket—"

Tonneman waved his hand. "I'll take care of paying the fellow, and I'll arrange with the Mayor to make it all right with your Alderman."

"Then, yes, sir. I'd like very much to go."

"First thing in the morning you make the arrangement for your substitute and I'll talk to the Mayor. Have you a horse?"

"Yes, sir."

"We can ride up in the morning if you'll meet me at half ten right here."

Goldsmith nodded, then flinched at the pain. As he opened the door he said, "I pray it wasn't one of our soldiers." He left quickly.

Jamie was glaring at the door with loathing. "I don't like that Hebrew."

"I don't think he likes you, either."

Jamie snapped his fingers. "That's how much I care. He's also in sympathy with the Rebels."

"He's just a poor man trying to do his job." Tonneman packed away his instruments and tried to make the surgery presentable. In spite of his dismissive words about his practice, there might be patients waiting to-morrow when he returned. "Would you like to come along to Kingsbridge tomorrow? It will give you a chance to see an American countryside."

"I think not. The position of Chancellor of Medicine comes with a house and a housekeeper. I'm going to see how soon I can move in."

"I had thought you'd stay here."

"Face it, John, I'm a reprobate, beyond salvation. I need women, I want women, I will have women. And you, my friend, are a bit of a stick. I need a place where I can wench away the hours without worrying about your—or, heaven help me, the Amazon's—disapproving eyes upon me."

CHAPTER 23

It was bitter cold and the sky was overcast with gloomy, moisture-laden clouds as Tonneman and the Constable set out for Kingsbridge. A brisk wind blew from the northeast. Tonneman's black gelding was lively, much preferring the weight of a single rider to the Tonneman carriage. Goldsmith's tired brown mare, Rifka, wanted to be friends but the gelding, Chaucer, wasn't having it. Whenever the mare nuzzled Chaucer, the gelding increased its speed. At that rate, Tonneman thought, amused, they would be in Kingsbridge before they knew it.

Politically, Kingsbridge was part of Manhattan. The bridge for which it was named was built by Frederick Philipse in 1693, after the Dutch King William III granted Philipse permission to build a bridge over Spuyten Duyvil Creek and collect tolls.

Tonneman's medical bag was attached to one of the many hooks on his father's old campaign saddle. In the saddlebags were a loaf of bread, hard chocolate, and a bottle of brandy.

Goldsmith's saddlebags were a treasure trove of cakes and cheeses and dried apple. The Constable had insisted on displaying them before they left. "My wife, sir. She thinks we'll starve to death between here and Kingsbridge and back."

"Women are like that. Be glad of it."

"I am."

"How's your head?"

"It's been better."

"And so it will be again."

"If I may say so, sir, your father was very respected."

"Thank you, Goldsmith."

Tonneman had thought to make quick work of the morning, reporting to the Mayor and getting Hicks's authorization to take Goldsmith with him. That had been simple enough. What had been difficult was listening to the Mayor's tirade against a certain wealthy merchant, John Hancock of Boston. This Hancock, who was president of the rebellious Continental Congress, had sent a letter to the Provincial Congress of New-York, which had somehow fallen into the Mayor's hands.

"Listen to this outrageous seditious cow shit," the Mayor bellowed. "Hancock wants directions given for immediate removal of all the sulphur now in the City of New-York, to a place of greater safety, at a distance from the City, and they are to please inform the grievance collectors in Philadelphia where they've hidden it."

The Mayor's face was apoplectic. He hobbled around his office, cursing the Rebels. Tonneman guided him to his desk. "If you continue like this you'll have a seizure."

Mayor Hicks shoved the letter at Tonneman. "This is an outrage. You know what he wants that sulphur for, don't you? Of course you do. To blow us off this continent, that's what."

The Mayor was still fuming when Tonneman left.

The town of Kingsbridge on the Haarlem River was a distance of thirteen miles via Bowery Lane and the Bloomingdale Road, which ran up the west side of Manhattan. Beyond Kingsbridge was the road leading to Albany and Boston. Though unpaved and filled with ruts, the way was much traveled. The name Bowery, from the Dutch word for farm, came from the old Pieter Stuyvesant estate which Stuyvesant had owned when he was the last Director-General of New Amsterdam back in 1664, at the time John Tonneman's ancestor Pieter, was Schout. Now, over a hundred years later, Stuyvesant's descendants had divided up the original property, which ran from the Bowery Lane to the East River.

Tonneman and Goldsmith rode through rocky wilderness terrain, gradually climbing to higher ground. It began to snow.

Goldsmith slowed when they came to a fork. "We turn right here. If we go left we'd end up in Bloomingdale's." He referred to the sprawling lands belonging to the rich farmer.

When they made the turn, crawling ahead of them was a cart stacked high with furniture and bedding. Three young children peered out from under the bedding. The children waved; the two men waved back and rode around, touching their hats to the young man and his wife driving the cart.

Tonneman took their slowing down as a good excuse to bring out his bottle. When he looked at his pocket watch, much to his annoyance, Abigail invaded his thoughts. Angrily, he cast her memory aside. They had been on the road for an hour. He drank and offered Goldsmith.

"First cake, sir. I never drink on an empty stomach."

The Constable passed Tonneman a honey cake. Tonneman passed Goldsmith the bottle. And so it went until the cakes were gone.

"Dr. Tonneman, what time do you expect to be back?"

"Depends on who we talk to and what they say. I would hope about sunset."

"That's what I thought."

"Do you have a problem?"

"Yes. I'm not religious, but my mother-in-law . . . Coming back after sunset means I'll be breaking the Sabbath."

There was no comprehension on Tonneman's face.

"For Jews the Sabbath falls on Saturday."

Tonneman nodded, still not comprehending. He reached for his saddlebags. "I have chocolate and bread, but if I bring them out we'll finish the damn bottle and never get to Kingsbridge." He put away the bottle.

"I'm afraid you're right, sir. They'll go fine with my cheese and dried apple on the trip back. We are a bit more than halfway to Kingsbridge."

Tonneman, humming the melody of a song Abigail had once sung to him, urged Chaucer forward.

The route ahead was overlaid with snow but otherwise clear. Travelers had packed the road hard. Old snow was being covered by new. Progress was slow as they picked their way carefully, wary of any quagmires that might exist just beneath the tranquil snow.

And thus they traveled until just outside Kingsbridge. "There's a shortcut," said the Constable, setting out over an untouched white field. "We can save half a mile."

Tonneman followed, steering his gelding in Rifka's path through the snow.

In spite of their previous caution, neither Goldsmith nor Rifka saw the first trench till they were upon it, but Goldsmith, being a fair horseman, avoided going head over heels into the ditch. "I should have remembered," he said, as he walked the mare back and forth and cooed comfortingly into her ear. "That's a good girl." He pointed left and right. "See, trenches all around. That's in case of attack by the King's men."

Tonneman shaded his eyes from the snow's white glare. Beyond the trenches he could now see the cannon, metal sentinels, also waiting for the attack. "So, it's come to this? Trenches and cannon in Kingsbridge."

"It came to this before this, sir. Nobody's died in Kingsbridge yet, as they did in Concord and Lexington and Bunker Hill. But they could. And they will if they have to."

"Enough politics." Fortunately the trenches weren't continuous. When they found a break, the two continued slowly across the field. They had no further words until Tonneman pointed to a two-storied broad-bodied house of stone and shingle across the road from a barn. "Is that the Cross Keys?"

"Yes. I was here once last year." Goldsmith directed his horse from the field back to the road.

The snow had grown heavier. It fell in thick clumps as if someone were pouring it from the heavens. "Let's rest the horses in that barn," Tonneman said, already riding for the shelter.

A little Negro boy, who could have been the twin of Abigail's Rudy but in coarser clothing, came racing out of the barn. "Watch out for the hole!" he shouted.

As he spoke the snow started drifting away from Chaucer's forefeet. Tonneman jerked on the reins and rode around the increasingly apparent cavity in the ground.

"Fire pit," the boy said calmly as he opened the barn door.

"Then put a fire in it or some rocks around it," Goldsmith told him peevishly.

"Yes, sir."

"Dry them off and give them some feed." Tonneman handed the boy a penny.

The boy led the horses to the stalls while Tonneman and Goldsmith trudged across the road to the stone building. Snow clung stubbornly to their clothing, making them walking snow statues. Tied to the railing in front of the tavern was a lone horse. The snow formed a white shell over all it came in contact with, including the poor beast.

The large room of the Cross Keys Tavern proved to be a wide low-ceilinged chamber of booths and small tables. A huge brick fireplace with a welcome but smoldering fire gave off the only light, except for that of the whale oil lamp on the counter, whose light glanced off the grease-stained, rough-hewn beams.

The barkeeper and the other traveler, a man in a red fox fur hat standing at the bar, stopped talking when Tonneman and Goldsmith came in and sat at one of the eight empty tables.

"Good day to you," called the barkeeper in a hearty, high-pitched voice. He was a fussy knob of a man with curly black hair and bushy gray eyebrows. "What will you have?"

"Any soup?" asked Goldsmith. He shrugged out of his coat and hung it on an empty chair to dry.

"Just cold beef and chicken till tonight."

"Some chicken then." Tonneman looked to Goldsmith who nodded. ". . . Mulled ale?" The Constable nodded again. "And two mulled ales." Tonneman rose and stood before the fire. He removed his sodden coat, shaking it of moisture. Then he returned to the table, hooking his coat to dry on the back of another chair. "Mr. Wares, is it?"

"No, I'm Alfred Abbott, the barkeeper. David Wares should be down in about an hour."

The other traveler threw a cape over his shoulders and collected his saddlebags. "Have you come from Albany?" he asked Tonneman.

"No. New-York."

The traveler went to the door without another word or gesture. He opened the door, cursed the snow, and plunged outside.

"Godspeed," Abbott called after him. The barman picked up a log and threw it on the fire, poked it in place, and left the poker to heat in the fire. "He has a way to go in this bad weather. Albany. I don't envy him." Abbott laughed, showing three brown teeth, two atop and one at bottom. "But the post must go through." He laughed again on his way back to the bar. "Ale and chicken in a minute."

Tonneman laid some coins on the table. "You're the guest of the Coroner, Constable, and hopefully the Coroner is the guest of the City."

The barkeeper looked from one to the other for only a moment before fetching the ale and chicken. With little steps he ran to the fire, brought back the hot poker, and heated the spiced and sweetened ale. "What brings a Coroner and a Beak to Kingsbridge?" he asked in his high voice, his eyes brimming with curiosity.

"Beak?" asked Tonneman, bristling for Goldsmith. "You have no call. Merely because the Constable is a Hebrew—"

Goldsmith touched Tonneman's arm. "Beak doesn't mean Jew, sir. It means Constable or Justice of the Peace."

Abashed, Tonneman shook his head at his error.

"So what brings you?" the barkeeper repeated, smirking.

"New-York City business," Goldsmith answered, pulling a leg from the chicken. Eating with gentiles was becoming a habit with him. First the soup, then, may his father rest in peace, the ham, now this gentile chicken. If his wife, Deborah, and her mother, the ever-righteous Esther, ever dreamed he was not eating suitable food, he would never hear the end of it.

"How goes it down there? The Governor still hiding on the King's ship?"

"He is," Goldsmith said flatly.

Tonneman drew his knife from his belt, held the bird firmly on the wooden plate, and cut the chicken down the center, then tore the bird in half. The spicy odor of burning juniper berries filled his nostrils. He pushed one of the coins at Abbott. "Do you know Jane McCreddie?"

Abbott scooped up the shilling. "This will cover the chicken and the ale."

"You're not serious," said Goldsmith. "For a shilling I can buy a whole chicken in New-York."

"Then that's what you should have done," Abbott retorted. "These are serious times. There's a war, you know."

"No war has been declared," said Tonneman.

"Nevertheless," squeaked Abbott, "it's here. Some people just don't know it, is all."

Tonneman pushed another shilling toward the barkeeper. "Jane Mc-Creddie."

"You know she was indentured here and ran off, otherwise you wouldn't be asking. Is that worth a shilling?" Abbott's fingers danced on the table near the coin, but he didn't touch it.

"Afraid not," said Tonneman, pulling the coin back.

Obviously Abbott was bent on having the shilling. He searched his mind for some titbit to throw them. "Did you know that this is General Washington's favorite tavern? He stays here when he comes this way."

"Very interesting," said Tonneman.

"Actually," Abbott continued, "never see much of him or his men. Leave the food and drink outside the door. Not friendly types."

"The girl," Tonneman insisted.

"Mr. Wares was sore sorry to lose her. She cost him a pretty penny, I'll tell you, and she was good for business. The boys came around her like bees to honey."

"Names," said Tonneman. "Who came around her?"

"The soldiers, by God. Who else?"

"I'll give you two coppers for every name you give me."

"And I'll give you two kicks in the arse every time you open your mouth," roared a new voice.

Startled, they all looked over to the stairs. Coming down them was an elderly man of great girth. The top of his head was bald as a hen's egg, but he had brown hair to his shoulders. "The name is David Wares. I run this establishment. And it's a Patriot establishment. I don't care if you are Constable and Coroner of New-York or the Lord High Mayor of London, you Tory bastards. Anything you want to know you ask me."

Goldsmith, offended, got to his feet. "I am a Patriot, sir."

"And you, sir?" Wares fixed Tonneman with a militant stare. "Declare yourself."

"I take no sides," Tonneman said. "I am a surgeon. I am neutral."

Wares laughed, a booming blast, with no mirth at all. "Neutral? There are no neutrals."

Goldsmith, seeing they were going to get bogged down in political differences, took the bit between his teeth. "King and country, or no King and country, notwithstanding, landlord, Jane McCreddie is dead and we're investigating her murder."

The belligerent Wares staggered as if struck by lightning. "Dead? Oh, my God." He clutched the banister.

Tonneman went quickly to the huge man, as did Abbott. The two helped the ailing man to a chair. "Rum," Tonneman shouted as he loosened Wares's clothes.

When Abbott didn't move, Goldsmith leaned across the bar, got the bottle of spirits, and poured a cupful which he set down in front of Wares. Tonneman gave it to the tavern owner to drink.

Wares sucked the rum in greedily. "I'm all right. You have to know that the money means nothing. She was my indentured servant, but as God is my witness, I would have made her my wife."

"The silk undergarments, did you give them to her?" Tonneman asked.

Wares nodded, then buried his face in his hands. "I loved her. Even when she took up with that damnable fellow."

"What fellow?" Goldsmith demanded.

Tonneman raised his hand. "Easy, Constable."

"Never had him in sight. But she was one to taunt me about him and his 'thick dark hair.' "

"Yes?" said Tonneman.

"I saw him once," Abbott admitted.

Goldsmith was normally a patient man. It was all he could do not to throw the rum bottle at the barkeep. "What did he look like?"

"Don't know about his coloring. Black as black hair, I think. Strutted like a soldier. Can't say naught more. He was standing in the shadows with Jane." Abbott pointed. "Over there, under the stairs."

"Bastard." Wares shook his fist at Abbott. "Why didn't you tell me?"

"Wouldn't have done any good, you old fool. He would have killed you or you him. Either way, where would you be?"

"Please stay to the point," said Tonneman. "Did you ever hear the man's name?"

"No." Abbott coughed and spat into a earthenware cuspidor near the bar.

Goldsmith took a sip of his ale to calm his nerves. In even tones he asked again, "What did the man look like? Fat? Thin? Tall? Short?"

"That Jane, she was a tall girl, maybe five and a half feet. He stood head to head to her. I'm only guessing, but I reckon he was maybe ten, ten and a half stone."

"Sound like anyone you know, Constable?"

"No, sir."

"How about someone you've heard about?"

"Sir?"

"What was it the Negro, Quintin, told you?"

"That man at the Collect, not a soldier but like a soldier. Maybe five and a half feet, not heavy."

"Exactly."

CHAPTER 24

Tonneman was awakened by Gretel's morning sounds in the kitchen. They seemed louder than usual. Different. The rumble of booming laughter mixed with Gretel's merry giggle. Tonneman hugged the quilt closer. His chamber was frigid. With his usual cold morning leap he tossed the quilt aside and scrambled into his stiff near-frozen breeches and shirt.

Opening the shutters he saw a light-streaked sky, and Mrs. Remsen from across the way with her daughter at the public well that did for the Rutgers Hill neighborhood.

He pushed his finger at the disk of ice in his pitcher to loosen it, dribbled the water into his bowl, and washed his face. He'd left his towel damp last night, and now the beads of moisture were frozen droplets of ice against his skin. He ran a comb through his hair and tied it back with the black ribbon.

The hallway was dark; Jamie's door was closed tight. Once more the booming laughter and the high giggle rose from Gretel's kitchen.

Tonneman found Gretel pouring steaming sage tea steeped with honey into a large cup held by Bear Bikker, who, if anything, looked more massive than he had two days before. Tonneman's initial reaction, a flicker of jealousy over Gretel's attention, was driven away by his cousin's sheer good humor.

"—and he says to me, boy, I'll not give you an argument."

Bikker was seated, booted feet sprawled toward the fire. A musket, its barrel wearing the farmer's yellow knit stocking cap, lay on the table near the plate of johnnycakes he was heartily consuming.

"Who in his right mind would give you an argument?" Tonneman felt himself thawing in the warmth and conviviality of the kitchen.

Bikker grinned, his mouth full of food. "I was telling Mrs. Gretel here about my sergeant. A little bit of a fellow from Brooklyn." Bikker stood and seized Tonneman by the shoulders. "By God, coz, it's good to see you."

"And good morning to you, too."

Gretel handed Tonneman a cup of tea. The chamber was aromatic with the smell of baking bread, honey, and the spicy sage tea. "So, Johnny, I have to hear from your cousin about Thursday night."

Tonneman's look was incredulous. "You know my cousin?"

"No. Your father's father knew young Bikker's grandmother, the Dutch cousins in Haarlem. Alas, old people die off. But how would you know? Young people get caught up in their own spinning." She started another pile of cakes on Bear's empty plate.

"What brings you here, cousin? And so early." Tonneman's manner was cool.

Gretel stopped between johnnycakes, thrust her hands on her hips, and stared at Tonneman. He refused to meet her eyes.

Bear ignored the rebuke. He forked another mouthful of cakes and shook his great head at Tonneman. "*You* bring me here. I cannot, I will not accept what you said about the Cause. Where do you stand, John Tonneman? With the people or against the people?"

"I take no stand."

"God in Heaven," Gretel uttered.

Bear Bikker shook his blond head again. "I used to think the world was just my farm. But it's not. It's the next farm and the next, far past where I can see. If a blockhead farmer like me can sort it out, so can an educated man like you. It's not like the old days. The modern world is too small for you to take no stand. No one will let you. You were born here. Your ancestors lived and died here on their own land. They're buried here. In the name of God, John Tonneman, you're an *American*."

"Amen," Gretel said fervently.

"Pretty speech for a clodhopper. May I have my breakfast now?"

"No," said Gretel. She folded her arms defiantly.

"I'm not taking sides and that's the way it is."

"Are you for the King, then?" Gretel demanded.

This made Tonneman think. In spite of the fire he felt chilled.

"We need no kings here to tell us what to do," she said. "Your father—"

"My father wasn't political." Tonneman pulled out a chair and sat opposite Bear. He drank his tea.

Gretel smiled. "You're almost right, boy. But when the time came to choose, he chose his country." She opened the oven door to inspect her bread, then with a long, flat wooden paddle began drawing out crusty brown loaves.

Bikker studied Tonneman thoughtfully. "Tell me something, coz."

"If I can, Bear." The dialogue, at least, was stimulating.

"What does a king have to do with me? What I know is he taxes me so he can keep on being a king. We don't need him or his kind here. We're free men. And so it should be for our children and our children's children." His voice became clogged with emotion.

"You're not a farmer, Bear, you're a politician. No, better—a philosopher."

"Mock me all you want—"

"I'm not mocking you, cousin. I simply believe there's yet time to make peace with the King." Tonneman stared down at the table, then across to Bear Bikker's earnest face.

"No. You still don't understand. The time has been spent. And to no one's profit. They've drawn our blood already in Massachusetts." Bear's passion brought his fist to the table, rattling plates and cups.

"You've been away too long, Johnny." Gretel stood with her back to the fire. "You have lost touch with your country, with your countrymen. Worse, you have lost touch with freedom. But you are home now. This is your land, your City, your country. If the King and his corrupt toadies have their way, it will be his land, his City, his country."

"Listen to the woman. We all have a stake in this." Bear leaned forward, his blue eyes startling in his weather-worn face. "Who are you? An Englishman or an American? You choose."

"I can be both," said Tonneman, his jaw set.

"Not any more," said Gretel. "They won't let us. Don't you see that? You must choose."

Tonneman's thoughts roiled inward. He appreciated what they were saying. But it was all words. Words that obviously meant a great deal to Gretel and Bear. This was understandable. They were simple people. He suddenly recollected the moment the *Earl Of Halifax* had entered the Narrows and how he had felt on seeing New-York after all those years. Was that what they were talking about? No, that was merely homesickness.

"Pick a side, Cousin John. There's going to be fighting in the streets soon." Bear took his cap from the musket.

"I'm a physician. To take human life is wrong. That's why I'm so against fighting."

"If we don't fight the King, old George'll bleed us till we're dry and throw away the husk. We'll be his slaves in our own country."

Tonneman, listening to Bikker's ringing words, felt again his excitement when he and Jamie had first stepped onto Water Street and he smelled the harbor, the roasting potatoes, the briny oysters, hard against the mixed accents of Dutch and others who had come to New-York to make new lives in the new land. At that moment he was a New-Yorker. But that was just nostalgia. And hunger.

He crossed to the fire, ostensibly to warm his hands. Gretel, Bear, Goldsmith, and even his own father had taken up the Rebel cause. Perhaps it was his attachment to Jamie that made him feel the outsider. As each day passed, however, it was growing more and more difficult to hold to his center path.

"Agh." Bear Bikker got to his feet. He was a full head taller than Tonneman and almost half again as broad. But their hair was the same pale shade of yellow and they looked like brothers. Bear clamped his cap on his head and gestured with his musket. "Are you with us? Yea or nay?"

Sharp, cynical laughter overrode Tonneman's response as Jamie entered the room. "Think twice before you answer, my friend. A yea will get you the hangman's rope."

CHAPTER 25

Emma Greenaway missed her grandmother. Grandmama was home in England, and all Emma had of her was the onyx cameo with Grandmama's profile carved on it. Emma adjusted the chain that held the cameo about her neck and peered at herself in the looking glass while Betty, the young maid Aunt Abigail had given her during her stay in New-York, worked diligently at shaping Emma's hair so it would look like Emma's mother's beautiful tresses.

"See, Betty," Emma whined. "It just won't stay. My pathetic mop is too fine and thin. It never holds."

"Stop fretting, Miss Emma. There, I'm done. And you are lovely."

Emma sighed. Her hair did look nice. Oh, no. "See." Stray wisps and strands were beginning to appear. "Mama's going to scold me . . . and you, too," she added wickedly. "I can hear her now." Emma raised her voice to imitate her mother's aristocratic tones. " 'You look the slattern. Slattern. Slattern.' " Emma kept repeating it till she was giggling, and tears were rolling down her cheeks.

Betty, caught up in the fun, lightened her voice and repeated the word, "Slattern, slattern," till she, too, was laughing and had collapsed on the chaise.

Emma stopped and blew her nose. "Nothing I do ever seems to please Mama. She doesn't like the way I look at all. Ever since I was a snotty brat I've been hearing—" Again she imitated her mother's voice "—'I can't believe a lump like you came from my womb.' It got worse after Papa died. 'I never had skin like that. Look at the way you walk. Why can't you walk gracefully, as I do?' " As she spoke the last, Emma flounced about the chamber in an exaggeration of her mother's court walk, causing Betty to go into another fit of giggles.

"Would I had the lovely cream skin of my Aunt Abigail, the thick golden hair. Would I had her poise."

"Then you'd be your Aunt Abigail and not you," Betty ventured through more giggles.

"That would be wonderful. To be someone else. I'd love to be you."

"No, you wouldn't."

"Yes, I would. I could walk out and about the City with no one the wiser."

Betty's eye grew bright. "Be right back." The maid ran from Emma's room, stifling laughter.

Emma had liked New-York the moment they'd arrived two weeks ago. There was something about the City—even with the grumblings of its people—that made her happy. No one watched her critically here. Except, of course, Mama.

The truth was Mama hated her. Emma had known that since she was very young. She was ugly and awkward and, as Mama often said, a sorry trial. Mama was constantly finding fault, reprimanding her for her awkwardness, her doltishness.

She had turned seventeen on board the *Rosamond* in the middle of the Atlantic. Mr. Jones, the tobacco grower from the Carolinas, had been charming to her, but Mama had to have him for herself. That's why when the young midshipman, Mr. Barrow, had presented her with a nosegay of tiny blue forget-me-nots—what did it matter that they were limp and edged with brown—she was so taken with him. He was tall and handsome and had such a lovely way about him.

Of course, Mama had been furious. In the hand mirror, Emma's face blotched several shades of unbecoming red and tears came to her eyes. Mama had declared her a slattern, and confined her to meals in their tiny cabin for the five days left of their voyage.

Sighing deeply, Emma remembered herself in the dreadful dowdy gowns Mama had had made for her before their voyage. They flattened her bosom and made her look like a man in women's clothing. Resentfully, Emma knew she had every bit as good a bosom as Mama, who was always showing hers off, insisting that her necklines be cut lower and lower.

The first night when she came down to supper, Emma sensed by the expression on Abigail's face that she was a friend. Emma hoped she was. Jesus knew she needed a friend.

Eventually, perhaps sooner than anyone realized, Emma would be married, with her own home. What did it matter if the man she was destined to wed was poor? She had enough money from dear Papa for them to live in luxury in this wonderful City and have enough left over for two husbands. But she would only have one. And children, so many children. She would be a wonderful mother.

Betty pushed Emma's door open. In her arms were duplicates of Betty's clothes.

"What have you there?"

"You said you wanted to be me. Here's your chance."

Emma considered what Betty was offering. She clasped her hands across her breast. "Why not?"

Amidst more giggles, Emma quickly removed her dressing gown and put on the black dress, white apron, and white lace cap.

Emma twirled, laughing softly. "How do I look?"

Betty put her hand over her small crooked mouth to cover her own laughter. "You'd pass below stairs right off. Do you want to go out into the world?"

Emma's heart beat wildly. "I can't—"

Betty wrapped Emma in the maid's green cloak. "Yes, you can. I dare you."

Emma knew she couldn't let a dare go by. With a great spirit of adventure she said, "Yes."

Betty led Emma to the servants' back staircase that led to the street and handed her a market basket. "This will make you look real."

Emma hung back, her cheeks hot with excitement. "I'm afraid."

Betty gave her a little push. "Go."

Emma had no place in particular she wanted to go. It was the idea of doing it that was so exciting. All she wanted was to walk through the streets of New-York and see the people.

She strolled through the Common carrying the market basket.

A pimply-faced boy carrying a load of bundles made rude noises at her. A soldier even pinched her bottom and called her "Lovey." Frightening but wonderful. No one took her for a privileged lady.

Emma was walking hurriedly away from the soldier when she bumped into a fine-looking man. "Excuse me," she murmured, casting her eyes to the ground, part in embarrassment, part playing the maid. "Sir," she remembered to add and covered her mouth with a shy hand.

"Well, you're a pretty young thing."

His words brought deep pink spots to her cheeks. Before she could comment, he bought her roasted chestnuts from the monger.

"Come walk with me in the Common." He offered his arm.

Too timid to speak, she merely nodded and took his arm. She strolled with him through the wintry field of the Common, oblivious to the cold and the dusting of November snow.

He told her wickedly wonderful tales of his adventures. But there was a serious side to him, too. He said he was prepared to cast off his youthful audacious ways and settle into the sedate existence of a husband. He was more than ready to marry and have children and lead an exemplary life.

"What sort of woman did you have in mind for your wife?"

"You would ask me that?" He lifted her hand to his lips. Her hand trembled.

From that point she could refuse him nothing. So when he took her to his room she allowed him what he called the glory of fondling her breasts. After all, she was dressed as Betty, she was Betty. Wasn't she doing what Betty would have done? And when he wanted more, how could she refuse? He was so handsome, like a prince.

To Emma, as she hurried back to the house on Crown Street, time had flown on enchanted wings. Seeing herself through his eyes was a revelation. She, plain Emma, had a lover, and if he would ask she was ready to run off with him. She had often thought that marriage—to anyone at all—no matter whom Mama chose—would allow her to escape from the prisoner's life she led. But this was beyond her wildest dreams. Heaven. What could Mama do or say if she returned a married woman? Quietly, she climbed the back stairs and returned to her room. Papa's legacy would come to her husband on her marriage. There was no way Mama could stop that.

CHAPTER 26

The day began like any other Thursday at *Rivington's New-York Gazetteer,* with the presses rolling at dawn.

Approaching the print shop at noonday, Tonneman and Jamie were watching Ben Mendoza and two other apprentices loading the wagon with this week's *Gazetteer* when they heard what sounded like distant thunder. The rumbling grew louder, closer and closer. Ben peered at the sky. No sign of a storm. The boys looked at each other, shrugged, and finished loading the wagon.

James Rivington stepped outside. "What is that racket?" When he spied Tonneman he called, "Dr. Tonneman, what can I do for you today?"

"Has anyone else reported seeing the girl Jane McCreddie?"

Before Rivington could answer, the noise grew louder. They all turned. Beyond the buildings to the north flew a scatter of frosty spray. Out of it galloped a great band of mounted marauders entering Hanover Square, with bayonets fixed, scattering all in their path. The shouting banditti came to a clamorous, ice-showering halt in close order before the print shop. Some of the riders had scarves over their faces, hiding their identity. Others didn't give a damn.

A small detail dismounted and entered.

"Gentlemen," Rivington said, pushing past the intruders. Tonneman and Jamie stood with Ben just outside the shop. Tonneman had heard of Illegals such as these. Only last week a band of Rebels had attacked and burned the home of a Loyalist judge in Westchester, tarring and feathering him.

Rivington remained calm. Even polite. "How may I help you?"

"How about leaving the frigging country?" one called.

"Stand aside, Rivington," said the leader of the detail. "We have a message to deliver."

When Ben slipped inside the door to the print shop, Tonneman and Jamie followed. The boy was quite upset.

Tonneman had been hearing diverse talk about Rivington. Though many disagreed with the printer about the direction America should take, they couldn't help but admire the man. Rivington was an out-and-out Tory but, some Patriots admitted, he was fair. What he put in his newspaper wasn't only pro-King. The *Gazetteer* reported each side of the issues dividing Tories and Whigs.

Tonneman still wasn't sure where he himself stood. But politics or no, it bothered him greatly to see outlaws wreck the business and life of any man. And wreck they did, beginning when two large fellows lifted the press handily and threw it to the floor. At this point Tonneman made a move to intercede. Only Jamie's firm grip kept him back. "I'm with you, my friend, but the odds are wrong," Jamie whispered.

Rivington remained stoic throughout, though from what Tonneman had heard of Rivington he knew the printer felt that was one of his children lying broken on the floor. He considered the press sacred.

"How dare you do that, you ruffians?" Mr. Morton, Rivington's clerk, screamed. "You are trespassers, violating the King's law!"

"*That* for the King's law," a short bandetto in a hide coat said, leaping high like a frog and pouring ink over poor Morton's bald pate. This was the signal. Things all around went crashing. Tables were overturned. Copies of the new *Gazetteer* were thrown about, some into the fire, others mangled on the floor. The ginger tomcat, now ginger and ink black, went screeching up the stairs to the sanctuary of the watchmaker's shop. Providentially, except for Mr. Morton's dignity no person was hurt.

In about three quarters of an hour the detail was done with its destruction and had carried away most of Rivington's type.

"Do you understand the message?" the burly leader demanded of Rivington.

The printer kept his clenched fists at his side and said nothing.

Morton was not so composed. "We know you, Isaac Sears, of Connecticut!" he shouted. "Why don't you stay in your own backyard?"

"If New-Yorkers tended to their messes we wouldn't have to come down here and clean up."

Morton was more incensed than before. "Judgment Day will come!"

"To us all, brother Morton. To us all."

The bandetto in the hide coat wasn't content. "What say we tar and feather Mr. Rivington and the lot of them, just so they'll remember we were here?"

This time even Jamie's strong grip couldn't still Tonneman. The younger surgeon shouldered himself directly in front of the short bandetto. "What say you don't?"

"Who's going to stop me?"

"We will." Jamie came to his friend's side.

"No need for heroics, gentlemen," the burly man said, "but I must say I admire your spunk." He inclined his head ever so slightly and led the detail from the shop, where they rejoined the rest of his company.

Tonneman and Jamie stood at the door and watched as the company faced, wheeled to the left, and rode out of town, singing "Yankee Doodle" at the tops of their lungs. They were cheered and followed by the crowds who had observed the raid, all the way to Coffee-House Bridge, where another crowd had gathered. The encouragement of the throng could be heard all over the City and most clearly by those who stood in the wreckage of Rivington's print shop.

"Hip, hip, *Hoorah,* Hip, hip, *Hoorah,* Hip, hip, Hoo*rah.*"

Tonneman turned to Rivington, searching for something to say.

The printer stood there, waiting for the painful echoes to fade. Then he said, "Arnold, help Mr. Morton clean up. Ben, write this down. We can manage one more copy of the *Gazetteer* before I go and get drunk."

Mr. Morton and Arnold set about their task. Ben took pen to paper. "Yes, sir."

Rivington took a soulful breath. He scratched his cheek and noticed Tonneman staring at him. "I'm thinking about how I'm going to tell my wife. Well, that's later. This is now. Ben: 'Rivington's press on Hanover Square was wrecked by the Connecticut "banditti" and was put out of business on Thursday, 23 November, 1775.'"

CHAPTER 27

With its abundant lighting, New-York was a splendid example of the new world metropolis, making night almost day in the densest areas. A whale oil lantern burned nightly at every seventh building in most of the City. Lamplighters made frequent tours, and the Night Watch diligently reported any lights out.

Of course in certain derelict parts just beyond St. Paul's, looking at the lower portion of the Common and surrounding King's College, illumination was not so bright. This area was called, with the dark humor of New-Yorkers, "The Holy Ground," in honor of the five hundred prostitutes who plied their trade there.

The gracious brick home and estate of Richard Edward Willard were on Crown Street just west of Broadway, in a section of the City where the wealthiest citizens lived.

Here, night was practically day, with street lamps in front of every third structure. The illumination continued as one approached the Willard home, the three-storied house garnished with two carriage lamps at the entrance.

The balustraded tile roof of the house was also lit, revealing a promenade with an unobstructed view of the North and East Rivers and New-York Bay at the foot of the island.

"Amazing," commented Jamie, eyeing the broken pediment over the substantial front door. He and Tonneman dismounted and turned the reins of their mounts over to the Willards' groom. "This street might have been lifted directly from Grosvenor Square."

The wind tore at their cloaks and played havoc with head covering as they hurried for the front door, delaying their entrance only briefly to readjust their clothing.

"The climate of your beloved City leaves much to be desired." Jamie readjusted his recovered tricorn.

"Anyone who lives on the Thames . . ."

Jamie was not to be silenced. "My blood would not freeze in Virginia, or for that matter, the West Indies."

The great hall they entered had a beautiful, sweeping staircase with mahogany rails and banisters.

Tonneman laughed. "This is only the beginning. You'll get used to it. And, I promise, learn to enjoy it."

Grumbling good-naturedly, Jamie gave his cloak and hat to the liveried footman. Tonneman followed suit. A bewigged butler in blue satin breeches and coat, and a ruffled stock took their cards and led them from the spacious center hall to a chamber on the left.

Inside, more light came from the graceful brass chandeliers. These candles that lit the paneled sitting room were supposedly protected from any sudden drafts by little glass globes. Still, when the butler opened the double doors, flames flickered, throwing an ominous cast over the room. All those inside looked up expectantly.

The butler announced in stentorian tones, "Mr. John Peter Tonneman, Coroner and doctor of surgery. Mr. Maurice Arthur Jamison, doctor of surgery, late of London, appointee of his illustrious Majesty, King George the Third, as Chancellor of the College of Medicine of King's College."

Although the fireplace and the shimmering gold damask curtains with ornate valances kept the room most fittingly warm, the four ladies therein wore woolen shawls over their colorful silk and taffeta dinner dresses. Or perhaps the shawls were a concession to the mild immodesty of the very European low-cut bosoms.

Tonneman and Jamie were greeted by a burly, authoritative gentleman who seemed quite familiar.

"I say," Jamie exclaimed. "You're the chap—"

"I remember," said Tonneman. "The fellow who managed the mob around the effigy last week." The man in claret velvet.

"And you're the hero of that day, Dr. Tonneman. We meet again. Richard Willard. Your servant, gentlemen. Sherry?"

So this was Abigail's husband. Strong, much older than she, but obviously a man of great power and wealth. The callow young physician of seven years before had been no match for this man. And now? Tonneman took a deep breath. He had no time for that sort of mooning nonsense.

His roiling thoughts were intruded upon by a footman at their elbows with a tray. Tonneman and Jamie took glasses, and Tonneman watched his friend with amusement. "Mr. Willard, you delight my day. Thus far my friend Jamie's constant song has been that New-York can never compare to his beloved London. This evening has already made certain he'll sing a different tune."

"I'll drink to that," said Willard. "So long as the tune isn't 'Yankee Doodle.' Har-har."

The carpets were French, the furniture solidly English Chippendale. In fact, Tonneman thought, everything about the Willard home was solidly English, even to the patterned wallpaper of French design, which showed rural scenes of gay ladies and gentlemen in beautiful gardens. Silver and porcelain accessories abounded.

Introductions were made. Abigail, again in blue, always in blue, re-membered in blue, watched him closely from behind a blue fan. Her pale hair was set in the fashion of the day in London, piled high on her head in bounteous curls. On a sofa next to her sat an attractive woman close to the age of Richard Willard, whose dark red hair was similarly coiffed. This was Grace Greenaway, Abigail's sister-in-law. She wore a richly trimmed nar-row-waisted gown of pale green which forcefully displayed her ample bo-som. Jamie bowed and kissed her extended hand, holding it a trifle longer than was proper. Grace Greenaway took immediate notice and flashed him a sultry smile.

Willard described, somewhat dramatically, Tonneman's coming to the aid of the fallen young woman with the market basket the previous week.

Abigail smiled knowingly and shook her head. "Just like John. Even as a boy he was always saving stray kittens up a tree. We've heard you were at it again today. Is that true, dear John?"

Willard's eyes flicked momentarily. Tonneman studied his sherry.

The moment passed.

Mrs. Greenaway fluttered her silver lace fan coquettishly at Jamie and patted the side chair beside the sofa, inviting him to sit.

Jamie winked at Tonneman and sat immediately. Grace Greenaway tapped his knee with her fan. "You are the image of my late husband, Stuart, in his youth."

"Charming," said Jamie, leaning closer.

"My late husband . . ."

Indeed Mrs. Greenaway enjoyed talking, but Tonneman did not enjoy listening to her, as she was a coarse woman who thought she was genteel. The latter was the worst offense. She was overdressed and had on layers of paint to disguise her true age. In the hollow of her throat was an enormous ruby set off by a chain of diamonds. Rubies and diamonds hung from her earlobes and glittered on her fingers. She was apparently not a recent widow, for she was very gay, with a rolling laugh, and she was stalking Jamie the way a terrier stalks a rat.

Further introductions were started but then interrupted by an unfortunate incident. Jamie's sherry glass suddenly shattered in his right hand.

"Oh, my dear!" Grace Greenaway cried. A servant came forward immediately and cleaned up the broken shards and sherry.

Jamie, his face white, stared at the blood issuing from a deep cut on his thumb. Tonneman took his friend's hand. "Isn't she a bit long in the tooth, old boy?" he whispered as he wrapped the wound with his silk handkerchief.

"Once more to the rescue, dear John." Enthusiastically, Jamie slapped Tonneman on the back with his left hand. Everyone laughed.

The third woman in the room was Grace Greenaway's daughter, Emma. She was as plain a girl as her mother was gaudy. Tall and ungainly, she had the blotchy raw complexion that cursed some red-haired women, and a large nose in a plump face. Self-consciously, the girl kept pursing her lips in an effort to hide her two upper front teeth, which were snagged, one almost completely obscuring the other.

Her yellow dress gave her skin a sallow hue. The only trait she shared with her mother was her enormous bosom, which she hid unsuccessfully under her shawl. Huge, gauche pink pearls hung from the girl's earlobes and about her plump neck.

Emma appeared awkward and ill at ease and colored unprettily when Jamie tried to extend the conversation to her. Yet she hung on his every word, barely taking her eyes from him.

The other man in the room, Philip Apthorpe, was irate over the Sons of Liberty. His wife Sally, a tiny woman in lavender, had all she could do to keep him mollified. Apthorpe, it seemed, was on Governor Tryon's provincial council and he was outraged over the mistreatment of Governor Tryon.

"Hear, hear," Willard proclaimed. "These Sons of Liberty are treacherous rascals. I'll doodle these Yankees till Armageddon and three cheers for King George." His ire vented, he went back to explaining to Jamie and the women how it was proper for the Colonies to pay for the housing and upkeep of the army which brought order to the turmoil. "Order, first and foremost, is essential in His Majesty's Colonies."

Tonneman was listening vaguely, standing, elbow perched on mantelpiece, when he caught Abigail watching him.

When their eyes met she looked away, but not before her husband noticed. With a set of his jaw, Richard Willard continued expounding on the need for order and keeping the rabble in line. "Liberty, bah."

"Agreed," said Apthorpe. "They have all the liberty men need and more."

"I'll go you one better." Jamie gestured with a fresh glass in his left hand. "The rogues can have all the liberty they want in hell."

When summoned to supper, Jamie escorted Abigail; Tonneman, Mrs. Apthorpe; Mr. Apthorpe, the timid Emma; and Richard Willard, his sister.

The formal dining room, lit by two candelabra, contained a beautifully proportioned table, with crystal, china, and silver set for eight. The centerpiece was an ornate Limoges affair of many levels and plates which held sweets and glazed fruits.

Courses of oysters, chicken and roasted lamb, winter greens and potatoes were served by the ever-diligent footmen. The wines were French and plentiful.

"Emma, take your nose out of your plate and stop playing with your food," Grace Greenaway scolded. "My daughter, Dr. Jamison, is such a trial."

Emma flushed horribly.

"If I may be so bold, Mrs. Greenaway," Jamie said, "why don't you bring your daughter to Dr. Tonneman's surgery? I could pluck that extra tooth of hers before you could say George Washington."

"And who would want to?" Captain Willard demanded.

Stammering, Emma said, "A—a—I—Irene wrote to me from London. She—She—She says those that know c-c-consider the p-p-potato dark, dirty, and highly s-s-sinister."

Grace Greenaway emitted a long-suffering sigh. "Don't be a silly goose."

"Irene says potatoes cause leprosy, syphillis, and scrofula."

"I am distressed to hear you speak that way in front of— Where did you hear that dreadful word?"

"Scrofula?"

"Emma . . ."

"Irene says—"

"Bother Irene."

The two medical men, Tonneman and Jamie, wisely offered no comment. The subject of poor Emma's snag tooth was forgotten. Talk happily shifted from Irene and potatoes and syphillis to the lack of entertainment —the diversion of the shuttered theater on John Street was sorely missed— to the difficulty of obtaining goods and services with so many of the shops closed and the citizens packing up and moving to the country.

After they were served Stilton cheese and stewed pears, followed by sweet pudding, curds, and cream and coffee with brandy, Apthorpe said, "Quite a to-do with Rivington today."

Willard cleared his throat loudly, an obvious signal to Apthorpe to mind his tongue.

"Pish tush, Richard," Grace Greenaway exclaimed. She wagged her fan. "The whole of New-York knows that two hundred armed Rebels descended on poor Mr. Rivington's print shop and threw his—what were they—his letters—"

"Type," Abigail supplied. She cast a shaded look at Tonneman, which he found disquieting. This time her husband seemed not to take notice.

Grace Greenaway nodded her head, her bosom nodding in accompaniment. "—his type into the river."

"No," Mrs. Apthorpe rejoined with informed glee. "I understand they took the type with them to melt for bullets. It's lead, you know."

"Gossip, nothing but malicious Rebel gossip," Willard said hotly.

"And the whole of New-York has heard that a brave physician"—Mrs. Greenaway looked at Tonneman—"saved that poor man Rivington from being tarred and feathered."

When Tonneman didn't respond she turned to Jamie. "Doctor?"

"Not I, madam," Jamie answered. "As you well know. I would not be nearly so brave, nor so foolhardy. It was my friend here who saved Rivington. He stood up to those banditti today and saved Rivington's arse from being covered with tar and feathers."

Abigail gasped.

Tonneman showed Jamie a fist. "You scoundrel. You were there, right by my side."

Jamie grinned. "But you were the brave leader. And I, just a humble follower in your shadow." Eyes resting on Mrs. Greenaway, he laughed boisterously. Then he turned to Emma and winked.

Emma blushed.

"Oh, my dear," Abigail said to Tonneman, "you might have been badly hurt." She turned to her husband. "Am I not right, Richard?"

With a sour look to Tonneman, Willard said, "These Rebels are naught but murderers and thieves, the lowest element of our society. They respect no law, nor their own governor. Worst of all, they do not respect the King. And that is intolerable."

Grace Greenaway's laugh was a delighted shriek. "Again a hero! How grand. Sooth, we should hang the bastards all and have done with this anarchy."

Willard looked pointedly at his wife.

"Ladies." Abigail rose in a sweep of perfumed blue silk. "Shall we leave the gentlemen to their cigars and take coffee in the sitting room? Not too long, gentlemen. We have a small musical evening for your pleasure." She smiled prettily, showing her dimples, and led the women out.

A footman brought Richard Willard an earthenware jar. A second footman poured the brandy into crystal goblets. Willard took a cigar and while the servants made the rounds of the other men, he bit off the end and dipped his cigar into his brandy before lighting it from one of the candelabra. His guests followed suit and leaned back in their chairs contentedly.

Apthorpe shoved his chair from the table and blew a haze of blue smoke into the room. "I've given some thought, myself, to moving to my country estate some miles up along the North River." Nodding to Tonneman and Jamie, he added, "Until we clear out these turncoats, these so-called Sons of Liberty, and hang them on their own Liberty Poles. My wife is constantly vexed by rumors from the servants and the tradespeople who remain."

Willard blew smoke rings, then poked his cigar through one. "It's not a good idea to let the women get too involved in politics. They are frail creatures who are easily fearful."

"Surely not Abigail—" Tonneman began. He was halted by Willard's keen stare.

"Lovely cigars," interposed Jamie, lightly. "I would hazard a guess that your sister is not one of those easily frightened."

"My sister is my twin," Willard responded. "Grace has the brain and often the wit of a man. Unfortunately I cannot say the same for my niece. The child needs a husband with a strong hand. What say you, Tonneman? She'll bring her husband an excellent dowry."

Tonneman shook his head. "I'm not a marrying sort of man," he said thoughtfully, realizing as he spoke that he indeed meant what he said. He stood, suddenly feeling uncomfortably warm. "I'm going to get a breath of air."

The central hall was empty. From the sitting room he could hear the murmuring voices of the ladies. When he moved to the front of the house, a draught of cold clawed at him. Without thinking, he followed the chill wind to the rear of the house. The back door was partially open and a man, his back to Tonneman, stood in the opening, leaning on a violin case, in whispered conversation with someone outside.

"Congress is worried. The damned Tories."

"We are united against them. New-York will not go down."

Hearing Tonneman's footfall, the musician closed the door, but not before Tonneman saw the lean form of Ben Mendoza slipping into the darkness.

CHAPTER 28

Emma smiled, rubbed her lips with the rouge she had filched from Mama's rouge pot, and kissed the onyx cameo about her neck for luck.

"Step lively, girl!" Her mother's piercing command to Lucy, the lady's maid they had brought with them from London, sliced through the sitting room she and her mother shared in Uncle Richard's home. The abrasive tone made Emma tremble, in spite of the fact that for the first time since the death of her father three years earlier she felt someone cared for her alone, really cared.

She waited for what seemed like forever, until she heard no further sound from her mother. Opening the door to the sitting room, she peeked out. The door to Mama's chamber was closed. Gathering up her skirts, Emma tiptoed to the door and listened. If she'd had her usual mulled wine, Mama's soft snores would be clear. Sure enough, they sounded through the door like the sawing of wood. Mama would doze till teatime, unaware that her good, pliant daughter had a lover, a wonderful handsome lover.

More than pleased, she returned to her room and impatiently waited for Betty to appear.

The house had grown still since the noonday meal. The children were napping, as were the adults. Only if one listened carefully could the soft tread of the household staff going about their business be heard. Emma knew for certain that Lucy had had her own mulled wine, and would be drowsing as well in a corner of the kitchen, her darning basket in her lap.

Parting the draperies, Emma looked out. The day seemed raw. There'd been more snow. What did she care? She would meet her man in the Common.

The sitting room door opened. Emma tensed. A light step, a knock at her door. "Miss?"

Betty. Emma flung open her door, pulling the maid in. "Hurry, hurry," she whispered hoarsely.

Betty giggled as she set the folded linen on Emma's bed. "Oh, Miss." Hidden among the linen was Betty's clothing. Betty dressed Emma in her worn blue muslin day dress with the low-cut bosom.

Emma clamped Betty's hat, a garish affair of many peaks and ruffles, on her head and tied it under her chin. In the hand mirror she saw that the hat quite covered her red hair. On first glance no one would know she was not Betty. Except her love. He would know.

Emma watched anxiously as Betty rolled and plumped the bedclothes to make it look as if Emma were asleep beneath them. Satisfied, the girls slipped out silently to the back stairs.

Inside the landing was the market basket, this time fitted with homespun. Betty handed it to Emma. Under the homespun was Emma's personal linen and a white silk nightdress.

Impulsively, Emma gave Betty a quick hug and ran lightly down the stairs into the cold. She wanted to race through the streets shouting, "I have a lover, I have a lover."

She did not race. Ever so sedate, she walked east, eyes down, past citizens and soldiers and noisy coffeehouses and taverns. Emma was constantly amazed how clean the streets were here compared to London. Where the shops were not boarded up, the apprentices were constantly sweeping the walk and the street, polishing brass, cleaning glass windows. Nothing here wore the blackened grit and centuries-old grime of London buildings.

Her step quickened as she neared the Common. Where was he? Would he not come? She wandered the icy stone walks with care. The trees were outlined in frozen snow. Then she saw him in the distance with his crisp walk. As he drew closer, her heart began to pound.

Emma knew that from this day on her life would be forever his.

CHAPTER 29

Gretel's day had started early, when, wrapped in her greatcoat and wool scarf, she had taken her basket from its nail in the kitchen and had gone out to the market on Broadway. Every day was a joyous occasion now that her Johnny was home. Well, he wasn't really her Johnny by blood, but she had brought him up after his poor mother died, hadn't she? And she would live, with God's help, to dandle Johnny's children on her knee.

But now she worried about him. He'd gone off to London a laughing, excited lad and had returned a sobersides. All that time in London had been unhealthy for him. Physician, heal thyself, indeed. The poor benighted boy was a dyed-in-the-wool Loyalist. Well, not really. But he thought he was. Like a kitten whose eyes hadn't opened yet. A Loyalist, but thanks be to God, not yet a Tory. And Lord willing, really a Patriot. Gretel sighed. Time, she knew, would make it right.

On Broadway the farmers had set up their wagons in a loose circle on the street as protection against the cutting wind. Eyes stinging from the cold, Gretel joined the other women to look over the goods. She stopped in front of old man Van Griethuysen and studied his chickens in their cage.

The hens, picking and clucking, tilted their heads first this way, then that, studying her with one bright eye at a time. They ruffled their thick red feathers and pushed against the treen slats of the cage. Gretel pointed to one particularly fat hen. "That one."

Old man Van Griethuysen opened the cage, caught the fat bird's legs with one hand, and held it upside down. While Gretel felt the plump flesh through the feathers, it screaked indignantly. The chicken stretched a long outraged neck, trying to peck Van Griethuysen. But the farmer was too quick and the bird went after Gretel.

Gretel smiled at the bird. "That's a good beak you have there. Good fertilizer for my garden." She gave a nod; the old man laid the bird on a low board, held it down with his knee, and chopped off its head with a hatchet. The headless creature twitched and struggled and when the old man lifted his knee, it jumped off the board, ran for a few moments, then dropped. Van Griethuysen scooped it up, shook the blood from the wound, tied its extremities with twine, and handed it to Gretel, who wrapped it in a greased cloth and put the package in the bottom of her basket. She picked out two dozen eggs, paid for them and the chicken, then moved on to buy butter, milk and cream, salt pork, potatoes, turnips and carrots and onions.

She was on her way back to the house from the market, her basket filled to bursting, when she saw a strange woman emerge from her front door and come down the street toward her. They passed each other, both staring boldly. Gretel could not believe it. The woman was obviously a hussy, her face smeared with rouge and powder. Her hand clutched her cloak, not tight enough, for the pale skin of her bosom showed. A heavy aura of sweet perfume drifted in her wake.

She must be a patient, was Gretel's first protective thought. The wickedness and impracticality of the woman's attire struck Gretel equally. A person could freeze on the way to hell.

Gretel trudged with her bundles to her side door. It was clear the woman was no patient. Patients did not walk through the house and leave as bold as paint by the front door.

In her kitchen Gretel filled her next-to-biggest pot with water and set it to boil so she could clean the chicken. She could hear Dr. Jamison moving around upstairs. Shortly thereafter he was in her kitchen for her cornmeal johnnycakes and a tankard of ale, a self-satisfied gleam in his eye.

The making of the johnnycakes distracted Gretel for a moment. Her little Johnny had always thought the cakes were named for him. He would dart into her kitchen demanding a plate of his cakes. Oh, how she loved that boy. Gretel missed the old days when he was young and Dr. Peter was so alive, always busy with his patients. But the past was gone and should be buried.

"I'm off to see to my almost complete new lodgings." Dr. Jamison helped himself to a ladleful of honey.

She pursed her lips and piled another batch of cakes on his plate. He smelled of the same sweet perfume as the rouged trollop, and there were traces of white powder on his green satin waistcoat.

At noonday, with her chicken stewing, she went out to the community well on the street with her water buckets. Young Henry Burton, the wheelwright's lad, was outside waiting for a chance to earn some pennies. She gave the ten-year-old a copper to help her bring the filled buckets back to the house.

Her friend Charity Woodstock had become a grandmother two days earlier, of a fine, strong boy. Gretel had baked shortbread to take to them this day so she could have a look at the fat-cheeked baby. So it was in the early afternoon that Gretel set forth, walking briskly across Broadway and taking the shortcut through the Common, which was only sparsely attended because of the unseasonable cold. The bare branches of the trees wore a coating of ice, bending and crackling in the wind. She stayed with the happy but exhausted mother and grandmother only a short time and then back she went through the Common.

Much to everyone's dismay, the west end of the Common had become a meeting place for soldiers and whores, what with the population of the City almost doubled by the presence of so many soldiers. Head bowed against the wind, Gretel was rushing homeward along the stone path when she came upon a crowd of people swarming about and shouting. Then flames licked above her, reaching to the sky.

Her pulse raced with fear and her body was drenched with sweat. It had been a long time, but fires still frightened her. She could manage her stove and fireplaces, but real fires brought back the memory of Kurt dying and the terrible pain of her burns. *"Ach,"* she uttered. She was better now.

Gretel had known two good men in her life: Kurt and Dr. Peter. And she had lost them both. But now she had her Johnny back and life was sweet again.

Calmer, Gretel realized that the fire was only a burning effigy of the King hanging from a tree.

"Treason!" someone shouted.

The shouter was answered by catcalls, jeers, and hisses. Soon several young men set upon him and roundly thumped him.

The clanging of a fire bell announced the coming of the firemen. The eight volunteers arrived, six in front, each pulling on the whippletree, towing their fire engine. Two pushed behind. All panted and puffed in the cold.

While four men held the hose on the fire, the other four pumped heartily at the double rack. But the water in the tank was frozen solid.

Soldiers, who'd been drilling on the Common, came to watch and make clever remarks and offer advice. They did not, however, offer assistance.

Only after the volunteers had set their own fire to thaw the tank were they able to pump the water and douse the blazing straw man.

Some citizens arrived toting leathern buckets and cloth bags, which all inhabitants of the City were obliged to keep suspended in the halls of their houses. If fire were to break out, citizens would come at the greatest speed, carrying water in their buckets and using the cloth bags to help save the personal effects of the victims. But there was no need for any of this now; the fire was out.

As she turned away from the excitement and started for home, Gretel caught a quick glimpse of Dr. Jamison. Jamison turned as if he felt Gretel's stare. Then he looked right through her and moved his eyes away. Was he with that woman again, the rutting goat? A woman's pale face was shadowed by his arm, undoubtedly the same scented hussy who had been in Gretel's home that very morning.

They were heading in the opposite direction, but he turned back for a moment, and the face he showed Gretel was the Devil's own.

CHAPTER 30

Hickey wiped his mouth with the sleeve of his coat. He'd just had a quick beer in Benson's Brew House on the East River waterfront, and was on his way to take care of business when he overheard with great interest a trio of soldiers in front of the Brew House discussing the trenches up in Kingsbridge. The way these boys talked! He loved it. The soldiers went inside and Hickey was on his way again. Out of nowhere a water vender pushed his cart in Hickey's path.

"Out of my way, bugger."

"I'm from the Tea Water Pump on Pearl Street. Would you care for some water?"

"And I'm from the other side of hell. Would you care for some fire up your arse?"

The water vender, a gaunt codger with a white beard and thick spectacles, moved closer. "I speak for the Fat Man."

Now Hickey remembered the game. "The water you sell. My friends tell me it's piss."

The vender's smile crept from his white beard. "What kind of piss is that, sir?"

Hickey looked about the waterfront. "Royal piss. What else?"

The vender took a wooden cup from among the others that were secured at his waist and started to pour Hickey a drink.

"Not for me. It'll rust my insides. What do you want? I've got to get back before Lieutenant Plunkett trips in a hole and kills himself."

"The Fat Man needs to see you tonight."

"Very well. Tell him here. Down the road. Latham's Boat Yard. But it will have to be after midnight."

"He won't like that."

"A lot I care what he likes. I've got personal business to attend to. Tell him I'll see him about half one."

"But—"

"Tell him."

Hickey was feeling very good about himself. The Mayor, having gotten wind of John Hancock's order of the 17th to seize and collect stores of sulphur, had had some of his stalwarts round up much of the stuff and store it in a near, yet remote, unsuspicious place. But Hickey had been busy over the past week and knew people who loved to talk.

About a half a mile from Fort George, Broadway ran into the triangle-shaped Common. There, on the west side of Broadway, between Weasyes and Partition Streets, facing the bottom end of the Common, stood St. Paul's Chapel, which had been completed in 1767. The church was situated in the middle of an unpopulated, thickly wooded area. Since there were perhaps twenty churches—including two other English, one being Trinity, three Presbyterian, two Dutch Lutheran, two Dutch Calvinist, one French, one Anabaptist, a Methodist, a Quaker meeting hall, a Moravian, and the synagogue on Mill Street—all in the densely settled tip of the island, New-Yorkers who were wary of danger in those rarely traversed woods worshipped elsewhere in the heart of the City.

It was in the basement of St. Paul's Chapel that the Mayor had cleverly hidden the sulphur. But not cleverly enough.

Hickey had duty this night. Feigning illness, he'd convinced Lieutenant Plunkett to replace him. Since Hickey often supplied the officer with spirits and tobacco, this was not difficult.

So while someone else protected New-York, Hickey and his six cohorts stole the sulphur out of the basement of St. Paul's. As they were working, a lookout brought word that the Sons of Liberty were on their way on the same mission: to steal the sulphur.

Leaving three men to continue loading the bags of sulphur into their two wagons, Hickey and the other three lay in wait for the Sons.

Hickey and his men were treacherous but, fortunately for the Sons, not very good shots. The clamor of shooting and shouting filled the darkness.

"There! Get 'em, get 'em!"

"I can't see. Where? Where?"

"There, you fool!"

"Ow! God damn it!"

After a final spurt of firing, a cry of pain sounded from the Patriot side. "I'm hit!"

"Can you walk?"

"Hell, I can run."

The skirmish was over. Hickey and his men had won the night with no wounded or dead. The Sons were in retreat with one wounded.

It had been great sport. Hickey and his three confederates each laid claim to the shot that had winged the one Son.

"And what kind of Son is he?"

"A one-armed Son, that's what."

"A Son of a bitch, that's what."

"A Yankee Doodle Son of a bitch!"

Hickey sent his three men back to St. Paul's with instructions to settle for what sulphur they had in the wagons and leave posthaste. He had other sport in mind.

Whistling "Yankee Doodle" to himself, he pulled his collar up around his ears and set off apace after the Patriots. The Fat Man would pay a lot to know names of the Sons and where they could be found.

The Rebels weren't hard to trail. Within minutes Hickey had them in earshot. By their sounds they had separated, going in different directions, but one of their wagon wheels had flattened and he could hear the telltale clank in the darkness ahead of him each time the wheel turned. When Hickey drew close enough to see in the street light and moonlight, he could make out only a driver and perhaps one figure in the back. He followed the wagon to a house on Maiden Lane.

The driver broke bits of ice from the house and threw the fragments at the closed shutters of a second-floor window. Almost immediately, as if someone had been waiting, the shutters were flung back.

"Mariana, it's me, Joel. Ben is hurt. Come and help me."

"Stay there," a soft voice from the window answered.

Within minutes a slight figure joined those in the wagon. Hickey followed them to another house a short distance away on Rutgers Hill.

The slight figure, bent under the weight of the wounded Patriot, led him into a house via the side door. The wagon that had brought them left.

Hickey rubbed his hands, part with cold, part with greed. The Fat

Man would be delighted with this information. There was a sign hanging over the side door. Hickey went closer but it was still too dark to read. He continued to watch the house. It would be a good idea to return in the daylight and have a better look at the sign. And everything else. When he calculated that nothing more could be learned this night on Rutgers Hill, Hickey left, intent on still another kind of sport.

CHAPTER 31

Tonneman was a boy again, bare of foot, digging for oysters along the river, putting more in his mouth than in the basket, still filling the basket to take home to Gretel.

He loved raw oysters, shimmering sweet in their half-shells. He would have just two more, he decided, and slurped one after the other. He didn't stop till he'd finished half a dozen.

When he had his fill, he skimmed the empty shells across the swirling miniature whirlpools of the East River and watched the terns dive for them, cawing raucously. Then he lay back in the grass and closed his eyes. The sun caressed his face like a hot honeyed breath, and the sweet grass whispered songs in his ears and feathered his arms.

He woke suddenly, jerked into the cold present, in his own bed. He was not alone. The candle he remembered smothering before he slept was lit, borne by a shadow. The shadow murmured something, set the candle down, bent over him, placed a hand on his shoulder.

Was he dreaming? The touch felt real. But like a dream. His hands moved swifter than a dream as he grabbed the intruder and pulled the shadowy form squirming down on top of him.

Instantly he realized he was holding a woman. On his bed. Shocked, he released her as suddenly as he'd grabbed her. She raised herself to her knees. "You had no call to do that," she whispered faintly. He could feel her trembling. "I was only going to wake you."

Tonneman sat up. "What do you want?" he demanded, his sleep-marked voice harsh and loud.

"Please be quiet," she whispered urgently. "Come down to the surgery. We have need of you." She slipped off his bed and her pale face caught the light. Tonneman snatched a noisy breath. Even with her hair exposed, he recognized the boy from the tree. Now, staring into that face in the candlelight, his heart beating faster than it should, he wondered how he could not have known, and marveled at his doltishness.

Muttering, searching among the bedclothes, she found her hat and slipped it over her head, tucking the lustrous dark hair up in a swift, sensuous gesture, becoming a lad once more—but never again to him. "No one must know," she whispered. "Please hurry." She opened his bedroom door, peered into the dark hall, and slipped out.

In haste now, he cast off the covers and pulled on breeches, shirt, and hose. Cracking the ice in his pitcher, he poured frosty water into his bowl and splashed his face. The cold wash brought him fully awake. He dried himself quickly, incompletely, on the band of clean white cotton, then doused the candle between wet fingers.

On the landing, as he padded by Jamie's door in stocking feet, he could hear his friend's snores. Guardedly, Tonneman came down the stairs in the pitch darkness and made his way to the surgery.

Someone had set a candle stand on the floor so that the light rose in an arc only a short way, certainly not to the windows, which were shuttered against the cold night air.

The girl was curved over a seated figure, its feet splayed on the floor. She straightened at Tonneman's entrance, and once again he was amazed that he had not realized she was a girl the moment he'd seen her the first time, despite her boy's clothes and hat and all. She shifted the candle and Tonneman saw her double from Rivington's print shop and remembered his name. Ben Mendoza.

Ben's face was white and drawn in the candlelight, his dark eyes glazed. Blood seeped from a thick bandage on his right forearm onto a coat he was using as a cushion and onto the pine floor.

Quickly Tonneman used the candle to light an oil lamp.

"No light."

"Be still. Do you want him to die?" Tonneman took some bandage cloth and a candlestick and twisted the cloth above the wound with the candlestick as a tourniquet. "Hold that taut. Understand?"

"Yes." Her concern was clear but she was not hysterical. That was the last thing he needed at a time like this, an hysterical female.

"What is your name?" he asked as he got the fire going. He left the poker deep in the burning wood.

"They'll see. Mariana Mendoza."

"Who? Never mind." He placed his hand on the tourniquet. "I've got it. In the cabinet—"

"The brandy," she said, leaping up.

"Smart girl."

"Your father taught me some . . ." Her hand was back on the tourniquet. ". . . I should have known about stopping the bleeding."

At that moment Tonneman felt a pang. Was it envy? He was no longer amazed at his father for making her his secret apprentice.

His patient moaned. He didn't want the boy awake while he did what he had to do next. Trusting Mariana to deal with the pressure, Tonneman unbound the saturated bandage and poured the brandy over the wound.

Ben came awake screaming. With her free hand Mariana covered his mouth. "No, Ben."

Ben, fully awake, stopped at once. Tonneman gave him a healthy drink of brandy, then put a roll of cloth between the young man's teeth. "Bite. One more time." He poured the brandy over the injury again. The boy shivered but made not a sound. Tonneman held the oil lamp to the ugly wound. Ben was lucky. The ball had gone through. Nicked the radial artery, but the bone was untouched.

The wound needed more precise cleaning. Tonneman jumped up and found that Mariana had laid out his father's instruments on a counter. He found the probe and tweezers and returned to his patient. "Hold fast, Ben. I see some flecks of powder in there. I have to get them out in case they're bits of metal. If I don't, you could end up with a sack of pus for an arm."

"Go ahead."

"Good lad." In spite of Mariana's consternation, Tonneman lit another candle and painstakingly picked out as much debris as he could. When Tonneman was forced to probe deep, not a peep from Ben. All the while Mariana soldiered through as good as her brother, never once looking faint. Tonneman poured a final brandy bath over the forearm.

"Will you stitch it now?" Mariana's face was drawn with worry.

"Too large a wound. And I have to control that artery." Tonneman took the poker from the fireplace. "Hold him. Bite hard, boy." Tonneman laid the hot metal on the boy's flesh and seared the wound closed. This time the boy whimpered, then mercifully swooned. The smell of charred flesh filled the small chamber. Tonneman smeared grease over the burned wound and bandaged it, neat and clean.

"All done. You may remove the tourniquet."

Mariana was as pale as a ghost. "Is my brother going to live?"

"If there's no infection." Tonneman put his arm around the young girl's thin shoulders and tilted the bottle to her mouth. Mariana swallowed, gasping. He was conscious of his arm about her. Emotions soaring and greatly confused, he took a long nip himself.

She moved to cover her brother with his greatcoat, but stopped when she saw how bloody it was.

"In the cabinet, blankets."

"I know," she snapped, getting one.

"You won't trust me with your secrets, but you trusted me with his life. How did you know you could do that?"

Mariana drew herself up tall, which made Tonneman smile. She was all of perhaps five feet. In boy's clothing she was very much the urchin, her brother's blood smudging her cheek and chin. A girl urchin, but an urchin nonetheless. "How old are you?"

Receiving no reply, he broke through the thin film of ice in the pitcher and cleaned the instruments in a bowl. She was on her knees, wrapping her sleeping brother in the blanket, whispering in his ear. She kissed his forehead and stood. She looked at Tonneman as if she'd been all alone with her brother and was surprised to see this stranger.

"How did this happen?"

She shrugged. Faint color had returned to her cheeks.

"Why the secrecy? I'm no Whig, but I won't tell."

She stared at him for a long time. So long he assumed she was not going to respond. Then she said, "Your friend is a Tory."

"Jamie?" A month earlier he would have found that amusing, but now he wasn't at all certain. "I suppose so." Tonneman took another pull from the bottle. "Is everything politics in this damn city?"

"Don't you know what's happening around this country? It started long before April but that's when it began. On Sunday, April twenty-third, at four in the afternoon, Mr. Revere came riding in from Boston, and church bells began to ring. I ran to Broadway with the men to hear the news. It was so exciting. Drums rolled: To arms. That night the arsenal was raided by the Sons of Liberty."

Tonneman was enchanted by this little woman, for that was what she was, not a child, not a little girl, but a woman, a passionate woman, who, though she spoke with a child's exuberance, felt things with all the emotion of a strong, intelligent woman. "Was Ben with them?" he asked, prompting her to continue.

She ignored his question. "What Mr. Revere told us was that four days before, early in the morning in a place called Lexington Green in Massachusetts, the King's troops ordered the people to disperse." Mariana struck a pose like an actor and brandished an imaginary saber over her head. " 'Lay down your arms, you damned Rebels,' " she declaimed, " 'or you are all dead men.' " Louder and even more dramatic she orated, " 'Disperse, ye villains, ye Rebels.' "

She grew quiet, all sense of acting gone. In a fragile voice she said, "Then the first shot rang out, and eight men died. Ten were wounded. The lobsterbacks went on from there to Concord. This time it wasn't so one-sided. We were waiting for them, atop houses and barns, from windows, behind walls and trees and stones, men, and women, too. We drove them off. We won that one."

"We did indeed." He kept his face serious.

"In May our Ethan Allen and General Benedict Arnold took Fort Ticonderoga . . . up on Lake Champlain."

"I know where it is."

"Then in June, on Breed's Hill in Massachusetts, there was a battle that made the first two at Lexington and Concord look like squabbles in a tavern. General Washington told me it was the first major battle of the Revolution."

"Told you?"

"Well . . . me and a lot of other people. He was talking to a bunch of us, making a speech. You know."

"Yes, I know." It was hard not to smile at her fervor, but he didn't want to insult her.

"The British Regulars shelled our boys nearly to hell but they were steadfast. Lord, they had to be. Not much ammunition. Fifteen musket balls per man. I ask you. Is that a way to run a war? You know what our boys were told? To hold their fire until they saw the whites of the lobsterbacks' eyes. Now I ask you, amidst all the smoke and stuff that goes on with cannons and mortars and muskets firing all over the place, you're lucky if you can see three feet ahead of you. And people trying to slash your guts out. If it's got a red coat and moves, shoot the damn thing. That's what I say."

This time Tonneman felt no urge to smile. The anger in her voice chilled him.

"We retreated from Breed's Hill to Bunker Hill. It was slaughter. Over four hundred of our men were slain or wounded. The Redcoats were hurt worse, but they took the day. Still, they didn't even expect us to put up as good a fight as we did, which goes to prove you oughtn't rankle the rabble." She cocked her head defiantly, as if daring Tonneman to rankle her.

Ben moaned. Quickly, Mariana returned to his side and pulled the blanket more closely about him. "That's the day everything changed. From then on, this was our City. Our *country.*" She stroked her brother's cheek. "Your father was one of us," she whispered, looking up at Tonneman.

Tonneman took a clean cloth, wet it, and knelt opposite Mariana over her unconscious brother's body. "There's blood on your phiz."

Staring at him with her huge dark eyes, she let him take her chin in his hand and gently clean her face. One candle flickered, sputtering, near its own conclusion. Something stirred within him. Her chin trembled in his hand.

CHAPTER 32

Buoyed by the evening's accomplishment, knowing there was a pretty penny to be made from the highest bidder for the stolen sulphur, Hickey hurried past Broadway to Church Street, then turned right to Barkley and King's College and the Holy Ground. He was filled with the wild fire of anticipation.

The bawdy houses across the way from the college were not for him. He wanted privacy for his roll and his tup. But not with the fat old slut, wearing a face covered with the warts, coming nigh.

"I know how to make you happy, love," she promised, breathing onions in his face.

"Die in a ditch, you old hag."

She backed off, then spat at him from a safe distance. "I hope the fires of hell roast off your cock."

As the Irish drew his fist, threatening to smash the old hag's face, she scooted across the street. Growling, Hickey wiped his face of frozen spittle. As he did, he saw the right one before she saw him. The woman was coming from the direction of Broadway. She was bundled against the cold in a heavy, hooded cloak.

He took some coppers from his purse and weighed them from hand to hand, relishing the clatter of the coins coming together. In moments she would recognize the sound and come to him.

His lips stretched across his teeth when he saw her shoulders straighten. As she quickened her pace, he put all but one coin in his pocket. Hickey could feel the whore's greedy eyes watching. When she sidled up to him, he was pleased to see that she stood taller than he by more than an inch.

"I'll be good to you, my fine beard splitter, I will," she said, smiling, with the Cockney sound of London strong in her voice. All the while she never took her eyes off the two-penny coin in his fingers. "But I promise I'm worth more than tuppence."

Hickey growled deep in his throat.

"Ah, but let's not talk of money, love. You just come along with me and you'll never regret it." She ran her hand downward from his chest to his private parts. "I'll make your bawbels hum." The Irish captured her wrist and applied pressure. Pain spun from her eyes. She didn't howl. He liked that.

"I don't go along with anyone, you cow." He thrust his face square into hers. "You want your tuppence, you'll come with me."

Hesitating only a moment, the tall whore said, "Whatever you want, Captain. Nancy's the one for you. This girl's got the stuff to make you happy as a oyster at high tide." She rubbed herself against him like a cat and he caught the tangy smell of her. The black wool scarf about her head slipped. A tangle of wild red hair escaped.

Hickey sucked in the cold November air. He was on fire. With her height and her red hair, tonight would be grander than he dreamed.

He had taken a room behind Gunderson's Butcher Shop on Little Dock Street because the smells reminded him of home and Dick Kineally's shop. He'd apprenticed to Kineally. All the while Hickey was scrubbing the chopping block, the bastard Dick the butcher was upstairs plugging his dick into dear old Ma.

There was not a sound from the dark and empty shop. Not even the cat. Gunderson had sent his family to Long Island and what with his being half deaf, he wouldn't hear a thing if Hickey and his whore frigged all the night long, singing "Yankee Doodle" till the cows came home.

But Hickey couldn't take all night long to do what he was going to do. He had an appointment with the Fat Man. So he would do her as pleased him to pass the time.

For the fun of it he took her into the butcher shop itself.

"Eh, what're we doing in here?"

"This is where I keep the spirits." He lifted her high and set her on the butcher block. "You like spirits, don't you?"

"I'll say I do. A dram of spirits for the girl with spirit."

"Right back."

"What?"

"Got to take a leak."

On this pretext Hickey pretended to go out back to the privy but instead ran to his room for the peach brandy.

In a short bit he and Nancy put away the bottle. She was lying on the block singing some fool song about love and flowers, all the while smirking at him, legs spread. The Irish pressed his hands over his eyes. He cackled. The drunken bitch looked just like his mother.

Sweat poured from him. The slut's song gurgled when he grabbed her by the throat. Then he tore away her clothes and had her on the butcher block, frigging her hard, all the time cursing her for the mean whore she was.

She cursed him back and gave him a furious ride until they collapsed in exhaustion.

He awoke not knowing the time. Nancy, snoring loudly, lay on the block, on her back, her mouth agape. He smacked the side of her head to wake her. She whimpered and her eyes opened. Confusion brimmed, then recognition. She held her arms out to him, cooing. "Come to Mama, my big beautiful boy."

He chopped off her head with the butcher's long-bladed cleaver.

Hickey brought the butcher's cart to the front of the shop and loaded his bulky package into it. The night was colder than a banshee's tit, but that aided him with his chore. He was planning on dumping her where he'd left Jane, until he remembered the house on Rutgers Hill. "Get on, horse," he said with a self-satisfied snort, "I've got a present for the Rebels."

The sky was dark with no stars. The only light came from the street lamps. The City was eerily still. His cart made little sound on the snow-covered roads, where even the nag's hoofbeats were muffled.

When he arrived at the house on Rutgers Hill, Hickey separated the two parts of his package and rewrapped the larger piece. He climbed down, carried his burden to the front door, and dropped it on the stone steps, laughing. "A bit of meat for the Patriot's soup."

The Irish went back to the cart, whistling "Yankee Doodle" softly. He picked up Nancy's head by its blood-matted red hair. The angry dead eyes caught his for a brief moment before he threw it.

CHAPTER 33

Gretel lay on her back, cap on her head, the bedclothes up around her ears, snug as a baby. But sleep would not come. She had set her kitchen to order and gone to bed early, having spent the long afternoon scrubbing floors and boiling linen in her large copper, then hanging it in the scullery to dry.

Neither Johnny nor Dr. Jamison had been home for the evening meal, so she had not needed to interrupt her work. When at last she had come to her bed, her back ached and her knees had gone stiff. She closed her eyes and rolled over on her side.

Half dozing on her back, her musings kept returning to Dr. Jamison. What she would like to do was take the eminent Mister Doctor Jamison by his Tory neck and chop it off like the rutting rooster he was. "*Ach,*" she muttered, "a man cannot jump over his own shadow." Unhappy all around, she rolled over on her stomach and commanded sleep to come. But it wasn't meant to be.

Johnny didn't need Dr. Jamison about, that was for sure. What her Johnny needed was a wife and half a dozen fat children. The nice young daughter of a good Patriot, a houseful of happy children she could hug and kiss and make sweets for. The notion made Gretel so happy that she found herself smiling from ear to ear. Then she sighed.

The stinking trollop and the bold look of her kept invading Gretel's mind. Where had the hussy been coming from? Gretel knew in her heart it wasn't Johnny. He would have more respect than to bring a jade into their home. Besides, Johnny had left early that morning. It had to have been Dr. Jamison.

Gretel had mixed feelings concerning Johnny's friend. She would be very happy when he moved on. Doctor he might be, but he was not a good man. Her *Fingerspitzengefühl,* her intuition, told her so. Tangled in the bedclothes, she thought: When the Americans drive the British from New-York, Dr. Jamison will return to England.

She had been enraged earlier in the day when she'd gone upstairs to do the bedrooms and empty the chamber pots. The harlot's perfume filled Dr. Jamison's chamber. There was rouge on the bedding, and the smell of a man and a woman, which had given her pause. Dr. Peter had never brought a woman into the house from the time Gretel arrived until he died. It just wasn't the way he did things. But, and she sighed heavily, times had changed. She was living in a new age. Men and women did not go by the old rules.

She missed the old doctor, even though he'd gotten a bit odd in his last year, like taking up with the Mendoza girl. Gretel herself had said to him it wasn't seemly for the girl to dress in boy's clothing and for the old doctor to spend so much time with her, let alone teach her medicine. She knew from her friend Deborah, who worked for the Mendozas, that the family despaired over the girl. Soon it would be time for her to wed, and who would marry such a peculiar lass, even if her father was a rich merchant?

Gretel dozed again, and woke when she heard her Johnny come home, the stairs creaking as he climbed them. She heard him tap on Dr. Jamison's door, but she could have told Johnny the doctor was not home yet. Then she heard Johnny's door close, and silence fell over the house again.

Some time later as she lay on her sleepless bed she heard Jamison return. After that she slept the sleep of the just.

What woke her, Gretel could not have said. Quiet as a mouse, she left her bed, wrapped herself in a shawl, and opened the door. The Mendoza girl in her boy's garb was creeping into Johnny's room. Gretel was stunned. What was this then? Obviously Dr. Jamison was a terrible influence.

She made ready to return to her bedchamber and put this awful night behind her, when the Mendoza girl came out of Johnny's chamber, down the stairs. Only minutes later Johnny followed her. Gretel put her feet into slippers and followed them. When she discovered they were tending to a wounded boy, she realized this was all for the Cause.

So, this was good. Johnny is taking up for his father, she thought with satisfaction, and retired silently to her room.

But the solace of slumber was still not to be hers that night. She dozed again, and woke again with a start.

A strange scraping noise was coming from outside, from the front of the house. She rose from her bed and opened the window that faced the street. The shutters squealed noisily. She saw the silhouette of a man standing near the well. He looked up at her, laughed, then sauntered off into the night.

CHAPTER 34

South of Division Street, near the Jews Burying Ground, were the shipyards. At this hour, shortly after two in the morning, they were all but deserted, and the warehouses were dark sentinels between the yards and the East River.

Hickey had chosen Latham's as the meeting place because it was the farthest out of the yards. When he was done with the Fat Man, he could rouse Benson, have that pickleherring open his brew house, and drink to the top of his bent. Private Thomas Hickey was well into his cups.

He tied his shivering black mare to the rail next to the dapple gray. His mare pawed the frozen earth. "You'll eat later, you old bitch." He walked the short distance to the dock. There, a white specter in the falling snow, stood the Fat Man.

Hickey whistled the first seven notes to "Yankee Doodle" sharply. The Fat Man stepped out. When they were face to face, Hickey said, "Ready then to have it done?" He ran a dirty, gnarled finger across the Fat Man's throat. The Fat Man slapped the offending digit away. Hickey laughed. "He's back north. I'll jump on my nag and ride for Cambridge."

"You are a bloodthirsty soul, aren't you?" said the Fat Man with some disgust.

"Bloodthirsty I am. That's what you pay me for. Soul? I sold it to the Devil a long time ago." The Irish laughed bitterly. "And he paid me poor, I'll swear to that."

"I'm not fond of these late hours," the Fat Man said haughtily. "At two in the morning I need my bed."

"I had business to attend to."

"Business?"

"It is none of yours." Hickey let his eyes probe the darkness, taking in the silent warehouses, the empty black waters, then the docks themselves. Coiled ropes and boxes and the bare bones of an unfinished ship made eerie shapes in the snow-choked darkness.

As the Fat Man followed his glance, Hickey could barely suppress a laugh. He'd recently learned who the Fat Man was, and he knew full well that the scurvy bugger had an interest in some of those very same warehouses. This war could make the Fat Man rich. If Hickey played the bastard right, much of those riches would fly out of the Fat Man's pockets into his own.

"Washington will die," said the Fat Man, turning his attention back to Hickey. "That's a surety as certain as Kingdom come. The only question is when. And that depends on many things not yet determined."

"You do go on, sir. I have information."

"What is it?"

"This is good stuff. Ought to be worth a few dollars."

"You'll be paid."

"The sight of the King's coin would oil my tongue."

The Fat Man patted his greatcoat pocket. "Soon enough, you covetous rogue."

Hickey grunted. "On Wednesday, fifteen November, the General met with a fellow from Connecticut at The Queen's Head Tavern . . ."

"Add Sam Fraunces to the list of those who will hang when this is finished."

". . . Name of David Bushnell. Went to the Yale school. This Bushnell says he's invented an underwater boat that can row up to a ship and place a mine below the waterline. Calls it the *Turtle.* Ain't that sweet? Claims he has black powder that can ignite under water."

Hickey's mount whinnied and prodded the dapple gray with her head, nipping the gray in the process. Hickey grabbed a handful of snow, squeezed it into a ball and threw it at his horse. The black neighed angrily; the gray snorted and stamped.

"That beast of yours is too mean to live."

Hickey smiled. "Just like me."

"We know about Bushnell and his Water Machine."

"Kiss my arse, if you do. You trying to cheat me out of hard-earned cash?"

The Fat Man pulled out a plump, clinking cloth bag from his coat pocket and handed it to the Irish. "Ten sovereigns. Is that enough to keep you quiet for the nonce, you greedy snap?"

Hickey shook the bag at his right ear. "I do love the tinkle of gold. For ten sovereigns I'll be quiet all night long." He opened the bag and peered inside. There was only half a moon in the starless sky and the nearest street lamp was out, which made it impossible to see. But he enjoyed prodding the Fat Man when he could. "Not that I don't trust, mind you."

They moved toward the horses. A cat howled, another answered. The waterfront reverberated with the sound. The dapple gray shied away from Hickey's mare.

"Settle, settle, you useless knacker," the Fat Man growled, laboriously climbing on his animal, "or I'll sell you to the butcher."

As he mounted, Hickey thought he heard another sound in the echo of the cats. A thin, strange wailing. He twisted in his saddle to see in all directions. The wail came again, and then a figure appeared perhaps thirty feet from them on the dock. At once the figure was gone. Hickey crossed himself. "Blessed Savior." All he could hear was the water, lapping at the piers.

"What's wrong?" the Fat Man asked impatiently. With some difficulty, he too, had shifted in his saddle to observe what Hickey was looking at.

"Did you see that?"

"What? Where?"

"Yonder. It was a banshee, a wailing woman of death. When a banshee walks and wails, you know what that means?"

"No. I do not."

"It means one of us is going to die." The Irish crossed himself again, even going so far as to kiss his thumb, a dim, half-forgotten childhood observance.

To the Fat Man this was vexing but also amusing. He had never before seen Hickey frightened. "We're all going to die. You Papists take everything too seriously."

"Can't we get inside? The jangle of coins will wake Benson."

"No. The less we're seen together the better."

They stayed that way for a moment, the only sounds the river and the horses pawing and snorting restlessly, their breath fogging the night air.

As if there had been no fright or mention of banshee, Hickey spoke. "You were saying, sir?"

"Correct me if I'm in error, but you were a corporal of Sappers and Miners at one time?"

Hickey nodded. "The last time I was serving His Majesty the King, before I had a disagreement with an idiot, name of Fleming, about how much powder to use with a field mine."

"Sergeant Fleming is no longer with the world . . ."

Hickey flashed his yellow teeth. "Blown to bits and bobs for his stupidity."

"After the explosion you were reduced in rank."

"Well, that's the army, ain't it? Such things never bother me."

"Then why'd you desert?"

"I had my reasons."

"How long were you in jail for counterfeiting?"

"Who says I was?"

"It's not your proficiency as a counterfeiter we're depending upon. There'll come a time when we'll want your miner's skills."

"Speaking of which, I've come across a fair supply of sulphur. Would you be needing some for your powder-making?"

"I don't come out in the dead of a winter's night for you to talk like some bloody chapman, hawking this and that. We're here on important business. There are things that will need blowing up."

"Such as generals."

"Such as *one* General."

CHAPTER 35

Gretel peered into the shimmering darkness for a long time, unaware of the cold. She'd seen Lucifer himself this night. There near the well.

She was not a religious woman, but she was shaken to the bone. Rousing herself, she closed the shutters, lowered the window, and crawled into bed, pulling the bedclothes over her head. She felt as if she were freezing to death. Never in all her life had she felt such a presentiment of evil.

"God in heaven," she prayed, "keep my Johnny safe." Gradually, her limbs relaxed and her blood warmed her body. But sleep was impossible; she was fully awake. She prayed again, fervently, her supplicating hands pressed together under the covers. She said her amen, pushed back the bedding, and swung her feet to the chilly floor. She would dress and get an early start to her daily chores.

Washing her face with what water she could squeeze from a sliver of ice, Gretel dressed quickly, placing her shawl high about her neck.

The stairs creaked as she descended. When she paused at the closed door of the surgery and heard Johnny's and the Mendoza girl's voices, she was tempted to tell Johnny what she'd seen. She stood debating this, and it came to her that the girl was not a deranged child or a wanton but another Patriot for the Cause. That was something to be wished. Like many women, Gretel knew the frustration of having to tend to woman's work when she had as much at stake as any man. She wished that she could wear a man's clothes and toil for the Revolution. This gave Gretel a momentary smile. Imagine her in breeches.

Still, the girl should wear fitting clothes. Dressed properly, she would be presentable indeed.

Gretel mused on the path her thoughts were taking as she plucked Johnny's beaver hat from its place on the maple knob near the front door. She plumped the hat on her head and strode to her kitchen.

Homer licked her hand. When he saw there was no food in it, he settled on the hearth and went to sleep.

"And where were you with your big voice last night, I ask you?"

The dog wagged his tail. He was old and deaf now, but a good companion.

Adding hot coals from the *doof* pot, where they'd been kept glowing overnight, Gretel stoked up the fire. Then, lighting a lantern, she went out the side door with her bucket. A moderate crust of fresh frozen snow covered the ground, but at least it wasn't snowing now. A few gray streaks in the sky foretold dawn.

The lamp glow flickered in the wind. Hoping the well water hadn't frozen, she gave the rope a hard tug to bring the bucket up. It wouldn't budge. She peered down the well. The bucket was hovering over the water. Sure enough, it was stuck. Gretel set the lamp on the ground and grabbed hold with both hands. The rope moved. *"Ach,* good."

It was hard pulling, but bit by bit the bucket came into view.

In the vague light of coming dawn it seemed as if there was something in the bucket other than water.

Gretel lifted her lamp. Horrified, she lashed out, sending the bucket whence it came.

Her scream flew high like an eagle's flight, slicing through the frozen sky.

CHAPTER 36

Gretel's terrible shrieks penetrated wood and stone. Tonneman came rushing out of the surgery, Mariana Mendoza right behind him with a candle; the flame blew out immediately. At the same time Jamie ran from the front of the house, almost falling over Homer, who was running in circles and howling.

Across the street, Chester Remsen slammed open his shutters. "What's happened? Have they begun killing us?"

Tonneman and Jamie came upon Gretel at the same moment. She was sitting on the frozen snow, Tonneman's beaver hat askew on her head, staring sightlessly, hugging the glowing lantern in her lap.

Even allowing for the lamp light, her skin was ashen. And despite the cold, she had broken out with sweat. Tonneman kneeled and put his fingers to her throat; her pulse was weak and slow.

"Gretel. What is it? Are you all right?"

"I'm very well, Herr Doctor Tonneman," she said tonelessly. "And you?" Homer, tail down, whined and licked Gretel's face.

"Blankets!" Tonneman shouted, taking the lamp from Gretel and gently pushing her head between her knees. "Get away, Homer."

Mariana ran back slippy-dash to the surgery for blankets.

A door slammed. From across the way Remsen, brandishing a musket, ran to them. "What's happening?"

"And spirits," Jamie called after Mariana. "Who is that girl?" He looked at Tonneman curiously.

Tonneman marveled at his friend. Mariana was dressed in boy's clothing with her hair hidden under her hat, and still Jamie knew she was a girl. Why hadn't *he?*

"The well . . ." Gretel said softly.

"Never mind the well."

Her arms thrashed about as she attempted to sit up. "I beg you. The well." Her voice grew to another shriek. "Look in the well!"

"All right," Tonneman said. "Stay calm."

Jamie held the lantern high over the well. Tonneman looked down. He saw only the bucket in the water. "Just the bucket down there," Tonneman said, humoring her. Remsen came over and stared into the well. So did Homer.

Jamie lowered the lamp so it shone in the well. "There's something in the bucket," he said in a low voice.

Tonneman pulled at the rope. The rope wouldn't give. When he saw that it was off the runner, he gave it a vigorous tug.

"That's got it," said Jamie.

Tonneman drew the bucket up. He had it in his hand before he realized it was streaming red. The mastiff leaped at the bucket. Tonneman jerked it away from the animal. "Homer, no." The dog slunk away.

"Sweet Jesus," Remsen cried.

"Good God," said Jamie.

Inside the bucket was the severed head of a red-haired woman.

CHAPTER 37

The Mayor of New-York sampled the coffee. Finding it to his liking, he took a further sip, then set his mug down on the scarred cherrywood table. The Queen's Head was busy. He shifted his aching right foot to a more comfortable position on a low cushioned stool. "You know how much pain I'm in?" He unfolded his copy of Rivington's *Gazetteer* and fitfully glanced at its front page. "What do you want?"

Alderman David Matthews put a finger to his lips. "You'll see. By and by, you'll see."

"Very well. Has Rivington had any luck getting more type?"

"What do I care about such things?"

The Mayor lowered his voice. "What did you want to talk about?"

Matthews spread peach preserves on a crumpet. "I'm having difficulties with Waddel."

The Mayor groaned. "What's your complaint with Alderman Waddel?"

Matthews cleared his throat. "The South Ward, my ward, and the Dock Ward, his . . ." Matthews stopped to take a bite of his crumpet. "He will not cooperate."

The Mayor beckoned to Elizabeth Fraunces, who had just finished serving a table nearby.

"Yes, Mr. Mayor?"

"Put a drop of rum in my coffee, there's a good girl."

She curtsied. "Yes, sir."

Matthews watched her with suspicion until she was out of earshot. His eyes skimmed the room. It was fairly certain that he and the Mayor were the only Loyalists in the room, maybe even in the City. That was a dangerous position to be in these days. "I've decided this place needs watching."

The Mayor's eyes darted about. He recognized everyone—well, almost everyone. Well before this Rebel nonsense, New-York had been his domain. The problem was that it was a kingdom of troublemakers. "How so? Why does it need watching?"

"That's not the issue, Mayor. Let's just say that Governor Tryon and I agree."

"Oh, is that the way it is?" Mayor Hicks gave his companion a hard look. There was a clear threat in what Matthews had just said.

"Yes, sir. That's the way it is."

Elizabeth, armed with the rum, poured the dark, sweet liquid into his mug.

"More," said the Mayor. "I'll be needing it." With Matthews and Tryon in the same bed, he knew his days as Mayor were numbered.

Elizabeth poured some more. "Will that suffice?"

"For the moment, Goodwife Fraunces. Thank you."

"Alderman?"

"No. Nothing. Go away."

"Yes, sir." Elizabeth's comely plump face registered nothing, but as she turned toward the kitchen, the fire caught the glint of anger in her dark eyes.

"Very well. What have you and the Governor decided?"

"This tavern, being on Broad Street, is on the dividing line between my ward and Waddel's. With the Governor's approval, I'm having my Constable and the Night Watch keep an eye on the place. I want Waddel to do the same."

"What seems to be his problem? Waddel's a good Tory."

"I wonder." Matthews' eyes narrowed. "No. He's just a hardhead."

Mayor Hicks looked about. "We are in the minority, you know."

Matthews looked grim. "Things will change sooner rather than later."

"I hope you're right. We think we're running the City, but if the Sons or one of those damned committees orders us to jump, we'll have to ask how high."

Matthews' response was to spit, and not at the cuspidor nearby but on the floor.

"I'm surprised they haven't sent you and me and the entire constabulary force packing," said Hicks. He sighed. "What do you expect me to do?"

"Advise Waddel to cooperate. The King's men will be in power again in New-York, maybe before spring. And what he does or doesn't do will be remembered. . . . What everyone does will be remembered." Matthews watched Black Sam come out of the kitchen with a large stew pot and sit at a table of men in hunters' shirts and leather pants. A cheer rose, and laughter.

The Mayor took a deep draught of his rum coffee. "Have your friend Tryon tell him. It was bad enough him interfering when he was on land. You'd think once he was on that damn ship . . . No matter where the glorious Governor is, he keeps trying to run the City. My City."

"Their City, you mean." Matthews jerked his head toward the other patrons of the tavern. He paused, then took a new tack. "Do it for me, Whitehead," he wheedled.

"All right, I'll talk to Waddel. Just leave me in peace."

"Thank you, Your Honor." Matthews was pleased with his small victory.

At that moment, Maurice Arthur Jamison, Doctor of Physick and Surgery, entered The Queen's Head. The Mayor waved him over. "Ah, Dr. Jamison. David, you remember the good doctor? Young Tonneman's friend? He's our new Chancellor of the College of Medicine."

Matthews smiled, almost pleasantly. He could afford this munificence. With Waddel's Constable and Night Watch and his own, he'd have a true picture of the goings-on in Sam Fraunces's tavern. And when the situation turned—and it would—he'd hang that Black Sam bastard from the highest tree in the Common.

"And you remember Alderman Matthews?"

"Of course."

"Will you join us, sir?"

"I'd be delighted." Jamie's attention was taken by the display of weaponry on the whitewashed walls opposite his chair.

"Something to eat? Drink?"

"Coffee will be splendid. Mayor, a moment please."

"Goodwife," Matthews bellowed.

Mayor Hicks leaned into Jamie.

"I'm afraid there's been another head, another woman with her head chopped—"

"What?" The Mayor glared at Jamie.

"Early this morning, Dr. Tonneman and I found a—"

"Good God, man."

"He sent for the local authority and for Constable Goldsmith, too."

"As if I didn't have enough on my plate. And I did want to go to church. I'll have to get over to Tonneman's house as soon as—"

"An interesting coincidence, gentlemen. She had red hair. So did the first one."

"Good God, man, no more." The Mayor's face was as white as his powdered wig.

Taking the Mayor at his word, Jamie stood and crossed to the wall of African objects. The last time he'd been here he'd been captivated by the two curved, single-edged serrated swords. As a surgeon he had a fascination for all sorts of blades, but he thought the scimitars to be particularly exquisite.

This time the sight of the two blades side by side made him draw an uneven breath. He nodded his head slowly and rejoined Hicks and Matthews just as Elizabeth Fraunces brought his coffee.

"Thank you. Ah. We meet again." Jamie touched her wrist with two graceful fingertips. Was her pulse beating wildly? Or was that his?

She smiled demurely. "You have me at a disadvantage, sir." She did not move her hand.

"The broken eggs. Ten—eleven days ago."

"Oh, yes. Your gallant friend."

Jamie frowned. "Tonneman," he said to the Mayor.

Damn it if the girl wasn't looking about, delighted. "Is he not with you today?"

"No, he's not. The rascal. Even in his absence he distracts your thoughts from me." Jamie kept his fingers on her wrist with a light pressure. It was *his* pulse that was going so swiftly.

"Do you suppose I have thoughts of you?"

"I would hope so. I have had thoughts of you."

"You flatter me, sir. And you forget that I'm a married woman and the mother of two daughters." With great poise and composure, she withdrew her hand from under his. "If you'll excuse me, people are waiting." She bobbed prettily and went to attend another table.

"Charming wench."

"She's most likely a darky, too." Matthews produced a box of snuff from his coat and offered it to Jamie, who shook his head. Matthews jabbed snuff in his mouth, up between cheeks and gum.

"What a shame." Jamie sighed. "Yet, the touch of the tar brush is fairly light in her. I doubt it would come off in one encounter."

Matthews stared at Jamie, at first uncomprehending. Then he roared, spraying snuff and spittle while the Mayor chuckled quietly.

Clapping Jamie on the shoulder, Matthews cried, "You're a good fellow, Jamison. We're going to enjoy having you here, I can see that. Quite droll. Doubt if it would come off . . ."

"Is our business finished?" Mayor Hicks asked Matthews.

"As far as I'm concerned."

"No need to mind your tongue in front of the doctor. You're a good Tory, are you not, sir?" His finger was still working the snuff.

"Better than that. A good Royalist."

Matthews cleared his throat. "That's a fine distinction." To the Mayor he said softly, "I want a sharp eye kept on Samuel Fraunces, because the Rebel son of a black bitch is playing cozy with the Continental Congress and George Washington."

Jamie raised an eyebrow. "Here, too? I was at Burn's Coffee House ten days ago, and was even attacked by a group on the street. I showed them what a Royalist kick in the arse was. Seditious bastards, all of them. . . . I had heard it said New-York was a nest of Tories. More like a hive of Rebels, if you ask me."

"My sentiments exactly," said Matthews. "And what do you do with a hive? You smoke it out."

The Mayor moved abruptly, bringing great pain to his sorry right foot. "Can't you two get it through your thick skulls? Excuse my bluntness, Doctor, but we are no longer the masters here."

"Maybe you're not," said Matthews, "but I still am. Things change. And they will."

"Everything in order, gentlemen?" Black Sam towered over them, a grin on his face, but a menacing presence all the same.

Jamie measured the big man. He was swart all right. Matthews was certainly correct. Back along the line somewhere, a nigger was in the hay.

"Fine," said the Mayor, "perfectly fine."

"I'm glad to hear it."

Matthews cleared his throat and spat at the metal cuspidor nearby. He missed and spattered the stained oak floor. "You have an interesting clientele, innkeeper."

"I would hope that those who drink and dine here have discerning tastes."

"It's not taste I'm talking about, but rather politics."

Black Sam grinned. "You're a bold bastard, I'll give you that much. If that's the matter at hand, then one would wonder what *you're* doing here. A man could get killed."

"Yes," Matthews answered pointedly. "Couldn't he?"

"Why don't you do us all a favor, Alderman Matthews, and take your leave."

"I haven't finished my coffee."

"I don't mean the tavern, or the City. I mean the country."

Matthews chose not to respond to this. "One more thing," the Alderman said ponderously.

"Yes."

"The matter of your being open on the Sabbath. You know that such practices are frowned upon."

"Very well. I won't do it any more."

"You've said that before. This time be true to your word."

"I like his being open on Sunday. The Mayor whined, "Where else will I get my breakfast?"

Matthews looked at Hicks disdainfully.

Black Sam turned to Jamie. "I saw you admiring my collection."

"Yes. The scimitars are very impressive."

"They're African, made by a primitive tribesman. But I've been told the steel was hand-wrought in the Damascus style, repeatedly folded when in the fire and fused, then finally etched with acid to display the resulting grain. Come, have another look."

Jamie's eyes rested on Matthews and the Mayor for a moment. Then he shrugged and rose, following Black Sam to the whitewashed wall. He ran his surgeon's fingers over the wavy metal of the scimitars.

"That shimmer is the sign of true Damascus steel."

Jamie nodded deferentially. To the swords, not to Black Sam.

"Somebody made off with one last night." Fraunces's face was impassive.

"Oh?"

"Yes. I had three. Two I kept on this wall. A third I kept in my room." He caressed the gleaming blade on the right. "See. This sword isn't quite the same as the other . . ."

"Jamison. We're going," Matthews called. Jamie turned. Mayor Hicks, carrying his cushioned stool, was limping toward the front door, mumbling to himself. Matthews tossed some coins on the table and followed the Mayor out.

"If you'll excuse me," Jamie said, lowering his head, ever the gentleman.

"Of course." Black Sam didn't lower his head at all. He'd learned the best way to deal with Tories was to keep one's eye on them at all times.

As Jamie was leaving, he literally bumped into the huge man just arriving. "I beg your pardon."

"Good day to you, sir," Bear Bikker said. He was also polite.

"And good day to you, Bear. Come right in." Jamie made a sweeping gesture with his right hand. "This place should suit you perfectly."

CHAPTER 38

Tonneman saw the object behind the lilac bushes on the kitchen side of the house. It was wrapped in white silk and was as one with the snow. He would have missed it completely if just a little bit hadn't been exposed, glimmering in the morning sunlight. He bent over and plucked it from behind the stiff icy branches, knowing what it was even as he unwrapped it. The familiar sweet smell gave it to him before his eyes did, as the white cloth showed deep dark red rinds with each unfolding. It was a sword. A single-edged, serrated scimitar encrusted with blood.

Matthews, on the dapple gray, rode up first. The gray pranced about impatiently as the Mayor's carriage pulled in.

"Have you found the rest of her?" These were the first words out of the Mayor's mouth.

Tonneman nodded glumly. "At the front of the house near the steps."

"What have you there?" Jamie asked as he stepped out. "May I, old chum?" He reached for the curved sword.

Tonneman released the weapon, but held on to the blood-blemished silk. The cloth fell away completely, revealing the finely etched, albeit gruesome, blade.

"Now where, gentlemen, have you seen a weapon like this?" Jamison asked in his best lecturing voice.

Tonneman, spent, sighed heavily. "Jamie, if you know something about this, please inform us. I'm in no mood for your Socratic games."

"I know." Matthews beamed, dismounting, not even troubling to glance at the weapon. "It's that black bastard's." The Alderman was beside himself with satisfaction.

"Precisely," Jamie answered. "This is the sword of Samuel Fraunces.

It's identical to one of the two that hang on the wall in The Queen's Head Tavern."

"Thank you for that information, Jamie. But . . ." Tonneman took the sword. "Mr. Mayor."

"I can't move," Hicks groaned. "This damn gout."

Tonneman shook his head. "Have you been taking the medicine I sent you?"

"No, the cramps were like knives. Purged me till I thought I'd die."

"If you had listened to me you might be rid of your gout by now."

"All right." The Mayor groaned as he stepped from the carriage. In his hand was his cushioned stool.

Tonneman nodded abruptly and trudged to the side of the house. Here the body was stretched out on the green leather apron in which it had been wrapped. The others followed in his wake. Standing near the gory shroud were Goldsmith and Fred Hood, Constable of the East Ward. Hood was lean of stature, with a face full of crevices and an angry mouth. A wagon waited to cart the corpse off.

"Your Honor," Goldsmith said.

Hood lifted his bicorn. "Sir."

"The head, Goldsmith." Tonneman stared down at the pathetic dead woman, naked under the bloody wrapping. The snow around the bundle was stained a foul pink.

Goldsmith went to the wagon and produced an Indian basket. In the basket was the head.

"Show it around, please," Tonneman said in *his* lecturing voice. "What do we see, gentlemen? In the basket and on the ground."

"Tonneman," Hicks protested. "No riddles, damn it. I'm late enough for church as it is."

Matthews smirked. "I believe you, Whitehead."

"Well, I am," the Mayor insisted. "And I'm in agony with this damnable foot."

Matthews made a point of studying the head and then the body. "What we really have here—" The Alderman walked to the wagon and scraped bloody snow from his boots on a back wheel, "is a head, chopped—" He nodded in the direction of the corpse. "—from that woman's body by an African sword belonging to Black Sam Fraunces, that filthy Rebel, son of a bitch nigger, jackanapes, rogue scoundrel."

Jamie was chewing his lower lip. "Correction. They don't go together."

"Oh, my God," exclaimed the Mayor, staring peevishly at Tonneman. "I thought you said they did?" He wheeled to Jamie, wincing at the distress it caused his gouty right foot. "Are you saying the head and the body don't match?"

Jamie shook his head.

Tonneman rubbed his eyes. "No," he said tiredly. "The head does in fact go with the body."

"It's the sword," said Jamie. "The sword has a serrated edge. And it is obvious that the head and body were cut by an even-edged blade."

ℭHAPTER 39

℘he day, for Constable Daniel Goldsmith, had begun inauspiciously. An argument had ensued in the kitchen between Deborah and her mother, the ever-righteous Esther, about whose fault it was that the fire had gone out. Goldsmith had wisely hidden in his bed, feigning sleep to avoid their usual strident demand for him to choose a side.

His daughters, Ruth and Miriam, were his one bit of solace. He'd dressed and was sipping his sage tea and playing tops with the girls when Deborah got after him about caulking the kitchen window.

"You should have done it last week when I told you the first time. The wind coming in keeps blowing out the fire."

There. Now the fire going out was his fault.

Constable Fred Hood of the East Ward came to his rescue by pounding on the front door, calling for him. "The Mayor wants us," he bellowed.

Goldsmith grabbed his coat, scarf, beaver hat, and a piece of dry bread and headed for the door.

Deborah, her hands on her ample hips, stood in his path. "Where are you going, Daniel Goldsmith, without your groats and herring?" She opened the front door. "Good day to you, sir."

"Fred Hood, ma'am." He doffed his bicorn. "Beg pardon. The Mayor." He scraped his boots, stepped in, and urgently whispered into Goldsmith's ear. "Meeting about the madman chopping the women's heads off."

Goldsmith scratched his wound. The white patch had fallen off the top of his head, but the short bristled area drew attention to where he'd been struck. "Please, Deborah. The Mayor wants me." He put on his coat. "Right, Fred?"

"That's correct, Mrs. Goldsmith."

"You'll take sick without your breakfast in this cold, and you'll die. Then who will care for your helpless wife and her mother and your poor innocent children?"

Goldsmith watched his wife as he wrapped his scarf several times about his neck. Helpless? Not bloody likely. "I'll have my cut seen to by Dr. Tonneman, and Gretel will feed me." Unwilling to hear yet again about the unfit food that gentiles ate, he clamped his hat on his head and escaped with Fred. Or so he thought.

"Daniel. Daniel."

He turned slowly. "Yes, dear."

Deborah stood on the stoop in her shawl, shaking his wallet at him. "At least take the victuals I worked so hard to prepare." Shivering, she thrust the wallet of food at him. There was no smile on her face. He offered none in return. Her eyes stabbed at him and she went back into their house.

The cold day was crisp with the smell of hearth fires and the tang of brine and seaweed from the East River. The two Constables waited as a squad of fledgling Continental soldiers marched by, then briskly walked the short distance from Water Street and King to the City Hall on Wall Street.

Goldsmith felt the same sense of apprehension he'd been feeling lately. Since he had reason to believe Constable Hood was a Loyalist, he was cautious when he said, "I wonder what they're up to."

"Hear say they're loading out for Boston."

"They'll get a good fight in Boston, that's for sure." Goldsmith cocked an eye at Hood. So much for caution.

Hood frowned at him but did not comment.

When they arrived at City Hall, they found Tonneman tying his horse to the rail in front. "Good morning, Constables." The physician's apparent weariness notwithstanding, there was an exuberance about him that Goldsmith had not seen before. Extraordinary for a man who'd had all that carnage dumped in front of his house. The body, the head, the sword. The sword?

Entering the Mayor's office, Goldsmith pulled at Hood's sleeve. "The bloody sword," he whispered. "Where is it?"

"Why ask me? I don't have it." Hood was first puzzled, then defensive. "I thought you had it."

Goldsmith scratched his fiercely itching head. "*I* don't have it, man. It was entrusted to you."

Having caught a bit of the whispered altercation, Tonneman looked from one man to the other.

Mayor Hicks turned away from the large window where he'd been watching the varied goings-on of the departing troops, and limped to his desk. A half-filled bottle of rum awaited him. He poured a splash into his mug.

"How's the foot?"

"Stop pestering." The Mayor was obviously agitated. "I have too much to worry about, with a madman running loose and Matthews and his political intrigues, to listen to you about taking medicine that keeps me pooping all the time."

"You haven't given it enough time."

"My only comfort is that they are all tarts. Heaven help us if he starts cutting up quality." The Mayor dropped his body into his slat-back armchair, then eased his sore right foot onto his cushioned stool. "Sit. Sit." He groaned and moved his foot gingerly, trying to find comfort. "Perhaps we've seen the last of our head-chopping fiend."

"Let us hope," said Tonneman.

"I've talked with Black Sam. It's been verified that he reported one of his African blades missing. It's most probable that that bloody sword you found, Tonneman, was his. I told him he could have it back by and by. No death has been associated with it. Am I correct?"

"None that we know of. I'd like another look at it."

The two Constables eyed one another while Tonneman and Hicks waited expectantly.

Hood whacked himself on the thigh with his bicorn. "You don't have it, Mr. Tonneman?"

"No, Constable, I don't." Tonneman turned to Goldsmith. "I gave it to you."

"Ha," said Hood.

"You did," Goldsmith agreed. "And I turned it over to Constable Hood, as it was his jurisdiction."

"You did not." Hood's malevolence was palpable. His hat was being twisted into a two-cornered lump.

"I did." Goldsmith looked pained.

"Let's not argue the point," Tonneman ordered. "It's probably where one of us left it in my barn or thereabouts."

The Mayor was no longer listening. He was more concerned with his distressing foot. Pouring himself more rum, he said, "Tonneman, I'm putting you in charge of returning the sword to Sam Fraunces. And we'll have done with all this." He shifted his gouty foot on its stool and took a hearty swig. "God willing, we've seen the last of this killer."

"I'll get on rounds, then," Hood said, eager to be off. He glared at Goldsmith and, with a nod to Tonneman and the Mayor, was gone.

"I have to go, too," Goldsmith mumbled.

"Goldsmith, first come with me to my surgery and have those stitches removed."

"Yes, sir."

They walked to Rutgers Hill, Tonneman leading his horse. Goldsmith said, "I know I handed Hood that sword. He's a drinker, you know. A bad apple. And a Tory."

"Don't worry, Daniel. You'll see, we'll find it in the barn without a doubt."

"I hope so, sir. I feel responsible."

In front of Tonneman's house on Rutgers Hill they found the Negro Quintin hard at work, attempting to dig up the frozen ground with a pickax.

"Good morning, Quintin."

"Good morning, Dr. Tonneman. Constable." Quintin's demeanor was respectful but chary. Just as it had been eleven days before: the day Goldsmith had gotten his head broken, the day Quintin told Goldsmith about the soldier near the Collect and Goldsmith insulted him by asking if he'd been drinking.

"What are you doing?" Tonneman asked.

"Digging a new well. Lady inside told the Mayor the well was poisoned by the bloody head in it. Mayor told me to dig a new well."

Goldsmith took off his beaver hat and scratched around his stitches gently. "Wrong time of year."

"Don't tell me, tell the Mayor." The black man went back to his labors.

Inside the surgery it was exceeding cold. Tonneman placed some wood on the charred embers of the fire and stirred them. "There," he said when the fire caught. "Gretel must really be upset to let it get so low." He found his pipe and lit it. "That's better," he said, clenching the pipe between his teeth. "Let's see to those stitches." Goldsmith sat on the examining table. "Hold still, now. When I finish my report on the new victim, I'll let you see it before I send it on to the Mayor."

"Thank you, sir."

"There you are, good as new."

"That's what you said last time."

"Now it's true. Shall we go out and find that sword?"

But they couldn't find it. After a thorough search of the barn and grounds, Goldsmith caught himself staring at the well. "You think it might be down there?"

"Perhaps. Are you going to go down and look?" As Tonneman spoke Homer appeared, slowly traveling up Rutgers Hill, tail between his legs. "Homer."

The dog barked, ran to Tonneman and nuzzled him.

Tonneman patted the mastiff.

"No." Goldsmith knew the sword wasn't in the well. He was certain that Hood had taken it.

"Come back to the surgery, Constable. We'll have a drink."

After a sip of brandy and a puff of his pipe Tonneman said, "So, we have two similar murders."

"Do you believe in evil, Doctor?"

Tonneman thought for a moment, pulling on his pipe. "Yes. But it's not enough to say this murderer is evil. He's got to have a reason. No one goes around chopping off heads simply because he's evil."

"Forgive me sir, but yes, they do."

Tonneman waved his hand dismissively. "What do you plan to do about it?"

"Well, this situation of the two red-haired women seems like two peas in a pod to me."

"Agreed," said Tonneman. "There were bite marks on this woman, too."

The Constable bobbed his head. He knew.

Tonneman puffed away. "The only irregularity is the bloody sword that couldn't possibly have done the deed."

"Yes, sir." Goldsmith made a face. "The missing bloody sword," he said bitterly. "What do I owe you?"

"On the City. Line of duty. Where are you off to?"

"First to the Holy Ground to ask the whores if they knew her. But first I'd like to talk to Gretel about Saturday night and Sunday morning."

"I don't think she's ready to talk about what happened."

"Well, I left my house without any breakfast. Perhaps she'll give me a hot drink and some porridge."

"Not a bad idea, Constable. I'll join you."

The kitchen side of the house was oddly silent. "She must have gone to market," Tonneman said, as he walked to the dining room and out to the front hall. Homer followed closely at his heels, almost tripping him.

Goldsmith caught himself staring at the unlit kitchen fireplace as he'd stared at the well. The room was bone-chilling cold. He could barely swallow. For no reason he could discern, he had a horrible, uncertain sense of foreboding, as if someone was walking over his grave.

CHAPTER 40

Tonneman had to hunch over to get through the low door, then he had to stay bent because of the slanted ceiling. The small room on the top floor of the house on Crown Street contained three narrow rope beds close together. Two were unoccupied. The girl lay prone on the bed just left of the door, whimpering and thrashing. Tonneman set his black medical bag on the second bed. The sour smell of vomit was strong in the room.

Abigail stood behind him in the doorway, repeatedly pulling at her right sleeve. Her face was pale and there were dark circles under her moist blue eyes. Only an hour before, as Goldsmith had been leaving Rutgers Hill, she had summoned Tonneman and his medical bag to the house, to the servants' entrance. They had used the back stairs.

Tonneman lifted the girl's limp wrist. He could barely find her pulse. A draught of freezing air leaked from a cracked window pane. "Come in or not," he said to Abigail, "but close the door."

Abigail, after a moment's hesitation, still fussing with her silk sleeve, stepped into the room. At once Tonneman saw what she'd been trying to conceal. Abigail had a purplish welt on her right wrist. She closed the door. "John—"

The girl's face was a swollen mass of contusions, continuing around to the right side of her neck. Her nose was broken and her lower lip split. He was sure he could straighten the nose with one twist, but now was not the time to do it, not until he knew more about her condition. Gently he sat the girl up and undid her dress.

When Tonneman examined her, she cried out, "Please, no! I don't know. Please!"

Abigail gasped. "Dear God."

The girl's back was covered with nasty contusions and lacerations.

"It's too late for God," Tonneman said angrily. "What happened here? This girl has been near beaten to death."

Abigail couldn't meet his accusing glare. "John, I—" She waved her hands crazily.

"Who did this, Abigail?"

"Will she die?"

"I don't know."

"My parents will take her in."

"Isn't it safe for her to stay here?" Tonneman stroked the girl's battered face. "What's her name?"

"Betty."

"Betty." Her swollen lids fluttered, barely able to open. Terrified at seeing Tonneman, her eyes darted every which way. When they fell on Abigail, she shrank back on the bed and whispered, "Don't let him—"

"Don't let him what?" Realizing he'd raised his voice, he said in kinder tones, "I'm Dr. Tonneman, Betty. We're going to take you where you'll be safe."

He mixed laudanum with some of the tepid water in the cracked and chipped pitcher standing on the unpainted pine chest at the end of the room. Betty winced when the alcohol touched her torn lips; her eyes closed. Tonneman lowered her to the bed.

Tonneman stood, banging his head on the slant ceiling. Rubbing the bump he passed through the door, head low. Abigail followed him out.

In the hall he said, "I'll need a carriage. Have someone get her ready and I'll take her to your parents. And have a runner inform your parents. Ask them to heat water so she can be bathed, and have them prepare a room with a good fire. First thing I want to do is straighten that nose before the laudanum wears off."

"Tilly."

A young maid came into view on the staircase, where she'd been standing just out of sight. Abigail gave her instructions. The girl climbed the rest of the way and disappeared into Betty's room.

"Who did this, Abigail?" He caught her arm at the elbow; she didn't speak. "Your husband?" He saw by the red flush raising from her neck to her cheeks that he'd been on the mark. "Why?"

"She . . . lied."

"But to beat her like that. Why not just dismiss her?"

"You don't understand, John." Her exquisite eyes pleaded with him.

"Richard is a good man. He has a violent temper, I'm afraid, and in particular when it's a family matter."

"What lie could she—"

"Forgive me, but it's none of your business, John. Richard and Grace—"

"What does your sister-in-law have to do with this?"

Abigail pressed her lips together. "Come down to the kitchen. We'll send Braxton up for Betty." She seemed to have settled something in her mind.

As he followed her down the stairs, he realized she wasn't having the usual effect on him; the quickened heartbeat, the dizzying desire were gone. Of course he had been concerned about the girl. Still, all the amorous pining-for-Abigail nonsense had quite disappeared.

At the foot of the stairs, Abigail stopped and said, "Emma has run off. With a man. It seems she met him in the Common. The disgrace. Betty was her personal maid. She helped Emma to do this stupid thing, dressing her in maid's clothing. It was only yesterday that Grace got the story from her."

"How? By beating her half to death?"

"I'm afraid she did strike her. After all, Grace is Emma's mother. But only once across the face."

"And your husband did the rest."

Abigail cringed as if he had struck her. "Betty had come to tell Grace about Emma because her conscience was bothering her, and she was concerned for Emma's safety. After three days. A little tardy I would think."

"Have you called in your Constable?"

"And have the entire world know our shame? Richard made discreet inquiries; he learned a young woman of Emma's description, accompanied by a gentleman, was seen boarding the coach to Philadelphia."

"Then that would be that, it would seem."

"It would seem."

"And what about *your* bruises, Abigail?"

"He's my husband, John."

"More's the pity."

Her eyes glistened. "More's the pity."

CHAPTER 41

Two soldiers were coming out of Jew Molly's door as Goldsmith approached Barkley Street. They were unshaven, unkempt, drunk, and mean-looking.

The taller of the two leaned into Goldsmith's face, spraying him with spittle. "Could you direct us to the Boston Road?"

"That's a piece from here. You'd best sober up first, else you'll freeze your arses off." The Constable gave them a hard stare.

The little one seemed unable to keep his eyeballs from rolling in toward each other. He rubbed the chapped skin on his lumpy nose. "We're off to join the Continental Army."

Goldsmith couldn't help but grin. "By what little uniform you have," he said, referring to their blue coats, "you're *in* the Continental Army."

"Oh," said the little fellow.

If these two were a sample of what was going to be fighting for liberty, it was going to be a long fight up a steep hill. "Good luck."

He watched them stagger toward Broadway, then knocked on Molly's red-painted door. His stomach gurgled, reminding him he still hadn't eaten. Gretel hadn't been at Dr. Tonneman's house to feed him, and the doctor had been called off on an emergency.

"Enter, sweetheart."

He opened the door. "Guess again. Not a sweetheart." A cozy warmth was coming from the fireplace, and the rich smell of chicken soup filled the chamber. Molly grinned at him. She was bare to the waist and had her skirts tucked up as she bathed herself from a large earthenware bowl. "Oh, Daniel, you can be my sweetheart any time and I won't charge you a penny."

Goldsmith tore his eyes away from her voluptuousness and turned his back. "I would thank you to clothe yourself so I can speak to you officially."

"Tut-tut, Daniel love." She mocked him, but the sounds of her movements told him she was completing her ablutions. At last, she said, "All right, Master Pure, you may put your virtuous eyes on me again."

He turned. Her bosom was still bare. Angry and red-faced, he turned away again.

She laughed. "All right. For truth now."

Goldsmith turned cautiously. She was covered. He was about to speak when his stomach made such a growl, the black kitten dozing on the hearth sat up and peered about. "I—"

"Hungry, sweetheart?" Jew Molly winked at him. "I could offer you a tup or a sup. Molly or chicken soup. Or both."

"I'll have a cup of your soup," Daniel said, blushing. "And none of your smart talk."

"But I thought it was my smart talk you wanted."

Goldsmith gave up. The woman ran rings around him all the time, and he could not keep his head straight. He watched her ladle soup, rich with little egg yolks, and took the cup when it was offered. Then, since she had claimed the only chair in the room, he found himself sitting awkwardly on her rumpled, oft-used bed.

"Ah," she exclaimed, eyeing him mischievously, over the rim of her cup, "I do love the look of you on my bed."

Flustered, he took a sip of soup and burned his tongue. "Would you know a tall red-haired whore?"

"Why? Do you want to?"

"Molly!"

"There are a score or more, that's what. Well, maybe five. You asked me about her before."

"This is a different one. She was very tall, maybe a head or more over you." When he realized what he'd said, he stopped.

Molly was frowning. "Is she dead? Has another one had her head chopped?" Agitated, she went to the pot on the hearth and poured her soup back into it. "When?"

"Saturday night, Sunday morning."

"Well, then, it's not Mary Red Beard because I saw her not two hours ago. She's not been well. I made the soup for her." Molly paced the small space for a moment, then stopped in front of him. "Tall, you say?"

He nodded. "You know her?"

"Nancy Leach, for sure." Molly picked up a basket of shiny fabric and began sewing neat little stitches.

"Are you being careful who you lie with? Those soldiers seemed fairly nasty sorts."

"Don't speak of soldiers to me. Nasty I can deal with. They're all so niggardly. Worse even than the Redcoats were." She grinned at him again. "Worried about me, are you?"

He finished his soup. "Just be careful."

"Daniel." She looked up at him. "I saw Nancy Saturday night, talking to a man."

"Describe him."

"Dark hair."

"Black? Brown?"

"Couldn't say. Not quite your height, six or seven inches over five feet. Nancy towered over him by maybe this much." Molly showed him about three inches above her head.

"How tall is she?"

"Don't know, but tall."

"Thank you, Mol, you've been a big help."

"Always here at your beck and call."

"Molly!"

Goldsmith hurried down Barkley Street to Broadway. He noticed Louise Bauer, with her market basket, watching him. "So, Constable. That's how you spend your day. With the whores."

That's all he needed. Louise Bauer was Deborah's mother's second cousin and would tell her at the first opportunity. Of course, he could always say he'd only stopped in for the chicken soup. Deborah would have to be glad about that; at least he was getting suitable Jewish food. Goldsmith scratched where his stitches had been and left the West Ward.

With Molly's description ringing in his head, Goldsmith started his rounds. The man she'd described sounded like the one Quintin and that barkeep up in Kingsbridge saw.

By noonday he'd finished his first circuit of the Out Ward and was headed back to the Collect. The pond was frozen over; a boy and two girls were skating, their boots tied to wooden soles on steel blades. Too soon, he thought. That's all he needed was a fall through the ice and a drowning. He ambled to the edge of the pond. "Get off there, you kids."

"We'll take care, Granddaddy."

"I'm the Constable. The ice is not set yet."

With much grumbling the young people left the ice. Goldsmith watched them as they removed their skates and went south, laughing and shrieking, probably making jokes about the mean old Beak.

He kept on walking. As was his custom, the first leg of his walk along the Collect was on the east side. Passing the rope yard he was hailed by young Roger Braitwaith, the son of one of his Watch. "Constable!"

"Roger?"

"Papa told me to tell you he's sick. Retching and shaking something fierce."

"Hell," Goldsmith mumbled. Now he'd have to walk Braitwaith's route, unless he could get one of the part-time Watch to fill in. Another day he would have tried to do with one man short, but this lunatic cutting off heads made that impossible. Alvord Luria was in Brooklyn today. His only hope was Stoutenburgh. "Roger, I want you to find Ned Stoutenburgh for me. If he's not home, try him at Burn's. Tell him to meet us at assembly on Cross Street at sundown."

"Yes, sir." The boy sped off on the run; Goldsmith kept walking. As usual, except for the workers on the Rope Walk there were very few people about. He was approaching the tar huts when it occurred to him that he was still hungry. He had food in his wallet; he would stop at Quintin's tar hut for a bit of warmth. On leaving Dr. Tonneman's house, he'd seen that the Negro had given up on the new well. If he was back at the tar pit perhaps he'd let bygones be bygones and offer him some birch tea. Goldsmith was more than willing to share the cold chicken he knew Deborah had packed for him.

Quintin was not about. The Constable stopped to warm himself at the ugly tar fire pit, the sour acids filtering through his nose. The sun had dipped precipitously, leaving a dreary gray sky and a dusky haze.

Turning, he plodded the short sludgy path to the tar house. "Quintin?"

The door was ajar. The Constable pushed it open, eager to get food in his belly and to thaw his weary bones.

This time it was Goldsmith who found the head.

WINTER

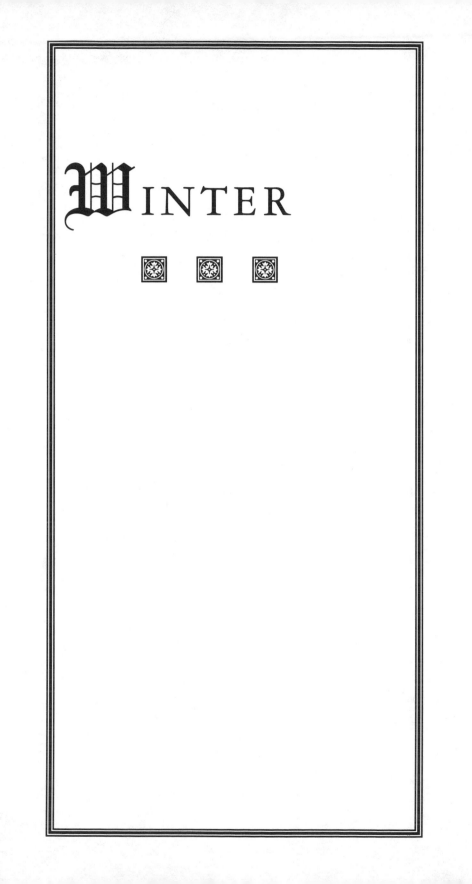

CHAPTER 42

Goldsmith sat up in bed. The banging and clattering of the women knocking the kettles about and setting up the coppers and tin tubs for the day's wash were enough to waken the dead. Fridays were the worst because everything had to be done earlier, faster, and therefore more loudly, in order to prepare for the Sabbath.

He waited, then he heard what he expected, the opening of the front door. He shivered, knowing the frosty wind would surge through the house. This was the first of many trips his daughters would make that day to the public well for water.

Twenty-five days had passed since he'd found Gretel's head in the tar house, skewered on the particular serrated African sword Hood had misplaced; twenty-four days since he and Hood had been dismissed from the constabulary for nonfeasance.

Because the head had been found in Quintin Brock's hut and the body in the nearby marsh, Quintin was the obvious suspect. At first the black man insisted that he'd been trying to dig a well on Rutgers Hill that morning, but Goldsmith knew Quintin hadn't been there when Goldsmith had left Dr. Tonneman's surgery.

Just when it looked as if Quintin was going to be arrested for all three murders, Goodwife Fraunces came forward and swore that Quintin had been with her in the kitchen of Fraunces Tavern during the period of time in question.

This was a revelation even to Black Sam. There was nothing improper about Quintin's being with Elizabeth. It seemed that Quintin had ambitions to be a cook.

With Elizabeth Fraunces's alibi for Quintin, Goldsmith was no closer to finding the killer and, therefore, no closer to redeeming himself and getting his job back. It was just plain bad luck. No one could tell him where Gretel had been that day. No one on the approach to the Collect had seen her, and the Watch Man at the well hole reported nothing untoward the previous night.

And now, on this cold, noisy Friday with the war coming closer every day, his head was aching, his stomach was cramping, and his purse was empty. It was a bad time to be out of work, but so he was. No work, no money, except for the few pennies his wife and mother-in-law earned in their new trade as laundresses. Unfortunately, most of their custom came from the few Loyalist families still in town.

The City itself was in turmoil; Tories were leaving by the wagonful. Soon they would all be gone. That pleased Goldsmith. It had not made him happy to think of depending upon the enemies of the Cause for his subsistence. The ever-righteous Esther had predicted that the Continental soldiers would come to them, but the Continentals weren't spending the money they didn't have on laundry. The few coppers they had went for food and beer.

Robert Scarborough had been named Constable in Goldsmith's stead. A nice enough fellow, Scarborough was not inspired to do anything about finding out who the head chopper was. What he did was walk about all puffed up with his new job.

Another clatter of pots. "Will you stop making such a racket, for God's sake."

"I wouldn't have to if you would bring money home to feed our children." Deborah's strident voice could shatter glass.

"And don't use God's name unless you're praying," called the ever-righteous Esther.

"Good morning, Papa."

Ruth and Miriam entered the bedchamber bearing hot sage tea and a crust of yesterday's bread.

"Thank you, my little birds. Would you like me to read to you?"

"Oh, yes," Miriam, who was but seven years, shrieked.

"Can't." Nine-year-old Ruth was already stern. "Work."

Miriam took on her sister's dour look and sour voice, a present from their mother. "Work."

They marched out, leaving Goldsmith with an almost overwhelming feeling of guilt. He ate quickly, dressed, and tiptoed down the stairs, heading for the front door.

"Where are you off to?" demanded the ever-righteous Esther. "We need firewood."

"I thought I'd stop by the Rope Walk to see if I could pick up a day's wages."

"A likely story." His mother-in-law made no secret of her deep disapproval of him.

"Will you be home for the midday meal?" Deborah stood facing him, her hands on her hips.

"No." He'd rather sit in Quintin's tar house and freeze his arse than put up with the ever-righteous Esther's interminable tormenting. The woman was constantly reminding him that he was in disgrace and not earning money.

The streets were deserted. Many shopkeepers had left town; those who remained had few customers for their wares or services. Then there was the cold. He could not remember such an early freeze and continuous, penetrating cold.

No need to go to the Rope Walk. He'd asked the day before; they'd let most of their men go. Perhaps Sam Fraunces needed someone to peel potatoes. He'd get no money for such work, but a bag of potatoes would be a fair return.

He had another motive—the stolen African sword that had killed Gretel. Exactly when had it been stolen and under what circumstances?

When Goldsmith arrived at Fraunces Tavern, as it was now called even though Queen Charlotte's head still greeted all comers, he found that someone had beaten him to the job. Quintin was sitting in the kitchen, big as life, smiling broadly at Elizabeth, listening to everything she had to say, and peeling a peck of potatoes. The fat black-and-white cat sat poised to pounce on any errant bit of potato skin that might fall to the floor.

"Constable," Black Sam said cordially. "What can I do for you?"

"Looking for some work."

"Quintin was going to chop wood, but I reckon you could get started while he does the potatoes. I'd offer you the potato job, but I don't think I could get Quintin away from Elizabeth." Sam roared with laughter.

"I'll be happy to cut the wood."

When Goldsmith had chopped for an hour and had worked up a rich sweat and sore arms, and a respectable stack of wood had evolved, Sam called him in. "I'm having some coffee. Join me."

Goldsmith gladly accepted the invitation. He was weary and his sweat had turned to chill. In the kitchen he stood near the stove, shivering and hugging himself.

Sam was hefting a big pot of coffee. "Let's go out to the dining room. Elizabeth, call me if the gravy gets too thick."

"Or I could add some water."

"Mind your tongue or I'll have you in the stocks with a placard on you, calling you wag-tongue." He kissed her. "I'll be happy if you just watch the pot."

The main chamber was empty save for two men in separate corners. Choosing a table near the kitchen, Sam called out, "Jem, Bushnell, hot coffee, come join us. Courtesy of Fraunces Tavern. Constable Goldsmith, I think you and Mr. James Rivington, our public printer, know each other. Gentlemen, this is David Bushnell. Mr. Rivington's friends call him Jem, but being a pathetic Tory he has no friends. Still, I have charity in my heart, so I call him Jem, too."

Jem Rivington nodded his powdered head at Sam's remarks but did not comment. As Sam filled the cups Goldsmith said, "I'm not Constable any more."

"Ah, yes, the sword," Sam said.

Rivington smiled. "There's no shame in not being what you were yesterday. I'm no longer the public printer. Sorrow, yes. But no shame. 'To thine own self be true,' that's my motto." He drank his coffee.

"Quintin," Sam shouted, "bring me a bottle of rum, will you?"

Quintin came out with the bottle, disapproval in his scowl.

"Thank you."

When Quintin was gone Sam said, "Man can't abide spirits, which is not an asset for working in a tavern. What am I going to do? My wife took pity on him, so here I am teaching him my trade. He's a little old to be an apprentice, but he has the makings of a good cook."

Goldsmith raised his eyebrows. "He's not working tar any more?"

"Oh, he's doing that, too. The man has the strength of a horse; he never gets tired."

Goldsmith shook his head. "Lucky chap. Two jobs. A lot of us don't have one."

"Not really. I don't pay him anything. Just food." Sam held the rum bottle up; when no one objected he poured rum all around into the coffee cups. "Goldsmith found my sword. Stuck in a woman's head."

"I heard about that," Bushnell offered, sipping. "When you have a garrison town these things happen. Good rum."

"It's a dastardly deed, but not necessarily that of a soldier," said Rivington. "Or of a Loyalist," he said mockingly to Sam.

"Are you saying the killer's a Patriot?"

Rivington made a steeple of his fingers. "He sounds as if he has a Patriot's brutish temperament."

"And I suppose the Tories are all friends of Jesus."

Rivington grinned. "Of course."

"Well, so was Judas. Ha. Got you, you Royalist oaf. And for that you get another drink." Laughing loudly, Sam poured a generous round.

In the lull that followed Goldsmith meant to have the advantage. "Sam. When exactly was the sword stolen?"

"I can tell you exactly. The day before you found the head."

Goldsmith nodded and drank. The next day he'd been sacked. He drank again, a great swallow. "How was it stolen? Was the tavern broken into?"

"Not that I could tell. I came down one morning and it was gone."

Goldsmith placed his cup on the cherrywood table. The coffee was black as tar. "Then perhaps one of your customers took it?"

"That seems to be the case. Someone just walked to the wall, took it down, and walked out with it."

"With no one noticing?"

"That I couldn't say. I told all this to the Ward Constable. I don't remember his name."

"Freemont," Goldsmith supplied. "Did he look around? Did you hear from him again?"

"No to both questions. Tory bastard." Sam raised a cup to Rivington. "My respects, sir."

Rivington grinned, and raised his cup. "And mine to you. You're a better friend to me than most of my Royalist comrades. Those that are left. I think you're all mad. I certainly don't agree with what you're all about, and I don't wish you well in your endeavor, but you should have the right to speak freely. Perhaps if you'd been given that right, things wouldn't have gotten so out of hand and events wouldn't have come this far toward disaster."

"Voltaire," said Bushnell.

Rivington blinked, uncomprehending. "I know his work."

"Voltaire says, 'Think for yourselves and let others enjoy the privilege to do so too.'"

Sam poured more rum all around. "Is that what they taught you at Yale?"

"Yes."

"Good school. I'd love to continue this philosophical discussion, but while you may all be gentlemen of leisure I have work to do." He stood.

"I'm not going anywhere," said Bushnell.

"Nor I," said Rivington.

The two made a strange, even comical, pair. The abundantly powdered Royalist, Jem Rivington with his great corpulence, and the thin, light-haired Patriot, David Bushnell.

Sam thought for a minute. He picked up the bottle and left the pot. "My compliments, then." He started for his kitchen.

"Sam?" It was Rivington.

"Yes, Jem."

The printer walked the few steps and put his arm about Sam's shoulder. "I'm leaving soon—for London. Perhaps in two or three weeks. There's something been troubling me and I need to get it off my chest before I go."

"Yes?"

Rivington looked about, then lowered his voice, but Goldsmith could still hear what he had to say. "I know no particulars. I only know what I have heard."

"Which is?" the tavern owner asked.

"They're going to try to kill Washington."

"That's not news."

"But what is news is that they know he likes to eat here. An attempt to poison his food is very likely. In your tavern."

"Is this a joke?"

"I swear not."

"Well, nothing to fear. The General is well north of here."

"When he returns, be wary of anyone who comes near his food."

"Thanks for the advice. You're not a bad sort, for a Loyalist, though a bit mad."

" 'Tis true, 'tis true, 'tis pity, and pity 'tis, 'tis true," Rivington declaimed with a wry smile. Then, more simply, "And you're a good chap for a Patriot."

When the printer rejoined Bushnell, Goldsmith followed Sam into the kitchen. Elizabeth had a bag of potatoes and turnips for him.

"Thank you," he said.

"Don't mention it," Sam said. "Try me again in a few days. Quintin's got to keep to the tar fire for a bit."

Goldsmith saluted with two fingers and stepped outside, ducking against the wind.

"Mr. Goldsmith?"

Goldsmith turned; Quintin had come after him. "Yes, Quintin?"

"I know you're not a Constable any more, but there's something you should know."

"What's that?"

"I saw that fellow near the Collect again. I told Constable Scarborough, but he couldn't have cared less. Told me not to bother him."

"Which fellow is that?" It was Sam; curious, the tavern keeper had followed Quintin.

"The one I saw before. The one that looks like a soldier."

CHAPTER 43

Both the North and East Rivers were frozen over.

As the City of New-York simmered politically in the midst of what seemed an endless freeze that had started in November, British ships hugged the shore to evade the treacherous chunks of floating ice.

This made life difficult for a City that could only be reached by water except at Kingsbridge, where a narrow wooden bridge connected the Island of Manhattan with its neighbors to the north. Food and other necessaries were in short supply.

Still, venturesome travelers and traders were able to walk or ride across the ice to and from New Jersey. Many truly industrious souls harvested oysters through the ice in the Bay.

In the Narrows but bound to the shore, the *Duchess Of Gordon* remained the home of Governor Tryon, who continued to pretend that he, as the King's representative, was still governing the City of New-York.

Daily the City was losing population; half the people had fled. Firewood was sparse. Soldiers, squatting in empty houses, used flooring to feed their fires. What they didn't eat or burn they dumped out the windows.

In spite of the departure of many New-Yorkers, John Peter Tonneman, doctor of physick and surgery, dentist, and oculist, had a fair practice. Patients arrived sporadically at his surgery from early morn till late afternoon.

Mariana Mendoza had become a mainstay, appearing every day but the Jewish Sabbath, helping, learning, ministering as Tonneman did with care and devotion and remaining at his side until late afternoon. Patients had come to accept the slim girl in her odd clothing. It was, after all, a time of crisis.

There was great discussion about Dr. Tonneman. Everyone knew his father had been a Patriot, but the young physician was another story. Mariana Mendoza was sister to Ben, a loyal Son of Liberty, but Tonneman's good friend was the imperious Dr. Jamison, late of London and presently the Royal Chancellor of King's College. Tonneman was also known to dine at the home of that lobsterback Captain Richard Willard.

Six months earlier, many had had friends on both sides of the fence, but as that fellow from Philadelphia said, "You and I were long friends: You are now my enemy, and I am yours."

For Tonneman, as he approached his twenty-ninth birthday, the comfortable life he had known as a boy, the life he'd expected to resume when he took up his father's practice, was ruptured forever by the horrible death of his beloved Gretel.

Something, perhaps it was the connection to his childhood, the very artery of his existence, had vanished with Gretel's sudden, hideous death. As Coroner it had fallen on him to perform the autopsy. He had done so, tears rolling unashamedly down his cheeks. Jamie had come from his new lodgings and stood with him, elbow to elbow. Tonneman had been so distraught that he'd missed the obvious. It was Jamie who pointed out the skewering sword and the difference in the sword cut. Gretel's head had been severed with a serrated blade. This was the sword that was discovered and then lost after the head had been found in the well.

The how of it had hardly mattered. She was gone. The only mother he had ever known. He would never hear the rolling laughter, never again receive her loving hug, never again hear her call him Johnny, never again see her stooped over the hearth. She had loved him, unequivocally, and he had always known it. She had asked for little in return, not even berating him, as she should have, for staying too long in London. For not being at his father's side. And for crawling along the center of the road when he should have shouted as she had, that he was a Patriot. Was that his worst betrayal? Not coming out against the King when all along, deep down, he knew the Patriot cause was just and the only path for a honorable man to take.

Now he had lost both his father and Gretel. He—a grown man—felt abandoned, orphaned.

He'd buried Gretel beside her long-dead husband, Kurt, not far from the Tonneman family plot. The service was simple, for the November cold was intense and the wind howled throughout, whipping and snapping skirts and shawls and threatening hats.

It was Bear Bikker and Mariana Mendoza's concern he felt more than any others. Bear had bawled like a baby when he arrived at Tonneman's house after the news of Gretel had spread through the City; he had sat for long hours with Tonneman in the kitchen, a garrulous but reassuring figure.

And Mariana Mendoza, whose ghostlike presence hovered silently, had guided him through his duties to his patients, of which there were many due to the scarcity of physicians and the scourge of Influenza.

John Tonneman understood the decay of the human body, that it was part and parcel of life itself. He understood that Nature bred her own violence and foisted it on man with floods and pestilence and the like. But man's violence against his fellow man? That was an obscenity.

After Tonneman had pulled a festering tooth from Sam Fraunces's throbbing jaw on New Year's Day, Sam suggested that Tonneman hire Quintin Brock until he was able to find a new housekeeper. The tavern keeper had taught Quintin to cook tolerably well; Quintin would do the cooking and also the housekeeping chores in exchange for food and a warm, clean place to sleep until the spring.

In the two weeks that Quintin had been with him, the chaos Tonneman felt had begun to subside. Order had returned to the Tonneman house.

Along with the order in his house there was harmony in his surgery. That, of course, was because of Mariana.

It had been a long, hard day. Tonneman sat at his desk in his study, writing his notes about the day's cases. A steaming cup of sassafras tea sat near his hand. A second cup rested next to it. From the surgery he could hear the soft clatter of his instruments being cleaned.

He placed his quill on the standish. How had this happened? He couldn't rightly say. After Gretel's murder, Mariana, this strange young woman, had made herself his assistant, and he no longer questioned her eccentric dress. These were eccentric times and America was an eccentric country; here, men and women did what was demanded of them, and then some.

Tonneman closed his patient book and took out the pamphlet Mariana had given him two days earlier, claiming everyone in New-York was read- ing it. He'd read it quickly and put it aside. But the words of the anony- mous author wouldn't be dismissed.

The pamphlet was called *Common Sense,* and the writer very skillfully addressed the issue: The disagreement with England had to lead to sever- ing the relationship between King and Colonies. He began to read it again.

"What do you think?"

Tonneman, startled from the depths of his thoughts, looked up to see Mariana in the doorway. She had taken her hat off and tied her lustrous dark hair back with a blue ribbon at the nape. He pointed to the cup next to his. "There's Yankee tea."

"What do you think?" she asked again, holding the cup to her lips. When he didn't answer she leaned closer to him.

"It has merit," he replied cautiously.

Her face was flushed and her lips pink. He thought about their softness and the woman's body he knew was hidden within the oversized boy's clothing she wore. "Merit?" she cried, waving her arms passionately, splattering tea. She slammed the mug down on his desk. "Balderdash. That's holy writ. It speaks for Independence."

Suddenly, he knew not how, he was on his feet, holding her, kissing those lips. There was no caution to him. Her mouth moved under his, responding.

"It is with the utmost regret I interrupt this great passion, old boy."

Mariana's eyes did not blink, and she did not move from Tonneman's embrace.

Jamie, highly amused, his smile verging on a sneer, continued. "I have a bit of important business to discuss and precious little time to do it in."

Mariana eased from Tonneman's arms, snatched up her coat and hat, and went into the surgery. With regret Tonneman heard the outside door close.

"I see you've been busy adding a mistress to your house." Sitting at Tonneman's desk, Jamie opened his patient book and studied his notes.

"Jamie—" Tonneman neatened his coat and perched on the edge of the desk. "She's not my mistress."

"She will be, John. She will be."

"And I don't intend her to be."

"More's the pity. There's something rather appealing about her costume, don't you think?" He cast his eyes around the room. "You could use a dab of the female touch around here. I quite miss the old Amazon."

Tonneman stared at his friend, his copper hair captured under a new, obviously costly, white wig and topped by a scarlet tricorn. The Chancellor of King's Medical College wore an elegant scarlet velvet coat, richly trimmed with black braid. Tonneman took it all in with growing confusion. Who was this monied fop? Surely not Jamie. "What urgent business do we have?" His tone was colder than he meant to reveal.

Jamie, ever alert, had caught it. He stood and brushed at his velvet sleeves. "Come, my friend, you've lost your humor." He slapped Tonneman on the back. "Be of good cheer. Whatever else happens, remember: Our friendship will endure."

Jamie was right. Shamed, Tonneman took his hand.

At that moment Quintin put his head in the door. He held a wooden spoon in his hand. "Excuse me, Dr. Tonneman, Dr. Jamison. Mr. Tonneman, you partial to garlic?"

"I have no objection to it."

"After you taste it in my cooking, it will make your tongue happy and your heart light and chase the blue devils away. Wait and see. It's good for what ails you, too. Cleans the poison from your blood, calms the stomach, and makes your heart mighty."

Tonneman smiled. "Anything you say, Dr. Quintin."

The black man grinned, bobbed his head, and backed out.

In contrast to Tonneman's cheerful countenance, Jamie was frowning. "I don't like that nigger."

"You don't like any black people."

"True. But I don't like that one in particular. I have this unsettling feeling that he's the one who's been cutting up these women."

Tonneman laughed. "Quintin? Don't be ridiculous."

"Scoff all you want. Murder is like an illness. The symptoms guide you to the cause. Dead women without their heads always seem to be in his vicinity. What more evidence do you need?"

"A motive would be helpful."

"Bah, these black heathen don't need a reason to kill. It's what they do. I wouldn't be surprised if that sham white man Sam Fraunces didn't have a hand in it, too."

"How about getting rid of all the Africans on this island?"

"Throw in the Rebels for good measure and I'll be content." Jamie smoothed the front of his scarlet coat. "Where are the halcyon days of old?"

Tonneman patted his friend's shoulder. "Yes. These times are unsettling, to say the least."

"And that's why I've come. We've learned that the Rebels are sending troops to New-York." Jamie snorted. "So, I may have to make a hasty retreat." He pinched his nose delicately with two slender, tapered fingers. "I suggest you come with us."

Tonneman was shaken. He and Jamie had come to a crossroads; indeed, they now saw everything at cross purposes. "I wouldn't consider it. This is my home." After a pause Tonneman said, "Us?"

"Yes, Captain Willard, his lovely wife, and his sister, my bride-to-be."

Tonneman laughed. "You a married man, Jamie? I can't see it."

Jamison frowned. "John, I have asked the lovely Grace Greenaway to be my wife. She has accepted. We are affianced."

CHAPTER 44

Goldsmith studied the Liberty Pole which stood where its less stalwart predecessors had in the Common. This one was braced so sturdily with metal supports that it would take an explosion to rock it from its moorings. He stood with Ben Mendoza and a cluster of other Patriots.

Ben's face was fiery with anger. "The Tory bastards went after the pole again last night. I'm off to Fraunces Tavern. We've called a meeting to decide what to do about it. Coming?"

"No," said Goldsmith, "I've got business."

"More important than what to do about the Tories?"

Goldsmith squared his jaw. "It needs to be done."

"You're not turning Loyalist on us, are you, Daniel?"

Goldsmith's hand clenched but he did not raise it to the boy. "What's that supposed to mean?"

"Your wife and mother-in-law do wash the shit out of their English drawers."

"It's that or we don't eat."

"Some people would rather starve."

"Easy for a rich Mendoza to say," Goldsmith retorted fiercely. He pushed his way through the crowd and kept going. Every day over the last month, prompted by what Quintin told him, Goldsmith had been asking all he met if they'd seen a swarthy white man with dark hair, about five feet six inches tall, who might be a soldier. He was at the Bayard Camp so often the soldiers there told him he might as well join up and get the soldier's money and the rations. That was in jest, of course; these days, the soldiers weren't eating that much better than the civilians.

Goldsmith stopped to inspect a group of soldiers coming along. Most were fair-skinned. One was dark, but too short. Another seemed right. Goldsmith stared intently.

"What you looking at?" the man demanded truculently in a rich Irish accent.

"Where were you on twenty-six November?"

"Dancing with Her Majesty, the Queen," the Irishman hooted.

"Who wants to know?" asked one of the other soldiers.

"Constable Goldsmith," he said, brazenly.

"Well, Constable, we all came in from Connecticut only last week if that will help you."

They were wearing blue coats as some Connecticut regiments did, but then, so did many New-York troops.

Goldsmith shook his head in despair. It was an impossible task. To find one soldier. "Thank you."

The soldiers sauntered off, laughing.

"What's your name, Irish?" Goldsmith called after them.

Without turning the Irishman yelled, "George Washington!"

Where was he going? Goldsmith turned around a full circle and remembered. Molly. Since his dismissal he'd picked up work at the Rope Walk and at Fraunces Tavern. He'd even worked a few hellish days with Quintin at the tar fire. Most of his time was spent wandering about, asking questions, getting negative answers. His nights were spent tossing and turning, for Gretel came to his dreams and said two words over and over: "Avenge me. Avenge me." It was as if he was being haunted by her soul.

Between his dreams and his wife and mother-in-law's hectoring, the only rest he got was when he visited Molly. He'd stop by Sam's and get some vegetables. For his children, of course, but he'd take out some for Molly, too. Then he'd visit her on the pretext of gathering information. After they ate their small repast, she would sing to him or tell him silly stories. Then, and only then, would he drift into dreamless sleep sitting in her chair.

When he knocked at Molly's door, there was no answer. He knocked again. "Just a minute," came a hoarse, barely audible voice. She opened the door just a crack and ran back to the warmth and shelter of her bed.

"No *sweetheart?*" he chided.

Molly coughed violently; tears came to her eyes. Her face was red with fever. "I don't feel well. My throat's sore, my head aches. My back and legs feel as if I've just had twenty men."

Goldsmith winced at her crudeness. He put his hand to her brow. He'd never touched her before; the deed incapacitated him for a moment. "You're very hot."

"I wish the heat would go to my feet: that's where I need it." She shivered just as violently as she'd coughed. "I'm so cold."

He put his coat over her bedclothes and sat on the bed. "Better?"

"Yes," she said, but he knew she was lying.

"I've only got potatoes and parsnips today. It will make a thin soup but I'll cook it if you want."

"That's sweet, Daniel." She coughed again, but this time, mercifully, the spasm was short. "There's birch tea. Let's just eat them raw and drink the tea."

He tucked her up as best he could and fed her. When they had finished the scant meal, he asked, "Anything else?"

"Anything?"

He nodded somberly. "Anything."

"Now he offers. When I'm too sick to make him keep his word."

"Molly."

She coughed.

"Molly?"

"I'm all right. Read to me."

"If you wish. What?"

She dug under her pillow. "Mary Red Beard gave me this pamphlet. A visitor from Philadelphia left it with her. And since she can't read . . ."

Goldsmith took the tract. " '*Common Sense,* written by an Englishman.' " He flipped through the pages. "Looks like dry stuff."

"Here's something that caught my eye," she said, taking the thin book from him. "Ah, here. 'The authority of Great Britain over this Continent is a form of government which sooner or later must have an end . . .' "

"He's talking about here. America."

"Yes. Could that be? Could we have our own government?"

"I guess so."

"Without the King?"

"Why not?"

"He says it's downright silly for Americans to give allegiance to a British Sovereign." Molly looked and found a page. " 'Every quiet method for peace hath been ineffectual.' That means he thinks we're going to have to fight."

Goldsmith nodded. "They tried to tear down the Liberty Pole again today. If it's a fight they want, then it's a fight they'll get."

"Daniel, you're frightening me." She coughed.

"I have to go now. But I'll be back—"

Suddenly she burst into tears. "No, don't go. Stay just a little . . ." This time the cough was so severe she spat blood into her hand.

"That settles it," Goldsmith said. He pulled Molly up and layered her with as many clothes as he could find. "Where are your boots?"

"Under the bed." She clung to him, all vigor gone. "What are you doing?"

"I'm taking you to Dr. Tonneman."

CHAPTER 45

Chaucer spied his barn and galloped the last twenty yards in a surge of desperate energy. When Tonneman reined the black gelding in, the weary animal neighed gratefully and stopped dead. It had been a long day. Many of Tonneman's new patients were ill with Influenza.

Dismounting, he led the heated horse into the barn. So abstracted was he by his own thoughts, he didn't see or hear Goldsmith follow him until the former Constable was at his elbow.

"She can't get her rest."

Tonneman started; then, seeing who it was, he set about removing Chaucer's saddle and giving him a rubdown. "Good God, Goldsmith," he said, handing the man the saddle, "what ails you? Molly is the one who's sick." After wiping the horse with bits of hay, he stroked him with the brushes.

Goldsmith set the saddle on a crossbar and sighed heavily.

Too tired to continue, Tonneman stopped his ministrations and threw a blanket over the horse. He broke the ice in the bucket and gave the horse his water. The gelding gulped noisily. "Too much, too much, you'll blow up like pig bladder." He took the bucket away and substituted the feed bag.

All the while Goldsmith watched him. "I don't mean Molly. It's Gretel. She can't get her rest. She comes to me in my dreams." Goldsmith laughed sharply. "Then *I* can't get my rest."

"Superstitious twaddle." At Goldsmith's woebegone expression Tonneman took pity on him. "Come into the house. We'll have a glass of Port and talk about this. Your eyes look terrible, all shot with blood."

Goldsmith grinned suddenly. "Like red piss holes in the snow, right?" He rubbed his eyes. "How is Molly?"

"The fever broke this morning. Sooner than I expected, I'm glad to say. It might have been the Pneumonia. That would have been a different story. But she's fine and sleeping like a babe." Tonneman measured Goldsmith for a long moment. "She is very frail, almost starved. Her recovery will be slow."

A glimmer of joy flitted over Goldsmith's face. "But she will get better."

"Yes."

"Praise God." Goldsmith's near lifeless eyes lit up and his morose mouth lifted into a smile. "I will have that Port."

"Come along, then." Tonneman's joy mirrored Goldsmith's. There was a spring in both their walks. For Tonneman, the reason was the girl he expected to see behind the door of his surgery. Mariana had awakened him from a long slumber that had crept upon him unawares and had threatened to consign him to a living death with Gretel's horrible murder.

But except for the low fire in the surgery grate the chamber was quiet. Disappointed, he walked through to the study and dropped his cloak on one of the wing chairs in front of the blazing fire. Goldsmith kept his coat on and trailed behind Tonneman.

From the kitchen, Tonneman could smell Quintin's wonderful spicy chicken stew along with his malodorous corncob pipe. Tonneman shuddered. Revolting idea, to smoke from a cob. The kitchen fireplace had a spritely fire, making the room warm and cozy.

The African, working furiously with a mortar and pestle, didn't look up. From the heady fragrance Tonneman knew the substance in the mortar was garlic. "Miss Mariana is upstairs feeding the other barley soup."

"Sit down, Goldsmith." Simply knowing she was here in the house pleased Tonneman. Quintin was a good man, knew just what to say to him. Had he read his mind? Perhaps Negroes did have second sight. But of course, he didn't believe in superstitious twaddle.

He sauntered into the dining room, and brought back the last bottle of Port wine. It was half full. He poured two generous glasses. There was perhaps one hearty drink left in the bottle. "Any more of this around?"

"Can't tell by me, Dr. Tonneman." Quintin had his stern countenance on. "I have no truck with spirits."

"My error." Tonneman knew if he wanted to seek out any more of the Port his father might have left, he'd have to search the cellar himself. He certainly wouldn't be able to buy any; with the British ships encircling the

City there wouldn't be another bottle of this stuff from Europe for some time to come. He sipped slowly, savoring the sweet, dark red wine from Portugal.

Goldsmith downed it like so much water. "The pattern is wrong."

"What?" said Tonneman, jarred by the interjection.

"Gretel was not young."

Tonneman had thought of this himself; he reconsidered it now. "You're right, of course. Perhaps she wasn't killed for the same reason as the others. Or even by the same man."

Goldsmith appeared ready to weep. "But why would anyone want to kill Gretel?"

"Because she knew something."

The two men looked at Quintin in amazement. Tonneman shook his head. It was obvious. But he'd been so immersed in his grief he hadn't seen it. Quintin was correct. Absolutely correct. "Anything else?"

"It would be the soldier, wouldn't it?"

Nodding agreement, Goldsmith said, "Perhaps it was something she saw."

Tonneman finished his wine. "Let's have a look at the patient." He climbed the stairs rapidly; once more Goldsmith was at his heels. Tonneman felt a certain kinship between them that for the moment he couldn't fathom. Then, in an instant, he knew: Mariana and Molly.

He knocked lightly on the door to his boyhood bedroom and pushed it open. The strong aroma of tar greeted them. Mariana was pouring hot water through a tar cloth; Molly was breathing in the steam.

"Enough," cried Molly. "This muck stinks."

"Quiet," said Goldsmith, "it's good for you."

A quick gleam of pleasure spread over Molly's wan face when she caught sight of Goldsmith. She patted her drab black hair, which Mariana had washed and combed. Mariana put the tar cloth aside and sat on the bed. Gently, she spooned soup into Molly's poor blistered mouth.

"How is my patient?" Tonneman asked, lifting Molly's wrist to take her pulse. Rapid. This concerned Tonneman, until he realized that Goldsmith was the cause.

"I'm improving, Mr. Tonneman."

Mariana's color deepened as her gaze found Tonneman's. When she stood, he saw that the bottom of the soup bowl was dense with garlic. "You didn't eat your garlic," he said.

"If I did I'd smell worse than that tar."

"I'd think better of it if I were you. Quintin swears by garlic. He claims it will cure anything."

Without thinking Goldsmith added, "According to the Talmud, it will enhance conjugal love." He blushed.

"Give it me, then," cried Molly, taking a spoonful and shoving it into her mouth.

Everybody laughed. Goldsmith looked at the floor, then moved to the foot of Molly's bed.

Tonneman beckoned to Mariana; the two started for the door.

"Mr. Tonneman."

He turned. "Yes, Molly?"

"When can I go back to my place?"

"Molly!"

"Leave be, Daniel. I have to earn my living."

"You're just getting over the Influenza. Others have it; they're not as lucky as you. If you go back to your old life, the Pneumonia would be a certainty. That would kill you."

Goldsmith glared at the ceiling. "Lord save me from stubborn women." He fixed his glare on Molly. "Listen to him."

"If Goldsmith hadn't found you and brought you here, you might not have lived through the night."

"Oh, oh," Molly wailed. "What's to become of me then? I'll die anyway."

"No," Goldsmith cried. He stared pleadingly at Tonneman.

Mariana, her back to Goldsmith and Molly, spoke softly to Tonneman. "Quintin will stay only until spring. You'll need someone." She clasped his hand.

Tonneman felt his heart turn in his chest. This tiny person had such a rational mind. He held onto her hand. To Molly he said, "It seems I am in need of a housekeeper."

CHAPTER 46

The water vender was waiting for him on the corner when he came out of the Gunderson house.

"Water from the Tea Water Pump, sir? A good way to start the morning."

"What?" Hickey demanded irritably of the water vender.

"The Fat Man wants to see you."

"Where and when?"

Those who remained in the City of New-York, whatever their reasons, were a people under siege from inside and out. On the waters surrounding them was the might of the British King. On land, two forces, one loyal to the King, the other steadfastly rebellious, were agitating for a confrontation. New-York was like a woman with two lovers. The King. The Rebels. Each wanted her exclusively.

When the first copies of *Common Sense* appeared and were read by the Rebel population, the flame for independence became a conflagration. *Common Sense* had put into words what men were dreaming, wishing, thinking in their secret thoughts, but not saying. No more placating. Freedom now. Independence. This war that had begun in Lexington and Concord the previous April was now not only a war the people wanted, it was a war they needed.

Major General Charles Lee, Washington's second-in-command, rounded up two regiments of six-week volunteers in Connecticut, aiming to move into Westchester. The foreboding was that if more Rebels entered

New-York, it would be a signal for a bombardment from the English ships. One of the many City committees that flourished during the war communicated this to Lee.

Lee bridled, but delayed.

Hickey wasn't worried about any of this war nonsense. He was the true professional soldier. Wars came and went. Life and death would go on. All that mattered to him were his pleasures. Beer and spirits that quenched and wenches that screamed and coins that tinkled.

He drove Gunderson's butcher wagon up to Harrison's Brewery on the street of the same name. The day was clear but cold. The familiar dapple gray was tied up in front of Harrison's, which meant the Fat Man was close at hand. "Harrison," Hickey bellowed.

One of the wide doors to the brewery pushed open. A tall, gaunt fellow stepped out to the street. "What's your pleasure?"

"Four barrels of your best."

"That will cost you."

"Just load them in."

"Who'll pay?"

"I will." The Fat Man stepped out the brewery.

Harrison bobbed his head deferentially. "Yes, sir. Pounds or dollars?"

"Continental dollars." The Fat Man took a fat wad of bills from his purse.

The brewer frowned. Hickey was not pleased either. He did love the tinkle of English coin.

"Bring the wagon," said Harrison, going back inside. "I'm not breaking my back."

"We're right behind you," Hickey called.

"Not so fast," said the Fat Man, climbing on board the wagon.

Hickey looked at Harrison trudging ahead of them, then he surveyed left and right. "You're Matthews, ain't you?"

The Fat Man showed no surprise at Hickey's knowledge. "Yes."

Hickey flicked the reins; the butcher's horse followed Harrison slowly. Hickey grinned and whistled a few strains of "Yankee Doodle."

"If that is meant to vex me, you're succeeding."

"People I know say that the Committee of Safety is suspicious of you."

"They're suspicious of all Loyalists and I make no secret of my sentiments," the Alderman said.

"My informants tell me you were entered on the list of the suspected as early as May."

"Suspected of what?"

"They haven't worked that out yet."

Matthews laughed. "Nor will they, the fools. They preach revolution but haven't the sense to come out of the rain."

"Don't be so sure. There are rumors that forces are arriving from all directions."

"Bah. Like the rumors of the pox I've heard. Something to frighten little children with."

"This is not rumor. I have it on very good authority that Washington has ordered General Lee to rescue New-York City from the King's blockade."

"Go on."

"There are two regiments in Connecticut right now." Hickey, puffed up, waited for a response from the Fat Man.

"We know that."

That was not the response Hickey wanted. "You always say you know what I tell you after I tell you. If you know so much, why don't you do something about it?"

"That is precisely our intention. If you'll shut your gob for a minute I'll tell you."

"What do you want?"

"Very simple. I want Washington dead. And by God, I want it to happen in New-York."

"But he's nowhere near New-York."

"We can wait."

"Is that it? If I'd known it was going to be that simple, I wouldn't have recruited so many."

"The more the merrier. No, that's not it. Quiet." They had come to a platform which was crowded with beer barrels.

"Give me a hand," said Harrison. "I'm alone here today."

Hickey backed the wagon in and helped the brewer lay down three planks. Together they rolled the four barrels onto the wagon.

Matthews handed Hickey the sheaf of paper money and Hickey paid Harrison. When he offered the thick wad back to the Fat Man, Matthews shook his head. "Keep it."

"You're very generous," Hickey said as they drove out. "What's this paying for?"

"On the same day you kill Washington, I want the Rebel cannon in New-York and Kingsbridge blown to hell. You will also blow up Fort George and the King's Bridge. Can you manage that?"

"Can I manage that?" Hickey laughed. "Is the Devil a red-haired woman?"

CHAPTER 47

Tonneman had always esteemed Sundays. When he was a boy it had meant release from studies. All over the City church bells would ring, calling the different congregations to worship. But of late when church bells rang, it was to summon people to Broadway with news of the war. Illness had never been respectful of the Lord's day, but now it was worse than usual. He was one of the few physicians left in New-York, and though many people were leaving, soldiers were arriving daily, many of them sick.

He'd been out all day, seeing patients. A broken leg, a serious head injury at the shipyards, and, of course, the Influenza in its severest stages. He'd heard rumors of the pox in the southern Colonies and was girding himself for that. If the pox should come, it would defeat them more efficiently than the King's troops could.

The soldiers he'd been seeing, mostly at the Bayard Camp, were a sturdy lot. He couldn't say the same for the poor wretches who lived nearby along the Collect. Wealthy Richard Willard and his family could find sanctuary during this crisis. The poor could not, having no means and no haven.

Six from the Collect had died in the past week, two of them infants. The intense cold and the lack of firewood and the Influenza were taking their toll. At this rate no one need worry about the Pox or the English.

When he'd seen what he hoped would be the last patient of the day, an utterly exhausted Tonneman headed for home. Continental soldiers were everywhere on the roads and streets of New-York.

The broken leg he'd set had been for Kate Schrader's grandson. From her he'd received the scrannel chicken now clucking feebly in his arms.

The poor bird would probably expire before Quintin took the ax to her. His other wages consisted of five eggs, a bag of vegetables, and five pence.

Tonneman put Chaucer in his stall, fed but did not brush the animal, and hurried across the snow into the surgery. There he found Mariana picking splinters from a near-festering wound on a carpenter's forearm. Tonneman set down his loot, handed the limp chicken to Mariana, and took charge of the wound. The carpenter, John Webb, seemed intensely relieved.

"Not that the lad here wasn't doing the job."

Tonneman raised his eyes from his task and grinned at his assistant, who had flushed crimson at the carpenter's remarks. She tugged at her hat.

"Many thanks, Doctor. No money, I'm afraid. Any work I can do for you?" The carpenter looked covetously at the chicken.

"The front steps need mending," Mariana said.

Tonneman relieved her of the chicken and gave it to Webb. "Take this bird and the food on the floor to the kitchen." He pointed. "Through there. Ask Quintin what needs fixing."

The chicken began screaking as if in protest. With one twist Webb snapped its neck. "I will, sir."

Tonneman watched the man leave, wondering if he would bolt out the front door with the fowl. Mariana started cleaning the instruments.

"Leave that for me," said Tonneman. "I'll see you home while it's still light." He didn't want her going home alone; the City was crawling with soldiers. He smiled then, for in that clothing who but he would know her for a woman?

This time she was not as vehemently negative as she had been in the past.

His father's carriage had been chopped up for firewood, so they would travel double on Chaucer. The horse was not happy to see the saddle again, but suffered it patiently.

Tonneman mounted and reached down for Mariana, scooping the tiny body in the bulky greatcoat up to sit sidesaddle-fashion with both feet on the left side of the horse. But the young girl flipped her leg over and sat like a man.

Tonneman was beguiled by her action. She never did what was expected. He put his arms around her to handle the reins, and marveled at the joy he experienced feeling her rapid heartbeat merge with his.

As they traveled toward Maiden Lane and her home, he lowered his head to hers so that their cheeks touched, heat amidst cold. She turned slightly; their lips touched, skimmed away, touched again.

They rode that way for the rest of the short journey, Chaucer's hooves echoing on the narrow cobblestone street, the two of them unmindful of the City's cold, mindful only of each other and their own heat. Maiden Lane was quiet but for a group of drunken soldiers who were showing two equally inebriated New-Yorkers how to load their muskets. One soldier aimed his weapon at Tonneman and shouted, "Let me see the whites of your eyes, lobsterback."

"I'm no lobsterback," Tonneman said evenly. "I'm a physician on my rounds."

"Pass, physician." The soldier saluted him drunkenly.

The other soldiers took up their comrade's words. "Pass, physician, pass."

Tonneman gave Chaucer a nudge with his boot and they rode past the boisterous men.

She was trembling in his arms. Or was it he who trembled? Tonneman didn't know. He did know that the drunken louts were not the cause. "Mariana," he whispered. She turned to him; he kissed her soft lips.

Mariana broke from his grasp. "My house." Before the animal had even halted, she swung her leg and slipped agilely to the ground. Without a stumble she ran to the fine brick house that was her home.

He watched her until she disappeared behind the door, then turned Chaucer and rode home. Was he mad? What was to come of them?

CHAPTER 48

The home of the merchant, David Mendoza, was quiet. A candle in its silver stand glimmered. Her brother Ben was surely out with the Sons of Liberty, as he was almost every night, and her father was undoubtedly sitting with her mother, at least that's what Mariana fervently hoped. She might be able to get to her bedchamber without his hearing her.

She tiptoed past the sitting room, and put her foot on the first step. "Daughter?"

"Yes, Papa."

His voice came from the dark sitting room. "Come here to me, and bring a light."

"Yes, Papa." She picked up the candle stand and carried it ahead of her into the sitting room.

Her father was sitting in a wing chair, his feet on a low stool. He moved his feet and said, "Sit here, daughter."

Mariana set the candle down on the side table and sat on the stool at his feet. She loved her father; he was a fine-looking man, and she was proud of him. David Mendoza had never understood her need to study medicine, nor did he understand that times were changing.

He touched her face gently. "Daughter, what will become of you?"

His voice was so sad, she felt tears in her eyes. "Papa, I will be all right, you'll see."

"You wear your brother's clothing, you work in a surgery with a man we don't know."

"But I know him, Papa. He's a good man. He needs me."

"Ah." There was a catch in Mendoza's voice. He leaned forward and took his daughter's face in his hands. "And how do you feel about him, daughter?"

Mariana's heart thundered. She could hardly hear her father's voice over the noise. She heard him ask again how she felt about John Tonneman.

"Papa, I—I—" She stammered.

"Do you love him, daughter?"

"Papa—"

"If you do, daughter, I will not stand in your way."

And suddenly, as if a dam had burst, Mariana found herself saying in a voice she didn't recognize as her own, "I do, Papa. I love John Tonneman with all my heart."

CHAPTER 49

At home Tonneman supped early and lightly on Quintin's root vege-table stew and heard the good news that John Webb, the carpenter, had repaired the front steps.

As he sat in his study writing in his casebook, intermittently dozing, his mind kept harking back to her. She was different from any woman he had ever known. There was no doubt in his mind that were she a man, she would be a physician. She was caring, she was brave, she was determined. And in the less than four months he had known her, she seemed to grow more beautiful daily in spite of her penchant for boy's clothing. Did no one but he see it?—Well, Jamie had seen, even before he—that she was a woman.

There would be problems. Her people married only within their reli-gion.

He looked at his watch. Almost seven. Laying his watch on the desk he finished his Port and corked the bottle. He'd been very fortunate. A Tory patient, on the way out of town, had paid him handsomely for easing the pain of his rheumatism. The payment had been six bottles of Port wine.

An authoritative *rap rap* on the surgery door woke him. Tonneman lifted his head, blinked, and peered down at his watch on the desk. Half seven. He took his candle to the surgery door and opened it. A black velvet night but for the high moon and his candle.

A stocky man, his dark brown hair showing slightly under his white wig, removed his tricorn and came into the surgery.

"Sir?"

The man's blue cloak was the finest of mohair; the simple green velvet jacket and breeches beneath also appeared costly. The face was familiar enough. Ben would look like this when he was older. And possibly Mariana's children. "I am David Mendoza." The man closed the door behind him.

"Are you ill, sir?" Tonneman was alert. All traces of sleep left him. Had the problems he'd anticipated come already?

"No, sir, I am not." Mendoza looked about, openly curious.

"Your wife? I'll get my bag."

"My wife is as well as she'll ever be, sir."

"Then?" Tonneman paused. Mendoza was staring at him intensely, but not with anger. "Some Port?"

"Yes." The merchant unwound the green wool scarf from his neck.

"Will you come into the kitchen?" Tonneman called on his way.

Mendoza followed only as far as the study. "I'd prefer to stay here." He proceeded to scrutinize the shelves of medical books.

"Excuse me for a moment while I get another glass, then."

When Tonneman opened the cabinet, the glasses gleamed at him. Molly had taken to her new position with great eagerness. She and Quintin were keeping his house almost as well as Gretel had.

No day went by that he did not think of the woman who had raised him, and grieve for the violence of her death.

He took the glass and hurried back to his study. Mendoza was reading the *Common Sense* pamphlet from Philadelphia. The merchant returned the tract to Tonneman's desk and stood waiting.

"My manners, sir." Tonneman pointed to the chair in front of the desk. "Please be seated." Mendoza sat and watched, perhaps faintly amused, as Tonneman poured the wine. Tonneman sat behind his desk and lifted his glass. "To liberty, Mr. Mendoza."

"To liberty, Mr. Tonneman. And to life." Mendoza drained his glass and set it down. "You've heard the news?"

Tonneman scratched his head. "You're referring to the new English warship in the Narrows?"

"Yes. The King of England bids enter our home."

"So it seems."

" 'The poorest man may in his cottage bid defiance to the Crown. It may be frail—its roof may shake—the wind may enter—the rain may enter—but the King of England cannot enter—all his force dares not cross the threshold of the ruined tenement.' William Pitt said that in Parliament twelve years ago.—The warships in the Narrows do not frighten you?"

Tonneman smiled. "I'm not that brave, to be so nonchalant; I'm exhausted. I've been on my feet or on horseback since cock's crow. It's been like that of late, day and night."

"My daughter says you are brave."

Tonneman was wide awake now. "Mariana has talked to you about me?"

"All in due time, young man. The English ship we speak of is the *Mercury.* It has brought Sir Henry Clinton from Boston with three hundred fighting men under his command."

"How do you know all this?"

"My Tory friends like to frighten me with such information. The hope was that the ice would deter Clinton, but it did not. He is at the gate. More of our people are leaving the City. The ice did not stop Sir Henry, but the cold and the snow on the road will bring misfortune to many."

Tonneman was not sure whether, by "our people," Mendoza meant Jews or Patriots.

Mendoza made a light smacking noise with his lips. Then he said, "But there is good news, too. General Charles Lee has come to New-York to save us. He has been sent by General Washington to supervise the construction of our defenses."

"Thank you for saving the good news for last."

"Unfortunately, General Lee arrived not at the head of his Connecticut volunteers but on a litter. Still, I understand he's a good General and will do right by us."

"That's quite a bit of news for one day. You've missed your calling, sir. You should publish a newspaper. I am in your debt."

"No, Dr. Tonneman, I am in your debt."

"Sir?"

"I am tardy with my thanks by more than two months. My son, Benjamin, tells me you saved his life."

"I had," Tonneman said cautiously, "a very able assistant."

Mendoza looked directly into Tonneman's eyes. "I've come to speak with you about my daughter, sir."

Tonneman was at a loss for words. It was suddenly very warm in the study. "Your daughter, sir?"

"She's still my daughter, sir. In spite of her peculiar behavior, her choosing to wear her brother's clothing, and her attachment to your father and now you. What's more, she is my only daughter. Her mother and I worry about what will become of her." He lifted his glass to his lips. When he saw that it was empty he stopped, uncomfortable.

Tonneman poured the man more Port. He, too, was uncomfortable. His clothing contrived to smother him.

Mendoza sipped, then rubbed his lips with his forefinger. "I am a man of some means, sir, and after this war is over and the English are gone from our shores I can provide an ample dowry."

Tonneman stood and leaned toward Mendoza, his palms on his desk. "I would have her as my wife without a dowry, sir." He sat abruptly, astounded at his passion, at his declaration. "Would she have me?"

Mendoza smiled. "She's a good girl, but she has a mind of her own and I think will not be so pliant as a good wife should . . ."

"But, will she have me?"

"She will, sir." Mendoza rose, his hand extended. "She will be fifteen next month. The same age her mother was when we were married."

Tonneman was flabbergasted. He stood and shook Mendoza's hand. "You know, of course, that I am not a Jew."

Mendoza wrapped his scarf about his neck and set his tricorn on his head. "These are special times and all of us must trust to good men."

Tonneman followed Mendoza to the surgery door. Neither man spoke a word.

Mendoza opened the door and turned back to Tonneman. The Jew's eyes were sparkling. "To you and your people, you are not a Jew. But to me, you are a Jew."

"Sir?" Had he heard correctly?

Mendoza stepped outside into the crisp February night. He assessed his future son-in-law's fair hair and coloring. With more than a little pleasure, he said, "Go, look for the bones of your Dutch ancestor Pieter Tonneman and his wife. You will not find them in the Christian cemetery."

CHAPTER 50

It was the kind of cold that seeped through your clothes and even your skin to rattle your bones. Hickey left the warmth of Benson's Brew House and started the trek toward the Collect, whistling "Yankee Doodle." Soon enough, soon enough, it would be warm.

It had been quite a day. The Mayor of New-York had announced that he was "tired of the mayoralty and desirous to retire from the town." And who was the new Mayor? It was all Hickey could do not to burst out laughing. The new Mayor was his sometime employer, the Fat Man: Alderman David Matthews, by the grace of His Majesty the King, through his servant, Governor Tryon. Take that and frig you, Patriots.

As a matter of fact, it had been quite a fortnight. First Sir Henry Clinton had stationed his ship, the *Mercury,* in the Narrows, then General Charles Lee had come to town and a thousand Rebels attacked the Fort and took away cannon and stores. Hickey had watched them from Bowling Green. All day long men and boys of all ages had loaded wagons and dragged guns through the streets to the Common.

In the Bay, the captain of His Majesty's Ship *Phoenix* knew of the attack but did not fire on the Rebel forces. Hickey sneered. Did the man fear harming friend as well as foe? Oh, if the Rebels only knew.

Meanwhile Tryon, the coward, sat on his arse in the bosom of the *Duchess Of Gordon* under the watchful eye of the *Asia,* still giving orders, all the King's men in New-York rowing out to receive them. What fools they all were. General Lee demanded these visits cease, but Oliver De Lancey and other Council members protested. They were still clinging to their connection to the King. Hickey spat on the frozen ground. They were no different from him. Everyone was out for the coin.

Immediately upon becoming Mayor, the Fat Man had sent word to

Hickey. Plans were to be moved up. Hickey should be ready to go at any time, even if that pickled rogue Washington didn't oblige by coming to New-York.

Which was why, Hickey thought, cursing, he was out here in this cold, freezing his bawbels off. He'd thought to fill his needs by stealing from the Powder Magazine, but it was too well guarded. Well, that didn't trouble him much. The Lord had provided. Or the Devil, by the name of Hickey.

He walked slowly northward, a heavy canvas bag strapped to his back, stopping frequently to look and to listen. Sounds of raucous singing came to him from the Bayard Camp off to his right. He stopped whistling. If there was a guard posted, the fool was probably drunk and asleep. Hickey smiled, secure in his knowledge of the frailty of men. Still, he was cautious, wary of the Night Watch.

Soon the icy marshland crackled beneath his feet. Except for the nigger he'd passed on the road, nary a soul was about. The going was precarious without a lantern, but some light came from the camp and the moon was bright. Besides, he'd been here so often he could find his way blindfolded.

The tar fire was smoldering as he knew it would be. It gave enough light for the work he had to do and was perfect for what he had in mind. He swung the bag from his back and unloaded it.

The new black powder he'd made was untested. Close to the camp or not, this was the best place and time to find out. And while he knew his bomb would work, he lacked the practice of making one. Not that he could ever really forget. Like frigging. He snorted and whistled "Yankee Doodle" again under his breath.

A sudden clatter and creak halted him dead still.

CHAPTER 51

The thumping awakened Goldsmith. He had taken more often than not to sleeping downstairs on the stiff sailor's hammock hanging near the fireplace, to be away from his wife and her constant badgering. Not that the fireplace was any help; it wasn't lit. Actually, tonight he had been for once in his own bed, and Deborah had banished him because he was tossing and turning again. Just as well; he had to be alone to think. As for sleep, Gretel wouldn't allow that.

Tomorrow he would take a wagon east to the stump line and cut down some trees. That would keep them warm for the while, and the work might make him tired enough to get some sleep. The loss of his job, which he'd been so proud to hold, was killing him. It was more than not being able to feed his family, though Lord knew that was bad enough. Without work a man was only half a man.

The thumping again. Who could it be at this hour? Oh, God. The English? Falling from the hammock, he grabbed his musket from its place over the fireplace and hurried to the door.

"Who?"

"Quintin."

Goldsmith opened the door. For a moment he was blinded by the light from the Negro's lamp. "What is it?"

"I just saw that man again."

"What . . . ? The soldier?"

"Yes, sir."

"Where?"

"At the Collect."

Goldsmith searched frantically for his boots. "Wait," he said, thrusting the musket into Quintin's hands. He ran up the stairs.

"Daniel? What is it? Is it the English?"

"Go back to sleep." He found his boots under the bed and put them on.

Deborah, looking like a ghost, was sitting up in bed clutching the bedclothes, her hair not visible under her white nightcap. "You're going to see that woman of yours. I know about that. Louise Bauer told me about seeing you coming from the Holy Ground. I didn't want to believe her, but I believe her now."

"Be still, woman." He turned his back on her and strode to the door of their bedchamber.

"What? You dare talk to me like that! Mother!"

The ever-righteous Esther, holding a candle high like the light of God, came charging into the room and stood in his way. "Are you harming my daughter?"

Goldsmith peered up beyond the ceiling, imploring. "Why me?"

CHAPTER 52

Not stirring, not breathing, Hickey peered into the darkness. Minutes passed and the sound was not repeated. He made his way to the tar house and looked inside. Empty. He went back to the fire.

Hickey put his spade to the buttery earth only two feet from the tar fire and dug his hole. The heat of the fire made the tar-saturated ground accessible. The hole didn't have to be too deep or wide, just large enough to hold the cannon shell he'd filled with gunpowder and fused with a match made of twine soaked in saltpeter and spirits of wine.

He dug a channel from the tar fire to the hole, quickly blocking the channel with a brick. Now Hickey brought the flask of peach brandy from his greatcoat and contemplated his handiwork. He was disappointed that his experiment would have to be so small. He'd love to be blowing up the Powder Magazine, or better still, that damned Liberty Pole in the Common.

No, here was best. He had a long taste of the brandy. The Devil's own truth was, he was doing this because it tickled his fancy. He loved the idea of testing his powder so close to the Bayard Camp, a thumb in the eye of the Rebel army. And . . . it would draw attention where he had done the other.

Hickey, softly whistling the "Yankee Doodle" melody again, set the shell in the hole and replaced the brick with a wedge of wood and tar. The fire would eventually burn away the wedge. When that happened, the flame would course through the channel to the bomb fuse. The fuse would ignite, and—

"Bang," Hickey whispered. "Bang."

CHAPTER 53

Goldsmith rushed headlong down the stairs to join Quintin.

He grabbed his beaver hat from one of the pegs next to the front door and jammed it on his head. A cane his father had used lay across the pegs. Feeling the need of a stout club, he seized that, too, on the way out.

As they proceeded at a brisk pace along King Street, Goldsmith shouted, "When did this happen?"

"No more than thirty minutes."

"And you waited this long—"

"I was helping Goodwife Fraunces. She takes food to people thereabouts. Kate Schrader's grandson was sick, so she sent me to get Dr. Tonneman. That's when I saw the soldier. Just the back of him. He was going toward the tar houses. But I had to get the doctor first. Now I'm telling you what I saw."

They turned right on William Street. Goldsmith was out of breath. His mind was racing faster than his feet. He was finally going to get his hands on the man who butchered Gretel. Then her soul would get some rest, and he would get some sleep. If this was the man who killed Gretel. If this was the man who killed anyone. He was only the man Quintin had seen that night and this night.

When they got to Frankfort Street, Goldsmith was panting, and, in spite of the frigid air, sweating profusely. He stopped for a breath and steeled himself to think only of capturing the man. It was a waste of time to think of what came next.

Quintin waited patiently.

"Where?"

"T'other side." The African gestured with his lantern. "I told you, toward the tar house."

They started again. The night was suddenly still. No sound came from the camp. Nothing. Except . . . whistling. "Yankee Doodle."

As they approached the tar house, they saw a man running east toward Bayard Street and the camp. Ahead of them on the ground, a flicker of light. The howl of a dog cut the silence of the night.

The ground erupted in a floor of flame. A hundred candles flared right before Goldsmith's eyes. Rockets and cannonfire. The war had started. Get home. The children. Molly. Quintin's lantern flew past him. Home. The children. Sleep. Was he dying? Was he dead?

SPRING

CHAPTER 54

Forever after Goldsmith would associate the event of that night in February with "Yankee Doodle." It had been five weeks to the day, and his head still ached when he was hungry or tired or out of sorts. And of late that seemed to be all the time.

For Quintin that night was inexorably bound to the Devil himself. He had told Goldsmith that he'd seen the Evil One's light, flashing blood red. And old Satan, the great adversary of humanity, grinning, waiting to scoop up their lost souls.

Tonneman had been first on the scene. He had been tending to Kate Schrader's grandson and was at the tar fire minutes after the explosion. He found Goldsmith and Quintin moaning, their clothes half burned away. The two were black with tar and crimson with blood. The wonder was they weren't dead. Only when they'd been carried to Kate's hut and cleaned up did Tonneman recognize them.

Goldsmith took particular pleasure in telling the story time and again. At first Deborah and the ever-righteous Esther treated him with concern and respect, but after the first week they grew weary of listening to him. So it was no wonder that the former Constable sought Molly out in Tonneman's kitchen to tell his tale, albeit each time with more embellishment. Molly was an avid listener.

This wasn't to say that Goldsmith was idle. Word had come from Boston that the British were leaving that city and probably heading for New-York. So Goldsmith had toiled with a good many of the men and boys remaining in the City, building fortifications on Bayard's Hill near the Bowery. From the hill one had a clear view of much of the City, and so trees were felled and a lookout post set up there.

Other men were put to building barricades across Broad, Cortlandt,

Wall, and Crown Streets. Batteries of artillery were hauled to Reed Street, overlooking the North River, to behind Trinity Church, to behind Whitehall Dock, and to Coenties Slip on the East River. One was even placed on Rutgers Hill. A third of the population was striving to make the City a fortress.

That morning, Goldsmith had been helping dig trenches, and his muscles were sore; his hands burned with calluses.

The previous Friday Governor Tryon had published an appeal addressed to "The Inhabitants of New-York." The British were no longer in the harbor, but they were close enough.

Broadsides appeared all about the City: *"A door is still open to honest but deluded People who shall avail themselves of the Justice and Benevolence which the supreme Legislature has held out to them of being restored to the King's Grace and Peace . . ."*

Roving bands of Patriots tore the broadsides down. But the Patriots had bigger game. They were also hunting Loyalists. Those Loyalists who hadn't yet fled did so now.

Eight thousand men had poured in from Pennsylvania and New Jersey and the Connecticut militias were on the alert. The City anxiously awaited the arrival of the New England Regiments.

So many people had escaped from New-York that now there were more soldiers than New-Yorkers, each in the different uniform and hat of his regiment. The City had an almost festive aura.

Soldiers laid their blankets where they could. The lucky ones found shelter in the abandoned homes of the wealthy. Those not so fortunate slept in muddy fields all the way up to Kingsbridge.

"Where's Dr. Tonneman today?" Goldsmith groaned and shifted in his chair. His back ached.

"Over at the Bayard Camp again. Dozens of those poor boys have come down with camp fever. Three dead already yesterday. Dr. Tonneman is helping move them to King's College. It's a pity they made the new hospital a barracks. No matter. The college was just standing there. Students sent home. Books and things packed away in City Hall. Have some more toddy, Daniel." Molly tilted the pitcher of hot sweetened spirits into his cup. Setting the pitcher down she stroked his face. The cuts and bruises had healed, but he would forever wear scars from the hot tar. Still, Goldsmith had been lucky. His beaver hat pulled over his head and tight about his ears had protected him; poor Quintin had lost much of his hearing.

Molly kissed Goldsmith's cheek. He did not protest. "Just your bad luck you were there when that tar fire decided to blow up."

He shook his head. "I keep telling you it was no accident. That soldier was out there. I'm positive he's responsible. He had a reason that I don't know yet. But I will. He did it. I'm sure of it."

"Doesn't it make sense that the British blew up the pits?"

"But why? If they were going to send a raiding party, doesn't it make more sense to blow up the Powder Magazine?" Goldsmith busied himself with his drink. Women. They didn't understand such things. He sneaked a look at Molly. She was wearing one of Gretel's dresses, which she had altered to fit her smaller figure. The woman had filled out some since her illness. To Goldsmith she was beautiful.

"You had better tell Dr. Tonneman what you're thinking." Molly went to the fire and stoked it. Then she inspected the contents of every pot. "If you stay awhile you can taste my mother's sorrel soup."

"I can't . . ."

"Yes, you can. Dr. Tonneman doesn't mind." She stared at his still-singed eyebrows. "Dear Daniel. Why you were there in the dead of night I'll never know."

It was a wonderment to Goldsmith. When Deborah nagged it was a cat-o'-nine-tails. But when Molly nagged it was a velvet caress.

"One good reason. Give me that and I'll never ask again."

"I was trying to get my job back."

"And attempting to clear his name, Molly."

Neither had heard Tonneman. The physician stood leaning on the kitchen door, weary and hollow-eyed. Even Homer on the hearth had been slow to notice. Like Quintin, the old mastiff was deaf, and a milky screen of cataracts had fallen across his eyes. "And the most important reason."

Goldsmith and Tonneman exchanged sad grins. "Yes. To let Gretel have her peace."

Molly snapped two fingers to her mouth and made a spitting sound to keep away the evil spirits.

This time the grins the two men shared were lighthearted.

While Molly ladled up bowls of sorrel soup, Tonneman asked, "Mariana? She's not in the surgery."

"Her mother was feeling poorly again, and since it was quiet here—"

He drank directly from the bowl and made as if to stand. "I'd best—"

Molly placed a firm hand on Tonneman's shoulder. "Have your soup like a real person and rest a bit or you'll be as sick as your patients. She said she'd send for you if need be."

Goldsmith smiled behind his hand. She bossed Tonneman around the way she bossed him. "You'd better listen to her, Doctor."

"That's right," Molly said, sternly. Then she winked. "I have things to do upstairs, so I'll leave you men to talk." She stared at Goldsmith pointedly, then left.

"What is it, Daniel?" Tonneman raised a spoonful of soup to his mouth. "Good soup."

Goldsmith tasted his soup. "Yes. I like soup." He smiled. Molly had proven to be not just a fine cook but a fine housekeeper. Tonneman's house was spotless. Goldsmith laid his spoon down and pushed his chair back, waiting for the doctor to finish.

"What *is* it, Daniel?"

"The man who set the explosion is the murderer."

"What do you base that on? How do you know the explosion has anything to do with the killings?"

Goldsmith shook his head. "I have no proof. It's merely a feeling that the murderer is one of our own soldiers."

Tonneman thought for a moment. "When the first killing happened— Jane from Kingsbridge—there weren't that many soldiers about. Nor were there many when Gretel was killed. Now there are more soldiers than New-Yorkers. No one keeps records. We'd never find a soldier . . . the needle in the haystack. Why do you believe so?"

"What Quintin said. And just before the explosion, I know I heard 'Yankee Doodle.' Who else but a Patriot would be whistling that tune?"

CHAPTER 55

The spring thaw had brought rain and more rain. The unpaved streets around the Collect were steeped in mud. Matters were made worse by renewed work on the wells for the municipal water supply system.

In the Bayard Camp, foul with the remains of dead animals and human waste, Dysentery and Putrid Fever raged. Soldiers were now crammed six men to a small tent. The exposure, poor food, and lack of physicians were as punishing as any British cannonade. Clothing never had a chance to dry before the rains came again. Fortification trenches flooded, collapsed, and had to be shorn up. And the wetter it got, the sicker the soldiers became.

There was just so much one physician could do. These were modern times, but Tonneman was overburdened and ill-supplied. And even if he had all the medicines known in the world, some things could not be cured. Tonneman led Chaucer through the camp along Bayard Street, the gelding's hooves splashing in the deep puddles. If he tried to ride the poor beast, it would founder and sink into a wallow of mud.

The news was that General Washington was en route from Boston. If his troops were facing this sort of weather, it would be hard going. Tonneman dreaded to think how many of Washington's troops would arrive ill, if at all.

The weather notwithstanding, New-York had settled into its new incarnation as an armed camp. Even the incidents of Tory Riding—Patriots tarring and feathering Loyalists—had subsided somewhat after stern reprimands from the Continental Congress, which was meeting once more in Philadelphia.

At the Bowery, Tonneman reined in to read a broadside nailed to a chestnut tree. One Samuel Louden was announcing that his circulating library now contained two thousand volumes, and a catalogue would be sent to all subscribers. Tonneman took in a contented breath. It was things like this in the midst of all the madness that let him know the world was still sane.

He mounted Chaucer. The rain had the sweet scent of spring to it. The trees on either side of the road were hinting green. Although he still grieved for Gretel, perhaps even more than for his father, Tonneman had much to be thankful for. Before summer's end, Mariana Mendoza would be his wife.

From Jamie, he'd received word that the Willard family had retired to Abigail's brother's estate in Princeton for the duration of the war. Jamie wrote that he had wed Grace Greenaway. There was no mention of Grace's missing daughter, Emma, who'd run off in November.

It seemed so strange to Tonneman that he had chosen a woman much younger than he, while Jamie had chosen a woman who was at least seven years his senior. But Grace Greenaway was an extremely wealthy woman, and Jamie was no fool. He had always been more fond of society and the fine life than Tonneman.

The rain dwindled to a fine drizzle. Bowery Lane was much traveled. Tonneman tried to maintain a distance from those fore and aft to avoid being splashed on as much as possible. His eye caught a movement in the woods to his right. He stopped. A deer? His pistol was in his saddlebag. Venison would be very tasty. He reached for the bag. The deer bolted. So much for a venison dinner. Sorrel soup again. He rode past the woods and realized he was not far from the Jews Burying Ground, below Division Street. He reined Chaucer in. It was still light, and he had no urgencies calling him home.

David Mendoza had implied that his ancestor Pieter Tonneman was buried in the Jews Burying Ground. Mendoza was wrong, of course. But with the cemetery so close at hand Tonneman decided to see for himself.

The Burying Ground was a large well-tended area behind a white paling fence. Tonneman rode up to the gate, dismounted, and tied Chaucer to the fence. A small stone house stood sentry off to his right just outside the grounds. To the south he could see the East River.

Tonneman stood for a moment on the soggy ground in front of the gate, thinking himself a trespasser; he lifted the latch and entered. Narrow white paths of flagstone, cutting between rows of gravestones, made the going easier in spite of the sodden ground. Some of the stones had worn worse than others with the years and were difficult to read. As he walked,

he saw the gravestones were simple, carved of marble or granite, the lettering in what he knew to be Hebrew and Dutch, some in Hebrew, Spanish,
and English. Many of the family names were familiar to him. Franks, Levy,
Hendricks, Lopez, Nathan, Gomez, Hays, Isaacs, Moses, Adolphus, and
others who he'd never realized were Jewish.

Actually, he had given little thought to religion, and his appearances
at the Dutch Reformed Church even in his father's and grandfather's day
had been rare.

The rain had stopped and a damp mist hung over the City. Tonneman
wandered further into the cemetery, a sense of peace in his soul, an unusual
sensation for him of late in the City of New-York. He was abruptly surrounded by the trilling of robins; a line of them had settled on a branch of
a birch tree and were serenading him. He paused to enjoy them.

"What seek ye here?" The hoarse voice was so close behind him, he
thought for a brief moment that a soul had risen from one of the graves
and spoken.

Tonneman turned quickly. Before him was a tiny hunchbacked creature in a hooded cape of coarse brown homespun. The gnarled hand, de-
formed by arthritis, fiercely clutched an oak staff. Hair sprouted from
assorted warts and wens on the hunchback's face, and the caved-in cheeks
indicated the absence of teeth.

Tonneman recovered from the unexpected appearance and lifted his
hat. A conundrum. What was this? Though he was a physician, Tonneman
was not certain whether the hunchback was a man or woman. Or perhaps,
he thought, amusing himself, he was merely Tonneman the dunce. After
all, he had mistaken Mariana for a boy. "Good day. I am looking for a
gravestone. A hundred years ago."

The ancient hunchback scrutinized him suspiciously through squinted
eyes, tottering back first to gauge his stature, then shuffling in close to
appraise his face. "The oldest are near the willows." The hunchback
pointed with the staff to a clump of willow trees lining the most eastern
side of the Burying Ground.

"I thank you." Tonneman made his way through the winding paths,
aware he was being followed by shuffling steps.

"You be the physician, Tonneman?" the hoarse voice asked, panting.

Tonneman halted to allow the hunchback to catch up to him. "Yes."

"You be looking for your forebears then?"

"Oh, no—I'm not Jewish."

The hunchback laughed a crow's call. "Your name be Tonneman?"
Tonneman nodded.

The hunchback stared up at him and smiled, exposing gray gums. "Bones were first planted here in 1683, but they moved the bones from the old cemetery here, too." Beckoning with a twisted hand, the hunchback shuffled down the path. Tonneman followed the small, limping bundle to the willow trees. The hunchback pointed with the oak staff again. "There."

Tonneman stepped forward. The gravestone said simply,

PIETER TONNEMAN

1695

מצבת

קבורת שמעון בן אברהם טנמן

בעל ואב אהוב

מכובד על הבריות

הנפטר שנת התנ״ה

תיניציביהי

The dates appeared to be correct. Tonneman glanced left and right. Other Tonnemans. He wandered the small cluster. Tonnemans were buried here until the early 1700's.

He was amazed. Mendoza was right. His ancestors had been Jewish. He returned to Pieter's grave. Lying next to him, so close they might have been in one grave, was:

RACQEL PEREIRA DE TONNEMAN

1704

מצבת

קבורת הזקנה

רחל בת משה פרירה

האשה והאם הנכבדה

הנפטרה ביום

כ״ח סיון שנת התס״יד

תיניציביהי

Although what appeared next was in Dutch, he knew enough to understand that she was Pieter Tonneman's beloved wife. Some Hebrew lettering followed the Dutch.

The hunchback sneezed, startling him. Without turning, Tonneman asked, "What does that mean?"

" 'Daughter of Moses Pereira.' See, he is buried there." The hunchback bent over a headstone and knocked aside bird droppings with the staff. "He was a physician, like you. This ancestor of yours."

Tonneman's jaw dropped with disbelief.

The hunchback grinned, then cackled and tugged on Tonneman's coat. "You might as well look in on the Mendozas. There's not much I don't know about Mendozas. I birthed the babies, now I care for the bones."

Well, one riddle solved. The hunchback was a woman. And a midwife. Midwives always knew everybody's secrets. Odd that one should be tending a graveyard.

The crone led him to the Mendoza plots further down the willow line and pointed to a gravestone that said:

BENJAMIN MENDOZA

1664

מצבת

קבורת בנימין בן אברהם

אח יקר לדוד

בעל לרחל

שהלך לעולמו

ביום י"יד לחדש אלול

שנת התכ"יג

ויהיו ימי חייו

תשע ועשרים שנה

תיניצייביהי

"What is the Hebrew?"

" 'Son of Abraham and beloved husband of Racqel Pereira Mendoza.' " She cawed. "That's right, boy, Racqel had both of them. First Benjamin Mendoza, then your ancestor, Pieter Tonneman."

CHAPTER 56

Thousands of American troops from New England and New-York filled the City to capacity. More arrived daily. The wharves were furiously busy with the arrivals and departures of farmers' barges, and there were even a few ships at the piers loading and unloading goods.

With spring the desperate need for firewood eased and a variety of foodstuffs became available again. On Whitehall and Broad Streets and Hanover Square a few shops even took down their shutters and reopened.

New-Yorkers, when they weren't worried about the British, were thinking about the choice of new delegates to the Continental Congress. The Loyalists cursed both the aristocratic conservative party and the craftsmen's liberal party. What would the new Continental government be? A democracy? An oligarchy? The conservatives, having been assured favored treatment when the British arrived, had sequestered themselves on Long Island and Staten Island, to wait for the English generals to strike.

In the kitchen of Fraunces Tavern, Elizabeth Fraunces was hovering over a simmering cauldron of pease soup, in honor of General Washington who was coming to dine. Daughters Lizzie and Catherine were picking berries in the yard and arguing over who would hold the basket.

General Washington had returned to New-York in mid-April with more regiments, and New-Yorkers and soldiers alike had stood three deep on both sides of the street to lustily cheer his arrival down Broadway.

Private Thomas Hickey, the General's chief guard, had been coming and going for days examining the doors, then making himself comfortable in the tavern kitchen.

"He's taken a shine to you, love," Sam Fraunces teased his wife. Only yesterday the guardsman had brought her a bag of flax and a wheel of sharp cheddar cheese, from New England, the size of a cannonball.

Elizabeth giggled. "War or no war, the man for me will have to come with flowers, not with cheese."

After going through his routine, with a great display of thoroughness, Hickey stood leaning against one of the columns on the front veranda of Fraunces Tavern waiting for the other guards to transport their valuable charge. A gray fog had covered the City and only now was beginning to burn off. The sun suddenly emerged clear and bright.

New-York was now fortified in such a way that the English would have to fight from house to house, street to street, and then up every mound and down every slope all the way to Kingsbridge, thirteen and a half miles away. Clever, Hickey admitted, but this was not his worry. His fighting was a different sort. And maybe after today there wouldn't be anything but surrender left for the Americans.

All ten thousand troops in the City, in the four brigades—Heath commanding the first brigade, along the North River and above Canal Street; Spencer the second, at Rutgers' farm and Jones Hill; Greene the third, on Long Island, and Stirling the fourth, in the center along the Bowery Road—All would lay down their arms and surrender. All because of one Private Thomas Hickey. The thought pleased him no end.

The Rebel cannon in New-York and Kingsbridge wouldn't blow today, nor would Fort George or the King's Bridge at Kingsbridge. But Matthews couldn't have everything, no matter what Hickey had promised. After all, a man only had two hands. Hickey was careful to hide his smile behind one of them.

He'd take care of the cannon and the Bridge and perhaps even the Fort tomorrow. As his sainted whore of a mother had taught him, one poke at a time, that was the way to take it.

When Washington's coach arrived, Hickey snapped to attention. The young aide in blue coat and buff breeches, a close duplicate of the General's own uniform, edged open the carriage door, stepped out, and waited for the guardsman to come off the driver's seat.

The guardsman, a plump farm boy from New Jersey, Foster Carpenter, was new; Ned Smith had died in February, a victim of the terrible Influenza.

"Hickey?" Carpenter called.

"Secure," Hickey responded.

"All secure, Lieutenant Dixon."

Only now did the aide open the door wide for the General. At once the cur, Rebel, bounded out, charging directly at Hickey, who managed a sideways kick before the General descended. Going into a feral hump, the dog snarled, but when Hickey opened the front door to the tavern, the animal scampered inside.

The General smiled at Hickey from his great height. "We are pleased. Good work, Hickey."

"Thank you, sir." Hickey fawned a humble smile and bowed his head. Was the General using the royal We? As he watched the tall man enter, he smirked again. Another King George. Ha!

Hickey's grand deed today would save the Rebels from that misfortune. The bastards should present him with a medal when this was done.

The clattering of hooves and wheels turned Hickey once again to the street. It was the coach with the other officers who would be dining this day with the General.

"Keep an eye open," Lieutenant Dixon ordered. He followed General Washington inside.

"Yes, sir." Hickey snapped his fingers at Carpenter.

"What?"

"Going around back. You mind the front." Quickly, Hickey made his way to the rear of the tavern and entered by the kitchen door.

The ugly nigger who helped out in the tavern was sitting on a stool next to the fire turning a venison roast on the spit. Elizabeth was tasting the soup she had made today in honor of their special guest.

Hickey sniffed the pungent air. Pease and pork and carrots, onions and turnips and sage, butter and cream, salt and pepper and mint. It smelled grand. Only one thing missing.

He sat on a small bench, lay his musket beside him, splayed his legs, and watched Elizabeth. The black and white cat left her litter of kittens on their straw bed near the hearth and rubbed against his boots, purring loudly.

"Quintin." Elizabeth raised her voice because Quintin had been hard of hearing since the explosion.

"Yes, ma'am."

"More firewood."

"Yes, ma'am." The nigger gave Hickey an odd sidewise glance and went out the back door.

Hickey thrust his hand into his jacket pocket and fondled the flask.

"Elizabeth." Black Sam stepped into the kitchen carrying bottles of Madeira, brandy, and ale in his massive arms. "Corn bread and butter for the General."

Elizabeth opened the door to the oven; the savory fragrance of fresh corn bread filled the kitchen. Hickey's stomach rumbled. He rose, took a cup from the side table, and let Sam fill it with ale.

"Are his teeth giving him any trouble?" Elizabeth cut the bread in squares right in the hot tin, holding the pan with a heavy cloth.

"Nary a grumble."

Goodwife Fraunces followed her husband into the main room.

Hickey set his cup of ale on the bench. Lazily, he strolled the short distance to the cauldron, whistling "Yankee Doodle" to himself. Out came the flask. Off came its cover. He lifted the lid off the soup pot, poured the full flask of brandy, strongly dosed with Paris Green, into the soup, and stirred it thoroughly. He raised the ladle to his nose. "Green to green." He snickered.

The door slammed; Hickey's hand slipped and he dropped the ladle, splashing pease soup on the floor just shy of the hearth. He turned to find the nigger giving him that same odd look. "Just having a taste." When the man made no response, Hickey advanced on him. "What are you staring at, nigger?"

Shifting his eyes, the African placed the logs in the bin. He set a large log in the fire, poking it till it took. The cat, at the hearth, was already making fast work of the spilled soup. Quintin went back to his stool and the roast while Hickey glowered at him, all to the mewling of the hungry kittens.

Elizabeth, smiling and flushed, returned to the kitchen. She uncovered the cauldron to stir the soup. "Where's my—" She spied the ladle on the floor where the cat was stalking it. "Shoo!" She snatched the ladle, tossed it into the basin, and replaced it with another from the rack above her stove.

Seeing the flask in Hickey's hand, she gave him a sharp look. Hickey took the hint and put the flask away.

Elizabeth set five bowls on a tray and ladled out the soup. Now she crouched, slid the tray on her strong right hand, stood, and sailed into the main room, balancing the heavy tray with ease.

Hickey smiled. He heard Sam Fraunces's booming voice. "Your favorite, General. Pease soup."

A sharp screech came from the cat— so sharp, in fact, that even Quintin heard. The kittens responded, standing, their tiny backs arched.

Quintin left the spit and stood over the tormented creature, staring. The animal retched violently, then went still.

"Just a fit," said Hickey. "I've seen it before."

"The soup," said Quintin, just as a joyous Elizabeth reentered the kitchen.

"The General dropped his spoon," she said, collecting a fresh spoon. "Everybody's dropping things today."

"Miss Elizabeth, the soup's no good. Don't let him eat it."

"What are you talking about? Of course the soup—"

The black-and-white cat gasped for air, shuddered, grew rigid, and died. Her five kittens gathered about their lifeless mother, mewling piteously.

Tears rolled down Elizabeth's cheeks. "Oh, my God." The spoon fell from her hands and clattered to the floor. "Oh, my God," she said again, as she ran into the main room.

Hickey raced after her. General Washington had borrowed a spoon from his lieutenant, dipped it into the soup, and was lifting it to his lips.

"General Washington! Stop!" Elizabeth screamed. "The soup is poisoned!"

CHAPTER 57

Hickey stood at Bowling Green where, facing the Fort, the gilded lead statue of King George garbed as a Roman emperor sat astride a prancing horse atop a marble base. As expected, the water vender was on the green hawking his wares. Hickey signaled the old man and the cart rolled to a stop in front of him.

"Water, sir?"

"Never mind that piss you peddle. I need to see the Mayor."

"I believe you can find him at City Hall, sir."

"That's the last place I want to go."

"Then, I'm afraid I can't help . . ."

Hickey seized the old man's shirt front and was about to say something particularly nasty when two soldiers in blue coats, buckskin breeches, white stockings, and half-boots, toting long rifles, approached the statue.

The first, a black youth with yellow pustules on his face, circled round the statue. "Look here, Luke." He spoke with the accent of a white Connecticut farm boy.

His pudgy white companion spat on the ground. In the same accent he said, "Ought to tear the damned thing down and melt it for bullets."

"Not a bad idea, Luke. Why don't you tell that to the sergeant?"

"Chester, you're an oaf. A mouth-farting oaf."

"So's your granny."

The two laughed boisterously and punched each other's arms.

Hickey was so outraged at the pair that he completely forgot his business with the water vender. "Why are you treating that nigger like your brother?" he demanded of the pudgy soldier.

"We don't want no trouble, mister," Chester whispered.

Luke glared at Hickey. "Speak for yourself, Chet."

Hickey glared back, his fists clenched. "You want a piece of me, boy?"

"No," the water vender said loudly, giving Hickey a shake of his head as a signal to desist. "He merely wants a piece of the statue."

"I'll say," said Luke, maintaining eye contact with Hickey. "What's the damn thing doing here anyway?" he added truculently.

Chester gave him an elbow in the ribs.

Luke grinned. His two front teeth were missing. "All right," he said, breaking off staring.

"Repeal of the Stamp Act," said the water vender.

Luke's brow creased. "What?"

"The Stamp Act was enacted by the British Parliament in '65."

"Bastards," Luke muttered.

The water vender, who'd been a schoolmaster before most of the population fled the City, happily continued his explanation. "The purpose was to raise revenues in the Colonies by requiring everyone to buy stamps and stamped paper for official documents, commercial writings. Things like that. It was supposed to go into effect on November first, 1765."

"Humbug." Luke tugged at his friend. "Let's get a beer."

"Wait," Chester said. "I want to hear."

The water vender smiled at Chester. He'd thought the Stamp Act was a proper way to raise money. He also missed practicing his profession; the last thing soldiers figured they needed was schooling. "People hereabouts didn't have much use for the tax. They made a fuss and the Crown repealed the act four months later."

Luke spat in the dirt again. "You sure do take the long way round, mister. What's this got to do with that statue?"

"Mind your manners, boy," said Hickey, who was still offended by the boy being in the company of a black and the two acting like they were comrades.

The water vender moved his cart so it was between Hickey and the two young soldiers. "Everyone was so relieved that the New-York Assembly voted to appropriate money for two statues. One for William Pitt, Earl of Chatham, who got it repealed, and this one here of King George."

"See," said Chester to Luke, trying to tickle his friend, but Luke edged away. He turned back to the water vender. "How long's it been here?"

"You've had your lesson," Hickey snarled. "Go away."

Luke set his feet and squared his chest. "Will not."

Hickey's face reddened ominously. Another word and he'd slice this little nigger-loving bastard's throat.

"Since August '70," the vender said quickly. "Ceremonies were held in Fort George there." He nodded his chin at the once formidable Fort and at the space where the wall had been. "Big crowd. I think you'd better move along."

"What happened to the wall?" Luke was stubbornly standing his ground.

The vender got his words out rapidly while Hickey fumed. "General Lee tore it down in February. Begone, boy. Go."

Chester tipped his tricorn to the vender and Hickey. "Thank you, sirs. Please don't mind my friend. He's still got pig shit on his boots. Good day."

The water vender and Hickey watched the two boys go.

"I should have killed them both," said Hickey.

The vender cast his eyes about, then started on his way. "Water from the Tea Water Pump."

"No, you don't." Hickey ran to head the man off.

"Please, sir, people are watching."

"If you want them to stop, tell me where the Fat Man is going to be. I need to talk to him."

"Sir."

Hickey pulled the vender from behind his cart, kneed him in his privates, and slapped him across the face. The man's spectacles flew off as he fell to the ground.

"Please," he groaned when Hickey raised a foot to kick him.

"I'll please you to death. The Fat Man."

"Serjeant's Tavern tonight at eight."

"That's more like it," Hickey said, dusting the vender off. He picked up the old man's spectacles and set them gently on the coot's nose. "See, when you're nice to me, I'm nice to you."

CHAPTER 58

Serjeant's Tavern sat, squat as a bullfrog, on Pearl Street at the extreme tip of the island. The taphouse was aromatic with hearty scents of ales and tobacco, and raucous with soldiers and merchants.

In a private chamber where the noise from the main room was but a muffled roar, the Mayor of New-York, David Matthews, talked with Mary Gibbons, a pert-featured woman of not thirty years, whose ruddy hair was all but hidden under her red bonnet.

"You agree, then?"

"Of course." Mary's freckled hands toyed with the glass of brandy before her. "You don't trust this Hickey, and I don't blame you. My past acquaintanceship with the General can help me to see him again. It was only a brief meeting at a dinner several years ago, but I'm sure it will suffice. As soon as I determine how best to accomplish my mission, I'll act. But only if Hickey fails. Then I'll deal with Hickey. In either case you will not be troubled again by either George Washington or Thomas Hickey."

Matthews grinned and tossed back his rum. "Good. We understand each other."

She drank her brandy with the same ease. "Was there ever any doubt?"

A knock on the door interrupted their exchange. Both fell immediately silent as a grizzled-haired waiter pushed open the door. "Excuse me, Your Honor—"

Suddenly, over the waiter's head, Hickey's face loomed. "It's me, Your bloody Honor." The Irish stumbled into the waiter, almost knocking them both to the ground.

"Beg pardon, sir." The waiter gasped for breath.

Matthews waved his hand. "Put him in a chair and get out."

"Yes, Your Honor."

"You're drunk," Matthews said, clearly disgusted, when the waiter had departed.

Hickey smiled. "Not yet. But I will be." He leered at Mary. "And who might this be?"

Matthews frowned. "Mary Gibbons. Thomas Hickey."

The Mayor scratched his ample belly. "Mary, I think our business is done here."

She stood and curtsied. "I'll take my leave then." The young woman swept out the door.

Immediately Hickey came up from his chair and followed her.

"Damn it," Matthews yelled. "I thought you wanted to see me."

"It can wait," Hickey shouted back. "I can't resist red-haired women."

CHAPTER 59

The brilliant afternoon sunshine on Dock Street dazzled David Bushnell's eyes as he considered the Bay through his spyglass. The Union Jack fluttered defiantly from ship after ship. No doubt about it, he mused wryly, the British were still out there. He lowered his glass. This was where he would test his Water Machine and himself.

The noise of the wharves filled his ears. Men called out to each other as they labored. Bushnell felt an odd sensation, as if the sun were burning his neck. He looked around. The waterfront was active with workers and traders and their wares. About fifty paces away, a man was staring at him. Bushnell knew the fellow. He was one of the General's guardsmen.

This made sense. Only a week before, Washington had returned to the City from Philadelphia. Headquarters was set up in the Kennedy House at number 1 Broadway.

Only now did it occur to Bushnell that this was the second time he'd seen the man in less than an hour.

The first occasion was when he left his room. The man had been bent over inspecting his boot; now Bushnell realized it was the same fellow. But the moment had passed without his giving any conscious reflection to the man's presence.

With deliberate steps, Bushnell walked toward the guardsman. The man at first seemed ready to bolt, then he stood his ground and called impudently, "And good day to you, sir. I was wondering if you'd recognize me."

"Hickey, isn't it? Did you want to talk to me?"

"No, sir. Simply walking by. Thought it proper to offer greeting."

"Of course." There was something about the swarthy man Bushnell didn't like, yet he didn't know quite what. The man looked him right in the eye, but his demeanor made Bushnell uneasy. "You never seem to be in uniform."

"No, sir. My duties often call for that."

"I see." Just what were his duties, Bushnell wondered, stepping back to let a steeve man from the docks, bearing a load of stinking hides, go by.

"Well, good day to you, sir." Hickey saluted, wheeled about, and left, dodging in and out among the dockworkers.

This so-called chance meeting with the guardsman continued to trouble Bushnell as he started back to his room on Bridge Street. How long had Hickey stood there before he'd felt his gaze? Could the man have been following him? Or was it just a coincidence? Bushnell shook his head vigorously. He was a mathematician and didn't believe in coincidence. Certainly not twice.

This had to be calculated. Hickey's actions had to have a purpose. Was General Washington having him followed?

Why? For the life of him Bushnell did not know. Perhaps that was the way of the spy game. Agents watching agents as a second line of defense to confirm loyalty. Seedy business.

Bushnell shook off these rambling thoughts and resolved to find Hickey and determine what his purpose was. Resolutely, the inventor started to retrace his steps to the waterfront. Then he stopped and smiled. He didn't have to find Hickey. It was so logical: If Hickey was indeed spying upon him, Hickey would find *him*. With this notion set firmly in his mind, Bushnell set off for Fraunces Tavern and a pot of chicory coffee.

Sure enough, when he came out of the tavern, there was Hickey in front of Johnson's Coopery, inordinately interested in barrels.

Pretending to be preoccupied, Bushnell hurried to his room.

From his window overlooking Bridge Street Bushnell watched Hickey set up his vigil. Bushnell lit a lamp and a pipe and waited. After a bit, he put out the lamp and waited some more. He was a patient man. Two hours passed before Hickey decided that Bushnell was in for the night.

And when Hickey left Bushnell was right behind him.

Hickey led him to Serjeant's Tavern.

When he saw Hickey vanish into a side room, Bushnell asked the stout, aproned fellow balancing a tray of tankards on his right hand, if there was a place he could have to himself.

The waiter gave him a broad wink. "Meeting a lady, sir?"

"That's it. A lady."

"I can fix it." The waiter gave him another wink and extended his left hand.

Bushnell had only a few shillings left, but this was certainly more important than tomorrow's breakfast. He pressed one of his precious coppers into the waiter's hand and nodded at a room next to the one Hickey had entered. "That would be fine."

The waiter looked down disdainfully at the single penny. Bushnell added a mate to the coin. The waiter sneered again, then shrugged. Obviously there'd be no more coppers from this one. "The room's yours. What are you drinking?"

Bushnell offered only silence.

The waiter spit. "You got to order something."

"Beer. In a glass."

Inside the chamber a single candle flickered weakly. Bushnell put his ear to the wall but could only hear sounds, no distinct words.

A sharp kick opened the door. The beer was slammed on the table. "Tuppence."

Bushnell had only a shilling left. He proffered it and waited fretfully while the waiter counted out his change. Eighteen pennies.

"You got one hour."

Bushnell swiftly drained his beer, then held the mouth of the glass to the thin wall. From the adjacent room, he could hear muffled words about a meeting with Governor Tryon, and foul talk against the Congress, Washington, and other notable Patriot leaders, but nothing he could make real sense of.

"I want more money." This he heard loud and clear. And no doubt about it, the voice belonged to the Irish, Hickey.

Then a laugh. "Money? Is that all you want? Here, take a case full. It was captured in Boston. Take it. There's lots more where this came from."

The door to his room opened suddenly, startling Bushnell, causing him to bobble the empty glass. He caught it and hid it behind his back. He peered at the waiter in the dim light. "Get out."

"No, I don't have to get out. You do. Somebody else wants the room."

"But I paid for it."

"Not enough."

"I'll pay more."

Voices were rising in the next room and Bushnell was desperate to hear. He emptied his pockets. "How much do you want?"

"Too late. I've got a fellow whose woman is already here. He gave me a shilling."

Defeated, Bushnell gathered up his few coins, quit the room, and waited in the crowd around the bar. Soon Hickey came out. Bushnell followed him to Little Dock Street. He watched as Hickey entered Gunderson's Butcher Shop. Bushnell stood outside for more than an hour waiting for Hickey to come back out, all the while thinking he had to get word to the General. Finally he tried the door to the butcher shop and, very cautiously, entered.

It was empty.

CHAPTER 60

The gate of Hell opened wide. He slammed it shut. It opened again. He closed it again. And hammered it down to keep it closed for eternity.

"Open up in there."

Hickey's eyes flew open. Groggy, he got to his feet.

"Open up."

"Who says?"

"The Provincial Congress."

He tottered to the door.

"What's this about?"

"You'll find out soon enough."

Since there was no other choice, Hickey unlatched the door. Two men stood before him, or rather one old man and one boy. The man wore the stylish blue uniform of the New-York Militia, the boy shabby breeches, with only the blue tricorn to identify him. Each stood with his musket at a trail from his right hand.

Should he run? The knife that was always there at the small of his back was not there this morning. That always happened when he was too drunk to think. He'd been pissed as a bear the night before. He remembered two bottles of rum. With the knife he could gut the old man in a trice. The boy would probably swoon at his first sight of blood, and he'd be gone. And if the dog hadn't stopped to take a shit he would have caught the rabbit. No, calm was the way. "What's this about?"

The man, who had to be sixty if he was a day, rasped his throat loudly and spit behind him. "Here to charge you."

"What do you have to do with me? I'm a soldier. I work for General

Washington. If I've done something wrong, it's up to the military to chastise me. Damn, it would take old George himself."

"Be glad of us, my boy. The army would lash your arse and fine you a year's pay. The Conspiracies Committee just wants to talk to you, is all. You'll probably be out in an hour having your morning pint."

"What's the charge?"

"Counterfeiting." The old man did all the talking. The boy, silent, stared at Hickey.

"Counterfeiting?" For once, Hickey was confounded. That frigging Matthews. Hickey had paid off his small group of mercenaries with some of the Continental paper that double-dealing duplicitous bastard had given him. The son of a bitch had put him in a deep well full of scum. "I don't understand what it has to do with me." He backed into the room. The knife was who knew where, but his pistol was under the bed, primed, ready.

Damn. He'd paid for the rum with Matthews' paper money. Hickey bent over the cot. Before he could move he felt the jab in the back of his neck. The old Militia man's musket. Hickey turned, slowly, snarling, "What the dickens do you think you're doing?"

"You are hereby charged with passing counterfeit bills and if you don't come willingly, we have orders to place you under arrest." The gaffer prodded Hickey again, this time in the chest.

There was nothing for it, then. Hickey belched loudly. He straightened the clothing he'd slept in and barked, "Let's go."

The Militia men walked him through the butcher shop, where Gunderson's wife and a daughter, who'd returned from Long Island in the spring, were scrubbing the shop prior to opening for the day. They watched mutely as Hickey was led away.

"What's this with counterfeiting, chaps?" Hickey asked with forced joviality. He didn't like the way this was going. Not at all. "You can put your guns up, you know. I'm a Patriot, too."

"I don't doubt you, lad," said the old man, not relaxing his weapon for a moment. "Word is there's a conspiracy to undermine our money. They say it's being printed on His Majesty's ship *Asia*—Well, whoever is spreading this bad money has got to be stopped or we'll lose this war before it's properly begun. You wouldn't want that now, would you?"

"Of course not," Hickey answered. They passed the heavy fortifications along Hunter's Key and Burnett Street. The streets were fairly empty. The boy's weapon was down and he wasn't paying attention. If Hickey was going to run, now was the time. The old man was keen, though. Even as Hickey had the thought to run, the old bastard shoved his musket deeper into his back. What a kick in the arse this was, thought Hickey, as the two marched him from Little Dock Street to Wall. Taken in by an old fart and a young squirt for a penny cunt charge of counterfeiting. The Militia men delivered him to the jailer and Hickey was locked in City Hall Jail.

The cell was small and he could hear the rats, but he'd been in worse. At least there was a candle. The Irish lay down on the dirt floor. This wasn't so bad, all he needed was a bottle. He had some money. After a while he'd bribe the jailer to get him some rum. Or better yet, brandy. And to get word to Matthews. The bastard had to know. The frigging rascal was the frigging Mayor after all. Matthews could get him out. He would get him out. If he wanted to. Of course he wanted to. Without Hickey there'd be no lovely explosions, and no dead General.

SUMMER

CHAPTER 61

The Fat Man, David Matthews, Mayor of the City of New-York, had spent early Friday evening at Serjeant's Tavern dining on fried cod and spuds with Ludwig Koppers and Philip Rattigan, two merchants who sang the Patriot tune, but only when the Rebel powers were listening.

But you couldn't count these two as Loyalists either. The only loyalty Koppers and Rattigan knew was to their own purses. The vermin were already tilting toward the Crown; they would be open about it fast enough once George Washington was eliminated.

Matthews was having his own private celebration. Of course he'd prefer roast beef and French wine, but that would come soon enough. The Mayor had dressed for the evening in a new outfit from London which Tryon had waiting for him on his last trip to the *Duchess Of Gordon*.

Tonight he was resplendent in an apricot velvet coat, black waistcoat with bone frogs, white stockings, and apricot breeches. At his wrist and neck was delicate Belgian lace. His tricorn was black with gold trim and gold ribbon. And he had a new walking stick. Its head was a regal ivory carved lion on which his hand could rest quite comfortably, thank you.

But he'd imbibed more brandy than was judicious, and he was having difficulty keeping the words of triumph from passing his lips as they dined and talked. Worse, his head felt as if someone were beating it with a hammer.

The tavern was hot as a smokehouse. The City heat was almost too much to bear. This time of year New-York was fit only for the rabble. Next year he'd have an estate further up the river in which to spend the summer. Matthews drew a lace handkerchief from his sleeve and mopped his sweaty brow. Damn, there were patches of wet crimson showing at the armpits of his lovely apricot jacket.

Hickey was worrying him. One word out of the Irish and all would be lost. Matthews had given some thought to having the Irish killed, and was still considering it, even though Hickey had assured him only yesterday that every requisite piece was in place and the plan would be carried out. All Matthews had to do was get him released from jail and out of the City after the General had breathed his last, which wouldn't be difficult in the ensuing panic. Hickey had been in a fury because he was in jail for passing Matthews's sham money in the first place. Now the Irish sod was demanding that every counterfeit bill be replaced with gold coins.

So, Matthews had arranged for the Irish's escape. He'd hired two Negroes to overpower the guards. It was cheaper to hire them for that than to kill Hickey. Besides, he needed Hickey. For the nonce.

All asmile, Matthews bade goodnight to the vile merchants and staggered home to Mrs. Laderman's boardinghouse, where he had a large well-furnished bedroom and sitting room on the second floor.

In his room he dropped his splendid coat to the floor and had a final draught of brandy. His teeth ached. He tottered to his bed and lay on his back. The chamber started spinning; his clothes were suffocating him. Clawing feebly at his neckpiece, he fell into a deep drunken sleep.

The glare of a lantern and the prodding of a pistol in his stomach awakened him with gut-wrenching alarm.

"Stop that. I'll be sick."

"You're going to be more than sick, you ill-formed Tory bastard."

"What is it?" Matthews could count six or seven among the shadows. "Who? What? Who are you?" He was sputtering. The room was stifling. Those damn Rebels had come to tar and feather him. Well, he would not stand for this. He was the Mayor of New-York. He pushed against the bed and got awkwardly to his feet. His peruke slipped off, exposing his egg-bald head. He groped for the wig, feeling naked without it. "What's the meaning of this? Damn it, I'm the Mayor."

"Not any more you're not." The man yelling in his face reeked of onions and ale.

Matthews felt ill. He clutched at the bedpost, swaying. It was then that he saw that the onion eater wore the uniform of a Captain Lieutenant in the Continental Army. Behind him, another officer, a sergeant, and four armed guards. One of the guards held the lantern aloft.

The second officer stepped forward, brandishing a stiff parchment. The guardsman with the lantern stepped with him, holding the light next to the document. The officer, sweat glistening on his upper lip, announced:

"David Matthews, we are arresting you in the name of the Committee of Safety. As is required by law I shall read their order: 'Whereas David Matthews, Esq., of the City of New-York, stands charged before us with being concerned in dangerous designs and treasonable Conspiracies against the Rights and Liberties of America; to wit: He is charged with conspiring with Governor William Tryon and others to assassinate General George Washington, to kidnap other general officers, blow up the Magazine at Fort George, spike the cannon in New-York and Kingsbridge, blow up the King's Bridge, and set fire to New-York in advance of the British attack. We do therefore in Pursuance of a certain Resolve of Congress of this Colony, order you to take and keep the said David Matthews in your Custody, till you shall receive further Order concerning him from us or the Congress.' "

Matthews sat heavily on his bed and groped for his wig. He'd been betrayed. Hickey.

The sergeant leaned over him. "What do you have to say to that, traitor?"

Damn Hickey to everlasting hellfire. "Traitor? You are the traitors." Matthews felt as if he were shouting, but the words that came out sounded so low he could barely hear them. He placed the peruke on his head. He was sweating.

The sergeant knocked the wig off.

"Sergeant." The command came from the second officer.

Matthews, hands shaking badly, set the wig back in place on his head. "You'll pay dearly for your treason once General Howe takes back the City. And soon, too."

"We'll not worry about that now," the Captain Lieutenant said grimly. He plucked the apricot coat from the floor and tossed it to the Mayor.

The men watched silently as the Fat Man put on his coat, straightened his wig, and placed his gold-trimmed and beribboned black tricorn squarely on his head. "To hell with you and your Cause," said Matthews.

"It's a pity you won't be around to see our victory."

Matthews was silent. There was still a slender chance Hickey had escaped—if the bastard hadn't been the one to betray him in the first place. And if Hickey was on the loose, all was not over yet.

CHAPTER 62

Hickey was getting tired of it. It had amused him at first, and he'd been certain Matthews, with his influence, would get him out of jail. Then again, it had been Matthews—maybe—and Tryon, sitting safe and sound on His Royal frigging Majesty's frigging ship, who'd passed him queer Continental bills. There was no trusting anyone. But he had plans.

He spat at a waterbug scampering along the damp floor. Missed. It was frigging hot and he needed his beer. All day long the Committee of Safety arseholes had been coming in and out, puffed up like roosters, like they'd done something special.

This was a new story. No more kind-speaking Militia men talking about a slap on the wrist for counterfeiting. This was the frigging evil-arse Continental Army going on about mutiny and conspiracy.

David Matthews says this, Goodwife Fraunces says that, David Bushnell says this, Quintin Brock says that. Who the hell was Quintin Brock? Had to be the nigger-man who worked in the kitchen of Fraunces Tavern. Two other niggers, Paul Swan and Davis Miller, had said Matthews paid them to help Hickey escape.

If it was true, Matthews was a bigger fool than he thought. Everybody knew you couldn't trust a nigger worth piss. And if one will bring you to harm, two will get you killed, sure. Hickey kicked the barred gate savagely.

The Committee now knew Hickey had tried to poison General Washington on Tuesday, the 7th of May, and they wanted him to confirm that it was David Matthews who had given the order to pour the poison in the soup. Hickey was not impressed with their knowledge or threats. Blunderers and fumblers all. They were so smart, how come it took them this long to get to him? More than a month. And they gave that nigger Quintin a harder time than they gave him. And all they'd asked Quintin was had he seen anyone suspicious around the kitchen that day.

No, sir, he was not impressed with the Committee of Safety at all. Shit, if he hadn't been arrested for counterfeiting, he would not be here in this frigging cell at all. If David Matthews had betrayed him, he would get him, he would. The fat bastard would sound the final rattle with Hickey's hands around his fat throat. And he could burn in Hell for all that. With this triumphant thought, Hickey curled up on the floor and fell into a deep and sweaty sleep.

By the light through the meager window it couldn't have been two hours later when they woke him and took him out of his cell, to a room where four buggering officers jabbered at him until the one behind a desk said, "Who are your co-plotters?"

He spat on the floor. He had no use for any of them, least of all Matthews, but he was no frigging informer. He'd get out of this somehow. And when he did, he'd handle Matthews in his own way.

The one behind the desk stood and said, "You are charged with mutiny and conspiracy. What have you to say?"

"I say I would like a beer."

After more jabbering, what it was he didn't know, and didn't care, the one behind the desk stood once more. "Thomas Hickey, you have been convicted of mutiny and conspiracy. Know that on the twenty-eighth day of June in the year of our Lord 1776, you will be hanged by the neck until you are dead, dead, dead."

A slow rumble started in Hickey's dry throat and finally broke through his lips in a terrifying laugh. "And you can go to Hell, Hell, Hell!"

CHAPTER 63

In the small shop, Karl Gunderson lay stretched out on his own chopping block like a lank side of beef.

Around him, in a symphony of crying and praying, were the butcher's third wife, Inga, and the sons and daughters from three marriages, their spouses, and the dozen or so children. Further crowding the little place were the goggling customers and the simply curious, who kept trying to elbow in to see the show.

The noise was enough to wake the dead. Gunderson was not dead, but he wasn't well, and he was in agony. Always a slight man, Gunderson was now a skeleton with skin.

His family, fearful that any move might kill him, dared not shift the man from the wooden block to his feather mattress in the house next to the shop.

It was this chaos that Tonneman came upon after he'd pushed through the noisy spill of customers and relatives gathered out on Little Dock Street. He'd been summoned by Gunderson's grandson, Seth, who was no more than twelve years, and was the typical skin and bones of the Gundersons.

"Make way, make way for the physician," one of the women cried. The human curtain parted with much handwringing. At once Inga Gunderson shooed relatives and customers alike outside.

The air was putrid with the smell of slaughtered carcasses. Still clutched in the butcher's right hand was a lean leg of mutton. At the base of the block lay a large cleaver. On either side of the block, neatly in their slots, were knives and cleavers of every description.

Tonneman bent over his patient, murmuring comforting words. Yellow-hued blood oozed from the man's nose. His breathing made the whining sound a saw does when cutting through knurly wood. His face was tinged blue, his left cheek and eyelid drooped. Now his breathing became unstable. Tonneman lifted the butcher's eyelids. His pupils were still, the left one smaller than the right. The man was dying. Tonneman had seen it all too often before. Apoplexy.

"Get me a pillow and blankets," Tonneman ordered as he stanched the blood with clean cloth from his bag and gently coaxed the bloody carcass from the dying man's grip.

"I'll go," young Seth called, already running.

Tonneman handed the carcass to the butcher's wife. He could see the butcher's arm was paralyzed. The man's pulse fluttered, stopped, fluttered.

Tonneman knew Inga Gunderson. He'd treated the lean woman several times. He'd gotten her through the Influenza that lengthy winter. In her last visit he'd lanced three boils and pulled her few remaining rotten teeth. She was twenty-five years old, and only one of the three children she'd borne Gunderson had lived and that one was sickly. Now he took the woman aside.

"There's little I can do, Mrs. Gunderson, but let Nature take her course."

The rasping breathing continued; the butcher's thin limbs twitched. One by one Gunderson's three sons and two daughters returned to the shop. They and the soon-to-be widow circled the body keeping watch. Predatory flies circled overhead, swooping down on the butcher, the carcasses, the knives and cleavers.

Seth returned with feather pillow and blankets. A daughter, Emily, as skinny as her father, placed the pillow tenderly under his head. A fine line of bloody drool slid from his mouth. She wiped her father's face with a cloth. "His apron," she whispered to her stepmother.

Inga Gunderson nodded, then the two women gently removed the green leather apron which covered his cotton butcher's smock and thrust it into the hands of his eldest, thinnest son and heir, Albert Gunderson.

As they were about to cover the wasted body, the dying man groaned loudly, setting off a tearful response from his family. Tonneman knew it was only a question of time, now. He reached for the narrow wrist. A faint flutter. Seconds later, Gunderson growled his death rattle. It was over. Tonneman pressed the butcher's eyes closed and folded his hands across his emaciated belly.

There was no more for him to do. In truth, there had been nothing for him to do from the beginning. The man had been dying; the man was dead. Tonneman moved away from the corpse, and the women took his place to prepare it for burial.

Albert Gunderson walked Tonneman outside to where Chaucer was tied to the rail. He watched as the physician hooked his bag to the saddle. The curious still stood outside, gossiping. The midnoon sun was hot.

Tonneman was thinking that if they didn't get Gunderson into the ground soon, the butcher would finally have girth with the poisons of death expanding inside of him. He suppressed a smile at the errant thought.

"Thank you, Doctor." The young butcher was rubbing his flat stomach and his supple green leather apron with both hands, in a slow, smooth stroke as Tonneman had often seen Albert's father do.

Impulsively, Tonneman reached out and touched the apron. Why had he not remembered this before? It was exactly like the apron that had held the body of the woman whose head Gretel had found in the well.

CHAPTER 64

"Albert, where were you on Saturday night, twenty-five November, last year?" Tonneman asked urgently. He was thinking that if one of the Gundersons was the murderer, it would have been so simple for him to do the deed in the shop. There would never be a need to explain the blood. But neither Albert nor his brothers, nor his brothers-in-law, nor their issue bore any similarity to the description of the soldierly dark man seen at the places the bodies were found.

The lean butcher wrinkled his forehead. "I can't remember what happened last week, let alone last year."

"Think back, man. Try. It's a matter of life and death. Are you a Son of Liberty?"

Although confused, the butcher answered with pride, "Yes."

"Then you were at St. Paul's that night in November. Remember? There was a fracas over some sulphur."

Albert shook his head, recalling. "No, I missed that. That entire week I was on Long Island buying venison. Didn't get home till late on the Sabbath. Missed church. The wife gave me hell."

Tonneman thought, one down of those who had access to the green apron. "Was your father the only butcher to use a green apron?"

"Only the Gunderson master butcher wears the green apron. It started with the grandfather's father in the old country." Albert rubbed his nose, squinting at Tonneman. "Why do you want to know all this?" There was just a trace of impatience in his voice, which Tonneman brushed aside, intent on his mission.

"How many aprons are there?"

"Three only. They was hard to come by. And when I came back from

Long Island, there was only two. With all the soldiers in the City it's no wonder things disappear."

"Albert, this is very important. I need to talk to all the men in your family, uh, over the age of fifteen."

"Why?" Sweat bathed the butcher's face. A thought suddenly became clear, and he was frightened. "Did my father have the Plague?"

"Good God, man! No, nothing like that."

Albert turned pasty-faced and clapped a bony hand over his mouth. "Oh, my God, we're all going to die."

"Please, Albert."

"The meat. The meat is tainted. I'll have to throw away all the meat? We'll be ruined."

"Albert, please calm yourself. I need Seth to take a message, and I need a place to talk to all the men in your family. And paper, pen, and ink. Can you arrange this for me?"

"Yes. You won't tell anyone our meat is bad. Promise me."

"I promise you I will be discreet," Tonneman said, only slightly ashamed of himself for taking advantage of the man's fears.

He sent young Seth with a message to Goldsmith who, he was sure, would be found in the kitchen on Rutgers Hill talking to Molly. Then he began interviewing the male members of the Gunderson clan who dutifully lined up in the sitting room of the small house next door to the butcher shop. All were anxious to be rid of the specter of disease that could close the shop and deny them all livelihood and sustenance.

When a breathless Goldsmith arrived, Tonneman had only to show him the green apron Albert, as master butcher, was wearing.

"That's the same . . ."

Tonneman smiled. "You're a smart fellow, Constable. Let's see if we can catch us a murderer."

The erstwhile lawman shuddered. The months of being out of work had hurt his pocket and his pride. He found little humor in the situation. Of late he found little humor in anything.

Tonneman patted Goldsmith's arm. "I didn't mean to rub salt in the wound. Perhaps we can get you your job back, too. You keep questioning this batch. Talk to the women, too. I've got patients to care for."

"You think one of the Gundersons is our man?" Goldsmith whispered.

"I have no idea."

Three hours later, when Tonneman returned, he found Goldsmith in the parlor with the entire family, including the dead man. Gunderson was wrapped in a winding sheet and laid out in a fresh-made pine coffin set on a low, paneled red chest, its balled feet painted black. On either side of the coffin candle stands held burning candles scented with lavender.

The occasion seemed a combination of wake and tea party. Goldsmith was being treated with awe by the men and boys, and fussed over by the women and girls, who kept feeding him sweet cakes. The unassuming fellow was a constant surprise to Tonneman. "What have you got, Daniel? Can we get you your job back?"

Goldsmith smiled. "Not likely. Not unless I can tidy my record and catch this bastard. The apron disappeared twenty-five November. The next morning Gretel found the head in the well."

Tonneman nodded. "At least we know we're on the right path."

"I never doubted it. Five of the men can't tell me where they were that night. Or at least they can't prove it. The old man Gunderson was with his wife." Goldsmith kneaded his nose. "Truth is, none of them feels right."

Albert was shuffling just outside the door to the room, trying to get their attention. "Albert?" Tonneman beckoned to him.

The spindly butcher rushed in. He was holding a sign on which was crudely printed ROOM TO LET. "Are we to be quarantined?"

"No, of course not."

Albert breathed a gusty sigh of relief. "Then no one else has got it. I'm so grateful, Doctor. I'll have the boy bring you two mutton chops in the morning."

"That's very good of you. I'm afraid we'll have to—" Tonneman paused, caught by the sign. "You have a room to let?"

Albert looked at the sign he was holding as if surprised to see it. "They told you about the lodger, didn't they?"

"Lodger?" Goldsmith shook his head at Tonneman.

"What lodger?"

"The soldier who was staying in the room behind the shop."

Tonneman and Goldsmith locked eyes. "The soldier?" Tonneman fairly shouted his words. "Where the hell is he?"

"Don't worry, Private Hickey's not going anywhere. They've got him over at the City Jail. You've seen the handbills about the fellow they're going to hang for trying to kill General Washington?"

Tonneman nodded. "Yes."

"That's Tom Hickey. They stretch his neck tomorrow."

CHAPTER 65

Molly knocked at his door early, but he was already awake, listening to a sound totally foreign to his ears. A hum as if of a million honeybees. He was already dressed.

"Dr. John, there's a boy, Reuben, to see you. He says it's important." Molly poured the hot water from her kettle into his basin and left him.

Tonneman yawned vigorously. It had been a late night and to no avail. He and Goldsmith had gone to City Hall to talk to Private Hickey, but those in charge couldn't or wouldn't give permission. They were presented instead with the handbill announcing that Hickey was to be hanged Friday, 28 June, the next day—this day—for mutiny and conspiracy, in the field near Bowery Lane. The audacious man had attempted to murder George Washington as part of a British plot to end the rebellion.

It had been well after midnight when he and a weary Goldsmith had returned to the house on Rutgers Hill. The former Constable was probably asleep upstairs. Or, more likely, in the kitchen letting Molly ply him with breakfast.

Tonneman shaved quickly and hurried down the stairs. He discovered Goldsmith where he expected, sitting comfortably, a mug of sage tea in his hand, talking to Reuben, the pock-marked lad who worked in City Hall. Reuben was twitching and bouncing like a marionette on strings. Homer, a little crazed by the youth's actions, kept nipping at his clothing. Reuben was too disturbed to notice.

"He won't tell me," Goldsmith said to Tonneman. "You better ask him quick before he busts."

"Yes, boy?"

The words rushed forth like a torrent. "I didn't know who else to tell, sir. But, oh God, I don't know, I mean, there's no new Mayor yet and you are the Coroner, aren't you?"

"Slow down, boy. You'll get there." Tonneman caught the boy by both arms to stop him from fidgeting long enough to get a clear story. "Now, talk."

"Oh, God," Reuben said, near to tears. "They've unearthed another head."

"I knew it." Goldsmith leaped to his feet. "What about the hair?"

"The hair, sir?"

"What color, damn it."

"It was red, sir."

Tonneman sighed. "Where?"

"Behind Serjeant's Tavern."

"Do we go look at the head?" asked Goldsmith.

Molly snorted. "What's a dead head going to tell you? The most important thing is to talk to that Hickey before he swings."

"She's right," said Tonneman. "Let's be off."

"Of course," said Goldsmith, slapping his thigh. "Sit down, lad, and Molly will give you some corn samp to fill your belly."

"Never mind the horses," said Tonneman. "We'll make better time walking."

"What's this?"

Mariana had come through the study and was standing in the door to the kitchen, her hair hidden under a tricorn.

"We're going to talk to Thomas Hickey, the man they're hanging today, about the murders. We're certain he killed the women. I have to know why he killed Gretel. She was different from the others. Tell my patients I'll return soon."

Mariana's chin inched forward. "I'm coming with you," she stated, daring him with her dark eyes to say no. Tonneman looked at her and smiled. He wouldn't dare.

"Molly, please tell my patients."

"Yes, Dr. John. Oh, I found a box in the attic—"

"No time now. Tell me later."

Outside, the hum had turned into a roar, as of thousands of voices all talking at once. Everyone, it seemed, was heading for the hanging in the field near Bowery Lane—soldiers, citizens, old men, women, and children. Tonneman, Mariana, and Goldsmith took hands so not to be separated.

They were swept up in the frenzy and were hustled by the ever-driving throng. The sun stood high above in an almost cloudless blue sky. The closer the three came to Bowery Lane, the harder it became to push through. People were milling about, up on tiptoes, leaning, looking, even though they were at a distance from the field and could see naught.

The blare of the multitude reached crescendo at Bayard Street. The pack of people was not to be believed: humanity, sounds, and smells as far as the eye could see and the ear could hear and the nose could smell, all talking, shouting, laughing. Venders were selling roasted corn and potatoes. Drink was abundant. This was a great event. A fair.

As they approached Bowery Lane, the three were forced by the dint of the crowd to release hands. In the glare of the summer sun, the unforgiving mob waited for the theater of hanging, amusing themselves, eating cold chicken and drinking warm ale, trading jokes. Laughter bubbled above the roar, and ditties ridiculing Hickey skipped from group to group.

Over twenty thousand—as many people as had lived in New-York— were there on Bowery Lane and stretched out in all directions. All had come to see the traitor Hickey hanged on this hot summer's day. Boys and girls ran about, as much as they could, in the crush of people, calling and laughing. Dogs joined in on the excitement with barks and howls. Overhead, two hawks circled slowly.

Men drank grog from bottles, passing them back and forth, impatient for the entertainment to begin. This was thrilling stuff, worthy of more than a few tastes. Hickey's was to be the first military execution of the Revolution and the first in the American Army.

Tonneman and Goldsmith pushed and shoved to get closer. Mariana was somewhere behind them.

Hickey wore only gray breeches and a clean white shirt. He was led by a major at the head of a six-man squad, and a drummer boy in full uniform, to the scaffold which had been especially erected for him in the field near Bowery Lane. A minister followed somewhat timidly.

Tonneman had now become separated from Goldsmith. The crowd kept him from getting close. Then he saw Goldsmith ahead, arguing with a Militiaman. "Goldsmith!" he shouted above the din. "Talk to Hickey!"

Goldsmith waved his hand to show he had heard. "Hickey!" he yelled.

At once, some in the crowd thought that was great fun and took up the call. "Hickey! Hickey! *Hickey!*" It was deafening.

Meanwhile the hangman, a black hooded mask over his head, went on about his business. He climbed the back of the ladder, pulled the rope taut at its nether end, and carefully secured it. At the limit of the stout rope hanging from the cross beam of the gallows was a noose with nine turns about the rope, a hangman's knot. The executioner stepped down, half lifted, half walked Hickey up the front of the ladder to the fourth step, and slipped the noose over Hickey's head.

"*Hickey, Hickey!*" the crowd yelled.

The executioner tightened the noose about Hickey's neck and faced front. The major called his men to attention. The drummer boy looked at the major. The major nodded.

A single drum roll.

The crowd grew still, Goldsmith and Tonneman as well, as if frozen in place. Overhead the hawks continued to circle, lower and lower, their wings slicing dark shadows over the crowd.

A lone voice cried, "Hickey, Hick—" then stopped midcry.

The major cleared his throat. "Thomas Hickey, you have been found guilty of mutiny and conspiracy. For these heinous crimes you are to be hanged by the neck until you are dead. Have you any last words?"

"Yes." Hickey sneered at the eager mob. "Beware of lewd women."

A slow, rippling laugh floated through the assembly.

One of the hawks circling overhead swooped down, as if to get a better look at Hickey. Startled, the minister removed his spectacles and squinted at the bird, now soaring high into the sky. He replaced his spectacles and turned his attention back to the doomed man. "Prepare your soul for God, my son."

"Go away, preacher. I wouldn't have a priest, why the hell should I want you? Go away and let a man die, can't you?"

All at once Mariana erupted from the crowd, rushing toward Hickey. "Hickey!" she cried. "The women who had their heads chopped off. Did you kill them?"

Hickey laughed, staring down at Mariana. "I'll be damned, boy, you tumbled to that. Yes, I killed the evil sluts. I killed them all and I'd do it again, given the chance."

There was a gasp, then the restless crowd as one voice now droned, "Hang him. Hang him."

Mariana drew as close as she could. "But why Gretel?" she screamed. "Why did you kill Gretel?"

Hickey frowned. His mouth twisted. He looked up at the circling hawks, then down at Mariana. "Which one was Gretel?"

CHAPTER 66

Hickey was dead.

Had he killed Gretel? they asked themselves and one another.

Mariana spoke first. "Of course it was Hickey. Who else could it have been?"

It had to be over. They needed for it to be over. There were other, greater, problems coming that would govern their lives from this day forward.

"Yes," Tonneman agreed. "Hickey killed her as he did the others, and that's the end of it."

Goldsmith sighed. "I suppose you're right. I hope you're right."

And so, because it had to be, the quest for Gretel's killer was concluded. And, most important to Goldsmith, Gretel's soul would find some peace.

All about them people were rushing through the streets yelling as if the world had come to some sort of glorious end.

Tonneman and Goldsmith saw Mariana to her door. She said nothing further, simply nodded to them and went inside. Her face was very pale.

"I reckon I better be getting home, then," Goldsmith muttered. "I have been neglecting my children of late." He walked away slowly, almost reluctantly. Then he turned and smiled. "But I will always have a craving for Molly's chicken soup."

"And?"

Goldsmith shrugged and trudged off.

Tonneman walked along the East River, listening to the sea birds. He looked out across the river where the hills of Brooklyn could be seen so clearly. The serene open view was an ironic reminder of the fleet waiting, waiting out in the Narrows.

The river proved no solace so he stopped at Fraunces Tavern for a brandy, but drink wasn't the answer to his heartache, nor was the sincere conviviality offered by Sam Fraunces. It was far too noisy there for a man to think straight. The way everyone was celebrating, you'd think all the troubles were over. Any fool could tell they'd just begun.

Tonneman walked again, remembering his youth and how peaceful life had been then, just him and Papa and Gretel. But that was the past, and it was fruitless to live in the past.

The blackened metal box was sitting atop his desk in his study when he arrived home. He ran his hand over the leaf design and wondered vaguely if Molly had put it there. She had said something about finding a box in the attic. But his thoughts would not stay with the box. Hickey's last words rang in his ears. *Which one was Gretel?*

He rubbed his eyes. It was late. Too late to ask Molly about the box. She was in bed. The house was quiet. He removed his coat and went into the kitchen. Homer, fast asleep, and deaf as well, didn't stir. The poor brute was getting old. He didn't even move when Tonneman tasted from the pot on the hearth.

Mutton stew. Albert Gunderson had been as good as his word. The stew was tasty. Molly was a good cook. Tonneman ate another spoonful, tempted to have his dinner directly from the pot.

He laughed out loud, remembering a time when Gretel had caught him doing just that. "Have respect for my food, Johnny. Eat from a dish, like a man." Homer snored loudly and shifted, but did not awake. Tonneman spooned stew into a bowl and took the bowl and an apple out to the barn.

Chaucer made quick work of the apple and then poked his muzzle at the stew. Tonneman rubbed the gelding's nose. "This is my dinner, friend, not yours." The animal lowered his head and nibbled bits of hay at his feet.

Dismissed, Tonneman sat in the doorway of his surgery eating slowly. The moon was only a little less than full and the summer night was clear and still but for the shrill buzz of the cicadas, the sentries calling to one another, and the answers of the City Night Watch. Fireflies flitted, making pinpricks of light on velvet.

"Eleven o'clock and all's well." The air was fragrant with strawberries on the vine and roses from Gretel's bushes. Tonneman set his empty bowl down.

The sound of a twig snapping to his right in the darkness drew his eyes. Bathed in ethereal lunar light was the outline of a woman on the low hillock. In an instant she was gone.

Good God, he was getting as mad as Goldsmith. For a moment he'd thought he'd seen Gretel's wraith. Tonneman took his bowl into the house.

The candle on his desk, casting a flickering yellow light on the black box, brought back the image of the wraith. Her hand was on the box. "Sweet Jesus," Tonneman whispered, closing his eyes. When he opened them, he saw only the box in the shifting candlelight. He set down his bowl and tried to lift the lid. But the hinge would not give. The metal was soft, but not tin. He pushed at the box with one hand and pulled and lifted at the hinge with the other. It opened.

Inside, the tarnish was less. The box was silver. Tonneman saw at once the Dutch inscription inside the lid. He raised the candle, the better to make out the simple words.

For our friends Pieter and Racqel Tonneman on the joyous occasion of their marriage. 30 August, 1665.
Conraet and Antje Ten Eyck.

Astonished, he set the candle stand down. Pieter Tonneman. His ancestor. Bemused by the notion, Tonneman began removing items from the box. Papers, a magnifying glass, a silver coin, a rolled-up parchment, a flat book-shaped object wrapped in blue silk. As he lifted the object, the silk slipped; there were fringes at the end of the silk.

He laid everything out on the desk, unrolling first the parchment. At once he saw the writing was Hebrew, and that although the color had faded somewhat, it was highly ornamented and had intricate and colorful designs. Beautiful, like the illuminated pages of a Bible.

There were names mentioned in the document. Racqel Pereira, Benjamin Mendoza. He recalled the name Abraham Pereira from the tombstone in the Jewish cemetery. He would have to ask David Mendoza to tell him what this meant. Or Mariana.

His hand, as if compelled by some powerful force, moved to the silk-covered object. Carefully, he unwrapped it, keeping the heavy silk in his hands.

Behind him came the barest sound: the surgery door opening and closing. He turned and saw a shrouded woman advancing slowly toward him. His hands, unknowingly, loosened the silk.

The woman gasped and caught the silk before it touched the floor. She threw back her shawl and grinned at him almost wickedly.

"Do you know what this is?" she asked.

He hardly knew her. She was wearing a gown cut to reveal the most beautiful clavicle he had ever seen. And the curve of her breasts was sublime. "You're wearing a dress." He moved closer to her and she to him. He placed his hands on her shoulders. Mariana.

She tilted her head and he kissed her, thrilling at the promise between them. A bond. Forever.

Finally she stepped back and held the silk out to him. "John, this is a tallis."

"A what?"

"A prayer shawl. Did my father . . . ?"

"No." He took her hand and showed her the silver box and the items on the desk. He smoothed out the parchment. "Can you read it?"

"Yes. They didn't want me to, but I learned everything Benjamin learned. And learned it better." She ran her fingers slowly over the ornate designs. "This is a Ketubah, a marriage contract. It delineates the mutual obligations between husband and wife. After it is read during the ceremony, it is handed to the bride. In the Ketubah the bride's rights are enumerated." Her eyes sparkled. "I think that is a marvelous idea."

"This, then, is the marriage contract of Benjamin Mendoza and Racqel Pereira?"

Mariana studied the writing. "Yes. How did you come by it?" She wrinkled her brow. "Ben was named for my father's father. I'm sure there was a Benjamin in our line before my grandfather. But who was Racqel Pereira?"

"Look." Tonneman showed Mariana the dates on the silver box celebrating the marriage of Pieter and Racqel Tonneman, some ten years after Racqel had married Benjamin. "This Racqel is Racqel Mendoza. I know, I've seen her headstone in the Jewish cemetery. She must have been widowed."

Mariana said softly, "This must mean that an ancestor of yours married the widow of an ancestor of mine."

Tonneman shook his head in wonderment.

Mariana was picking up the book that had been wrapped in the tallis. "A Bible. We have one just like it. It has been in my father's family for generations."

Tonneman opened the book. Again, in Hebrew. There was an inscription—so faded it was difficult to read.

Mariana held the candle up. "This Bible was given to Abraham Pereira by his father Victor on the occasion of his Bar Mitzvah."

Tonneman turned the heavy pages with care.

"What's that?" Mariana pointed to a piece of yellowed paper tucked between the two pages.

Tonneman studied the Dutch for a moment. " 'Beloved father,' " he read haltingly. " 'Benjamin is dead one year. Since you are gone from me, too, I have given myself to Pieter Tonneman, a Dutchman and a Christian whom I love beyond words. The children I bear him, God willing, will be of our faith. He has agreed. He is a good man.' "

Mariana put her arms about Tonneman's waist. "You're a good man, too, John, just like your ancestor."

Gently, Tonneman returned the letter to the Bible and took Mariana in his arms once more. "So," he whispered, "this closes the circle."

CHAPTER 67

Sunset this night found an exhausted and hungry John Tonneman riding home on the Albany Road from Kingsbridge.

He'd felt impelled to take the time from his full schedule to see David Wares and let him know the murderer of the Scotch servant girl, Jane McCreddie, had paid for her life with his at the end of a rope.

Preoccupied as he rode along, his mind was filled with a jumble of thoughts. Mariana, who would be his wife in less than six weeks. The war. Gretel's killer. All these ingredients combined with his long hours and his punishing routine to make him weary. He longed for the oblivion he used to find in the bottle and the high life of London.

Dawn had arrived that morning with a particularly beautiful sunrise, and the air was a warm caress. From window boxes, flowers blossomed in radiant colors. The people in the City, however, were too distracted by the rapidly changing political currents to take any notice.

It had begun to appear that His Majesty, or at least his senior officers, agreed with John Adams, the delegate to the Continental Congress from Massachusetts, that New-York was the key to the continent. Control of the North River was now more than ever paramount to both sides in the growing conflict. The City was a frenzy of worker bees erecting gun emplacements, stringing huge chains designed to prevent the British from going upriver.

There was no doubt that His Majesty's forces were planning a visit. It was common knowledge that General William Howe had arrived from Halifax with more than one hundred British vessels. Over the last few days more ships arrived. The General's older brother, Admiral Richard Howe, brought an army from England in another flotilla.

Admiral Howe was followed by Admiral Peter Parker from Charleston with his ships. Ships of the line, frigates, transports, and every vessel conceivable clotted the entrance to the harbor, waiting. The British army, which included 9,000 German mercenaries, was 32,000 strong.

Rumors floated on the air like dandelion fluff. On Saturday, 29 June, the always prudent Provincial Congress had cautiously adjourned and agreed to meet again on Tuesday, 2 July, which was tomorrow, at the White Plains Courthouse, a safe distance from the beleaguered City.

Tonneman had been on call day after day, all day, and much of the night, from one end of the City to the other. Now that the City was packed with soldiers, there were broken limbs, lacerations, shootings—on purpose and accidental—and dysentery. In the winter they had had to worry about the Influenza; in the summer, the threat of Yellow Fever plagued them.

Because of the scarcity of physicians, Mariana had become an accepted substitute. When Tonneman was out, patients were willing, if not overly content, to let Mariana treat them; she'd become more and more accomplished. Yesterday the girl healer, as some had begun calling her, had put as neat a splint as was ever seen on a young boy's broken arm while his mother held him, and went from there to delivering a baby when no midwife could be found.

Near the De Lancey estate the noise and dust warning him of many men ahead made him wary. Goldsmith had shown him a broadside telling of the encampment of Royalists in the hills prior to their departure for Canada. The dust settled and a company of soldiers on their way north trooped past him.

"What's the do?" Tonneman called to a private at the tail end of the company.

The soldier shrugged. "On our way to Kingsbridge. We've had word of British troop movements from Boston, heading for New-York."

Tonneman hurried Chaucer homeward. He stumbled into his bed and was in a shallow, restless sleep when General Howe at last entered the Narrows.

CHAPTER 68

In Philadelphia, where the heat hovered over that city like a heavy, moist blanket, the thirteen American Colonies began to vote.

Forty-nine members of the Continental Congress heard the resolution written by Thomas Jefferson of Virginia, which ended with, ". . . *That these United Colonies are, and of right ought to be Free and Independent States; that they are absolved from all allegiance to the British Crown, and that all political connection between them and the State of Great Britain, is and ought to be totally dissolved; and that as free and independent States, they have full power to levy war, conclude peace, contract alliances, establish commerce, and to do all other acts and things which independent States may of right do. And for the support of this Declaration, with a firm reliance on the protection of Divine Providence, we mutually pledge to each other our lives, our fortunes and our sacred honor.*"

Nine states voted "aye." Two states, "nay." Delaware tied. The thirteenth, New-York, did not commit. The delegates from New-York were waiting for instructions from the Provincial Congress now sitting in White Plains.

In the City of New-York, guns, drums, and church bells all gave warning of the imminent arrival of the British, but the third New-York Provincial Congress in White Plains did nothing but wrangle, unable to reach a decision.

Washington prepared to meet the foe. The General sent one regiment to Paulus Hook in New Jersey, directly opposite New-York Harbor. And General Israel Putnam led his men to Staten Island, prepared to meet landing forces.

Goldsmith brought a broadsheet to the house on Rutgers Hill, announcing that Long Island was alerted to stand ready to fight.

The deposed Mayor, David Matthews, was charged by the Committee of Safety with "dangerous designs and treasonable conspiracies against the rights and liberties of Americans." He was further charged with being cognizant of, or concerned in, Governor Tryon's plot to assassinate General Washington and blow up the Fort. Matthews was condemned to die and escorted by armed guards to Litchfield, Connecticut, to be imprisoned until the sentence could be carried out.

CHAPTER 69

In Philadelphia, the heat was broken by a violent thunderstorm, and the Declaration over which they had debated bitterly for more than three long weeks was agreed to. Twelve ayes. One abstention.

The sole abstainer was New-York.

CHAPTER 70

The heat had receded. A light breeze stirred trees along the Common. Tonneman and Mariana walked among other early evening strollers, hardly noticing the amusement of those who knew the Mendoza family and were seeing Mariana in women's clothing for the first time.

Before another month passed she would be his wife. Her hand in the crook of his arm burned like a blazing ember. His desire for her took his breath away. And to think he had once mistaken her for a boy.

His personal thoughts were not the only ones on his mind. The day before, the newly elected fourth New-York Provincial Congress had finally voted aye. As soon as the New-York delegates to the Continental Congress changed their abstention to aye, the acceptance of the new Declaration was unanimous.

Mariana's hand pressed Tonneman's arm, and he looked down at her sweet face. The passion in her dark eyes enveloped him like a fiery cloud. His mind soared. What if he took her back to Rutgers Hill now? In one month they would be married. What would it matter?

Suddenly, there came a great clatter of men's feet and horses' hooves. Whirlwinds of dust flew up and around. It seemed George Washington's entire army had entered the Common.

The foot soldiers formed a great square. In the center, General Washington and his officers sat astride their horses.

Mounted to the left of the officers were a standard-bearer and a crier with his large brass bell. The standard-bearer proudly displayed the billowing colors of the Grand Union flag of the Revolution: The red and white crosses against the blue field of the Union Jack were in the upper left corner, and representing the thirteen Colonies were the thirteen red and white stripes.

All assembled could hear General Washington cry out: "I order that the troops be read the Declaration Of Independence with an audible voice."

The crier prodded his steed forward, his right arm swinging vigorously, ringing his brass bell. "Hear ye, hear ye. Special notice from the Continental Congress."

"It's finally come." Tonneman's voice quavered with excitement.

Church bells began to toll, bringing men, women, and children to the Common. The crier rang his bell again, cleared his throat and read what had just arrived from Philadelphia.

"When in the course of human events, it becomes necessary for one people to dissolve the political bands which have connected them with another, and to assume among the powers of the earth, the separate and equal station to which the laws of Nature and of Nature's God entitle them, a decent respect to the opinions of mankind requires that they should declare the causes which impel them to the separation.

"We hold these truths to be self-evident, that all men are created equal . . ."

Up until this point there had been a hushed quiet. Now the crowd erupted.

"Hurrah!"

"Amen."

"Hosanna!"

Tonneman took off his hat and ran his hand over his hair. "At last."

Ben shouldered through the crowd, his face glowing. "Sister. John. This is a day to be alive. Can you feel it?" He gave Tonneman a bear hug and kissed Mariana.

Tonneman agreed. "But I hope we're up to the task that Declaration sets before us. The British will never tolerate this. They are bound to attack. I trust we're ready."

"They'll never put a foot in New-York," a nearby merchant said.

"I pray you're right." Mariana shivered and pulled her shawl about her shoulders.

"There's Joel," Ben cried. "I'm off."

Bear Bikker, sitting proudly on his horse, caught sight of his kinsman, the physician, and called out to him. His booming "Coz!" rose over the throng.

Tonneman, grinning, directed Mariana's attention to the giant on horseback who, with his new blue tricorn and slightly worn blue jacket, looked quite the soldier. They made their way through the congestion to where he was dismounting.

"Mariana Mendoza, my cousin Bear Bikker of Haarlem. Bear, this is my wife-to-be."

Bear raised his tricorn, beaming. "I will be at your wedding to welcome you to our family, God and the English willing. My company is leaving the Bayard Camp and heading for Kingsbridge today." He patted the Pennsylvania Rifle now in his saddle holster. "I call her Beauty. Isn't she? I won her in a dice game a fortnight ago. She's a far sight better than that old wreck of a musket I was issued." Bear chuckled. "I beat a couple of City boys who thought they could teach a country boy how to suck eggs." He embraced Tonneman and Mariana together in one swoop of his massive arms, then mounted his horse and rode off.

The crier rang his bell again; the crowd quieted. He read again. "The foregoing Declaration was, by order of Congress, engrossed, and signed by the following members. John Hancock is first with his name writ large, then there's . . ."

As the crier read off the names of the brave men who had put their necks on the line, Tonneman took Mariana's hand. They left the Common walking slowly, neither saying a word.

Then, Mariana sighed deeply. "I know I shouldn't feel glad with war looming. It's very frightening. But I am glad we know who killed Gretel and the others. And that the blackguard has been hanged."

"He didn't even know her name." Tonneman's sorrow was palpable.

Mariana squeezed his hand. "We will name our first child in her honor."

Tonneman looked down at this impossible woman with whom he would spend the rest of his life. "Our first-born will be a boy, and we will name him Peter."

"Our daughter Gretel will be a physician."

"Our son Peter will be a physician."

The sound of running footsteps and shouting behind them made them turn. Men pounded by. Soldiers. Civilians. They were carrying ladders, crowbars, hammers, and ropes.

"What's happening?" Tonneman called. "Are the English—?"

A man in a brickmaker's smock turned. Running backwards he called, "We're off to get King George! Come with us. Bowling Green."

In Bowling Green facing the Fort, where the statue of King George on a prancing horse was prominently displayed, a delighted crowd danced at the King's gilded feet, but not in supplication. The common people ogled the royal figure on horseback insolently, and made taunting gestures, thumbing their noses.

Soon Bowling Green was jammed with people, from old men and women to little boys and girls, all rejoicing, reveling, talking, swearing, praying, singing, celebrating the toppling of the King.

The crowd was hardly different from the day Hickey was hanged, death and the celebration. One of the old men was painting on the statue's pedestal, "Death to the King."

The citizens were eager, but doubting. One shouted above the cheering. "Now instead of being ruled by mad George Hanover we will be ruled by mad George Washington!"

"I am a man released from prison."

"We are all men released from prison."

What was talk suddenly became action. Black slaves under the orders of white Militiamen and civilians leaned ladders and tossed ropes and hooks. Then, with an enthusiastic hurrah and a tug, King George was down from his high horse.

One of the Militiamen shouted, "And we'll do the same to the real one if we get our hands on him." They then dismembered the lead body, passing little bits about to the crowd as mementos.

The people stood around the statue site in a great curve that continuously reestablished itself as men, women, and children came and went and stared and pointed at the empty pedestal, laughing and rejoicing. Children and dogs cavorted; there was an outburst of applause. Other children danced in a circle and sang "Yankee Doodle."

As if by magic, the smell of frying oysters and clams, roasting potatoes and corn filled the air. A feast of food and joyous human sound overflowed. The air was fragrant with foods and spices, noisy with the crash of the butcher's cleaver and laughter and song. As at Hickey's hanging, men were passing around grog bottles. Many clasped arms and danced.

"This is a shameful infamy," a brave Loyalist cried. "A manner of life is fading like a ghost."

A young Patriot stepped up to the Loyalist, his clenched fist in the Loyalist's face. Another Patriot pushed the first aside. "Leave him be. We all know what he said is not true," the second Patriot said ardently.

"When something is rotten, it has to be rooted out and destroyed. This is a time to dance in the streets."

An old man and woman carried a lit candle to the statue site and prayed over it as men with tools chopped away at the base.

Mariana pressed Tonneman's hand in hers. She looked up at him, but he was distracted, in awe, as he watched what was happening about them. New-Yorkers hung out of windows, stood on the rooftops, cheering, offering support.

The populace paraded through the streets of New-York carrying pieces of the royal corpse. They shouted, "We'll mold this lead into bullets for American muskets."

A horseman with a pike speared the King's head, albeit without its laurel wreath, and rode about with it to the enjoyment of the revelers. It was taken to the Fort, now renamed Fort Washington, and displayed in front of the Blue Bell Tavern on the pike.

"Ben is right," said Tonneman. He pulled Mariana to him. "What a time to be alive."

Mariana smiled up at him. "And we shall live forever."

$\mathfrak{F}$OOTNOTE

For all practical purposes, the Revolution began April 19, 1775, on the Village Green in Lexington, Massachusetts, when Minutemen and local militia exchanged "the shot heard round the world" with British troops.

The Continental Congress, a body of delegates representing all thirteen Colonies, and established principally to deal with grievances against the Crown, had begun its work in the fall of 1774, in Philadelphia. In June of 1775, the Continental Congress created the Continental Army with an appropriation of $6,000, and George Washington of Virginia was appointed Commander-in-Chief.

In the autumn of 1775, the City of New-York (at that time it was hyphenated) was a strange mix of Loyalists and Patriots, coexisting uneasily. New-York was a Patriot town, and was also referred to as a "nest of Tories." The government was Royalist. The King's Governor, William Tryon, so feared the Rebels and what they might do to him that he fled to one of His Majesty's ships, the *Dutchess Of Gordon,* and attempted to conduct the business of state as the ship sailed back and forth in the Narrows.

Coin of the "realm" was Continental dollars and/or English pounds.

What we have named the Kingsbridge Plot was known historically as the Hickey Plot. New Yorkers today will recognize the name Kingsbridge, which still exists in the Bronx.

Hickey is said to have tried to poison George Washington with Paris Green, an emerald green, poisonous, water-soluble powder composed of arsenic trioxide and copper acetate, which was used primarily as a pigment. Although various sources maintain the phrase Paris Green didn't come into the English language until 1870, we liked the designation too much to lose it. Other than that phrase, we have stayed with our determination not to use any words in the book that were not in the language in 1775.

George Washington did own at least one fox hound. We named ours Rebel because it seemed appropriate.

Samuel Fraunces's tavern still exists as Fraunces Tavern in its original location on Pearl Street, and is still a tavern. It also houses an extraordinary museum of Colonial history. As for Sam himself, his early history is sketchy. Supposedly, he was born in the West Indies in 1722 or 1723, and lived in Philadelphia before he turned up in New-York history when he was about thirty. He was said to be Portuguese. The appellation "Black Sam" did not necessarily have to do with race. It was common usage to describe someone of swarthy complexion.

A 1790 Census report at the New-York Historical Society lists the Fraunces family as free and white. Still, there are those who maintain that Sam Fraunces was black.

Maps of the period show us that by this time the North River was also known as the Hudson and the East River was sometimes referred to as the Sound River. We stayed with North River and East River to avoid confusion. Similarly, we chose to spell Broadway as one word. On maps of the day and in journals it was referred to variously as Broadway, Broad-Way, and the Broad Way.

There is a small Jewish cemetery at the edge of Chinatown, on St. James Place near Chatham Square. This second cemetery, under the jurisdiction of the Congregation Shearith Israel, an unbroken descending line from the first Congregation of Spanish and Portuguese Jews in New Amsterdam, was established in 1683. The first burial ground, which we described in *The Dutchman,* is gone.

Alderman David Matthews, who became Mayor of New-York after the resignation of Whitehead Hicks, was condemned to death. He was sent to Litchfield, Connecticut, and then on to Hartford, supposedly to be near his wife. One day, disguised as a woman, he escaped. He returned to New-York when the City was taken over by the Crown in September 1776, and became Commissioner of Chimneys for as long as the English held New-York.

James Rivington was a Tory and the printer and publisher of the *New-York Gazetteer.* Issues of this newspaper can be read on microfilm in the library of the New-York Historical Society. The raid by Isaac Sears did destroy Rivington's press. Rivington fled to London but returned to New-York after the British took the City. He named his new newspaper the

New-York Gazette. He ended his days as a successful salesman of musical instruments.

It is doubtful that George Washington met young David Bushnell at Fraunces Tavern. We don't know that the General met the inventor at all, for that matter, but Bushnell did indeed design and build the first American submarine, and it was called the *Turtle.*

On September 6, 1776, the *Turtle* attacked Lord Richard Howe's flagship, the *Eagle,* on the North River near South Ferry, attempting to attach a mine to its keel, but the keel with its copper sheathing resisted the drill, and the mission failed.

The British took secure possession of all of Manhattan Island on November 16, 1776. New-York remained in British hands and became a refuge for Loyalists until 1783.

The rest is history.

F   T13275
Me   24550

AUTHOR
Meyers, Maan

TITLE
The Kingsbridge Plot

BORROWER'S NAME

F   T13275
Me   24550

Meyers, Maan

The Kingsbridge Plot

DATE DUE		
MAR 3 1 2003		